JADE *and*
JEOPARDY

OTHER BOOKS AND BOOKS ON CASSETTE
BY LYNN GARDNER

Emeralds and Espionage

Pearls and Peril

Diamonds and Danger

Turquoise and Terrorists

Sapphires and Smugglers

Amethysts and Arson

JADE *and* JEOPARDY

a novel

Lynn Gardner

Covenant Communications, Inc.

Cover photograph by Lynn Gardner
Cover image (jade pieces) ® 2000, PhotoDisc, Inc.

Cover design copyrighted 2000 by Covenant Communications, Inc.

Published by Covenant Communications, Inc.
American Fork, Utah

Printed in the United States of America
First Printing: July 2000

07 06 05 04 03 02 01 00   10 9 8 7 6 5 4 3 2 1

ISBN 1-57734-650-5

Library of Congress Cataloging-in-Publication Data

Gardner, Lynn, 1938-
    Jade and jeopardy / Lynn Gardner.
        p.   cm.
    ISBN 1-57734-650-5
    I. International police—Fiction. 2. Terrorism—Prevention—Fiction. 3. Mormons—Fiction.
    I.Title.
PSPS3557 A7133 J34 2000
813'.54--dc21
                                        00-024112
                                          CIP

Acknowledgments

My thanks to Valerie Holladay and JoAnn Jolley, not just for moral support and editing prowess through the process of publication, but for going the extra mile with personal support on the battlefront. Thank you! Thank you!

To my husband, Glenn, and daughters, Nikki and Shelley, my chief critics and greatest advocates. Thank you!

To my critique group, Dorothy, Tanya, and Bev, who make me better than I am. Thank you!

And heartfelt thanks to the Originator of all gifts and blessings for opening doors that enabled me to tell my stories. Thank You.

CHAPTER 1

With trembling fingers, I unlocked the front door of the cottage and raced to check the answering machine. Had I missed Bart's call from Zaire? No blinking light. No call. Where was my husband? Had he penetrated the terrorist compound undetected? Or had he been caught?

I rubbed at the muscles knotted in my shoulders. Kicking off my sandals, I collapsed into the luxurious comfort of the navy leather sofa—our first major purchase as newlyweds. I needed some solid comfort. My day had been exhausting, physically and emotionally. Being probed, poked, and prodded by doctors was not my favorite pastime, and today's appointment had been particularly traumatic.

The little grandmother clock on the mantle chimed four soft tones as I closed my eyes, trying to block out the devastating words of Dr. Simon, dreadful words every woman fears. I could do nothing now, so I absolutely would not think about it.

Suddenly I was attacked by a tiny ball of soft white fur. Duchess, the newest member of our family, welcomed me home, reminding me it was dinnertime. While I stroked the purring kitten, I surveyed the new look of the cottage with a sigh of pleasure and contentment. After our marriage almost a year ago, we'd turned the caretaker's cottage of my parents' estate above Santa Barbara, California, into a cozy honeymoon nest.

Between Interpol assignments for Anastasia, we'd weeded out the pastiche of furniture Mom and I had lived with the last twenty years. Bart and I were putting our stamp—our personalities—on the decor and making it home. Our escape from the world. Life was good. It would be much better when Bart's call came. I worried when he was on assignment, and I had much to report. Some good news, some bad.

The ringing phone startled me from my reverie. I raced to catch it before the caller hung up, hoping, praying it was my husband. I needed to know Bart was safe—and I knew he was worried about the outcome of my appointment with Dr. Simon.

"Hello!"

"Alli. Thank heaven, you're there."

"Bishop O'Hare?"

"Don't talk. Listen. I have twenty seconds to relay this message from Bart. 'Anastasia's under attack. Leave house immediately. Pull "M" file, take notes you'll need for a month—nothing else. Repeat Mouse Island. You're in jeopardy. Disappear.'" He paused. "Call me at my office Sunday morning at 6:15. I'm your contact with Anastasia— your only contact until the crisis has passed."

"Bishop, what happened?"

The line went dead.

I dropped the phone on its cradle. Fear slammed through me as I digested the information and reviewed the message. *Anastasia under attack.* Another contract on the members of the anti-terrorist arm of Interpol? Apparently.

Leave the house immediately. It was being watched.

Disappear. Someone would be after me.

Take nothing. The cat! What about Duchess? I couldn't abandon her. She'd starve. I grabbed the basket I'd found in a Beverly Hills pet shop. Bart called it a frivolous purchase since the whole basket wasn't much bigger than a shoe box, but the kitten wasn't very big, either. The bottom held a tiny litter box in a pull-out drawer, with another small compartment for food.

"In you go, Duchess." I dropped a few nuggets of dry cat food in one corner and filled the small water bottle hanging from the side of the basket. Hopefully, my friend in Santa Barbara could keep her while I pulled a vanishing act.

I flew up the stairs and stuffed my swimsuit and shoes into a tattered old beach bag with a change of underclothes. What else should I take? *Leave the house immediately.* No time for anything else.

The reflection in the mirror startled me. I looked pale, ghostly, my ashen pallor accented by tousled black hair framing it. Dark half-moons under my green eyes created a cadaverous look. I turned quickly away from the specter, glad for the moment that Bart wasn't here to see his wife looking so ghastly.

On the way to the front door, I grabbed a handful of plastic bags and placed Duchess's basket in the bottom of the beach bag along with my purse.

It was then I spotted the unusual note from Alma on the roll-top desk next to the door, not in her usual neat script but scrawled across the front of the small package atop today's mail. "Allison—delivered this morning. Couldn't understand messenger. Leave quickly. Luv, A&J."

Alma and Jim. Bart's parents. Two more members of Anastasia. Already warned and gone. I dropped the package into the bag, locked the cottage door, and clicked the remote toward my little red convertible to lock it. I wished I could take it, but Bart had a good reason for directing me to leave another way. Anyone sent looking for me would have done their homework, would know what kind of car I drove, making it that much easier to find me.

It took less than a minute to cross the expanse of freshly mowed lawn to Mom and Dad's mansion at the top of the hill, overlooking the Pacific Ocean. I loved this place, abundant with aromas I associated with home, love, safety, and comfort: salty sea air, pungent pine, hot wind from the golden hills above us, and the roses Alma tended so lovingly around the estate.

Unlocking the huge front door, I stepped silently into the white marble foyer, waiting for the crystal chandelier overhead to stop tinkling before locking the door behind me. Removing my sandals, I tiptoed through the white oak French doors of the music room into the ballroom, listening, determining I was alone before proceeding to the white marble fireplace at the far end of the room.

A five-foot gold peacock with emerald eyes the size of my thumb covered the yawning opening of the fireplace, which was large enough to march an army through. Twisting one emerald eye up and the other down, I slipped behind the screen and through the elevator door that opened silently in the side wall of the fireplace.

Just as silently, the door closed and the elevator bore me swiftly down into the cliff on which the mansion was built. At the bottom, the door slid open into a dark, humid cavern filled with pungent smells of the ocean and the sound of lapping waves.

I touched a small cavity in the rock, illuminating tiny foot-level guiding lights to navigate the narrow rock passage. Midway down the passage, I fingered another indentation in the cavern wall. The tiny lights disappeared as a door in the wall silently opened. Stepping inside, I slid my hand down the interior wall until my fingers found the switch, depressed it, and the door swung shut, sealing me in utter darkness.

Only then did I activate a switch that flooded the room with fluorescent light—the Control Center of Anastasia, Interpol's anti-terrorist division. The air-conditioned room, filled with computers, radios, communication and monitoring equipment, and Anastasia's files, could have been the communications center of any modern industry.

On my way to the files, I checked the messages on the computer and found a one-liner from Mom. "Undercover for the duration. Remember your training and disappear." I deleted it.

Nothing from Bart. Except the message he'd been able to get to Bishop O'Hare. Why had he called the bishop? Because he couldn't reach me? Or was the FBI involved and Bishop O'Hare was working with Interpol? That sounded reasonable since he was to be my contact for the duration of this situation, whatever it was. A shiver ran through me. "The duration" had an ominous sound.

That message said to pull the "M" file and take enough notes for a month. The "M" file contained Anastasia's stash of ready cash. For a month. Just how far underground could I go, and how much would I need?

I grabbed a handful of hundred-dollar bills and slipped them under the liner in Duchess's litter box. Then I pulled a few smaller denominations and four credit cards with matching ID created for such a purpose as this.

Donning swimsuit and swim shoes, I wrapped my clothes in a plastic bag, put Duchess's basket in another plastic bag inside the tattered beach tote, plopped on a floppy hat, and headed for the door.

One last, important thing. I sent a fast, fervent prayer heavenward for the safety of all Anastasia's agents, especially Bart and my parents, and for guidance and inspiration on how to do whatever I needed to do. As I reached for the lights, I added a postscript that I'd be able to follow Dr. Simon's orders as closely as possible. The flash of irritation I felt at having to slow down when I desperately needed to be healthy and vital and strong surprised me, and I refused to acknowledge that it might stop me altogether very soon.

I scanned the room one last time. I didn't dare leave a message. There was always the possibility the Control Center could be discovered. Terrorists didn't send idiots to annihilate groups like Anastasia.

Bart's communication had said, "Repeat Mouse Island." I assumed he meant leave the estate by way of the ocean using scuba gear, as we'd done in Greece. I might have done that if it hadn't been for Duchess. No time to find a cat-sitter. No time to do anything but take her along. My tender heart wouldn't consider for a second abandoning the tiny, helpless thing.

I turned out the lights and opened the door. Waiting for my eyes to adjust to the darkness, I made sure I was still alone, then stepped into the cool, moist air of the cavern and closed the door behind me.

Crossing the passageway to the other side, I groped my way along the rock wall toward the sound of waves crashing against rocks, until the splashing seemed directly below me. Tentatively, I ran my foot along the floor of the cave until I felt the edge of the rock where the floor dropped away beneath my toes.

I descended the narrow steps, hugging the wall of the cave. When Dad designed the Control Center, he'd had this passageway open fifty feet above the ocean, then carved a slim set of stairs into the rock wall that led down to the beach.

Duchess decided at this point that she didn't much like being shut up in a basket with so many new scents to investigate. Her tiny mews wouldn't be heard above the sound of the ocean, but later, in a situation where absolute silence was required, I couldn't take the chance she'd inadvertently betray me.

The result of an experiment in cross-breeding, Duchess was, for all intents and purposes, a voiceless cat. She could still make small sounds—nothing compared to her Oriental forebears, but enough to be a danger. I hoped Mark, my Santa Barbara friend, was home and wouldn't mind cat-sitting, although his dogs probably would.

Inserting the beach bag inside the last of the plastic bags, I deposited it on the strip of sand while I retrieved one of the kayaks we kept hanging near the stairs. Securing the bundle in the front seat, I slipped into the back, and pushed off into the cold water.

The cave, through several twists and turns, led to open ocean. At high tide the opening and first few feet of the cavern were submerged, but with the tide out, we passed easily through the passageway. I paused at the entrance to the cave, checking for boats in the cove—for anyone watching the house. The only thing in sight was a sailboat out toward the Channel Islands.

Taking advantage of adrenaline-produced energy, I leaned into the paddle, clearing our cove in two minutes, pausing only briefly as I rounded the point to scan the open ocean ahead of me. A couple of pleasure boats too far out to be a concern and a couple of fishing scows returning to harbor were the nearest craft.

I couldn't resist one last glimpse at the estate—at the mansion perched atop the cliff and towering green pines silhouetted against cloudless blue sky. I couldn't see our cottage, nestled beneath those ancient trees, but I knew every corner, every nail hole in the cozy little place.

How long before I could come home? Before my family would return? If they did. As the dread word "if" surfaced, I banished it from my mind. They—we—just *had* to return. I couldn't conceive of any other possibility. Life couldn't be that cruel, could it? I realized that mortality was meant to be a series of tests, trials, and challenges to prove our faith in God and our worthiness to return to His presence, but I'd always pictured my family beside me during these vicissitudes.

Vicissitudes. Interesting word. Synonyms: life, experience. Just what did God have in mind for my "life experiences"? I'd certainly planned a different path than I seemed to be traveling right now. What was *His* plan?

Taking a deep breath, I plunged the paddle into the waves, stroking evenly, rhythmically toward Santa Barbara ten miles down the coast. No time for energy-draining worry. The afternoon was perfect for a workout—gentle breezes and smooth water—and this would certainly provide a good one. Barring any unforeseen obstacles.

As I settled into a comfortable cadence, my mind sorted over the unbelievable events of the last hour. The trauma at the doctor's office with its surprising, horrifying diagnosis. The frightening phone call from Bishop O'Hare. My frantic flight. Bart's call that never came from the Democratic Republic of Congo, formerly Zaire.

When terrorist unrest in the African nation had reached dangerous levels, Interpol had requested that Anastasia intervene. My husband and two other agents, Oswald Barlow and Mai Li, were sent to defuse the situation and destroy the terrorist grip on the area in any way possible. That usually meant infiltrating the terrorist group. Had they been successful? I worried constantly when Bart went undercover, risking his life each time he associated with the dregs of society bent on destroying the world.

Keeping one eye on the coastline, I moved farther out on the water. The assassin . . . I shuddered as I finally acknowledged the dreadful word . . . the assassin could see me with high-powered binoculars no matter how far out I got. The bright yellow kayak stood out on the water. But if he hadn't made it to the estate yet . . .

Who was after us this time? Many organizations would pay incredible amounts to have Anastasia annihilated. Powerful underworld leaders with terrorist connections continually plotted against this elite circle of agents—their deadliest threat. So many enemies for our little group who wanted nothing more than a safe world to live in, a quiet place to raise families.

My heart lurched at the thought. Would I ever have that opportunity? I glanced at the freshly healed scar on my leg, ugly and red—a memento of a bullet I took to save Bart nearly three months ago in Texas.

The doctor who'd repaired the damage to my leg also repaired the damage caused by a bursting fallopian tube. I'd lost the baby I didn't even know I carried. Worse still, it appeared that my chances of ever getting pregnant again were slight. Devastated as I'd been, Bart experienced our loss just as keenly. He had hoped for a houseful of kids.

At that time, the doctor recommended that we immediately begin the paperwork involved in adopting any children we wanted. In his opinion, they'd be the only ones we'd be privileged to raise. After much prayer and discussion, we'd decided to begin the long process to adopt those babies.

However, at the moment, raising children seemed a far-off dream. Surviving—suddenly on two different fronts—was the order of the day. Dr. Simon, in making a routine check after the fallopian surgery, had discovered a suspicious shadow on the x-ray. Today he'd done a biopsy. Now we awaited the test results. Of course, if the assassin found me, those results would be the least of my worries.

Strange that I'd felt so vital, so alive, so complete, just six months ago. Like a verdant green valley full of beautiful fruit and flowers and wonderful living things. A veritable paradise. My world wasn't perfect, but whose was? Now, with the news from Dr. Simon, I pictured myself as a barren desert—not the beautiful, blooming-in-the-spring kind, but bleak and empty, with an ugly malignancy lurking in the shadows, an alien monster waiting to destroy.

But I wandered unnecessary mental paths. I needed a plan. My flight had begun with nothing more in mind than leaving the estate as quickly as possible. I'd accomplished that. Now I must focus, concentrate on staying alive. I couldn't afford a single thought that didn't have to do with disappearing off the face of the earth for the next month. I shuddered. Would it be that long?

I stroked faster, increasing the rhythm and cadence of the paddle. My arms felt the strain of the continued dip and pull of the oar, first on one side, then the other. My back would feel it soon. I didn't want to think of the repercussions of all this forbidden activity.

I concentrated on Santa Barbara—on the marina. And calling Mark. Then I had second thoughts. Would I be leading him into danger if I contacted him? But what could I do with Duchess if I didn't? It might be better not to go into Santa Barbara after all. But where?

Too bad I'd never learned to fly. Anastasia's Lear jet was parked about two miles from here, just waiting for someone to use it. It wouldn't be me. But that gave me another idea. If I beached at UC Santa Barbara, I could blend in with the college students, catch the bus to town, then take the train or rent a car and get lost in Los Angeles.

It seemed like a better idea than rowing the rest of the way to Santa Barbara. Someone could be watching the marina. Or were they watching all along the coast? Hard to tell, since I didn't know who was after me, but usually a single assassin was sent for each target. Because I was Anastasia's newest agent, the least experienced, and a twenty-five-year-old woman, they probably wouldn't send more than one—and probably not even one of their best.

But I couldn't count on that. I couldn't plan on the natural prejudice that breed of men held against the intellect of a woman. That could be a fatal mistake.

I rested, stretched, touched the now tender area of the biopsy. It felt sore, swollen. Nothing I could do about it. I renewed my paddling. A wet suit would have been a better idea than a swimsuit. As the sun dipped toward the horizon, the temperature dropped. Even with steady paddling, the burn of muscles working hard didn't warm me.

Then I could see the University of California's Santa Barbara campus jutting out on the coast ahead. I'd need to pick my spot carefully. Would it have changed much in the few years since I'd been on campus? I glanced over my shoulder frequently, making sure no one followed, checking out each boat that came in sight, holding my breath until I'd decided it wasn't a threat. Finally I chose a secluded area of beach with tall, scraggly bushes and steered for it.

As I approached the headland, a huge bonfire flared on the beach at the spot I'd chosen to land. Figures moved in front, silhouetted against the bright orange flames dancing in the twilight. My paddle froze mid-stroke. I ran a mental checklist, reviewing my options, as the kayak sliced through the water toward the light and noise.

Then I headed for the beach this side of the fire. I needed the warmth of that blaze, if only for a minute, and I'd just had an idea. If it didn't work, what did I have to lose?

Only my life.

CHAPTER 2

I counted approximately twenty figures in various stages of dress and undress cavorting in and out of the water and romping on the beach. An impromptu game of what looked like volleyball, minus the net, occupied a half-dozen people clad in shorts or sweats.

A couple of girls in tiny bikinis raced toward the water with two guys in hot pursuit. The pursuit was the only thing hot about it. They'd freeze as soon as they hit the water. The Pacific Ocean off the California coast was never warm in May, and this year was no exception.

I beached the kayak on the brushy, rocky part of the beach with the least amount of action and watched the activities. No one paid me any attention as I pulled the bright yellow craft out of the water and deposited my big plastic bag behind some brush.

Removing my wedding band and emerald engagement ring from my finger, I tucked them inside Duchess's food drawer in the bottom of her basket, then hurried toward the blazing fire, shivering from head to toe. The couple nearest the fire looked up and smiled.

"Oh, I forgot how cold it can get when the sun goes down," I smiled, backing toward the fire and vigorously rubbing the goose bumps on my arms. "I've got to go get something over my swimsuit or I'll never be warm again."

The chill banished, and without waiting for the surprised couple to reply, I headed back toward the kayak, scooped up the beach bag, and fled toward the campus in the deepening twilight. Hopefully, they'd decide I had the wrong beach party and forget about me.

I stopped in the shadow of one of the college buildings long enough to shrug on the denim skirt and short-sleeved white cotton sweater I'd worn earlier in the day. Not smart to have forgotten a jacket. The evening breeze off the ocean ruffled my hair, sending shivers through me. But if I remembered right, a bus should be heading back to town soon, and I'd be out of the cold.

I caught sight of it about the same time I located the bus stop. I'd never make it—unless a compassionate driver waited for me. I yelled, waved, and broke into a run across the lawn. Too late. No compassion. The door closed and the bus moved slowly away from the curb. Suddenly, another shout rang across campus.

A wheelchair streaked down the sidewalk and into the path of the bus, which jerked to a stop as the man in the wheelchair grinned broadly and raised his hand to the driver. The door flew open and the driver's voice carried across the night. "Arnold, you're gonna do that once too often, and I'm not gonna be able to stop this vehicle. How many times I gotta tell you? This bus don't stop on a dime like your chair."

While Arnold got on the bus, I slipped in quietly, just another coed heading back to town after a day on campus. I made eye contact with no one, burying my head in my beach bag to pet Duchess and assure her that all was well. A little tummy tickling, and she was satisfied her world was still intact.

I wished I could say the same for mine.

Decision time. Should I get off the bus at the airport and rent a car, or go on to Santa Barbara and catch the train to Los Angeles? Which would help me disappear quickest, and be hardest to trace?

Reviewing my training at Quantico six months ago to become an Interpol agent, I opted for the latter, for the obvious reason. Invisibility. Exiting the bus a couple of stops before the Santa Barbara train station, I walked the rest of the way, locating a phone booth in a busy area outside a noisy restaurant. I called Mark, keeping my fingers crossed that he could come for Duchess and I could still catch the last train out of town.

The phone rang four, five, six times. Finally his answering machine came on. "This is Mark. I'm not home right now. In fact, I won't be home all month. If it's urgent that you reach me, you can call this number in Hong Kong."

The number in Hong Kong would do me no good tonight. I hung up the phone—and my hopes for an unencumbered run.

"Well, Duchess, looks like we're going on a trip. Hope you're a good traveler."

I dug a hair band from my purse, fashioned my unmanageable mane of black curls into a ponytail, tucked it out of sight under the wide-brimmed hat, and hurried the few blocks to the train station. With sunglasses hiding my emerald eyes and hat pulled low over my face, I bought a ticket to San Diego. If anyone inquired about passengers buying tickets to Los Angeles, I wouldn't be among those described. Fortunately in California, sunglasses were normal attire, day or night.

I glanced around the old Spanish-style station, studying the assortment of passengers awaiting the next train. A clean-cut young man in his late teens leaned against the brown glazed-brick wall, eyeing a sophisticated career-type woman in her late twenties with long legs and a short skirt, too intent on her cell phone conversation to notice him.

Two older businessmen, with ties loosened, smoked outside under large, tan adobe arches, avoiding the setting sun. Through glazed triangles of glass, I could see a harried mother corralling three active youngsters in a separate area to keep them from bothering people. A white-haired man read a newspaper, and a young Oriental couple were taking pictures of the famous Bay Town Fig Tree that spread its huge, white-wood branches over one entire portion of the parking lot.

No one observed me, nor did any of them seem the type I'd consider dangerous or potential assassins.

With an hour before the train's scheduled arrival, I left the station to wait elsewhere, but close enough to hear if it came early. This was not a train known for its punctuality, only for its spectacular views as it hugged the coastline.

Music, voices, and aromas emanating from a nearby café reminded me I hadn't eaten since lunch. The tables on the sidewalk were filled with an eclectic mix of diners: college students, beach bums, older couples, and a table full of young girls ogling the surfers at the next table.

I ordered comfort food—Greek fettuccini with garlic bread. When my meal was ready, I slipped out the side door and looked for a secure place to eat and watch. Across the street, a flower shop closed. As the shopkeeper drove away, I jaywalked to sit on a white wrought-iron bench where I had a view of the street in three directions but was hidden by the flower kiosk on the corner.

Before I began my own meal, I opened the lid on the basket and gave Duchess some fresh air and food. Content to observe me from the basket still nestled in the beach bag, she devoured her dry meal. I hoped it tasted as good to her as my feta cheese and black-peppered fettuccini did to me. The highly seasoned garlic bread would certainly keep anyone from getting close enough to strike up a conversation.

Then I had nothing to do but wait. Wait and wonder. Wait and worry. Had the rest of Anastasia successfully disappeared? Was Bart okay? Then one more worry surfaced: I was under doctor's orders—as of this afternoon—to rest, relax, and be totally stress-free for the next few days until the test results were analyzed. Where would I be a few days from now? And what damage would I do by disobeying my doctor's orders? Or had I already done it with all that paddling?

The sound of the approaching train interrupted my catalogue of worries. Dumping my Styrofoam dinnerware in the nearest trash can, I secured Duchess in her cozy habitat, then checked out all vehicles, moving or parked, and the shadows surrounding the station before stepping into the street. I hurried to the picturesque old station, recently revamped to its original 1905 design, and boarded the waiting train.

Choosing a seat in the corner, I plopped the beach bag in the other seat. From underneath the hat's wide brim, I could watch passengers boarding the train, as well as a good section of the platform.

As the train finally pulled from the station, I realized I'd barely breathed since I sat down. I took a long, deep breath, exhaled slowly, and stretched my legs. Flexing aching fingers I'd kept balled into tight fists, I rolled my head in a wide circle to relax my taut shoulder muscles. Think pleasant thoughts. Think about Bart.

I smiled as memories of my husband tumbled through my mind—the massive miscommunication during courtship, our explosive wedding, our newfound closeness since our baptism. I felt myself relax as I recalled our memorable Christmas on that unforgettable slow boat from Sri Lanka—an idyllic cruise that became the honeymoon we'd never had.

I thought of our ordeal at the hospital in Texas, where our appreciation and love for each other had only deepened. It was true—affliction and adversity were refining fires that burned away the dross and left something more precious as a result.

Feeling totally rejuvenated, I opened my eyes and spotted a newspaper someone had left on the seat across the aisle. In black, bold-faced type, its headline proclaimed an unsettling development: ***Ebola Imitator Unleashed. WHO Alarmed.*** I picked up the paper. WHO must be the World Health Organization.

"It's always dicey whether you make the last train out or not. The gamble keeps life interesting, don't you think?" The voice, unexpected and close—too close—startled me.

Whirling, I gazed directly into big, chocolate-brown eyes that hinted at an unrestrained sense of humor. Arnold, my knight in shining wheelchair who'd stopped the bus on campus, studied me with an unblinking stare.

I studied him right back: sandy hair skimming his collar, brown eyes the color of Hershey's kisses, a slight smile revealing nice teeth, muscular biceps one would expect from someone used to locomoting himself with arms instead of legs. And this was no college-age kid. My guess put him in the thirty-five to forty-year range.

My first impulse was to excuse myself and find another seat. I didn't need friendly conversation right now; I needed anonymity. My second was to find out why he'd approached me. His wheelchair would be a perfect disguise for an assassin.

I smiled back. "With either train, it's a gamble. I don't know which is worse, the San Diegan or the Coast Starlight."

"Don't put your money on either being on time, coming or going. But you've gotta love the scenery, and it sure beats the alternative—driving Highway 101."

"I didn't see you get on. Do you take the train all the time instead of driving?" I asked, still puzzled by his approach. People from this area were friendly, but not as outgoing as this man. It bothered me that I hadn't seen him on the platform.

"I'm special," he grinned. "Got my own boarding area. I'm taking a couple of graduate classes at UCSB. I review my notes on the way back to Los Angeles, finishing assignments in the three hours before we arrive at Union Station. Then I'm free. No stress and tension from the commute, I've eaten a leisurely dinner, and I'm ready to be a good guy instead of a grouch when I get home."

"Who's waiting for the good guy when you get there?"

His eyes softened. He pulled a picture from the side pocket of his wheelchair and held it out to me.

A skinny little girl with long blonde braids and a missing tooth beamed at the camera.

"Your daughter?" I handed the picture back.

"My life," he breathed fervently, a tone that brought a lump to my throat. He tucked the picture back in the pocket, avoiding my eyes for a moment—waiting, I felt, for the mist to clear before he looked up.

"She's darling. How old is she?"

"Six tomorrow. We're planning a special day, just the two of us." Then he laughed, bitterness obvious in the sound. "Of course, that's all there is—just the two of us."

I waited. If he wanted to tell me, I'd listen. But I wasn't going to ask. I wasn't going to get involved with anyone and their problems. Not now. I'd have a hard enough time taking care of *me* in the next month.

My training as an Interpol agent hadn't quelled the compassion I felt for any of God's creatures in need of help. This little quirk of mine—picking up strays, whether they be human or animal—had endangered several Anastasia assignments. Someone had always been there to bail me out. But this time I was on my own. I couldn't afford to get involved.

I closed my eyes. Maybe he'd go away. Maybe he'd think I was tired—sleepy—and leave. He didn't. He wheeled his chair to face me and started talking.

"Are you in grad school? I haven't seen you on campus before."

So much for slipping onto the bus unnoticed. "No, and I didn't thank you for stopping the bus. I'd have missed it if you hadn't made that dramatic swoop in front of it. Do you do that often?"

"Clyde watches for me to come out of my last class. He pretends he'll leave me, but he's never done it yet. What—"

I interrupted, pretending I hadn't heard the beginning of his question. "I'm glad he's more compassionate than I supposed. Tell me about your little girl. What's her name?"

"Morgan." His eyes crinkled in a smile before it reached his mouth. "She's an angel. One little bundle bursting with love."

He stopped and stared at my beach bag. Funny noises emanated from it. Arnold looked at me expectantly.

I glanced around the train. His wheelchair blocked the view of other passengers. I opened the beach bag, removed the basket, and withdrew the ball of white fur.

"This is *my* little bundle of love. Duchess, meet Arnold."

His eyebrows went up in surprise. "You know my name."

"The bus driver called you by name."

He nodded. "You take a kitten to class?"

I laughed. "No, although I could probably get away with it. Her litter is one of a kind. She's bred to be quiet. That little noise she made is the most you'll hear from her."

"Morgan would love her."

I shouldn't ask. I should terminate this conversation right now. *I should not get involved.* But I asked anyway, "Where is your daughter while you're in school?"

"She stays with an elderly neighbor next door. We trade. I fix her stopped-up sinks and do odd jobs for her, and she keeps Morgan while I'm gone. She's a widow, misses her grandchildren, and adopted Morgan as one of her own when she was born. She's the only grandmother Morgan's ever had."

As soon as he said it, I knew he regretted it. He turned away and fussed with the pouch hanging from one arm of his chair. I gave all my attention to Duchess, caressing her under her chin and rubbing her tummy, which elicited contented purring and licking of a finger by way of thank you.

I busied myself tucking her into the basket and placed the basket back into the ratty-looking beach bag. I really would have to replace this at the earliest opportunity. Especially if I planned to appear anywhere respectable.

Planned. How much planning could I do? Until I talked to Bishop O'Hare on Sunday and got more details, the only plan I had was to lay low, stay out of sight, and stay alive. At this point, I had no idea what that would entail. I thought of Bart, in the midst of terrorists, taking the time to call Bishop O'Hare with instructions for me.

Always thinking of me. How I loved the guy!

Suddenly feeling uneasy, I glanced at the man in the wheelchair. He leaned forward, gripping the arms of his chair, and stared at me, a frown creasing his suntanned forehead. "Who *are* you?" he asked softly.

When I didn't answer, he reached over, pushed up the brim of my hat, and took a good, long look at my face.

CHAPTER 3

My heart thumped wildly, my mind racing. One glance at those muscular arms, and I knew my only option was to avoid them. If I didn't have Duchess to worry about, I could dive over the empty seat in front of me and make it to the next car before he wheeled his chair around and caught me. If he really needed the chair.

Suddenly his hand darted out and grabbed my arm. "Whoa. I'm sorry. I didn't mean to frighten you."

I removed my arm from his grip, physically and mentally distancing myself from him.

"Let's start over," he said gently, backing his wheelchair slightly. "I'm Arnold Trent, grad student at UCSB studying criminal psychology. I'm the father of one beautiful little princess. And I've scared you."

I took a deep breath. "No," I stammered.

Arnold shook his head. "I recognized that 'fight or flight' look in your eyes. I frightened you. I'm sorry. Was it me, or . . . ?"

He waited for me to finish the sentence. I didn't.

Careful, lady. You don't know this man. You don't know why he singled you out from all the other passengers on this train. And until you do . . .

"Are you afraid of me, or is it something else?" he asked.

I'd never been a good liar. What could I say that had a ring of truth, yet wouldn't reveal anything about me?

I glanced at the beach bag, avoiding his scrutinizing stare, avoiding his big, brown, sincere eyes as I spoke. "I'm leaving home. No one knows where I am or where I'm going. I thought you might have been sent to stop me." All true.

I glanced at him. Did he buy the story? Did he know who I really was?

He sat back, elbows resting on the arms of the wheelchair, and laced his fingers together, watching me. Like a judge contemplating a sentence, I thought. Was this man my judge and jury? And executioner?

"Why are you running?" he asked.

"I'd rather not talk about it."

"What would you like to talk about?"

However he'd managed it, he was now on the offensive and I was on the defensive. I didn't like the shift in perspective.

"Actually, nothing," I said. "I'd like to sleep for an hour. It's been a rather harrowing day." I closed my eyes, hoping he'd buy that.

"Back to gambling," he said.

I opened my eyes and looked at him. "Gambling?"

"Catching the train—a gamble that kept life interesting. What would you have done if you hadn't caught the train?"

Why do you want to know? So you'll know how I think when I get away and you can find me again?

Arnold caught the hesitation and hammered back, softly, but with an intensity that made me squirm, *"What* are you afraid of?"

"Being cornered. Being caught. Having no options. Being on the defensive. Having control taken from me. Being questioned like a suspect. Take your pick—or all of the above." The words tumbled out as I reached for the beach bag.

In one swift movement, Arnold rolled forward and picked it up. Panic coursed through me. He placed the bag on my lap, reached in, and pulled out the basket. His eyes never left my face as he fingered open the latch, scooped out Duchess, and held her out to me with one hand while he dropped the bag to the floor with the other.

I reached for the tiny kitten with trembling hands, then shut my eyes as I held her to me. What was the matter with me? I used to be an adequate actress. Now I felt every emotion playing across my face in I-max proportions.

"Back to gambling," he repeated softly.

I looked up. A gentle smile filled his face.

"I'm not the big bad wolf, but if I were, your eyes would have told me where to find grandmother. They telegraph your emotions—al ost your very thoughts. Never gamble."

"Why did you do that?" I asked.

"What?"

"Take Duchess out of her basket and give her to me."

"Why do you think?"

I paused. "To give me something to think about besides myself. To give me something to concentrate on while I regained my composure. To make you look compassionate and caring instead of like the big bad wolf."

He laughed. "Are you studying psychology, too?"

I looked him straight in the eye. "Arnold, I'd rather not talk about me. Name a subject. Anything you want. Race, religion, politics, current events, the world situation—anything. But I'm off limits."

He laughed. "I like you better this way. The spark is back. The light. By the way, that's what started this whole thing."

"What?"

"The light. You have an inner glow. I want to know why. Who are you? Why are you special? You got on the train, looking little different from the other passengers, closed your eyes, did some little mental thing, and you were transformed. You glowed with some inner light that made you stand out. I watch people all the time. You're different."

"I don't want to stand out," I whispered, glancing around to see if anyone was listening to this incredible conversation.

"I know that now. And you're getting jumpy again. If we weren't on a moving train, you'd run. Fly away. Be gone before I had any answers."

"You're right there, buster," I said under my breath, wishing a stop was due. I *would* fly away. Run as fast and as far as I could from this disconcerting man who could just as easily be friend or foe.

Duchess wriggled in my hands. I'd been clutching her too tight. I settled her in my lap, and she snuggled under my hand, rubbing against it, a signal that she'd appreciate a tummy tickle. She must enjoy those as much as I enjoyed Bart's back scrubs in the shower. Just one of the many delights of wedded bliss.

I thought of Bart, remembering his tender ministrations to injuries sustained in our incredible adventures, tried to picture him in Zaire in his current assignment without me. When I couldn't call up a mental picture of the place, I suffered a pang of loneliness—or worry—or both.

"Where are you now?"

I studied the enigmatic man in the wheelchair. "I tried to wish myself to the other side of the world. I thought maybe if I wiggled my nose, or muttered some bewitching incantations, I could escape from you and your incessant questions."

He smiled. "I'm persistent. I'd probably follow you there just to find out about you."

My heart froze. "Don't." The tone sounded weak, frightened. "Don't," I repeated with emphasis. "There's nothing special about me. There's nothing interesting to know, except that I'm a married woman."

He raised one eyebrow. "Is that who you're running from?"

I looked him straight in the eye. "My husband is the last person I'd run from. If I could, I'd be running *to* him at this minute." *Stop. Don't let him drag your story from you. He's smart. He's learning to push the right buttons to get you to blurt out what he wants to know.*

"Go away. Please, just leave me alone. Let me run away in peace. I don't want your counseling. I don't need your help. I can't tell you what you want to know. Just go away."

Arnold folded his arms—and stayed.

Two could play this game. I hoped that was what it was—a game. *What if you're playing footsies with the very man sent to kill you? He'll needle under your skin, make himself a friendly pest, then when you get off the train—zap. You're history.*

I turned to the window and stared out into the night. Maybe if I ignored him, he'd tire of the game and go away. Unless he *was* the assassin.

Bart was right. I really wasn't cut out for these dangerous games. Oz was right, too. I should stay home with a houseful of kids. But that might never be an option.

I'd loved Bart all my life. We'd grown up on the estate together, his parents as caretakers of the estate, my mom as manager. I'd followed him around like a puppy, and all the time I'd been growing up, he'd been the perfect big brother I never had. Whatever he did, I wanted to do.

Just before we were married, I'd discovered that not only was he an Interpol agent, but my mother and father were, too. And my mother actually owned the estate. I closed my eyes and leaned my head against the seat. What a shock that had been: to discover I was heir to millions of dollars, and my mother was the famous movie star who built the mansion. My parents had worked together, undercover, for over twenty years, and I'd never suspected a thing.

That was when I'd determined I wanted the same life as my parents. Side by side, Bart and I could work to eradicate terrorism and make the world a safer place. But even after formal training as an agent, I didn't quite measure up. Just as you can't make a silk purse from a sow's ear, neither can you make a cunning agent from someone more cat than fox. Make that kitten. I wasn't even as smart as a cat. You never knew what cats were thinking.

What was Bart thinking now? When he said he thought of me constantly, I believed him. He'd even slipped away from infiltrating terrorists and the Tamil Tigers in Sri Lanka to arrange for a marvelous Christmas surprise when he discovered I'd be in the country. But was he worrying about me instead of worrying about his own survival in Africa? Wondering if I'd disappeared before the assassin found me?

Assassin. I blinked my eyes open and sat up straight. He was still there. Still watching me.

I hugged my arms close to me. "I thought you were going away."

"And miss the show? Not on your life," he said. "Besides, the light is back again. What were you thinking? What turns that glow on?"

I stared at him blankly. "I was thinking about my husband."

"What about him?"

"Sorry, Charlie. That's off-limits. Remember?"

"You're a paradox, you know. A pretty, puzzling paradox. One minute your face is radiant with an inner glow—peace. That's what it is. An inner peace. The next you're as nervous as a baby bird fallen from the nest, waiting to see if the cat's spotted her yet."

"Has he?"

"Has who, what?"

"Has the cat spotted her?"

Arnold laughed a little ruefully, and rubbed his hand over his day-old beard. "You still think I'm the big bad wolf, don't you?"

"You tell me. Are you?"

"I'd be pretty stupid to get this close—here—now—if I were."

"Or pretty smart," I countered.

"It's that serious, huh?"

I looked at him a long moment before I answered. "Deadly."

He didn't reply, just watched me, never taking his eyes from mine. I stared right back. He didn't look like an assassin. He didn't act like one. But then, how close had I ever been to the real thing? Terrorists I'd seen up close. But terrorists in general were different from assassins, who were sent specifically to eliminate one person in cold-blooded murder.

I did want to trust him. Then I asked myself why. *Why would I trust anyone when I'm running for my life, when I don't know who's after me, or how close they are? If this man isn't the assassin, which I don't know, then his life is in danger by his very proximity to me.*

I shut my eyes, asked for a little guidance from One who knew the truth about all things, then turned again to Arnold. "Where is Morgan's mother?"

"Why?" he asked. He looked surprised, as if I'd caught him off guard.

"Because if you are Mr. Nice Guy, your life's in danger as long as you hang around me. I wouldn't want to be the cause of making Morgan an orphan. Does she have a mother?"

Arnold's eyes narrowed quickly. "You weren't kidding about the deadly?"

"Not for a heartbeat. So I recommend you turn your transportation around and absent yourself from me for the remainder of the trip. That way, you won't be in the line of fire if, or when, I'm found. And unless I get better at playing these games fast, that may not be very long."

"That explains the fright. But it makes the other even more enigmatic. How can I see that peace so clearly in your eyes when you're . . ." He broke off, letting the sentence fall away and disappear into the sound of steel wheels on rails.

"Running for my life? Say it. Not saying it doesn't make it not so. Admitting it helps face it. Of course, I've just broken a major rule, since you may very well be the person I'm running from."

Silently he shook his head.

I leaned forward. "That's why, for Morgan's sake, if not for your own, you need to split, posthaste, and stay far away from me. That way, you just might get home in time to read her a bedtime story and help her say her prayers. And while you're praying, add one for me."

Arnold wheeled his chair close to mine and covered my hand with his. "Do you believe I'm the one who's after you?" he asked quietly.

I looked deeply into those chocolate-brown eyes and saw nothing but honesty staring back at me. I shook my head.

"No. But I could be wrong. I often am. My husband says I'm too trusting. He's right. I'm naive and gullible, and I want to believe that everyone is good and everything is what it seems. But that's a fairy tale, and you need to get home in one piece to your little princess so you can read her one. Go on, get out of here."

He leaned forward in his wheelchair. "Where are you going when you get to Los Angeles?"

I stared at him. Didn't this man ever give up? "Even if I trusted you, I wouldn't tell you."

"Can I help?"

"Like I said, say a prayer."

He persisted. "Do you have a place to go? I don't even know your name."

I sighed. "Arnold, if I'd wanted you to know my name, I'd have told you. But you seem very hard of hearing, so it probably wouldn't have done any good. Get lost."

"If you're planning to hide, I have a suggestion. You could come to my—"

"Your house? Arnold, how do you know what I've told you isn't one big lie, and I'm actually running from the police? You don't know anything about me."

He sat back in his chair and steepled his fingers. "Actually, I've learned a lot about you. And I'm sure it's not the police you're running from. As I said, you could come to . . ."

I interrupted him. "I'd never draw someone else into this, especially Morgan's father."

"You don't even know Morgan."

"Yes, I do. She has long blonde braids, an infectious smile, and a missing front tooth. And only a father to look after her."

He glanced down at his hands, then looked up with misty eyes and smiled. "Be safe. And when you finish this business, give me a call." He dug a card out of his pouch and handed it to me. "I want to know about that glow. I want it for Morgan. I want to see that look in her eyes."

I nodded and dropped the card in my bag. "I promise I'll tell you how she can have it."

He slowly wheeled his chair down the aisle. I didn't turn to watch, simply leaned my head back on my seat, closed my eyes, and stroked the purring kitten. It would have been kind of nice to have gone home with him and met his daughter. To have had some place to hide out.

I reached into the bag and withdrew the basket, snuggling Duchess into her bed. As I bent to put the basket back in the bag, I saw the small package on which Alma had scribbled her note. In the crunch of things, I'd completely forgotten about it.

It had no return address. It hadn't even gone through the mails. No postmark on the stamp.

CHAPTER 4

Puzzled, I unwrapped the plain brown packaging, struggling with the tape. The next layer was something that resembled Mylar—actually two separate layers of it. Under all that a sturdy box appeared, about four inches high, four inches deep, and five inches long.

Brown plastic wrapping tape covered the plain box on both ends. My fingernail wasn't sufficiently sharp or strong to split it. I dug in my purse for my fingernail file. Bart called it a woman's weapon, since I frequently substituted it for screwdriver, pry, lever, and miscellaneous other tools.

Inside the box, tightly secured by more than enough cellophane tape, bubble wrap covered something hard and angular. I glanced up to see if anyone watched, observing my curiosity and excitement. All the passengers were involved in newspapers, books, conversation, laptop computers, or sleep.

Piece by piece, strip by strip, I peeled away the clear tape until at last the bubble wrap unfolded like petals on a flower. Inside lay a black velvet pouch. I held my breath, loosening the drawstring.

Gently I shook a sizable chunk of gleaming stone from the pouch—an exquisitely carved green jade lion with colors ranging from deep emerald to almost translucent white. The lion appeared to be walking, one foot extended in front of the other, his head held high, mane full.

The figure wasn't much over three inches long, about two inches high, and possibly one and a quarter inches wide. It felt cool, and perfectly smooth to the touch, except for the pointed ears and indentations that comprised the mane. Even the feet had rounded corners.

It fit nicely cradled in my palm, the tail end toward the heel of my hand, the head poking out between my thumb and forefinger. Almost as if it belonged there.

Was this a gift from Bart? A curio? A memento of his Zaire assignment? Or was there something more to it? In our travels in the Orient, I'd seen almost everything imaginable carved from jade: dragons, elephants, Buddhas—even tigers, but never lions. Was there some significance in the figure?

While I searched each piece of the wrapping, my mind raced over reasons Bart would have sent it. It wasn't like him to send me gifts during a mission. He brought them home to me—personally put them in my hands to watch my face as I opened them.

Was he afraid he wouldn't return? Or was this meant to be a comfort during his absence as I underwent all the tests alone? To the Chinese, jade is considered the concentrated essence of love. Maybe the jade lion simply signified Bart's love for me. I could go with that.

Thus far, I hadn't found a word of explanation in all the layers of wrapping. As I poked my finger into the black velvet pouch, I felt something in the bottom. A card. A business card written in some language I didn't understand—not one of the dozen I spoke or read. I guessed it might be Swahili or Kingwana, languages of the Congo.

On the opposite side, Bart's small, tight handwriting filled the card. "Princess, tuck this in safe place in the Control Center, not with you or in house. Vital it not fall into wrong hands. Will explain when we talk. Good luck on tests." Almost illegible in the corner was a tiny caricature of a suit of armor: Bart's signature. My Knight in Shining Armor.

Well. That posed a problem. It wouldn't be in the house, so anyone looking there wouldn't find it, but I didn't know what to do about the other part. Why wouldn't he want it with me? Because someone would be after it? Big deal. Someone was already after me. But not because of the lion.

Or was it? I reviewed Bishop O'Hare's message: "Anastasia's under attack. Get out of the house. Pull the 'M' file, take what notes you'll need for a month—*nothing else.*" Did the "nothing else" mean the lion? Did he think I'd received it already? Actually, I had. I just didn't know it.

I carefully re-wrapped the stunning piece of jade exactly as it had been before. Why had he enclosed it in all these layers? The bubble wrap I understood, and the reinforced box. But why the Mylar? If that's what it was. And why two layers?

Computer diskettes were shipped in a similar substance to prevent erasure of data by magnetic fields. I unwrapped the jade lion and examined it more closely. Mega-data could be encoded on a surface not much bigger than the head of a pin. Had I missed such a microdot stuck on the carving?

I searched it carefully, scrutinizing every inch of the beautiful little lion. It was satin smooth, except for the mane and the indentations for the eyes—areas that were too deep or too small to be as highly polished as the broader portions of the jade. There didn't seem to be anything I'd missed the first time.

Once again, I wrapped the stone just as it had been packed and tucked it back in the beach bag. Then, on second thought, I retrieved it from the open bag and put it in the zipper pocket of my purse. I didn't need to leave it where it could easily be stolen if someone reached into the open top of the bag or lose it if it fell out.

Then I settled the beach bag next to me, looped my arm through the handles, leaned back, and closed my eyes.

I could keep a constant vigil and be less than alert when we arrived at Union Station, or I could relax and trust that the assassin wasn't on the train. Which was the wiser? That was the trouble with this business: so many choices, and the wrong one could get you killed.

I opened one eye at each of the stops, noting who got on and who got off. But I spent most of the trip willing my body into a state of repose while my mind worked on a feasible plan to stay alive.

I could hole up in some high-end hotel. Would they look for me there? Or would hunkering down in some scruffy motel be better? Or should I stay on the move? Who was looking for me? A single man who did his homework well, knew my habits, knew so much about me he could predict my actions? Or a network—cab drivers, bellhops, desk clerks, reservation agents, car rental personnel? The very people I'd have to deal with to move around. That made all the difference in what I did.

Anastasia used apparently homeless people on the street to watch for suspects, grocery clerks in neighborhoods the suspect frequented, gas station attendants—anyone dealing with the public who could spot the face on the pictures we passed out.

Therefore, I either had to alter the face, or not show it.

Next loomed the problem of lodging. I thought briefly of getting lost on the streets of Los Angeles—becoming a street person—but that thought lasted about two seconds before my better judgment took over. Too dangerous. I might luck out and pull it off, with a lot of help from my guardian angels, but in spite of my training as a special agent, I wasn't very streetwise. I lacked the experience that spelled the difference between life and death on the streets.

That brought up the next problem—doctor's orders for rest, relaxation, and freedom from stress. Fat chance. All I could do was be careful, more careful than I normally would have been, and pray I wouldn't foul anything up.

I considered several scenarios, discarded most, and still hadn't arrived at a concrete plan when the train arrived at Union Station in downtown Los Angeles. Sending a fervent plea heavenward for guidance, I stood to exit the train.

"Need a ride somewhere? Mrs. Pickins' daughter and Morgan will be waiting to take me home. We could drop you wherever you're going. Or you could crash with Morgan and me for a couple of days."

I turned to find Arnold directly behind me. "I thought you were going to be a good guy and keep your distance."

"Just wanted to let you know the offer still stood. Being alone in L.A. isn't good."

"Nothing about this situation is good."

"Not even meeting me?" Arnold grinned.

"Get lost. If you won't consider your own safety, think of your daughter."

"I'm listening. Just wanted to reiterate the offer, and remind you of your promise."

"I'll keep it. And thanks. I appreciate the offer. But I can't. I'll wait until you're gone before I get off."

I stepped aside and watched Arnold's powerful arms propel the wheelchair to the end of the rail car. When I was sure he'd cleared the platform, I slipped behind a couple with two teenagers and exited with them, not appearing to be a lone passenger disembarking. My pursuer should be looking for a loner.

The night air was balmy—typical Southern California spring weather. Keeping my face in the shadow of the floppy-brimmed hat, I mingled with the noisy group heading for the buses. I could hop buses most of the night until some guidance and inspiration came my way. I counted on that heavenly help.

Suddenly a cry punctuated the clamor, followed immediately by the screech of tires and a sickening thud. I rounded the bus in time to see a wheelchair, bent and broken, skid across the street and onto the sidewalk.

Arnold!

I ran into the street as two people rushed toward the crumpled figure of the man sprawled on the pavement—a little skinny girl with long, blonde braids and a woman in her thirties with a look of horror on her face I wouldn't soon forget.

"Somebody call 911," I screamed at the gathering crowd as I knelt at Arnold's side. I touched his neck, felt for a pulse. Found it. I looked up into the terrified blue eyes of his daughter.

"He's alive, Morgan. We'll get the ambulance here right away. They'll take him to the hospital." I wanted to promise that everything would be all right. I couldn't.

She threw herself at her father with an anguished cry, but I caught and held her, rocking her back and forth. "We'll stay right here, Morgan. But we won't touch him. We don't want to make anything worse by moving him."

Morgan clung to me until her racking sobs subsided, then she pulled away, wiping tears from her face, and looked at me.

"Are you a friend of Daddy's?" she asked between sniffles.

"Yes." You could say that. Acquaintance would be more accurate.

I looked up at the woman who'd brought Morgan to meet her father. She stood, not moving, not speaking, not even weeping. Just staring at the still form on the pavement as if she couldn't believe what she saw.

Then he moaned and moved.

"Daddy!" Morgan cried, and I let her bend and kiss his face.

"Don't move, Arnold. The ambulance is on the way. How do you feel?"

"Like I was hit by a truck," he whispered. A semblance of a grin flashed across his face for an instant, then disappeared as he winced with pain.

He reached out and grabbed my hand. "Stay with Morgan. Don't leave her. Please. Promise me."

"Arnold, I can't do that. You know I can't. Don't ask," I pled as his eyes fluttered and closed. "Arnold. Look at me. Open your eyes. Don't you dare die. You've got a daughter to raise."

He opened his eyes, motioned to Morgan to bend close, and whispered, "She'll take care of you, honey. Take her home. Be good for her. Ask her . . ."

The wail of a siren blocked out the rest of his words. The ambulance headlights blinded me when the crowd parted. I stood and pulled Morgan to her feet as the attendants jumped from the cab and rushed to Arnold's side.

Somehow we got through the loading of Morgan's father onto the gurney without major tears and asked the name of the hospital where he was being taken.

"Can we go with him, please?" Morgan asked the attendant as he prepared to close the doors of the ambulance. He looked over her head at me and shook his head. Then he knelt in front of the little girl.

"Why don't you go home with your mommy, and we'll call you just as soon as he can see visitors, okay? That's a good girl."

"Shouldn't we follow you?" I asked.

"Better take the little girl home to bed. Call the hospital later." Then he jumped in the driver's seat, and the ambulance left us standing in the middle of the street. He never heard Morgan's plaintive statement: "But I don't have a mommy."

That shattered my heart in a thousand icy fragments. Blinking away tears that stung my eyes and throat, I took Morgan's hand and we walked to the wheelchair.

"I don't know if this can be fixed, but I guess we'd better take it, just in case your dad can still use it when he gets home. Will you carry this for me while I put it in the trunk?" I handed her the beach bag and picked up the remains of the wheelchair.

The woman stood rooted in the same spot, apparently in shock. I should have had the EMTs check her.

"Morgan, what's your friend's name?"

"Angie. What's in here? Something's moving."

"I'll show you as soon as we get in the car. Angie, will you open the trunk?"

Angie didn't respond. I put the twisted mess of metal on the ground, popped the trunk from inside the car, and loaded it in. Then I got Morgan into the car and buckled in. Finally, I put my arm around Angie, guided her to the passenger side, and put her in the car. She just looked at me—actually looked *through* me.

"Is my daddy going to be okay?" Worry—and realization—hit Morgan again. She began to cry.

"Look what I have in here, sweetie. Will you hold her for me? I think she might be frightened by all the noise." I took the kitten from her basket and snuggled her into Morgan's frail-looking arms. It was love at first sight. She oohed and ahhed, and temporarily forgot about her injured father in the utter fascination of the soft kitten.

I climbed into the driver's seat. "Angie, where do you live?" Again no response. "Angie? I need to know where you live."

"She doesn't talk much," Morgan said from the backseat.

"Why?"

"Something about her throat. Grandma Pickins says she's . . . moo . . . no . . ."

"Mute?"

"Yes, that's it. What's her name?"

"Who?"

"The kitten."

"Duchess," I said absently. What had I gotten myself into? A mute woman in shock, a motherless child who could be fatherless before the night was over, and no idea where any of them lived. Could things get much worse?

A policeman tapped on the window.

They just had.

CHAPTER 5

My first thought was, *which ID shall I pull out? I can't be here. I can't be a witness. I can't be listed on any police report.*

My second was more lucid. I hadn't seen anything. I'd been behind the bus. And that was the story to which I stuck. I reported what I'd seen, asked if I couldn't please take the little girl and her baby-sitter home and give a formal statement later if they needed one. Morgan supplied her phone number.

I hadn't even thought about the pickup that hit him. Hadn't given a thought to the driver, who was nowhere to be found. And I hadn't thought when I moved the wheelchair from its position on the sidewalk. All I thought about was getting this child away from the scene of the accident and home. Major mistakes.

I lucked out. The officer had a little girl himself. Imagining how she'd feel if she'd just seen him hit by a car, he asked me to come in tomorrow, bringing Angie, to give a written statement. In rummaging through Angie's purse for her driver's license, I'd found a Mother's Day card addressed to Mrs. Clara Pickins, Tremont Street, Long Beach.

I pulled away from the curb and asked Morgan if she knew her address. She recited it in the sing-song voice children use when they've memorized something. The number was consecutive to the number on the envelope. So far, so good. Now where in Long Beach was Tremont? I couldn't hope Angie carried a Thomas Guide in her car, the indispensable street guide for Los Angeles and environs.

At least I was familiar with Long Beach. I'd worry about finding the street when we got there. Slipping into traffic on Highway 101, we crossed the Los Angeles River and merged with I-5, the Santa Ana Freeway, heading southeast. At 10:15 p.m., traffic was still heavy, but nothing compared to rush hour.

I watched for the exit to Highway 710, the Long Beach Freeway, and when we were on it, headed south. I tried to elicit some response from Angie. She was no longer in her former catatonic state, but neither did she seem willing to communicate.

"Morgan, does Angie live with her mother next door to you?"

"No. She visits a lot. Tomorrow she's taking Grandma Pickins on a trip."

My heart sank. "Where are they going?"

"To Arizona. Grandma's sister went to heaven. Then they're visiting Angie's sister."

My heart hit rock bottom. I'd planned on leaving Morgan with Mrs. Pickins and vamoosing pronto. A stab of conscience hit me. Well, I hadn't promised Arnold I'd stay with his daughter. In fact, I'd told him I couldn't. He knew I couldn't.

How did he know I would?

"Daddy and I have a whole week . . ." The sniffles started again, quietly at first, then became sobs.

"You and your Dad were going to have a special time all next week—just the two of you together?"

"Uh-huh," she affirmed between hiccups.

"What were you going to do?"

"Go to the aquarium, and the zoo, and then he had a really special treat. He said it was a surprise, so he couldn't tell me what it was."

"And what were you going to do tomorrow for your birthday?" I glanced in the rearview mirror and caught her surprised expression.

"How did you know it was my birthday?"

"Your dad told me, but he didn't tell me what you planned. Just that it was something special for the two of you."

The silence in the backseat became profound. I peeked over my shoulder. Morgan had her face buried in the soft fur of Duchess's tummy, and the kitten had both paws up on her face, appearing to hug the forlorn child.

I looked quickly back at the road and blinked away hot tears.

"I know what we can do tomorrow. We'll go see your dad." *Whoa, lady. That may have been a rash promise. What if . . . ?*

Too late. I could hear the quick intake of breath. And suddenly Angie came to life. She shook her head back and forth vigorously.

I glanced at her. She was glaring at me. Silently she mouthed, "No."

"We can't?" I asked quietly, hoping Morgan couldn't hear.

Angie shook her head again.

"Why?"

One word. She mouthed, "Dead."

I shook my head. "No, he isn't," I insisted. Morgan, entranced by the kitten once again, didn't appear to be listening, happy in the knowledge she could see her father the next day.

Angie put her hand on my arm. When I looked at her, she nodded solemnly. She believed he was dead. Had she been in shock the whole time we'd been talking to Arnold? Did she really not know he was still alive?

A shiver went through me. Was she prescient? Had he died on the way to the hospital? Or did she have a premonition that he wouldn't be alive tomorrow?

"Angie, he was alive when they put him in the ambulance. He talked to me. He talked to Morgan."

This time the head-shaking wasn't as adamant. This time there seemed to be some doubt in her mind.

"He is alive," I affirmed, hoping, praying that he still was, that his injuries were superficial, and that Morgan would have her father home soon. This was not a selfish prayer. It wasn't for me, though it would be more inconvenient than I could possibly imagine if he didn't live. It was for that little girl in the backseat who would be all alone. No one deserved that kind of break.

Angie touched my arm. I watched her mouth form the words, "Are you sure?"

"He was alive when they put him in the ambulance." I couldn't tell her I knew he was alive now. I didn't.

Tears streamed down her face. I could only guess that they were tears of relief. What was her relationship to Arnold? Friendly, concerned neighbor, or more? I was definitely in over my head in this.

Angie pointed at the Pacific Coast Highway exit, and I moved into the right lane. No one spoke for the next several miles, and I followed Angie's hand directions at each appropriate exit. Around the traffic circle on Alamitos, and right on Ximeno. I carefully noted each street so I could find my way out—or back.

At about 11th Street I saw a church spire resembling a lighthouse—without a cross on top. Slowing the car, I scanned the front of the white stucco building for the familiar logo—and found it. The Church of Jesus Christ of Latter-day Saints. A haven in a storm. *Thank you, Father,* I breathed. *I just might be able to handle this after all.*

At 6th Street, Angie pointed left. The street dead-ended in a right turn that became Tremont. I'd never have found it myself—at least not without a Thomas Guide.

I pulled into the driveway Angie indicated, not sure whether it belonged to Mrs. Pickins or Arnold and Morgan. Angie produced a key and headed for the house on the right. I hoped it was the key to Arnold's house, and that she wasn't planning to leave me in the car all night. I glanced into the backseat. Morgan's head drooped at an uncomfortable angle. She was asleep.

Angie opened the door, turned on the lights, and returned to the car as I put Duchess back in her basket and unbuckled Morgan's seat belt. Angie gently lifted the sleeping child and carried her inside. I followed with my dilapidated beach bag and the car keys, not sure who the car belonged to—Angie or Arnold.

I helped Angie slip off Morgan's shoes and jeans, and we tucked her into bed in her Winnie the Pooh T-shirt. No need to wake her for pajamas. Angie nestled a soft yellow Winnie the Pooh bear under Morgan's arm, covered her shoulders with a sunny yellow blanket, and turned off the bedside light.

I followed her into the hall. She pointed to the bedroom directly across from Morgan's, apparently indicating that was where I'd sleep, and got her first good look at me. I took the opportunity to study Angie at the same time.

She had gleaming shoulder-length auburn hair, blunt cut, that swung as she moved. She was not especially attractive, but neither was she homely—just an average-looking young woman, except for her penetrating eyes. Those dark eyes, so dark I couldn't determine their color, looked right through me.

"Angie, I need to explain something. I don't know Arnold. I just met him on the train tonight. I can't stay here. I have somewhere else I need to be."

She turned on her heel, auburn hair swirling like a shampoo commercial. I thought she was going to leave me standing there, but she crossed the living room with swift strides and picked up a legal pad from the cherry wood desk by the front window.

"Did Arnold invite you here?" she scribbled in large, looping letters.

"Yes. He thought I had nowhere else to go, but I . . ."

She started scribbling again. I waited in silence for her to finish her message. "Another lost puppy he's always bringing home. Did he say anything else?"

So Arnold was a kindred spirit—adopting the homeless and the helpless. "He said tomorrow was Morgan's birthday, and they were going to celebrate together. Morgan said they were planning fun things all week."

She studied me with those intense, dark eyes, evaluating, appraising, I was sure, deciding if I could be trusted with Morgan.

"And before they put him in the ambulance, he asked me to stay with Morgan until he got home," I added lamely.

She nodded and started scribbling again.

"But I can't," I protested. "I have to be somewhere else."

"If he asked, he trusted you." She flashed the line so I could read it, then scribbled some more. "Good judge of character. Mom and I leaving tomorrow for Arizona for week. Funeral. Can't miss it. Need you here."

I nodded weakly. What more was there to say? Morgan couldn't be left alone.

I held out the car keys to Angie. "Are these yours?"

She went back to her notepad. "Yes, but you'll need car while Arnold in hospital." I read the message, then she continued, "If you'll take us to airport in a.m., you can use car while we're gone."

"Fair enough," I said. "What time are you leaving?"

"9:00 from Long Beach Muni. Leave at 7:30," she wrote.

"We'll be ready."

Angie nodded, giving me another long, penetrating look. She smiled a faint smile that seemed more forced than friendly and whirled toward the door, her hair performing the shampoo commercial again. Before she shut the door behind her, she turned and mouthed, "Thank you," and pointed to the lock on the door.

"I'll lock it. Thank you, too."

When I saw her form cross the lawn in the light from the window, I locked the door, then sank against it, weary and weak-kneed. I didn't know whether to laugh or cry. From start to finish, this had been an unbelievable day. I sank slowly to the floor, and for want of anything else to do, I cried.

Tears for having to sit alone in the doctor's office, freezing, waiting. Fearful tears for what biopsy results might show. I touched the spot where Dr. Simon had stuck the needle to withdraw a sample of tissue from the cyst. It was still tender, still swollen.

Tears of concern—and frustration at facing the unknown—for Bart, for Mom and Dad—for all of Anastasia. Where were they? Were they safe?

Tears for Morgan, a child without a mother and now possibly a father, too. Tears for Arnold, a good guy who seemed to have more than his share of bad luck.

And finally, tears of exhaustion, and fear of what unknown tomorrows might bring. Did I cover it all? I hoped so, because I finally ran dry. I wiped my eyes on the hem of my denim skirt and got to my feet.

Opening the top desk drawer, I found the phone book, called the hospital, and asked for information on Arnold . . . I stopped. Arnold who? I couldn't remember his last name. I frantically combed through the drawers looking for a last name while I explained the accident to a tired but patient person on the other end of the line.

"Trent," I said triumphantly, finally finding the drawer where he kept his bills and bank statements. "Arnold Trent."

"Is this a relative?" she asked, knowing full well that it couldn't be if I didn't even know his last name.

"No, I'm not a relative. I'm baby-sitting his six-year-old daughter, and she wants to know how her daddy is."

"Just a minute, please. I'll transfer you to the emergency room."

"Thank you."

She didn't wait to hear my thanks. After an interminable wait, someone finally picked up the telephone. Another tired voice came on the line.

I repeated my request, and was again put on hold. I really hated the music you had to listen to when someone put you on hold. There ought to be a law against it. It took away your agency—forcing you to listen to something against your will.

Finally Arnold's deep, mellow voice came on the line. "Is that you, Morgan?"

"No, it's me. Morgan fell asleep on the way home with the kitten in her lap. You were right. She loves it. How are you?"

"It could've been worse. Broken arm, cracked rib, slight concussion, severe headache. Thanks for taking care of Morgan. By the way, I don't even know your name."

I paused a bit too long, trying to decide what to say.

"Your real name," he said before I could pull one out of a hat or remember any on the ID cards in my purse. My mind was too tired, too dull, to play games tonight. A very dangerous condition. One that could be fatal.

"Allison," I finally answered.

"Allison who?"

"Allison is enough for now. Any idea how long they'll keep you?"

"Since they're out of beds, they'd be happy to send me home right now, except for one grouchy old nurse who says I'm not going anywhere for at least twenty-four hours. But she goes off shift at seven. Could you pick me up right after that? Or are you taking Angie and Mrs. Pickins to the airport?"

"We're taking them to the airport, but we'll come for you as soon as we drop them off. Are you sure the doctor will release you?"

"Doesn't matter. I'm outta here the minute you show up. I can heal at home a lot faster than I can where they wake you every hour to see if you're sleeping comfortably."

I laughed. "I can tell you've spent your share of time in hospitals."

"Far more than my share. I have an aversion to them." He paused, then asked softly, "Was Morgan okay? Really okay?"

"She shed a few tears, but Duchess is a great comforter." I almost said good-bye, but thought better of it and asked, "Got a minute?"

"Let me check my calendar," he said with a note of sarcasm. "I'm not going anywhere, Allison. What do you need?"

"Tell me about Angie."

Slight pause on the other end of the line. "What do you want to know?"

"What happened to her voice?"

"When she was young, she had a rare form of cancer that affected her vocal cords. She chooses not to speak rather than use any of the forms of artificial voice available."

"Does she live with her mother?"

"No. She has an apartment in Belmont Shores."

"She lives alone?"

I could hear the amusement in his reply. "Yes. She spends a lot of her spare time at her mother's helping out whenever Mrs. Pickins needs something. She has Morgan call her Aunt Angie. She's got a real soft spot for the child."

And for the child's dad, I thought.

"Why?" he asked.

"Just wondered. She was in such a state of shock when she saw you on the pavement, she didn't respond to my questions until we were halfway home. She wasn't aware that you spoke to us. She actually thought you were dead."

There was silence on the other end of the line.

"Good night, Arnold. Put a 'do not disturb' sign on your door."

"I don't have a door. I don't have a room. They keep shuffling me from one cubbyhole to another, then into the hall and back again. It'll be a long night."

"Then you'd better get started on what little sleep you'll get."

"Allison," he started, then stopped.

"Yes, I'm still here."

"I hate to impose on you more than I already have, but I need another favor."

"Name it. I'll see if it's within the realm of possibility."

"There's a cake mix in the cupboard. Would you mind baking Morgan's birthday cake and having it on the kitchen table when she wakes up?"

"I think I could handle that. Any special requests? Just a plain two layer? Or a flat one in a nine-by-thirteen pan?"

Another pause. "How are you at decorating cakes?"

"Not wonderful, but I can handle simple things. What did you have in mind?"

"There's a cake pan in the cupboard with directions. Everything you'll need will be there. I'll owe you big time if you could take care of that item for me."

"I'll do my best. See you in the morning."

We hung up, and I dragged my weary body from the desk chair to the kitchen. Better see what my promise entailed before I put my head to a pillow.

I opened two cupboard doors before I found the cake mix—two cakes mixes, to be exact. Then I opened three more cupboards before I found the cake pan. Either the man was a culinary genius or an absolute novice. Only one or the other would attempt this.

Winnie the Pooh grinned at me from the picture on the new cake pan, shaped, of course, like the beloved Pooh bear. That part was okay. Baking the cake I could handle. But all those little dots and dashes and swirls and squiggles of icing that would paint the picture on top of the cake would present a problem.

Something—a noise—a feeling—a bit of intuition—made me turn around. Chills shivered through me from head to toe at the sight.

CHAPTER 6

The face peered in the open kitchen window not three feet from my face. Only the flimsy screen stood between us.

He was old, wrinkled, shaggy-looking, and from what I could see, almost toothless. A drooping eye on one side and a scar across his cheek on the other gave his features a malevolent look in the half-light from the window. I didn't stop to ask his intentions. I slammed the window down, locking it securely.

Then I ran for the back door and locked that. He met me there, opening the screen door as I threw the bolt. I hurried to each of the bedrooms and the bathroom, closing and locking each open window. Then I ran, breathless, down the hall to the living room and reached for the handle to wind the window closed.

He was there before me. My heart beat a million miles a minute, thudding so hard it hurt. I raced for the phone to dial 911.

"Where's Arnold?" he rasped. "Who're you? Don't go callin' the police, girlie. I ain't gonna hurt ya none. I just come for my supper. Arnold saves me the leftovers every night, and I come to get 'em when Morgan's asleep. I don't look so good and I don't wanna scare her."

I clung to the phone. Was he for real, or was this a stall? I didn't move.

"I ain't plannin' on comin' in. Go look in the icebox. Should be a tin plate all covered up with that there clear plastic stuff. Just set it out on the back porch and lock the door behind ya. Where's Arnold? He tells me when he's leavin' and he didn't say nuthin' about bein' gone."

"Why don't you stay right here while I check the fridge? If the plate's there, I'll put it out for you. Will you stay where I can see you?"

"Sure, missy. I know what I look like, and it ain't a pretty sight."

He leaned against the screen. He was right; he wasn't a pretty sight. More like something out of a B-grade horror movie.

I walked backward down the hall so I could watch him, then hurried into the kitchen and threw open the refrigerator door. There it was—in the middle of the top shelf. A foil pie tin heaped with spaghetti and meatballs. A plastic fork lay across the top of the plastic wrap.

I grabbed it and peeked out of the kitchen door. He still leaned against the window screen. I returned to the living room.

"Does he heat this for you?"

"No, ma'am. Just puts it out so's old Joe can eat it like that. Tastes just as good cold. Put it on the back step and lock the door again. Sorry I scared ya."

I unbolted the door, placed the meal on the back porch, quickly stepped inside, and shot the bolt again. Then I hurried back to the living room to close and lock the windows. I'd rather be stuffy than dead. Or scared to death.

Duchess was making little noises in her basket, so I let her out and pulled open the litter drawer. When she was through, I scooped it, then slipped an ID card and matching credit card from underneath the liner, along with three hundred-dollar bills.

With Arnold safely home, I'd leave immediately. I couldn't take a chance on leading anyone here. He didn't need any more trouble—especially that kind! Weary to the bone, I picked up Duchess and her basket and headed for the bedroom. Since there were only two, and Angie had pointed to the one opposite Morgan's, I took the time to look at it this time, instead of just flipping on the light to lock the window.

Definitely a man's room. No frills, ruffles, or pastels. Hunter green tailored spread. Vertical louvers on the windows—no curtains. Arnold was a neat man. No clothes strewn around, shoes in an orderly row on the closet floor. Why did a man in a wheelchair need so many shoes? To coordinate with his clothes, I guessed. Or could he stand—put weight on his legs?

Little goose bumps shivered down my arms. A wheelchair made a perfect cover for an assassin. Even his daughter wouldn't have to know he could walk. When he received an assignment, he left town and ditched the chair until his return, when he resumed his old disguise. I examined the soles of his shoes and felt relief rush through my system. No scuff marks. No wear and tear. I hoped that meant Arnold was legitimate. I wanted him to be, for Morgan's sake.

A built-in bookcase covered one wall, jammed with every kind of book imaginable. Arnold's taste was eclectic. Fiction, nonfiction, American and world history, all the sciences, biographies—name it and it had to have been there somewhere.

I checked on Morgan, still curled up with Winnie the Pooh. Her room was perfectly charming—all little-girl ruffles and lace with a cheery yellow polka dot comforter. The walls were even a shade of pale yellow.

She had a bookcase full of books—the usual stuff you'd expect in a child's room: Disney classics, Golden Books, Maurice Sendak, plus one whole shelf devoted to beautifully illustrated fairy tales from all over the world. This was certainly a reading family. Arnold went up another notch in my estimation. He'd better be legit. I hated to think I was that far off in my judgment of people.

Borrowing some toothpaste, I brushed my teeth with my finger. I'd definitely need to shop for essentials. And I couldn't sleep in my clothes or they wouldn't be presentable tomorrow, so I rummaged in Arnold's drawers, looking for pajamas. None.

I did find a T-shirt that looked several sizes too large for even his biceps and borrowed it. I was never so glad to get out of anything in my life as I was to shed the swimsuit, which was definitely not made to be worn for hours on end as a substitute for undergarments.

Putting Duchess's basket on one side of the bed with the litter drawer open, I collapsed on the other side, flipping the spread up over me for covers. I'd forgotten prayers.

I tried to roll off the bed, but my body just would not obey me, so I settled for a murmured "thank you" for having survived this day and a plea for Father's continued loving watchcare over me. I added a P.S. for Arnold and Morgan—and for Bart, wherever he was.

As my body relaxed, I expected sleep to come quickly. It was after midnight, and I'd been up early. That alone was normally enough to guarantee a good night's sleep, not to mention the added stress of suspecting—fearing—the test results.

Then the call from Bishop O'Hare had set the adrenaline pumping once again. Why couldn't I call him before Sunday? I mentally rehashed our conversation of last Sunday at church. This was his week to teach a seminar at FBI Headquarters in Quantico, Virginia. He planned to make it back in time for church this Sunday, so he must have called me from Virginia. Bart apparently contacted him there to relay the message to me.

Life was complicated enough without throwing in all the extra problems. The contract on Anastasia. Unknown test results. A barren womb. And now an injured good Samaritan with a darling little girl who had no mommy.

What had happened as Arnold crossed the street? It suddenly struck me that I didn't even see who hit him—or why. Had he not looked as he wheeled into the street? Was his attention on something else? Morgan, for example? Had the driver not been paying attention?

Or was this deliberate?

Now I was wide awake. As the possibilities paraded through my mind, I examined each of them. No attempt had been made on my life. I felt reasonably certain my location was still unknown to my pursuer. It had to have been an accident. I'd stayed clear of Arnold just to make sure no one could connect us.

But had a connection been made? Why would the assassin attack Arnold, with me only a few steps behind? Had someone else, another woman, been close to Arnold? Had the truck been aimed at her, the driver thinking it was me, and she'd avoided being hit? Or was this some sick mind playing psychological games with me, trying to scare me out of my wits? Trying to send me fleeing without thought, without careful planning? Just running helter-skelter so I'd make an easier target? So many questions, my head ached. No answers.

I left the unknowns and proceeded to the next matter: where to go tomorrow. One good idea might be the library. I knew next to nothing about jade, and this seemed a perfect time to uncover something pertinent about my beautiful little lion. Besides, that seemed as good a place as any to hide.

Wanting another look at the lion, I switched on a light on the nightstand and got the box from my purse. I started to unwrap it, then glanced at the clock. Two a.m. I'd been up twenty-one hours. I didn't know what time Morgan woke up, but if that cake needed to be waiting on the table when she got up, I'd have to start pretty early.

Then I remembered Angie and Mrs. Pickins and the airport at 7:45. I groaned. Maybe I'd better just get up now and bake the cake. If I'd put it in the oven after I fed Arnold's friend, I could have had it decorated by now. Instead, I dropped the box on the nightstand, turned off the light, and decided I'd better try for what little sleep I could manage in the few hours remaining before dawn.

So much for rest, relaxation, and a stress-free week.

I woke to find Morgan snuggled beside me, teasing Duchess with her blonde pigtails, and the kitten pouncing happily all over her.

"Good morning, Morgan. Happy birthday." Then I remembered the cake and sat straight up in bed. "Uh-oh. I told your dad I'd have your cake baked, decorated, and waiting on the table when you got up this morning. I'm sorry. I didn't get it done."

Her big, blue eyes looked up and she flashed a forgiving smile. "That's okay. Daddy doesn't want me to miss Mommy so much, so he does things he thinks I'd like. Know what?"

"No. What?"

"I really like ice cream cake. Tiffany had one at her birthday party, and it was yummy."

"Then how about if we go buy you an ice cream cake, and you and your dad can decorate Winnie the Pooh some other time? Would you like that?"

She beamed. "Can I choose which one I want?"

"Of course. Now, we'll have to hurry with breakfast and take Angie and Mrs. Pickins to the airport. Then guess what we're going to do?"

"Go see Daddy," she squealed, bouncing on the bed.

"Even better than that," I said. "He told me we can bring him home."

"Yippee!" Morgan did a somersault on the bed, then rolled off and ran to get dressed.

I headed for the shower. Same old clothes as yesterday, but at least I had clean underclothes today instead of a swimsuit. That was something to look forward to.

Breakfast consisted of a quick bowl of cereal with bananas on top. We'd barely finished when I heard Mrs. Pickins giving Angie instructions as they left their little house next door. Morgan ran for Duchess and the basket, so I could put them both in the beach bag to take along. As I reached for my purse, I noticed the wrapping on the box I'd left on the nightstand was slightly askew.

I looked at Morgan. She was watching me, her blue eyes filled with trepidation.

"I thought it was a present for me, so I unwrapped it."

"That's okay. It's something my husband sent me. We'll get you a present."

I tucked the box back into my purse, dropped the purse in the beach bag, and we hurried out the front door. With only two keys on the ring, one must fit the front door. It did. I felt better about leaving the door locked, safe neighborhood though it may be.

Mrs. Pickins fussed over Morgan, then turned her attention to me. Understandably curious, she made no bones about asking pointed questions. How did I know Arnold? What did I do? How long would I be here? I answered as truthfully as I could, evading as much as possible without appearing to do so. With great relief, we dropped them at the departure area of the airport and headed for the hospital.

Morgan, of course, had Duchess out of her basket playing with her. How would she have handled this without that tiny, cuddly kitten to capture and hold her affection and attention? I was actually glad I'd had to bring the cat along.

When we reached the hospital, Morgan skipped happily toward the building in front of me. She had done well dressing, but I hadn't had time to re-braid her hair. Oh, well. That could wait. We entered the emergency entrance, couldn't see Arnold anywhere, and inquired as to where we might find him.

"We've come to take my daddy home," Morgan announced.

The nurse glanced at the excited, dancing child, then looked up at me and frowned. "When did he tell you he was being released?"

"Last night about midnight. Is there a problem?"

The nurse glanced again at Morgan, held up her clipboard and said in a cool, efficient tone, "Let me see where you can find him. Would you like to wait over there?" She pointed to a row of chairs filled with people waiting to be treated.

The look on her face frightened me. Something was wrong.

CHAPTER 7

The nurse turned and walked away. Motioning Morgan to stay put with the beach bag and Duchess, I followed, catching the retreating nurse in two quick steps.

"Something has changed since last night. What's the problem?"

Serious brown eyes turned toward me. When Morgan was out of hearing distance, she explained, "He started having excruciating headaches about two a.m., violent vomiting, along with double vision. The doctor had already diagnosed a severe concussion, so he ordered several tests this morning to see if it's something more than that."

"Can we see him?"

"They've taken him upstairs. You'll have to check with admitting. I'm not sure where he is now, whether he's in a room or still being tested. Will you excuse me? I have several patients waiting."

"Thanks for your help." I turned back to Morgan. She wasn't dancing anymore. She didn't know what was wrong, but she knew something had changed since we'd walked into the hospital. Big blue eyes filled with worry, and her lower lip stuck out just enough for me to see it quiver.

"Come on, Ladybug. We've got to go find where they've stashed your father." I reached for her hand and took the beach bag. I really must replace it. I looked like a bag lady toting the tattered old thing.

Morgan slipped her little hand in mine and clung tightly to my fingers. "Where's my daddy?" she asked in a small, unsteady voice.

Should I keep up a pretense that everything was all right? Better not.

"The nurse said he had a bad headache, so they were doing some tests to see what caused it. He might be having those tests right now. We'll see if we can find him."

She could live with that. The tension disappeared from her face, and she skipped along as we followed signs to Admitting, where they directed us to the third floor, Room 345 D. That bed was empty. So was the one next to it. I checked at the nurses' station. Arnold Trent had been taken for an MRI. He wasn't scheduled to be back in his room for another hour, but he had left a note for his daughter.

I took the note, said a silent prayer to dispel the sudden foreboding that descended on me, and knelt beside Morgan to read it to her. I snuggled her against me while I quietly read it.

"'Dear Morgan: I knew you'd love that kitten when I saw it. Would you like to have one just like it? Maybe we can get one this week. I think the mean old doctor is going to keep me here today. I even told him it was your birthday, but it didn't do any good. He said I have to stay. But I want you and Allison to have a fun day. I'll call this afternoon and tell you if I get to come home in time for cake and ice cream. Don't eat it all without me. Save me at least one piece. I love you, my great big six-year-old. Dad.'"

I tried to fake a smile through tear-blurred eyes. Morgan didn't see because tears filled her big, sad, beautiful eyes and slid silently down her cheeks.

"Well, I guess that leaves just you and me and Duchess. What would you like to do first?"

She wiped her face with her fist. "Could we just go home and wait for Daddy to call?"

"We could." I stood, picked up the tattered bag, and held out my hand to the forlorn child. "Would you like to stop on the way and pick out an ice cream cake?"

"Okay." Her enthusiasm had disappeared.

We wound our way back through depressing hospital corridors, then outside to the car. Even holding Duchess all the way to Baskin-Robbins didn't do much to restore the sparkle to her eyes.

She picked out a beautiful ice cream cake, and we each had an ice cream cone. Choosing just the right flavor, tasting four different ones before she made up her mind, helped a little. She even managed the semblance of a smile when I handed her the sugar cone topped with double-decker bubble gum and chocolate mint chip ice cream.

Then we drove back to the empty house. That would be a pretty sad place today if I didn't think of something fast.

Turning onto Tremont Street, I spotted a car parked in front of Arnold's house. Strange; Arnold hadn't mentioned expecting company. Did he have a housekeeper? Trepidation trickled through me. Instead of stopping, I drove slowly by the house. The front door I'd carefully locked stood wide open. In the house that was supposed to be empty, I could see several men in sports jackets in the living room.

One turned to leave as I accelerated. The sun caught his blue-black hair and his face as he stepped out of the house. It was a familiar face, one I'd seen before.

I drove to the corner, trying not to speed or call attention to the car in any way. Where had I seen that face? Who were those men? Probably not friends of Arnold's. The way they were dressed, they belonged in one of two classifications: the really good guys or the really bad guys. I wasn't betting on the good guys right now.

"Allison, didn't you just pass my house?" Morgan peered out of the backseat.

"I did. I decided it's going to be a whole hour at least before your dad can call, and it's such a beautiful day, we need to go to the beach. Do you like the beach?"

"Yes," she said hesitantly.

"But you'd rather go with your dad." I glanced in the rearview mirror.

She looked up, caught my eye, and nodded silently.

"Then we can go twice. We'll go this morning, then we'll go back again when we bring your dad home. Will that be okay?"

"Okay." She returned to the ice cream cone dripping down her hand. Duchess obliged by licking what she could reach with her rough little tongue. Morgan giggled.

Think, lady. If they're after you, how did they find you so fast? If they aren't after you, why do you recognize one of them?

Arnold was studying criminal psychology. Were these people he'd arranged a meeting with? No. How did they get in the locked front door?

With a sinking feeling, I knew I could rationalize all day but it wouldn't change the truth. These were the really bad guys, and they were after me. In some way I couldn't figure out, they knew I'd been there. Had I left anything of mine? Could Arnold be traced in any way to me?

I reached into the backseat for the beach bag. A quick inventory accounted for everything—except the big floppy hat I'd worn. I panicked. Where had I left it? I didn't remember seeing it in the bedroom. I glanced into the backseat. It had slipped to the floor, under Duchess's basket. I breathed a sigh of relief. I didn't want anything left that would prove I'd been there, even if they knew—thought—I had been.

The jade lion should be safely tucked in my purse. I felt inside to make sure. The box was still there. But Morgan had opened the box! Had she put the lion back, or had she left it out and re-wrapped the box?

I pulled into the first parking lot I came to and stopped the car.

"We're not at the beach," Morgan observed, looking out the window.

"Nope. Not yet. I just need to check on something." With trembling fingers, I unwrapped the box, layer by layer. The beautiful gemstone lion was still there. But it wasn't wrapped exactly as Bart had sent it. The Mylar wasn't covering the lion. I redid the packaging as it had come to me.

My mind raced, covering my steps since the phone call from Bishop O'Hare. If anyone had tracked me, had known where I was, they would have come last night in the dark, when I was most vulnerable. Why wait until morning? And why so many?

Then I thought of Arnold. I could easily believe a setup—if he hadn't left me with his daughter, the light of his life.

Arnold. He was going to call home. He couldn't!

Slipping the idling car in gear, I headed for the strip of stores on the other end of the parking lot. Find a phone. Where are the phones when you need them? How I missed my cell phone!

I finally spotted one in front of a Mexican restaurant at the end of the strip mall.

"Morgan, I'm going to call the hospital and have them tell your dad where we are. If he gets through sooner than they thought, we don't want him to worry, do we?"

She agreed as she offered the whole cone to Duchess, then took a lick herself. I closed my eyes and shook my head. I didn't know what Arnold would say to that. I remembered doing it myself as a child until my horrified mother caught me.

I dialed the hospital. No answer in room 345. I dug out more change and tried again, this time asking for the nurses' station nearest room 345. When a nurse finally picked up the phone, the clatter in the background nearly drowned out her voice.

"Please listen carefully. I know you're busy, but listen. The patient in room 345 must *not* call home, no matter what. Take the phone out of his room. Give him this message. Write it down, please. Ready? 'Worst fears came to pass. We're fine. We'll call *you*. *Don't* call home.' Did you get that? Would you read it back to me, please."

She read it back. I thanked her and asked if there was any more word on Arnold. None. I hung up and got back in the car. I'd said the beach; we'd go to the beach while I formulated some sort of plan. And tried to figure out how they'd found me.

I zigged over to Pacific Coast Highway, heading south. This was one road I'd been on before, from one end to the other. I needed something familiar right now to regain my confidence —it had all just dissipated when I saw that man. That man with the familiar face.

First, one quick detour before the beach. I remembered a store in The Marketplace, an upscale mall in Westminster where a friend and I had stopped on an excursion a year ago. She'd found a dress I'd loved, but when she got it, I didn't. Now I needed it. If they still carried it.

G. Nonni's was an expensive little store with a huge fountain just outside on the plaza. Morgan wanted to throw pennies in and make a wish. I knew what her wish would be. I gave her all the pennies I had, plus a few nickels and dimes, hoping that would help make the wish come true. Then I pulled her away, promising this one bit of shopping wouldn't take long.

It didn't. I quickly found what I was looking for: a classic black dress, scoop neck, washable polyester georgette on one side, black and white print rayon crepe on the other. Totally reversible. Optional tie belt. Wrinkle-resistant. It could survive the beach bag crunch and still look good.

Convinced it was worth every penny in my current situation, I happily forked out the $125, and would have paid more. I dropped my acquisition in my ratty-looking beach bag and tossed the sales receipt in the nearest trash container.

Morgan insisted on watching the ducks on the pond that curved through the outdoor mall, and we walked the entire perimeter to be sure she'd seen them all. As we strolled, the gurgling fountains and tranquil pond eased some of the tension in my body, though my mind raced. The man. Who was he? A plan; I needed a plan. What was the best course of action?

From Westminster, we drove through picturesque Naples and across the canals to Livingston Street. When it intersected with Ocean Boulevard, I could see the surf. A few more blocks, and Morgan pointed out the window. "This is where we usually come," she announced.

I turned left on Allin, a one-block-long street ending at Belmont Plaza Olympic Pool, with the pale blue Pacific Ocean and golden sand straight ahead. Belmont Pier spidered out into the ocean on long, thin legs, reaching for a couple of islands fringed with tall, spindly palm trees.

I parked next to Belmont Shores Children's Center, which Morgan identified as a place she'd spent some time. Brightly painted murals in the windows of the colorful building marked it as an inviting place for children.

Glancing at the ice cream cake that would surely melt in the hot car, I grabbed the box and beach bag while Morgan put Duchess back in her basket, taking charge of kitten and container as if they were her very own. I twisted my long black hair into a ponytail, donned sunglasses, and crammed the floppy hat on my head. Hand in hand, we crossed the street to the wide cement steps leading down to sand and water.

The pavilion to the left—part swimming complex, part restaurant—contained a contingent of interesting characters. I looked each of them over carefully. My danger antennae were full up. I couldn't afford to get careless. The assassin assigned to me wouldn't care if a helpless, harmless little girl got in the way.

A short, plump, sun-bronzed man with curly gray hair, very white at the temples, and a bushy mustache hosed the sand off the steps of the Raguzzi Ristorante. His form-fitting, clean white T-shirt, with sleeves rolled up 50s-style, revealed a tattoo on one arm. Clear blue eyes looked up at me, smiled when he saw Morgan, and he waved. She waved back.

"Do you know him?" I asked.

"He's always washing the sand away. It's his job," she said matter-of-factly. "Let's walk this way on the boardwalk."

The "boardwalk" wasn't board at all, but a wide ribbon of concrete twisting and curving through the sand as far as I could see down the beach in both directions. In-line skaters, skate boarders, cyclers, and people on foot were colorful polka-dots decorating the gray ribbon. Bright blue lifeguard stations dotted the length of the beautiful beach, many with two or three tall palm trees standing high above them like sentinels watching the sea.

Morgan led the way to the Belmont Pier, and we sat on a bench overlooking white-crested waves gently lapping at the immaculate sand. There wasn't a speck of litter anywhere in sight.

"We come here a lot," Morgan said. "Daddy loves the water." She looked up with those trusting blue eyes and smiled. "Do you know my dad can surf?" she said proudly. I felt it was a statement more than a question.

"What does he do with his wheelchair?"

"He leaves it with me on the beach. He doesn't go out very far, and he doesn't stand up. He can't, you know, at least not very well. You know what I think?"

"No. What do you think?"

"I think it makes Daddy forget for a little while about his legs."

A very observant, intelligent six-year-old.

"See that big building with the pictures on it?" She pointed toward the Long Beach city skyline.

"The aquarium?" I asked.

She nodded. "That's where we were going today. Or maybe this week."

"Have you been there before?"

"That many times." She held up both hands, then closed and opened them.

"How many is that?" I laughed.

"Ten or twenty. If I hold them up like this, it's ten. When I hold them up again, it's ten more."

"In other words, you go there a lot."

She nodded, her feet swinging back and forth.

"Morgan, I think we need to start our celebration of your birthday right here. Since we didn't take your ice cream cake home and put it in the freezer, we need to eat it before it melts. When we pick up your dad from the hospital, we'll stop and get another one."

"Two?" Her eyes grew wide, and her whole face lit up.

"Two, just because you are being such a trooper about your father not being here on your birthday."

We opened the box on the bench between us, cut two large portions off one end with the plastic knife the clerk stuck in the box, and proceeded to eat it with our fingers.

"I didn't sing happy birthday to you," I said.

"It's okay. You can sing with Daddy."

Two men, probably in their late forties, strolled along the pier and stopped to lean over the railing not far from us, their conversation drifting on the breeze coming off the ocean.

"Why don't you think it could be in place already? Tom Clancy always writes about hi-tech stuff. He doesn't have to make it up. It's there. Hey, I've got the GPS system in my car right now. It's the same principle. Feed info into the system, send it to the satellite, and the satellite tells you where you are, right down to the house number."

"That I believe. It's just that the stuff in his book *Op-Center* was a little too sci-fi for me. No way will I believe you can feed a picture of a person into a computer, give geographical coordinates to be searched, beam it up to a satellite, and that satellite will locate the person for you."

The hair on the back of my neck stood up. Anastasia stayed on top of all the latest gadgets, all the spy technology. As soon as it was announced, we were made aware of it through Interpol bulletins: who had it, what they used it for, and whether or not we could use it, too. Had I missed that bulletin? Entirely possible.

That would certainly explain how they found me. And we had similar technology right now that we used. Even tracking me in the dark wasn't a problem for a system with a night vision lens.

Satellites took pictures every few minutes or seconds—whichever they'd been programmed to do. Someone could enter my parents' estate into the satellite's computer, direct it to take pictures at desired intervals, then track my progress to UCSB campus. With the big floppy hat, I'd have been easy to spot getting on the bus, and though I'd been careful to avoid being recognized on the ground, once the satellite locked on when I got on the train, all it had to do was scan each stop and they'd know when I got off.

We'd been using satellites for some time to photograph items as small as license plates. Whoever monitored the pictures saw the plates, checked the registration for the address, then sent a team to catch the sleeping bird in the nest. But why had it taken so long to get people there if that was how I'd been tracked?

I'd puzzle that one out later. Right now I had to change my appearance—drastically—and hightail it out of town in a different car. I glanced at Morgan, and at Duchess enjoying more ice cream. How fast and how far could I run with these two innocents along?

CHAPTER 8

"Morgan, let's run some errands, then see if your dad's ready to come home."

"Okay." She jumped from the bench, wiping her sticky hands on her pink T-shirt, and put Duchess back in her basket. I boxed the once-beautiful ice cream cake, now melting into an unrecognizable blob, gathered up the beach bag, and we hurried back to the car. The car I needed to get rid of pronto.

Morgan buckled up and settled Duchess back in her lap while I removed the front license plate from the car using my fingernail file as a screwdriver. I looked around to see if anyone was watching, then smeared the melted ice cream cake all over the back bumper and license plate, rendering the latter illegible.

I wiped my hands on the grass next to the curb, removing most of the gooey residue, but leaving them incredibly sticky. Oh, well.

We headed up Ximeno Street, passing the church on the way.

"Morgan, see that building right there? The one that looks like it has a lighthouse on top? In case I forget to tell your dad, that's where he can find the special light for you. Will you remember that?"

She watched it as we passed the white stucco building with a red tile roof. "Okay. What kind of light?"

"He'll know what you mean."

A group of white-shirted young men in helmets wheeled out of the parking lot on bicycles, followed by two girls in a white car. Must have been zone meeting for the missionaries.

"See those neat-looking young men with their shirts and ties and black name tags? They're the ones who can teach you about that special light your dad wants you to have. They have all the answers he's looking for." *And some he doesn't even know he needs,* I thought. How had our family ever gotten by without the gospel in our lives? We thought we were happy. We thought we had it all. Now we had so much more. My mind lingered on all the blessings attributable to the gospel as Morgan strained to watch the missionaries until they were out of sight.

But back to today's harsh reality. I remembered seeing a shopping center near the traffic circle, and I headed for that. It had two of the things I needed right now.

Yes! Better than I'd hoped—actually too good to be true. I was sure we'd have to take a taxi to find a rental car after we finished our shopping. But Avis had an office here. It became our first stop.

I looked at the map on the wall pinpointing all the Southern California rental offices while Morgan entranced Duchess with her long golden braids. By the time the service representative finally got off the phone and whispered, "How can I help you?" in a low, sultry voice that matched her shoulder-length sable hair and voluptuous figure, I had a plan.

My story, to account for my out-of-town driver's license: I'd driven to Long Beach to take my niece to the San Diego Zoo for her sixth birthday, but my car developed problems. I needed a rental while mine was repaired so we could continue with our plans. I filled out the paperwork, got the keys, and as we went out the door, Miss Luscious Lips called after Morgan, "Happy birthday, honey."

"Thank you," Morgan said, her eyes shining when she realized this beautiful stranger knew about her special day. "We're going to have so much fun."

I hustled her out the door before she could explain just exactly what fun we'd been talking about—and it didn't include the San Diego Zoo.

"We're going to play dress-up," I explained as we moved down the strip mall to the store I'd remembered seeing last night.

In Marshall's, I pulled a T-shirt and some jeans off the rack. No time to try them on; I just hoped they'd fit. Next I grabbed a pair of tennis shoes, a couple of pairs of socks, and finally a replacement for my rag-tag beach bag. On the way by the jewelry counter, I snatched an unusual pair of dangling earrings that looked like they'd brush my shoulders.

I chose a bright turquoise T-shirt and a cute little sun hat for Morgan, and selected a crushproof straw roll-brim hat for me, afraid to be seen in the large-brimmed floppy one again. After we checked out, I pulled the new shirt over her head. She put the hat on and modeled it for me. "This is fun," she giggled.

Everything else fit perfectly in the old beach bag, so when we left the store it didn't look like we'd purchased anything. Except this time Morgan was carrying Duchess's basket and looked like a different little girl with her bright shirt and her braids tucked up in her hat. I let her tag behind me, keeping one eye on her but staying far enough ahead that we didn't appear to be together.

Next stop: Strands, whose sign proclaimed they specialized in hair color. A girl with the most beautiful burgundy hair I'd ever seen greeted me.

"How long will it take you to cut my hair very short and change the color?" I asked.

"What color do you want?" She eyed my hair professionally.

"Any color but what it is."

She snapped her gum and grinned. "Come on back."

Morgan settled into a chair, took Duchess from her basket, and entertained herself for the next forty-five minutes while I got a completely new look. The cut took all of fifteen minutes, and the color—or stripping of my color, as the case may be—took only thirty minutes because that's all the time I dared spend in one place.

I plopped the new straw hat on my startlingly short, light-streaked new tresses, collected a few color bottles to take along, and sent Morgan ahead to Merle Norman's. When she entered, I followed, requesting a total makeover with the new eye makeup the stars were wearing. Sort of a modified Cleopatra look.

I used their rest room to change into jeans, T-shirt, and tennis shoes, then dumped everything into the new bag. Morgan was entranced as I paid for my moisturizer and new makeup. "You don't look like you," she giggled.

"Good. We'll go visit your dad and see if he recognizes us."

I couldn't believe my good luck in finding everything in one place. My guardian angels couldn't have done better if they'd laid the plan themselves. Now came the tricky part: getting myself and Morgan into the car, with the possibility that some "eye in the sky" was recording it on film.

Leaving her and the new bag containing all the old stuff with the Merle Norman lady, I strode to the parking lot to find my car, inventing a swinging new walk to go with my short cap of streaked curls, my new face, and a pair of skin-tight jeans. The jeans were my only mistake, but I didn't have time to exchange them for something that would let me breathe.

I located the rental car at the far end of the parking lot and drove back, pulled up next to the sidewalk, and opened the door. Morgan dashed to the car and tumbled in, a jumble of arms, legs, bags, and baskets. I reached across, swung the door shut, and pulled quickly away.

Morgan dived over the seat and buckled in. I handed her the basket containing a shook-up kitten, and she soothed the frightened ball of white fur while I headed for the hospital. Angie's car should be okay in the parking lot overnight.

On the way to the hospital, I tried to prepare Morgan for the very real possibility that her father might not be released from the hospital immediately. The more I thought about it, the more serious I'd decided his injuries could be. From what little the nurse revealed, which was usually only the tip of the iceberg, he could actually have a fractured skull instead of just a concussion.

Bed D in Room 345 was still empty, as was the one next to it. The man across the room smiled at Morgan, who returned his smile with a timid one of her own. We started for the nurses' station to see if they had any word on the missing occupant of Bed D when a gurney popped out of the elevator at the end of the hall, heading our way.

"Let's wait a minute and see if that's your dad," I whispered, pulling Morgan against the wall beside me.

It was. And he looked right through me. No sign of recognition at all. He couldn't see Morgan, who was below his eye level. I squeezed her hand, and we laughed.

Arnold raised up on one elbow as the gurney turned toward his room. His face was a mask of pain, but he'd heard his daughter's laughter. While the orderly checked the fit between the door jams, I put my finger to my lips. Arnold raised his eyebrows but settled back without a word.

"Morgan, when we go in to talk to your dad, I want you to whisper to him. We don't want to disturb the sick men in the other beds, okay?" I didn't want anyone in that room able to report any portion of our conversation.

She nodded solemnly and waited, fidgeting, until the orderly left. As we entered the room, I closed the door behind us, drew the drapes around Arnold's bed, and boosted Morgan up so she could give her daddy a big hug and kiss. He watched me over her head as she nestled against his chest.

"I wouldn't have recognized you—didn't recognize you," he said quietly. "What happened? I got your message."

"We were going to go back to the house—tell him what we bought, Morgan, instead of the Winnie the Pooh cake."

"An ice cream cake, Daddy," she whispered. "It was yummy."

"We changed our mind about going home and went to the beach instead, as there were some vermin at your house."

"What's vermin?" Morgan said, looking up at me, then at Arnold.

"Nasty little bugs, pests, undesirable things you don't want to be around," I said.

"I didn't see any," she said.

"You usually find them around garbage areas, or under rocks. We'll check them out when I get home and take care of them," Arnold explained. "So what are you going to do?"

"That depends on you. What's the diagnosis?"

"Undetermined, as yet. But they're not through poking, probing, or photographing, so it doesn't look like I'll get home tonight, maybe not even tomorrow night." His eyes bespoke an apology, as well as the pain I could tell he suffered.

"Morgan, do you want to sign your dad's cast?" I pulled a pen from my purse, and while she laboriously printed her name, I stood behind her and mouthed, "Is there anywhere you'd like me to take her?"

Arnold hugged his daughter to his chest with his good arm and thought for a minute. He pursed his lips and shook his head.

"We're sorry you're going to miss all the fun," I said, leaning close to the two of them. "Morgan and I are playing dress-up, and we're going on a little trip."

"Want to tell me where?" I was glad Morgan wasn't watching his face. She could easily have read the worry written there.

"North on I-5," I said. "There's a park with ducks and geese; we'll have a picnic, then catch the train home. I need to do some research . . ." I stopped and peered out of the curtain as the door creaked open. An orderly wheeled in the occupant of the bed next to Arnold.

"We need to go," I whispered. "Can't stay in one place too long. Say a prayer for us. I promise I'll take good care of Morgan."

Morgan clung to her dad, not wanting to leave. He kissed her head and caressed her cheek, not wanting to let her go. How helpless he must feel. How horrible to have to entrust your only child to a perfect stranger who was running for her life. That I was his only available baby-sitter troubled me as much as it did him. Terrible time for his usually dependable and helpful neighbors to leave town.

As a tear trickled from his eye, I looped my arm through my new bag, placed Duchess's basket in Morgan's hands, and scooped the girl into my arms.

"Be safe," he whispered hoarsely as I opened the curtains and we slipped quietly out of the room. When we reached the stairs, I set Morgan down and we walked silently down to the first floor and left the hospital.

Once outside, where I no longer felt every word was overheard by a dozen pairs of ears, I tried to cheer up the sad child.

I knelt in front of her. "Do you like to ride carousels?"

Morgan looked at me through her tears. "Like a merry-go-round?"

"Yes. Would you like to ride one? And stick your feet in some very cold water by a waterfall? And feed the ducks by a lake?"

She sniffled back her tears. "Could we?"

"We can do just about anything you want on your birthday—except bring your dad home from the hospital. From here it's about an hour—maybe a little more—to the carousel. Are you ready for an adventure?"

"Yes."

A simple yes. What a trusting child—or did she have any idea how unusual this whole fiasco really was? Probably not. But Arnold did. No wonder he had a blinding headache. If I were in his place . . .

We slipped onto the Santa Monica Freeway at two p.m., just ahead of rush-hour traffic. I found a radio station playing upbeat music, and we sang along while Morgan lavished love on Duchess. Suddenly I had an idea.

"Morgan, if you could buy anything in the whole world for your birthday, what would you choose?"

Her blue eyes met mine in the rearview mirror. "A kitten just like Duchess."

"How would you like to have the real Duchess, instead of one just like her?"

The child's blue eyes widened. Her little bow of a mouth formed a perfect "O," and a squeal of delight escaped.

"Do you mean it? Do you really mean it? I could have Duchess? I could keep her forever?"

"Forever and ever. Happy birthday, Morgan. I know you'll love her as much as I do, and you'll take good care of her."

"Oh, I promise I will."

So far, so good. One happy child. One kitten taken care of. I felt better, too. Until I remembered the spy in the sky. Was there more to it than I knew? Could I successfully escape detection by simply changing my appearance?

I spent the rest of the hour pondering places where I could disappear with a child, just in case Arnold didn't get out of the hospital in the next few days. The freeway merged with I-5 in the San Fernando Valley, and I moved into the far left lane.

The face of the man at Arnold's house kept coming back to me. Where had I seen him? Where did I know him from? It was there, just under the surface, but I couldn't quite pull it out of my subconscious. Maybe I was trying too hard.

We passed the Clarence Wayne Dean Memorial Interchange, built after the original overpass collapsed during the Northridge earthquake in 1994, severing the main traffic artery to the Antelope Valley. I never passed this point without seeing in my mind's eye the heroic cop on his motorcycle, rushing through the pre-dawn darkness to his duty station and plunging to his death off a road that suddenly ended in mid-air.

We exited on McBean Parkway, and I turned left. If I remembered right, there was a Chuck E. Cheese's close by. That should make a little girl happy on her birthday.

It did. Ecstatic, as a matter of fact. We watched the giant animated mouse, duck, bear, and whatever else perform while we finished off a pepperoni pizza. Then Morgan climbed through the tubes and tunnels and slid down the slides with another little girl about her age.

They played the games and she shared her tokens with her new friend while I asked the mother a few discreet questions about the area. One of the rules you're taught: never leave a trail by asking specific questions about a specific place—unless you want someone to find you.

I needed to find Bouquet Canyon. Bart and I'd discovered a delightfully cool babbling brook in the canyon one hot day when we were exploring, which led us to Antelope Valley—off the main highway. The more hidden I could get, the better.

When Morgan returned for her pink lemonade, I suggested we ride the carousel. With traffic heavy now, close to quitting time, it took nearly ten minutes to find Valencia Towne Center and the beautiful carousel in front.

Two rides later, I decided we'd need jackets in this mountainous community when the sun set. In the mall, we found one for Morgan and a black cotton-blend with hood for me. Then we headed up Bouquet Canyon, passing the Lombardi Farm and Texas Canyon Rangers' Station. A few miles up the winding road, I pulled over so we could play in the creek. I'd remembered a waterfall—actually, a series of waterfalls—so we piled back in the car to see if we could find them.

Traffic through the canyon was heavier than I'd imagined it would be. Commuters who worked "down below," as they called it, but lived in Antelope Valley, avoided the heavily congested Antelope Valley Freeway when possible. This shady, picturesque road was a beautiful, stress-free alternative.

Suddenly I rounded a curve to see flashing blue lights just ahead, and a policeman standing in the middle of the road, waving everyone onto a paved turnoff area.

My heart did a nosedive into my stomach. What now?

CHAPTER 9

I didn't see an accident. Why the roadblock? I watched with growing anxiety as the officer stopped at each open window, checked driver's licenses, and waved the car through.

This presented a dilemma. I'd rented the car with one of the fake IDs, then changed my appearance. And I had a child in the backseat who was not mine.

I scrambled to produce the car's registration, my fake driver's license, and a beautiful smile for the officer as he waved me up to the head of the line. Then I held my breath and said a silent prayer that he wouldn't question me—or Morgan—and that my papers would pass inspection.

"You look different in this picture," he commented dryly.

"Just had a complete makeover. Which look do you like best?"

He looked in the backseat and leaned down so he could talk to Morgan through the window. "Which do you like best?" he asked Morgan. "The new look or the old one?"

My heart stopped. I watched her in the rearview mirror, afraid to breathe.

She put her finger to her cheek as if thinking—some cute pose she'd picked up from TV, no doubt, and said, "I think I like this new look."

I didn't know what else she'd say, so I broke in. "Is there a special reason for the driver's license check, or do you do this often here?"

"Just routine." His face curved into a smile. "It slows traffic down through the canyon. Some people take these corners much too fast." He patted the car. "Drive safe, and have a nice evening."

As I pulled slowly back onto the narrow, two-lane road, I let out a long sigh of relief and thanked my guardian angels for getting me through that one.

We found The Falls, as the area was called, where a series of about five waterfalls cascaded from the top of a mountain to the lower elevation of the valley floor. Several other cars were parked there, with people of all sizes, ages, and persuasions clambering over the slippery rocks, taking pictures, wading in the icy water, and picnicking on the grassy banks.

While Morgan climbed on the rocks with a cute, fat little boy who couldn't quite get to the top, I pondered the face of the man whose identity kept eluding me. There was something frightening about him. Something I couldn't remember, but that produced a frisson of fear whenever I thought about him. I needed to remember. I needed to know who was looking for me.

We continued our winding journey through the canyon and came out in Leona Valley, a lovely, narrow green valley with cows, horses, an abundance of fruit trees, and beautiful homes climbing the hillsides.

I followed the signs to Lancaster, up over another winding, steep little pass that opened into a grand vista below. Houses spread halfway across the wide, flat valley, with a brown, dry lake bed stretching to the mountains on the far side.

A change in strategy would be necessary. I hadn't planned on everything taking twice as long as I'd estimated. But maybe that was okay. Maybe this was as good a place to hide as any. Until I remembered the identity of that man, until I knew who I was dealing with, I'd need to stay hidden.

I'd been to Lancaster a few times before: with friends to escape the foggy coast and find sunshine; last summer when we'd treated the Mayflower Gardens group, who'd saved me from Scarlotti in Hawaii, to a special luncheon; with Bart while I recuperated from a shattered arm during our San Francisco diamond caper. A ghastly experience.

I shook my head, remembering the numerous injuries I'd received since Bart had come back into my life. That I'd survived some of them seemed a major miracle. I missed him dreadfully, but I didn't miss the life-threatening situations in which we always seemed to find ourselves.

All I remembered about Apollo Park was 50th Street and something. As we left the pass behind us and crossed the California Aqueduct, we ended up on 60th Street. I love places that make it easy to find your way around.

Our secondary purpose for this trip was to feed the ducks, but we had nothing to feed them until we discovered a service station/mini-mart on 60th Street West and Avenue L-8. I refueled the car while Morgan got a loaf of bread for the ducks. We bought drinks, got on 50th Street West, and headed north. Apollo Park had to be somewhere close by.

Voilà! A right turn at Fox Airfield, past a fleet of fire-fighting airplanes, and suddenly we had more ducks and geese than either of us cared to see in one place. They attacked, racing toward us, wings fluttering, making the most fearful noises. Morgan screamed in terror and ran back for the car, wildly waving Duchess's basket through the air.

Someone came to our rescue with his sack of bread, and the fickle fowl honked and squawked and screeched around the old gentleman, who didn't fear getting nipped by the huge, well-fed, waist-high geese.

I grabbed Morgan by the hand and we raced to the safety of a picnic table, where we held court for a more sedate flock that didn't try to eat us alive before we could get the bread out of the package.

We walked around the lake, played on each of the playgrounds, stopped to examine the Apollo spacecraft after which the park was named, and had a brief history lesson. While Morgan climbed to the top of a playground rocket ship, I pondered the man I'd seen at Arnold's, trying to put a name with the face, and mapped out our strategy for the next twenty-four hours.

I couldn't call Bishop O'Hare until Sunday at 6:15 a.m. In the neighborhood of thirty-six hours from now. If we spent the day here tomorrow . . .

How I missed my cell phone! It was so easy to call from anywhere to anywhere. I needed a phone now. Needed to connect with Bart. Needed to know when the trains left for Los Angeles and when they arrived. Needed to know Arnold's prognosis and let him know we were safe and even having a good time—if you could call being chased by vicious, carnivorous geese a good time.

As the sun disappeared in a blaze of brilliant orange and purple and blue behind the Tehachapi mountains, the wind suddenly grew cold.

The next order of business—find a hotel. Morgan looked tired. Exhaustion hit me. Adrenaline spurts did that; I'd had more than my share of those, and little sleep last night. Plus, not knowing exactly how those men found me had me plenty worried.

We drove toward the heaviest concentration of lights and ended up by the Oxford Inn and Marie Callender's Restaurant. Its proximity to the freeway didn't make me happy; the restaurant did. But first, I needed to find the train depot. That should be easy: locate the railroad tracks and follow them to the depot. I hadn't seen any tracks on the west side of town, so I turned east, hit the tracks at Sierra Highway, and turned right.

Wrong way. At Avenue M, I decided I'd gone too far so I turned around and headed north, explaining to the sleepy child in the backseat that we were exploring and we'd get a room very soon.

There it was, between Avenue J and Lancaster Boulevard: The Lancaster Metrolink Station. I did a quick perusal of the area, locating spots where we could hide if need be until train time tomorrow, and drove back to the Oxford Inn.

Checking in, I purposely garbled the license plate number of the car. No need making it easy for anyone looking for us. We freshened up a bit, then walked next door to Marie Callender's. We decided on pie, but neither of us could narrow down the list of delightful flavors to just one. Finally we indulged in a huge piece of delicious strawberry pie, lingering over it to the very last smear of whipped cream I wiped from Morgan's cheek, then headed for the hotel.

I needed to make a phone call, but if they'd discovered Arnold's whereabouts and tapped his phone at the hospital, we'd be located instantly. How could I let him know we were okay without revealing our location?

As we walked through the parking lot, a couple of jolly-looking truckers were laughing and talking about their kids. One needed to be in San Pedro in three hours. He had a shipment to be loaded on a cruise ship at eleven o'clock, and he barely had time to make it.

That snitch of conversation gave me two wonderful ideas. San Pedro was immediately adjacent to Long Beach. I looked the big man over carefully, liked what I saw, and approached him.

"Excuse me. I heard you say you're on your way to San Pedro. Would you do me a huge favor? Actually, it's for Morgan." I pulled her out from behind me and she ventured a timid little smile at the tall, broad man who stared down at her before she backed away. "Her dad's in the hospital. I need to get a message to him that we made it up here okay, but no one else can know where we are. Would you call this number when you've completed your business and let him know Morgan had a wonderful birthday today, that she misses him, and we're just fine?"

I scribbled as I talked, writing the hospital's number, Arnold's name and room number, and a couple of sentences so he wouldn't forget the message.

He frowned at me, suspicion written on his face, until I whispered that Arnold's ex-wife had attempted to kidnap Morgan, and we were trying to keep her safe until her dad was released. I explained if we called from here, the ex-wife could trace the call, but if he called from San Pedro, she'd think we were still down there somewhere.

That did the trick. He must have had some experience in sticky legal maneuvering, because he readily took the paper, promising to call when he arrived in San Pedro while they unloaded his truck.

I thanked him profusely, and Morgan and I headed for our room. I'd tried to keep her from hearing the stories I'd been weaving all day. I hoped I'd been successful during whispered conversations, and she'd stayed oblivious to the tangled web I'd left behind us. Not a good example to set for a child. I'd been taught not to lie. Because of that, I wasn't very good at it, even when necessary in situations like this.

It was one of the many hazards of this unique lifestyle. I hadn't yet dared try to reconcile the contradictory demands it made on me as a member of the Church. But I couldn't put it off forever, and when this nightmare was over, I should make that a priority. Right now, I had another: simply staying alive.

On the elevator, we remembered that neither of us had toothbrushes or nightclothes. So we rode back down and asked at the desk for emergency supplies.

"What do you think of our adventure, so far, Morgan?" I asked as she took Duchess from her basket in our room.

She smiled a contented, if subdued, smile and cocked her head to the side. "It's been fun." She busied herself with the kitten for a minute, then asked in a quiet, wistful voice, "Do you supposed we'll be able to go home and get Daddy tomorrow?"

I sat down on the floor in front of her. "I hope so, but it will depend on whether or not your dad has to stay in the hospital. If he does, we'll find something exciting and fun to do so you won't miss him. Okay?"

"Okay."

When I came out from my shower, Morgan was playing with the jade lion. She looked up at me, uncertainty in her eyes. "I didn't think you'd care if I looked at it again. It's so pretty, and it feels so smooth. What did you call it?"

"Jade. Tomorrow we'll go to the library to read about it. But now, you need to take a bath."

Re-wrapping the stone figure in its many layers, I replaced the box in my purse. Should I ask her not to touch it again? What could it hurt if she did?

I began unbraiding her hair. "Morgan, will you ask me to help you next time? I'd rather you didn't get the lion out by yourself."

"Why?"

"It's very special. My husband sent it to me. I'd feel really bad if it got broken."

"Okay."

That was easy. The long, blonde, silky-fine hair was not. But we managed to get it untangled and re-braided after the shampoo without too much trauma.

Morgan and Duchess occupied one double bed. I took the other. Morgan fell asleep immediately. I tossed and turned and ran every mug shot I could think of through my memory. Then I catalogued all known assassins. Interpol's rogue's gallery was extensive. Somewhere in that vast collection of names and faces, this man must occupy a prominent spot to evoke such a reaction.

Quietly I got out of bed, opened the curtains slightly, and by the golden glow from parking lot lights I sketched his features, writing his description as I remembered it, a trick I'd been taught at Quantico. I'd forgotten one outstanding feature until I wrote the color of his hair. Raven black, with a narrow strip of snowy white above one temple.

Raven.

CHAPTER 10

The pencil slipped from my suddenly numb fingers. Chills swept over me. I was wrong. They hadn't sent just any old hit man for me. Raven was one of the top assassins in the world. And from the group with him at Arnold's house, I'd been wrong on two counts. They'd sent more than one.

I tried to call up the file in my mind, to remember everything I'd read about Raven. He usually worked alone. So why did he have help this time—and so much? There had been four or five men at Arnold's house that I could see. Were there others? Certainly I didn't warrant more than one man chasing me, much less all that extra muscle. Raven's reputation alone sent brave men scurrying under deep cover when he'd been given the contract on their lives.

If Raven was after *me,* the newest, least experienced, and most naive agent in the group, who'd been assigned to the rest of Anastasia? Suddenly I felt sick to my stomach.

It no longer mattered who paid the high price demanded by these professional killers. That they were willing to fork over big bucks, the *really* big bucks it would take to get someone of Raven's caliber—and then assign him to me—meant the rest of Anastasia now contended with those scant half-dozen assassins who commanded *much more* than a million dollars a hit.

Should I be flattered that I had a million-dollar price on my head? What made *me* worth a million dollars to anyone—besides my husband and my parents?

Then I thought of Jim and Alma. A chill enveloped me so completely that I had to snuggle back in bed and wrap the blankets tightly around my shivering body. Jim was the electronics genius who'd helped Dad design the mansion on the estate with its secret panels and Anastasia's Control Center, and he now kept everything operating efficiently.

Alma, his sweet wife, simply kept everything clean and polished and running smoothly for all of us. They had never undergone any professional training as Interpol agents, nor had any aspirations to do so. Unlike me, who had badgered my father until he finally relented and arranged my training at Quantico, they had no desire to do more than quietly serve behind the scenes and make life easier for Anastasia'a field agents.

Where had they gone? Did they know how to disappear? Would *their* trackers be Raven-deadly?

For the rest of Anastasia, this was old hat. There had been so many contracts out to eliminate the members of this elite anti-terrorist group that I'm sure my parents had lost count. They were accustomed to being tracked and hunted, having lived with the dangers of their profession for twenty-five years.

Bart's nearly six years with the group had honed his skills of becoming an illusive shadow instead of a moving target. He had a natural affinity for it. Oswald Barlow, former FBI agent, could probably take care of himself and Mai Li in Africa, though attempting to quell the terrorist-instigated trouble there would be difficult while they were trying to disappear.

I hadn't worried about Else, Anastasia's beautiful Norwegian agent. I considered her better than Raven at everything. And the other four—Dominic, Lionel, David Chen, and Rip Schyler—had ample experience in dodging assassins' bullets and bombs.

That left me.

Oh, Father. What possessed me to think I could compete in this kind of situation? Why did I ever imagine I could help make the world a safer place?

It had been a beautiful, exciting dream. Working beside my husband, we'd be the greatest crime-fighting team ever. That wasn't the way it worked in reality, however. Bart disappeared in some remote corner of the world on assignments everyone deemed too dangerous for me, and I stayed at home fulfilling menial responsibilities anyone could have handled.

The few exciting jobs I'd actually participated in had been serendipitous—I'd been in the right place at the right time with Bart, and he'd had no choice but to use me. *Or rescue me,* I thought ruefully.

Now I'm on my own, with one of the world's highest-paid bad guys trying to get me in his gun sights.

And saddled with a six-year-old girl. And a kitten.

I wanted to think things couldn't get much worse, but as soon as that thought crossed my mind, they usually did. Right now, I couldn't imagine it.

What could I do? The logical thing was to get as far away from California as possible. As soon as possible. I couldn't take Morgan with me. That meant I had to find somewhere to leave her—immediately.

Could I drop her at the hospital for Arnold to worry about? After all, she was *his* daughter, not mine. Would the hospital allow her to stay with her father? No.

I punched my pillow. Why did Mrs. Pickins and Angie have to leave town? Didn't Arnold have any other friendly neighbors? No family? Where was Morgan's mother? I'd thought of that so many times, had opened my mouth to ask Morgan, but shut it again.

How could a man just turn his daughter over to a perfect stranger?—also a question I'd asked numerous times. I pummeled and punched the pillow. Who in his right mind would allow his child to accompany someone who was running for her life?

What about the senior citizens from Mayflower Gardens Retirement Center we'd befriended in Hawaii? Would one of them keep the child? I was sure they hadn't forgotten the terrifying incident when my kidnaper, Scarlotti, tried to re-take me at gunpoint and they'd courageously intervened. But how would Morgan feel, being left in the hands of more strangers?

Face it. You're stuck with each other until Arnold gets out of the hospital. And in the meantime, you just have to become invisible.

Raven could have already located Arnold through the paper trail he'd left: police reports, possibly a newspaper article about the accident. It would be too easy to slip into Arnold's hospital room in scrubs, bug his phone, wait for a call—and trace the trucker to San Pedro!

If that bug was in place when the call was made, Raven could grab the trucker before his cargo was unloaded. What had I done?

Methods of making people talk were infinite and varied. To save his own family from Raven's threats, that good man would, I was sure, reveal whatever he knew about the strangers who'd approached him in Lancaster.

I glanced at the clock. Two hours since we'd talked to the trucker. He should be arriving in San Pedro any time in the next hour, depending on traffic. That meant a quick change of plans. If Raven himself came up to find us, we had two hours, three at the outside. If he had a contact up here, or called the police to report a kidnaping, we had no time at all.

Why had I involved that poor trucker? What had I gotten him into? From now on, I couldn't use anyone's help; it was simply too dangerous for them. I said a quick prayer for his safety, hoped I'd imagined the entire scenario, hoped Raven hadn't located Arnold at the hospital, but put Plan B into effect—just in case.

I tore a sheet of paper from the pad of paper by the telephone so no impression would be left on the pad before copying the number of the Metrolink. I checked for an alternate location, another office where I could leave the rental car, then stuffed the paper in my purse. I'd paid for the room in advance, so I had no checking out to do.

Dressing quietly, I packed our meager belongings. Since I'd given the kitten to Morgan, I removed all my money, IDs, and my wedding and engagement rings from Duchess's basket, put Duchess in her basket in my beach bag, then slipped Morgan's jeans on her.

That woke the sleepy child, but she was no help. Her legs and feet were like limp spaghetti, impossible to slip into shoes, so I settled for socks, adding the shoes to the already heavy bag. The jacket wasn't much easier. Car keys in one hand, the bag in the other, I scooped Morgan off the bed and we quietly abandoned the room.

Morgan snuggled on my shoulder and went back to sleep. I crept down the stairs to the side exit and slipped out into the parking lot.

Buckling a sleeping child in a seat belt must be something that comes more easily with experience. She wanted only to curl up on the seat and go back to sleep. We compromised. I pulled down the center armrest so she could put her head there, and got the seat belt tightly fastened before she relaxed against it.

Now where?

I turned onto Avenue K heading west, away from the lights of the city. Less light meant less people. I needed somewhere to park until morning, somewhere the police wouldn't patrol every hour, sending me on my way.

At the corner of 20th Street West, I pulled into Albertson's parking lot looking for a phone, found one, and called the Metrolink number. The recorded message said the first train on Saturday left at 6:41 a.m. for Union Station in Los Angeles. Too bad tomorrow wasn't a weekday. We could have left town at 4:30 a.m.

A mile west on Avenue K, I passed Antelope Valley College on one side of the street and an LDS church on the other—a warm, familiar link in a hostile, unfamiliar world. I briefly considered taking refuge in the parking lot, but there were still a few cars there, and I didn't want to answer any questions if someone thought I was in need and offered help.

You are in need. Of guidance, a friend, a hideout, a baby-sitter, and not in that particular order.

I continued west. Maybe Mayflower Gardens could help after all. I remembered one of those dear old people telling me they lived in a secure area where guards patrolled the streets at night. Did the guards know all the cars? Maybe not. Probably not.

Remembering only Avenue M, but not a cross street, I turned on 50th West and headed south. The tiny village of Quartz Hill had added another traffic light and a couple of antique stores since I'd been there last. I turned right on Avenue M, hoping Mayflower Gardens wasn't to the left—but what the heck? All I had was time. I could drive around all night—if I could stay awake. But driving all night wasn't the plan.

I crossed 60th West, afraid I'd overshot my target, but another half-mile west and *voilà!* there it was. I followed the cinder block wall to the entrance, turned in, and drove around the winding streets with overhanging trees until I found a parking lot off the street where there wasn't a light directly overhead. I parked, locked the doors, checked to make sure Morgan was as comfortable as possible, and curled up in the front seat to catch a few zzz's before dawn.

My plan had been to leave the rental car parked in front of the agency office on Rancho Vista Boulevard and 30th Street West, then catch a city bus to the train. But I didn't know how early the buses ran, or if I could connect with one in the time it would take the bus to get to the depot.

New plan.

The other Avis office was on 10th Street West, at the Essex House—should be about a mile and a half from the train depot. We could leave the car and walk. Poor Morgan; I didn't know how athletic she was, but I hoped I didn't have to carry her.

Sleep came, troubled, dream-filled.

I sat up with a start, flailing my arms to ward off the man who grabbed for me—the man with raven-black hair—and whanged my arm on the steering wheel.

Now wide awake, heart beating wildly, I held my watch up to check the time. Two a.m. I'd had maybe three hours of sleep. I needed six more.

Rearranging my very uncomfortable position, I tried to envision every scenario we might encounter tomorrow. Supposing Raven knew we were here, had come himself to find us, had checked the Inn and discovered we were gone, then what would he do?

He'd check the hotel registration for the make and model of vehicle I drove. The incorrect license number wouldn't slow him down much, but maybe a little. He'd be looking for this car, but I felt confident—at least reasonably so—that he didn't know about the change in my appearance. Even a spy in the sky couldn't catch everything, could it?

The sooner we ditched the car, the better the chance of eluding him—unless he was waiting at the train station or had someone staking it out. Therefore, Morgan and I couldn't be seen together. How do you tell that to a six-year-old who must feel you're the only familiar thing in her strange new world?

He could have reported that I'd kidnaped Morgan and have the police searching for us at this very moment. They'd pick us up, then with fake ID, he'd step in and arrange to transport the kidnaper—me—back to Precinct XYZ in Los Angeles, dispose of me along the way, and bingo, he'd collect his million bucks.

What would happen to Morgan? I didn't like that scenario.

Once again I thought about asking Mabel or Sarah here at Mayflower Gardens to take Morgan, to get her out of my hands and out of danger from Raven, but once again I felt reluctant to leave Morgan with strangers, though the kindliest in the world. Arnold had put her in my care. I might even have been responsible for his accident. And, I reminded myself, I could not involve or endanger these dear old people again.

What time did buses start running on Saturday? Probably not early enough to get us to the depot on time. Taxi? No public phones here that I'd seen. Or were there? Did I see a community center when we were here before?

Unfortunately, I didn't dare leave Morgan alone in the car, and I didn't dare move the car at two in the morning. About every thirty minutes, a white pickup drove slowly through the Gardens. I could avoid security on foot . . . I wasn't sure in the car.

Pondering the problem, examining it from one angle and then another, I'd finally dozed again when Morgan whimpered in the backseat. She was cold. I was cold. We were both miserable.

Four a.m. Two hours before we could show up at the train station. I started the car and turned on the heat. At least we didn't need to freeze. Might as well do a little exploring to see if I could find a telephone and call a taxi to deliver us to the Metrolink Station.

Taxis keep records, but if we were dropped a mile from the train station, would that be close enough to point the direction we'd gone if and when those records were examined?

I drove around the corner and down the block, found the community center, drove into the driveway, and circled around behind looking for a phone. A tall, lean man with a full head of snow-white hair stepped out of the bus parked by the double doors.

And right behind me, the white security pickup whipped out of nowhere, pulled up to my bumper, and stopped.

CHAPTER 11

Hugh. Could that really be Hugh? I pulled abreast of the bus and rolled down the window, ignoring the security guard getting out of his truck.

"Hugh?"

"Yes, ma'am?" The tall, white-haired man approached the car and looked in the window. I turned the light on.

"We met in Hawaii. In the Coconut Club. You called the police for me."

"Why, Mrs. Allan, you sure do look different with your hair that way. What are you doing here in the middle of the night?"

"What are you doing *up* in the middle of the night?"

He laughed and waved to the guard to get back in his vehicle and leave us alone. "It's a friend of mine," he called. Then he stuck his head back in the window. "We're riding to Los Angeles today on the Metrolink. Two-for-one special this month on tickets, so our whole group's going down. I sure enjoyed that lunch you and your mom treated us to after Hawaii."

"It was the least we could do. You saved my life. Hugh, tell me about the Metrolink. Are you taking the six forty-one train?"

"Yup. Been a big crowd every Saturday, so they told us to be there at least forty-five minutes early to get tickets. But we're all so slow, we figured we'd better get there more than an hour early. Takes some of us fifteen minutes just to cross the platform." He laughed, but I knew there was a grain of truth to what he said.

"What time are you leaving here?"

"We'll start boarding at five o'clock. Soon as anybody shows up.

Most of us don't sleep past sunup anyway, so it's no big deal to get up with the roosters. You didn't say what you're doing here this time of day."

I took a deep breath. "Would you believe I'm running again?"

Hugh shook his head. "Darned shame."

"Could I ask a favor?"

"Ask away."

"Is there any possibility we could hitch a ride to the train station? We'd planned to ride into L.A. today, too. But I'm afraid to drive this car in town."

"Who's 'we'?" He peered into the backseat.

"I'm baby-sitting a little girl. Her dad's in the hospital."

"And somebody's after you?" His wrinkled forehead creased even deeper.

I bit my lip. *Please don't show me sympathy. I can handle this,* I thought, *if you just don't feel sorry for me.*

"Yes. We need to get back to Los Angeles and find out if her dad's ready to be released from the hospital. I thought the train might be a good way to sort of get lost."

"Sure, Mrs. Allan. Just park your car down by the street, and come get on board. There's plenty of room."

I looked in the backseat. "Morgan, are you awake?"

"Yes," came a quiet reply.

"Do you want to get out here and get on the bus while I park the car? It's probably warm on the bus."

She shook her head, her eyes big and round and wide awake. She'd heard everything we'd said.

I drove down the short driveway, parked the car, extracted Morgan, Duchess, and our bag, locked the car, and we walked in the cold, crisp, pre-dawn air back up to the bus. When we got on, the warmth of the bus wrapped around us like a security blanket. Apparently no one else liked to be cold, either.

Hugh shut the door behind us and went to help someone out of a car that pulled up adjacent to the door.

"Who's after you?" Morgan asked when we'd settled into our seats on the very back row, Duchess's basket between us.

"Some bad guys."

"Why?"

What could I tell her without scaring her to death?

"Because my husband and I tried to stop them from doing bad things to people."

"What kind of things?"

"They blow up buildings and don't care if anyone gets hurt. They're called terrorists. We try to prevent them from doing that."

"I saw some terrorists on TV. They had guns and bombs and killed a lot of people."

"Morgan, do you want to help me fool them and get away?"

"What can I do?"

"When we get to the train station, I want you to stay with one of the people on this bus and get on the train with them. They're looking for someone my age—possibly with a child, but they wouldn't look twice at a grandma with her granddaughter. You'll need to keep your braids under your hat again, too."

"What will you do?"

"I'll get on with one of the other old people and pretend I'm helping them. Then when we sit down inside, you and I can sit together. I'll be watching you, and we'll be close, but we'll pretend we don't know each other. Okay?"

"Okay."

"Have you ever been on a train before?"

"No." She yawned.

"Then we're in for an adventure. Trains are fun. Do you want to put your head in my lap and go back to sleep? We're not leaving for at least thirty more minutes, then we'll have the drive to the station, so we've got an hour before we get there."

I moved Duchess's basket, and Morgan stretched out on the seat with her head in my lap. I stroked her hair, tucking little escaping tendrils back into their braid, and soon felt her small body relax. I leaned against the seat and closed my eyes, ignoring those who boarded the bus chattering with one another.

Thank you, Father, for this little island of refuge in a dangerous storm.

"Well, I think it really is her, Mabel. That darling Allison Allan we met in Hawaii. Hugh's right. She does look different with her hair whatever color it's supposed to be."

I opened my eyes. Sarah leaned over the seat and smiled. "I didn't think you'd get back up our way ever again, and suddenly you turn up on our bus. What's going on?"

"Hello, Sarah. How are you? Hi, Mabel. What are you two dears up to these days?"

"As little as possible," Mabel said with a mischievous twinkle in her eye.

"I don't believe that for a minute." I looked at the two octogenarians, wondering how long before they told everyone on the bus our story.

"You didn't answer my question, Allison," Sarah said. "And who is the precious little girl in your lap? Since you were on your honeymoon when we met you less than a year ago . . ." She let the sentence dangle, waiting for an answer.

"Okay, you two Miss Marples. I'll let you in on the story, but you're going to have to keep it a secret from the rest of the group. And I need your help."

I gave them a watered-down, very brief version of the story and asked them to help us get on the train so it appeared Morgan and I were with them but not together. When anyone asked, could they tell them we were relatives or something, and we'd planned to make the trip with them?

They loved the idea. Sarah, a feisty blue-haired darling, had called Scarlotti's bluff when he held a gun on her in Hawaii, and she'd insisted that Hugh call the police, whether that horrid man shot her or not. I'd fully expected Scarlotti, the most evil of men, to shoot her and drag me with him back to his island. But they'd stalled him long enough for help to arrive.

Once again these active, energetic, chronologically-gifted friends came to my rescue—although it scared the daylights out of me to involve them in any way. Hadn't I just vowed that I wouldn't ask for help so I wouldn't put anyone else in danger? Especially these old dears?

I kept questioning them about their lives, so they didn't have time to ask me about mine. The less they knew, the better. But Sarah was no dummy. She was still razor-sharp at eighty-six. As soon as we were alone, the barrage of questions would begin. In the meantime, I watched out the window as the bus headed for town.

The area around Lancaster, Quartz Hill, and Palmdale was one of contrasts. There were older brown or golden-beige stucco homes with cedar shake shingle roofs on lots big enough to keep horses; these were equestrian communities. Then there were the huge new California-style white stucco homes with red tile roofs and six-foot-tall cinder block fire walls wrapped around them like gray ribbons holding them all together. Empty blocks filled with Joshua trees, mesquite, and sagebrush added a rural flavor to an otherwise modern, thriving community.

In California, the two things most feared were earthquakes and fires; thus many homes were made of stucco, which withstood the shaking of the earth better than bricks or other building materials. Cinder block fire walls were common where a fire, whipped by the notorious desert wind, could race across several miles in a manner of minutes.

The sun was just coming up when we finally arrived at the station. I woke Morgan, introduced her to Sarah, and told her to pretend this sweet lady was her grandmother. I'd get off first with Mabel, then Sarah and Morgan would wait until the bus emptied to come.

I plopped the straw hat atop my streaked hair as Mabel bustled down the aisle, dragging me behind her. Only the most agile of the elderly passengers made it out in front of us. That was fine. Hopefully we'd get lost in the middle of this adventurous group of retirees. Mabel stuck close to the couple in front of us, introducing me to Art and Kay Krell, and we chatted as we made our way, a friendly foursome, to buy tickets.

Art was tall, craggy-faced and lean, his bearing dignified. I wasn't surprised to learn he'd been career military. His tiny wife, who didn't seem to come to his elbow, clung to his arm like a teenager in love and chatted nonstop. A charming couple who clearly still adored each other after sixty-plus years of marriage.

Would Bart and I live so long? Not if Raven and his kind had anything to do with it. Again I questioned the wisdom of our ridiculous lifestyle. But however much I wanted to opt out at this point, I knew my husband didn't share my sentiments.

I helped first one of the older people and then another, offering a hand up the step here, guiding another around an obstacle there as I scanned the station platform, the parking lot as far as I could see, and inside the tiny terminal for anyone who appeared to be watching the place. Maybe we'd get out of here without being recognized after all.

Sarah and Morgan alighted from the bus. Sarah was the perfect grandmother; I could see she'd won Morgan's affection already. I bought Sarah and Morgan's tickets, then wondered how to get them to the pair without being noticed. As I pondered the problem, Hugh guided a wheelchair around the line to the ticket dispenser.

"Will you hand these to Sarah and the little girl when they get here, Hugh? They're being awfully slow, and Mabel and I need to get seats on the train."

Hugh winked and held out his hand. "Go on ahead. I'll deliver the tickets to the slowpokes."

Mabel and I followed the Krells aboard the blue and white Metrolink, a clean, comfortable, double-decker commuter train that traveled seventy miles an hour from outlying areas into Los Angeles and back. When we'd found our seats, saving the ones facing us for Sarah and Morgan, I searched the station again.

People of all ages crowded the platform as more poured from the parking lots. The train would be filled to capacity, and a holiday atmosphere prevailed. Children raced ahead of parents to claim a seat, usually climbing into the upper level. The Mayflower Gardens group stayed together on the lower level, where there were not as many stairs to navigate.

I kept glancing at the big round clock on the tower atop Lancaster's neat-as-a-pin yellow and green station. It had been announced that the train would leave on time, and those still in line to purchase tickets from the vending machine would be left behind to catch the next train in three hours. Good. That meant we'd leave very soon—not after the crowd boarded.

The seats filled quickly. Some faced each other; some had small tables between them so commuters could work, read, or play cards. In this car, the seats were blue and plum tapestry-looking, with plum vinyl headrests and plum and blue carpeting. Large windows afforded passengers a panoramic view of the city, or countryside, as the case may be.

When Sarah and Morgan finally sat down, I breathed a little easier. Only minutes to departure time. I glanced at the headline of a newspaper some man down the aisle was reading: ***Scientist Murdered. Formula Stolen.*** The subtitle read ***World Endangered? Nation Panics.*** I knew about panic firsthand. I'd been in a state of near panic since Bishop O'Hare's call.

I worked the ache from my neck and shoulders, which had been tight with tension for the last hour. Even my fingers hurt from clenching my fists. I flexed them, took several deep breaths, and stood to stretch. I could see over the heads of those still crowding around the ticket machine. Congratulating myself on how clever I'd been, I glanced once more around the depot from this higher vantage point.

No. *No!*

CHAPTER 12

Shrinking back from the window, I moved into the aisle. A sandy-haired man in jeans and a navy Harley T-shirt conferred with the security man standing on the platform. I'd seen him earlier, but since he'd been helping direct people to the ticket vending machine or pointing out rest rooms, I assumed he was an employee of the Metrolink system.

As I watched, he signaled to someone who'd been out of sight in the depot—until I'd stood to stretch. Now the man in the depot stepped from the shadows toward the door. First, gray slacks appeared, then a white turtleneck and black sports jacket.

As the man emerged from the shadow into the light, the white streak in raven-black hair was all I needed to see.

Now what? Should I get off the train and leave Morgan with Sarah and Mabel? Draw my pursuers away? I glanced at Sarah and Morgan on the seat facing me. Sarah, petting Duchess in her basket, pretended to focus on the child and the kitten, but her eyes were on me. She'd seen my reaction.

"Morgan, have you memorized your telephone number and your address?" I asked quietly, turning back to the window.

The loudspeaker announced the train's departure.

"Oh, yes. Daddy taught me a long time ago."

"Will you show Sarah how well you know them?"

The man in jeans and the Harley shirt moved to a forward car. Raven headed for the end of the train.

Morgan recited in a sing-song voice her name, telephone number, address, and her dad's name.

As the final departure warning was broadcast, the two men moved out of sight. I leaned toward the window but couldn't see them. The doors closed, and the train moved slowly forward.

Had they made it aboard the train? I watched as we passed the end of the platform. No sign of the man in jeans. He'd made it. There was no doubt in my mind that Raven had, too.

"Sarah, what you are doing in Los Angeles today?" I tried to sound casual, but fear constricted my throat and a high, tight sound emanated instead.

"Family history research at the big library downtown." As she watched me, her hand slipped around Morgan's shoulders to pull the child close. Morgan looked up and beamed a sunny smile at her.

"I can't believe it. That's where we were going," I said. Maybe this would work after all. I formulated a plan as I spoke.

Kneeling in front of the child, I took her hands in mine. "Morgan, two of the men chasing me just got on the train. I think they won't recognize me, but I can't wait to see. I'm going to move around on the train, and if it looks like it would be best, I'll jump off at one of the stations. I'll meet you at the library. Will that be okay?"

Morgan frowned.

"You'll have to take good care of Duchess, and Sarah will take good care of you. I need your help on this. If anyone asks, you don't know me, you've never seen me, and Sarah is your great-grandmother. Can you do that?"

She nodded solemnly.

Watching both ends of the car, I scribbled a note for Sarah containing the name of the hospital where Arnold was confined, the phone number there, and a quick description of Raven.

"Don't try anything heroic like you did in Hawaii," I said. "This man is worse than Scarlotti, if that's possible. Just take care of Morgan, and if I have to get off, I'll see you at the library."

"We'll be down on the fourth level—family history and genealogy research. Be careful," she admonished with a quick squeeze of my hand.

I perched on the edge of the seat, pretending to visit with the Krells across the aisle while I watched for the men. They'd search each car, upper and lower level, converging in the middle. And this car was about the middle. I needed to leave here, and stay as far from Morgan as I could.

I blew the child a kiss, gave her a big smile, grabbed my bag, and headed for the guy in the jeans. Why tangle with Raven if I could avoid it?

Through the glass in the door, I watched the sandy-haired man saunter down the aisle in the first car, nodding at people, speaking to others like a goodwill ambassador. Not your normal, everyday bad guy. Smart.

As he neared the end of the first car, I ducked into an empty seat out of sight and waited for him to start on the upper level. When he climbed the stairs, I entered that car and slipped into the rest room on the lower level. I could hide out here until he cleared this end car. I'd only have one door to watch, and if either of them returned to this car, I'd spot them before they could spot me.

And what would happen if they saw through my flimsy disguise?

I looked in the mirror. Darkening the eye shadow and eyeliner, I accented both as the makeup lady at Merle Norman's had done yesterday, renewing the neo-Cleopatra look I'd been hesitant to paint on today.

Then I changed clothes, breathing a lot easier once I was out of those tight jeans. No wonder I hadn't slept in the car—besides being twisted like a pretzel, I'd been packed in like sausage in a casing. I donned the new long dress with the black and white print side out, then tucked, folded, and hiked it up so it was just at my knees and secured it with the sash, obi-fashion. The hairdresser had left me with two-toned hair—there hadn't been time to strip all color—so I teased my very short, lightened ends till my hairdo was poufy and full—as much as possible with what I had left to work with.

I peeked out of the rest room. Two jean-clad legs in leather boots descended the stairs. I pulled my head in quickly and waited, my heart pounding, until the footsteps receded down the aisle. I looked out.

Wrong man.

Way to go. Jeans are the national costume of America. Everyone wears them. Except Raven. But he wasn't American. I didn't remember his nationality. I should have recalled everything I'd read about him, but I didn't. Just that he made the list of top ten assassins Interpol published periodically, and that his success rate was extremely high. Very few misses. That statistic gave me chills.

Forgetting details could be fatal. From now on, I'd pay more attention to those little things that could make the difference between whether or not I lived to enjoy another sunrise.

No one pounded on the door wanting to use the rest room, so I waited with it slightly ajar until another step on the stairs alerted me to someone descending. This time I watched the feet. Navy Saucony athletic shoes below the jeans. Expensive. When the man walked down the aisle, I stuck my head out.

Navy Harley T-shirt. Right man.

He walked to the end of the car, but before he went through the door, he paused. He was watching my reflection in the glass!

I dropped my bag in the rest room, stepped out into the aisle, and stooped down by a little dark-eyed boy traveling with his mother, a baby, and two girls.

"Would you like me to tie your shoe so you don't trip and fall when you get up?" I smiled up at the mother, silently asking her permission.

"Thank you," she said with a heavy Hispanic accent. "They never stayed tied. Of course, kids these days think it's cool to leave them untied. He imitates everything his big brother does, but when you're only two years old, it's hard not to trip over them." The mother smiled affectionately at her small son.

"How old is your baby?" I asked in Spanish, glancing toward the end of the car. The man with the Sauconys turned and stared. I leaned over to look closely as the proud mother uncovered the baby.

"Three months. My mother's never seen him, so we're going to show him off." She smiled, replying in Spanish, apparently relieved that she didn't have to labor in a tongue still hard for her to speak.

The man ambled toward me, about halfway down the aisle now.

"I'll bet Grandma will be happy to see you today," I said to the girls, in Spanish, raising my voice slightly so the man could hear.

"Momma. I need to go to the bathroom," the littlest of the girls whispered.

"Can I help? I could take her in, or hold the baby for you."

She hesitated only a moment, apparently deciding that I looked trustworthy enough to hold her baby while her other children looked on. "Would you mind?"

"I'd love to." I reached for the baby, and as Momma took the dark-haired little girl by the hand, I said quietly, "I think I left my bag in there. When you're through, just bring it out with you, will you please?"

I sat down next to the little boy and talked to the baby, telling him how beautiful he was, how much like his handsome, two-year-old big brother he looked, crooning nonsensical baby-babble in Spanish.

I didn't raise my head, pretending to concentrate on the baby. I heard the footsteps approach. Heard them stop. Out of the corner of my eye, I could see the navy Sauconys in the aisle right next to me, feel the heat of examination on my skin.

He was looking for a black-haired, green-eyed woman. My hair was streaked blonde. But the eyes were still green. I should have grabbed my colored lenses. Why didn't I think of that before I left home?

Why was he still standing there? He needed to leave before they came out of the rest room with my bag. I could change everything but the bag.

Please go away.

I continued crooning to the baby, then reached out and tickled the little boy's knee and he giggled. I ignored the man, pretending to be part of this family. But that would only work until Momma came back.

Please leave.

The older girl, probably about eight or nine, hummed quietly while she watched me. Was she just curious about this stranger who had suddenly barged into their family, or didn't she trust me?

"I like that song. Will you sing it for me?" I said, never reverting to English.

She shook her head and looked up at the man, who retreated slightly.

"Come on," I coaxed. "I'll bet you know all the words to the whole song."

A little smile played at the corners of her mouth.

"You can sing it quietly, so just I can hear. I'd like that. Please?"

The navy Sauconys backed away a couple of steps, and as she began to sing a lovely Hispanic lullaby, I hummed along with her. The shoes turned, and I heard footsteps move down the aisle as the door to the rest room opened and Momma and little sister emerged with my bag.

We exchanged bag for baby, and I settled on the edge of the seat across the aisle, hurriedly donning sunglasses in case Saucony returned.

A scowling teenager gathered up the backpack and jacket he'd spread out, hoping to keep anyone else from sharing the seat. When I flashed a saccharine smile at him, he turned to the window and ignored me.

I liked being ignored. I'd have liked very much to become invisible so *everyone* could ignore me.

Picking up the Metrolink schedule the young man left on the seat, I studied it carefully. We'd arrive at Vincent Grade Station any minute, then it would be another thirty minutes before the next stop at Princessa Station.

How could I increase my odds of getting to Union Station without being discovered? How could I return Morgan to her father without endangering either of them? And how could I get out of Los Angeles without Raven knowing I'd gone?

I'd pictured this nearly two-hour trip as a relaxing respite from the fear and tension Raven's appearance incited. Instead, it had turned into a game of cat and mouse with a much-too-small playing board.

And the cat appeared to be closing in.

CHAPTER 13

Plan A: Work my way into this little family across the aisle and help Momma with her handful of kids. Raven was searching for a single woman, Caucasian, green eyes, long black curly hair. Did he know about Morgan? Add: possibly with small child. If I appeared to be part of an Hispanic family, as long as he didn't get a good look at me, I'd probably be safe. With my dark roots and lightened ends, I could still pass for Hispanic.

Saucony was a hired gun. He may not have studied my picture as thoroughly as Raven, who'd have memorized every inch of my face and profile, every freckle and mole. Given a chance to study my face, the hairdo and makeup wouldn't stop Raven for a minute. His trained eye would see through that thin disguise immediately.

Plan B: What *was* Plan B? I needed an alternate plan, something more than just keeping the requisite distance between Raven and me. And if I couldn't . . . ?

Bail out.

In the ideal situation, all escape routes would have been previously reconnoitered and alternate escape routes identified. Right. When did that happen? Only in the instructor's manual. Made me wonder how much training my instructors experienced, and how much of it came from textbooks written by some desk jockey who'd never been under fire in the field.

The little boy across the aisle became bored with sitting still and started climbing under and over the seat. Momma had her hands full. I introduced myself as Maria and offered to take him for a little walk down the aisle and to the upper level and back. Again she hesitated only briefly. Where could I go with her son while the train was moving? Yes, I could take him for a walk. She was grateful.

We ambled toward the door leading to the rest of the cars. Neither man was in sight. We climbed the stairs slowly. The two-year-old wanted to do it by himself. When he'd finally attained the top of the mountain, we hurried to the other end of the car and down those stairs.

I couldn't afford to leave my watch-station. If Raven approached, I had to disappear. How had Bart disappeared? And my parents? Where had they gone? It wasn't like they could hop a freighter to Australia and vanish into the outback for a couple of months. They had work to do.

The country formerly called Zaire was a hotbed of terrorist activity designed to overthrow the new government of the Democratic Republic of Congo and disrupt elections. Snipings, bombings, riots, strikes, disruption of public transportation—name it and it happened, over and over again.

Bart had been sent to infiltrate the terrorist organization; Oz and Mai Li were his support system, his communication with Anastasia and Interpol and one man in the government of the DRC.

Why did my husband have to have this unique ability to become someone else, to don another identity as quickly and easily as a new suit? He'd appear at the side of one of the terrorists at a critical moment, profess to be sent by someone known to these people, and quickly ingratiate himself into the group, usually by saving the life of someone of importance. That he managed to arrange all these details to fall so perfectly into place amazed me.

Of course, the plan had been rehearsed, revised, and every step, as far as was humanly possible, examined for faults. Then the plan was executed, with Oz and Mai Li orchestrating behind the scenes to put Bart into position.

After that, he was on his own inside the organization. Usually living with the enemy—an uncommonly vicious enemy, known to turn on its own in a heartbeat. One could only imagine their treatment of an outsider suspected of being a plant.

And he loved it. He relished the danger, the excitement, the adrenaline surge. Most of all, he loved the outcome—loved ridding the world of one more group of terrorists, one more danger to society and peace. Loved feeling he made a difference in the world, a contribution to freedom.

My father was the same. He slipped in and out of almost any culture without notice—the invisible man. His looks were so average, so unremarkable, that he faded into the woodwork and escaped attention, making him the perfect undercover agent. He'd done this for twenty-five years or more. What were the odds that he could keep going indefinitely?

Somewhere, didn't statistics eventually catch up? How long before his luck ran out? And Mom's with it. In all the previous contracts made to eliminate Anastasia, had there ever been such talent hired? Such expertise?

That brought me full circle. Why had Raven been sent for *me*—lowest on Anastasia's totem pole? His forte, if I remembered correctly, was high government officials who usually had a security system to thwart and bodyguards to circumvent. In spite of the security, he'd been very successful.

But he'd made one mistake. Some agent, somewhere, after days of boring, uneventful surveillance, had snapped a picture of Raven leaving a meeting with dissidents of a new African government. Then he'd been photographed as he fired on a cavalcade, assassinating the next prime minister of that country. Wounded, he'd escaped and disappeared for several months, apparently while he recovered.

Now his face appeared on every "wanted" list in the world, though I didn't remember seeing his sidekick in any of the profiles we continually received.

Raven had expensive tastes, stayed in the most exclusive hotels in the world when he worked, and after a job, vanished into thin air for at least a year. No one saw him—ever—anywhere—until he appeared for the next job, though every law enforcement agency in the world would be looking for him.

He had a couple of fetishes, one being germ-related, but idiosyncrasies weren't unusual for someone in his profession. And unlike many famous assassins known for a singular method of operation, Raven used different MO's to eliminate his prey, each one tailor-made to fit the assignment.

That's all I was to him: an assignment. A name on a piece of paper. A picture for identification. Not someone with a life—a story—hopes and dreams—potential.

At least two days ago, I thought I had a life. Today, that was questionable. If Raven didn't get me—if somehow, by some miracle, I managed to avoid him, outwit him, escape—would I end up, six months down the road, being a statistic on a medical roster?

That was a downer. In fact, this whole scenario had me wondering if the easiest thing wouldn't be to just step out of the train while it was speeding down the track and cheat both Raven and . . . who? Death? *Get a grip, lady!* Those thoughts were too morbid for words.

Momma needed help again. I quickly offered to hold the baby while she took the two-year-old with the dark, sparkling eyes to change a very aromatic diaper.

I used the opportunity to ask the girls their names, where they lived, where their grandmother lived. Did they take the Metrolink to see her often, or was this a special trip? Where did they go to school? Did they like school? What did they like best? What was the baby's name? And their little brother's? Their mother's? It wouldn't do to say "Hey, you" if I needed to appear on intimate terms with my newly adopted family.

My thoughts returned to Raven. What would he do when he met his sidekick and learned I hadn't been on this end of the train?

He'd search for himself.

I glanced at my watch. Thirty minutes since we left Lancaster Station. He was overdue. The two men should have met by now, having searched the entire train, and Raven should be on his way to this end. Princessa Station was still seventeen minutes down the track.

Plan C. Plan C. What was Plan C?

The training manual said to be prepared for all eventualities. That meant expect him to spot me, recognize me, and attempt to accomplish his mission immediately. Therefore, I had to be invisible when he got this far. I headed for the rest room again. The slight sprinkling of freckles across my nose didn't usually show up in pictures. But if I had lots of them . . .

With the newly purchased eyebrow pencil, I enlarged those freckles, using a light touch but making them noticeable at first glance. Not bad. All I needed was a blacked-out tooth, and I could pass for Daisy Mae.

With the lip liner, I added a couple of angry-looking zits. My peaches-and-cream complexion disappeared. That should do it. Only time would tell if I'd been clever—clever enough to fool a man trained *not* to be fooled by such cosmetic devices.

I took a deep breath, put on my sunglasses, and opened the door. Suddenly it was test time.

The gray slacks and black jacket registered before I raised my eyes and saw the man. I paused, dipping my head so he couldn't get a clear view of either my face or profile. I slowly, purposefully turned back to the door and pulled it closed, hoping to sidle back to my seat with the Hispanic family and escape further notice.

Right. *Dreamer.*

I took one step and heard him move behind me. He was being obviously noisy, waiting for me to turn. Waiting for the chance to examine my face. I was probably the only person on the train he hadn't checked out.

Time to hide in plain sight.

A normal reaction on hearing someone directly behind you would be to turn, identify, and get out of the way. I calculated about where he would be, whirled, and purposely bumped into him. Firing an apology in staccato Spanish, I ran my hands down the cashmere lapels of his jacket, as if to straighten anything I had mussed in my clumsiness.

He retreated a couple of steps. I advanced, repeating the apology in English, fussing over him, but never establishing eye contact, brushing his sleeves while I kept apologizing for my ineptitude.

He retreated farther and grabbed my wrists to stop the pawing of his person. Mumbling, "It's okay," he escaped to the rest room. I heard water running immediately.

I leaned my head against the window, squeezed my eyes shut, and tried to calm my wildly beating heart. When my legs stopped quivering and I felt I could trust them not to give out on me, I returned to my seat and sank into it, weak-kneed and breathless.

Remembering that idiosyncracy had temporarily saved me. Raven hated being touched—couldn't tolerate anyone's hands on him or stand to touch a stranger. He was at this moment probably lathering his hands with soap and water, or shaking my germs from his coat.

As soon as my emotions were under control, when my heart had slowed to a reasonable speed and I could think straight again, I offered to read the children a story from a picture book they had.

When Raven emerged from the rest room, I was holding the little boy on my lap; his sisters, one on each side, were intent on the story I was reading to them in Spanish. With a hurried glance in my direction, Raven ran upstairs, and in about one minute exited the car on the other end.

Safe—for the moment. But what would the next hour bring? Unless that was Saucony approaching from the other car for a second look.

CHAPTER 14

I spent the remainder of the ride into Union Station watching anxiously for Raven or the man in the navy Saucony athletic shoes and navy Harley shirt to return. Saucony made one more sweep, but I spotted him coming from the other car and busied myself with the children. As he walked by, they laughed out loud at a silly story I made up to entertain them, and he didn't seem to give me a second glance.

He didn't come back to this end of the train, nor did Raven. That gave me time to think. Time to develop a dozen scenarios, and discard half of them. It was one thing to be able to visualize a scene and what you'd do if this happened or that happened, and where you'd go if you had to hide—if you knew the layout of the city. It was another thing entirely if you were working in unfamiliar territory.

I'd been to Union Station—hoped Morgan wouldn't be traumatized by the scene of her father's accident. I'd been to the big Central Library downtown. But the blocks in between were mostly unknown. I remembered Olvera Street, Pueblo de Los Angeles Park, and the Avila Adobe Museum, historical Hispanic landmarks directly across from Union Station. And that was as much of downtown Los Angeles as I recalled at the moment.

I did remember city buses waiting outside the station, but it couldn't be more than a dozen blocks to the library. If I couldn't easily catch a bus, I could just hoof it.

Who'd think we'd be going to the library? That question brought up another. Why had Raven shown up at the Metrolink? How had he found me? If he'd monitored the phone call made by the trucker to

Arnold at the hospital, he'd have known we were in Lancaster and come immediately. But how had he found me at the train station at six o'clock in the morning?

Think, lady.

I wasn't thinking—at least not clearly. *Well, get it together, Allison. Your life depends on it.*

I picked up the thread of my last thought. How had Raven found me at the train station at six o'clock in the morning? He'd have checked the Oxford Inn first. I'm gone. Trace the car. Suppose he had a network of people looking for me. If someone spotted the car, Raven would show up. But who'd look in the Mayflower Gardens Retirement Center?

The security guard. If Raven arranged an APB on the car, and the guard monitored the police channel, which was entirely possible, the guard could have called the police and reported not only my rental car, but me getting on the bus. I needed transportation. Bus leaving Mayflower Gardens for trip on Metrolink to Los Angeles. Everything fell into place for Raven. I'd left a clear path for him to follow.

Right to the library. Not good.

But apparently my disguise had worked. Or had it? Had Raven or Saucony recognized me, but couldn't make their move until we left the train? My spirits sank with that last thought.

Then again, maybe they hadn't recognized me. Maybe Raven would think he'd made a mistake and go back to Lancaster to search some more if I hadn't appeared on the train.

No. He'd leave Lancaster to subordinates. His instincts would tell him that if I got on that bus to the Metrolink, I'd be on the Metrolink to Los Angeles. He'd think Los Angeles was more my "home ground"— familiar territory. That I'd know places to hide. People to hide me.

New plan. Get off the train and never get to Los Angeles.

But what about Morgan? I could run, but if he decided Morgan was the child with me, if he grabbed Morgan . . . If I got off, I'd never know. She'd be terrified. I couldn't leave her. If I stayed on the train, I'd at least know that she got safely off with Sarah and she hadn't been connected to me. Yet.

Curse you, Arnold, for getting me involved in your life! Curse me for letting you. Once again, I'd let my soft heart and compassionate nature overrule sound judgment. But if I hadn't taken Morgan, who would have? And what if I had been responsible for Arnold's accident? Then I owed it to him to care for his daughter.

I watched as we stopped at the San Fernando Station. The man in the Harley shirt and Saucony shoes came to the second car, got off the train, and watched passengers disembarking. Raven would be doing the same on the other end of the train.

Saucony repeated this at the Burbank and Glendale Stations. Not that many people to observe. But they'd have a hard time watching everybody get off at Union Station. If I could melt into the crowd, disappear in the throng, they might miss me. If Sarah could shield Morgan from Raven's scrutiny, we might have a chance.

Did Raven know what Morgan looked like? Probably. He'd been in their home, had surely seen her picture. But if she was with older people instead of a young person, and her blonde braids were hidden beneath her hat . . .

As we pulled into Union Station, the little Hispanic family began gathering up their jackets, books, and belongings. I offered to help carry the little boy and a diaper bag. Momma flashed a grateful smile and shepherded the little girls ahead of her, following me. A cozy little family.

I was wrong. Raven and Saucony weren't alone in monitoring the passengers exiting the train. As we got off, two men in suits and white shirts with two-way radios in hand stood directly in front of our open doorway, forcing passengers to go around them. They examined every man, woman, and child leaving the train. I glanced down the platform. Two more at the next car. The same scene would be occurring at each car.

The only thing I didn't know was the identity of the men. Who wanted me? Plainclothes police, FBI, or were these Raven's men? If he'd accused me of kidnaping, the FBI could be involved. But even if I knew they were the good guys, I wouldn't dare approach them for fear that they'd believe Raven and whatever phony credentials he used, and turn me over to him.

I was on my own. At least until Sunday, when I could turn to my own FBI man—the one I knew would believe whatever I told him. No matter who said otherwise. And the one I could trust not only with my life, but with my soul as well.

As I approached the men, I chatted in Spanish to the little boy I held, keeping my face as hidden behind him as possible, then turning at the last moment to talk to Momma, who made sure I was right in front of her with her precious, squirming son. She chattered about the little reunion "we" were minutes away from enjoying. I held my breath, waiting for someone to grab my arm. Waiting for Raven or Saucony to pull me aside and tell me . . . whatever assassins tell their victims before they blow them away.

But nothing happened. We crossed Alameda Street to historic Olvera Street without incident. I let out a long sigh of relief and turned to see white-haired Hugh pushing the wheelchair and ushering his elderly charges to a DASH bus. Sarah had Morgan by the hand, and they were laughing at something. Good. I hoped this wouldn't be a traumatic memory for Morgan. Maybe she'd even remember it as something of an adventure.

A tall, very good-looking Hispanic man with a few streaks of silver in his dark hair came forward from under a large, shady tree and greeted our group. The two girls squealed and rushed to meet him, throwing their arms around his legs. He picked them up, one in each arm, a smile spreading across his face that would put Julio Iglesias to shame. A much beloved uncle, apparently. Momma introduced me in her mother tongue and we nodded to each other congenially, both of us with our hands full of children.

Good. I could drop the pretense, leave my adopted family, and get on with my business. Momma had helped me avoid detection, and I'd helped her with her children—a mutually beneficial arrangement. But the sooner I got to the library and retrieved Morgan, the better. I had to get her back to her father, then disappear.

Just then, Grandma appeared. The girls ran to her, and the uncle with movie-star good looks reached for his wiggling nephew. As I started to hand the heavy little bundle over, the nerves on the back of my neck tingled and goose bumps raced down my arm. Still holding the diaper bag, I turned just enough to see what had caused my danger antennae to react so violently.

Saucony was crossing the street from Union Station, heading straight for us, watching our reunion intently. He didn't look like he was headed for Olvera Street to check out the little Mexican market, or to enjoy a leisurely lunch in one of the delightful restaurants that lined the tiny street. Or to play tourist at the historical buildings. He looked like a man with a mission. I was that mission.

I turned back and eyed the handsome uncle, praying I could trust him to help me. Feigning a kiss to his cheek, I whispered, "Please pretend I'm your niece. That man in the Harley shirt and navy athletic shoes has been bothering me. I'm afraid of him."

Uncle quickly put his arm around me, pulling me close against his side. He reached down and kissed my cheek. "How's that?" he asked in Spanish, a merry twinkle lighting his eyes.

"Fine. Thank you," I said, watching Saucony out of the corner of my eye. He stopped as he reached the sidewalk, not ten feet from where we stood, and seemed to waiver in his determination.

"I've got a better idea. How about if you are not my niece? I can think of a much better relationship we could pretend to have," my new uncle said quietly as he continued to hold me close against his side while balancing his bona fide nephew in the other arm.

I looked up into dark eyes that would make even my grand-mother swoon. "My husband probably wouldn't appreciate that. But we'll both be eternally grateful, if we can just keep up this little game until that guy leaves."

"Then let's give him a show," he said, turning with his arm still around my shoulder. "Lucia, and all you hungry kids, let's go eat. I have to go to work in a couple of hours, so let's get this party started."

He led the way with his little harem following, his arm firmly over my shoulder, propelling me along with him. We crossed the courtyard, and as we approached the restaurant, I caught Saucony's reflection in the window, still standing on the sidewalk watching us. As we moved to the door, my handsome uncle pivoted us and stepped aside, waiting for his mother, sister, and her children to enter in front of us.

I glanced back. Saucony took a step onto the plaza, heading slowly in our direction.

"He doesn't give up easily, does he?" Uncle said softly.

I looked up. Uncle was watching him, too.

"No. Is there a back door I can leave through?"

"There is, but what if he expects that and follows you?"

"I'll have to take that chance. Thanks so much for you help. Point me in the right direction, and tell your mother I think she has a lovely family."

"Sure you don't need any more help?" His dark eyes were serious now.

"If I do, I'll wish you were around. Thanks." I kissed his cheek and that of the little boy who was clamoring to follow his mother. As we entered the cool, dark interior of the Mexican restaurant, he pointed toward the kitchen. With a quick glance over my shoulder to see if Saucony had reached the front door yet, I hurried through the kitchen and out the back door into the bright sunshine.

Then I stopped. As soon as he saw I wasn't there, he'd know I'd come out this way and come after me. Rushing back inside, I found the rest room. Untying the fabric belt I'd wrapped around my waist obi-fashion to shorten the dress to knee length, I stripped off the dress, reversed it, and shrugged it back on. I now wore a long black dress instead of a short print one.

I dumped the contents of my bag on the counter and turned it inside out. It wasn't intended to be reversible, but it worked. At least it was a different color now. I scooped everything back into the bag, then brushed the teasing from my hair and wet it down, slick against my head. Scrubbing the Cleopatra eye makeup and freckles from my face, I opted for the fresh look. No makeup at all. A little dangerous around Raven, but hopefully he'd left me to Saucony. I could only hope this man wasn't as professional as Raven.

I walked out of the rest room, made my way past the table where my former "family" was being seated, even got a stare of appreciation from my new uncle, but there was no recognition in his eyes. Encouraged, I headed for the front door instead of the back. As I slipped my sunglasses on and rounded the corner by the cashier's counter, I came toe to toe with a pair of navy Saucony shoes.

Without looking up, I murmured, "Excuse me" in Spanish, slipped around him, and out the front door. Swinging my bag and my hips as I headed for the plaza, I stopped abruptly to look in the window of the store next door and glanced back. He hadn't followed me. I paused, checking behind me in the reflection of the window. He must have been alone.

Feeling the coast was clear, I cut across the plaza and headed for 5th and Grand as fast as I could walk. I had to keep holding myself in check. I wanted to run, wanted to put as much distance between me and that man as I could, in the shortest amount of time.

The exercise felt good. About nine blocks into the hike, my confidence returned. My head always cleared when I ran, and I did the nearest thing to that now without calling attention to myself on the streets of downtown Los Angeles.

As I neared the library, it dawned on me that someone could be waiting for me to show up there. That's where the Mayflower Gardens group went—with a little girl. Had they connected Morgan to me yet?

I skirted the block, entering the building across the street from the library—the back door to Carl's Jr. and The Green Burrito—through the office building entrance to the fast food restaurant. I stopped for a minute to check out the breakfast crowd.

At first I saw no familiar faces. Then as I headed slowly for the bank of cash registers, I heard a buzz of laughter and voices in a corner out of sight. I peeked around the drink dispensers and saw the entire Mayflower Gardens crowd, and Morgan, having breakfast. A quick glance at my watch told me why. It was only 9:30. The library didn't open until ten o'clock.

This would be a long day. It had already been a very long night—and an even longer morning.

I checked the rest of the diners, making sure none of them were watching the group waiting for me to show up, then stepped from behind the empty salad bar when I saw Sarah looking my way. Holding my finger to my lips, I motioned her to come to me. Then, before anyone else saw me, I headed out the door through which I'd just come.

Sarah came—slowly, but she came, bless her heart. I pulled her toward the ladies' room, found we were locked out—it required a token from the restaurant—and took her down the corridor and around the corner where we couldn't be seen.

"How's Morgan doing?" I asked.

"She's fine. What a charming child." Sarah put her hand on my arm. "I'm so glad to see you. I was afraid they might have caught you.

My, but you are a chameleon. I had to look twice to make sure it was you."

"Changing my clothes and hair will only work for so long. Then Raven will get wise to me. Have you seen anyone watching you?"

"A pair of nicely dressed men with walkie-talkies boarded the bus with us at Union Station. They came in, got some coffee, and went out. They're down by the corner where they can see both entrances to the library and watch the front door to the restaurant, too."

"Good girl, Miss Marple. You're terrific. Now I just need to know if Morgan's father will be released from the hospital today so I can get her back to him, but I'm afraid his phone is bugged and they'll trace the call."

"Can I call?"

"How would that help?" I thought about it, then shook my head. "They'll still be able to trace the call to here."

"But if his old aunt in town from the retirement center in Lancaster just heard about his accident and inquired how he was, they wouldn't connect it to you," Sarah insisted.

"I'm not so sure about that. Raven would probably make the connection—check it out in any case. But if I'm nowhere near Morgan, what can it hurt?"

Sarah turned to leave. "I'll go call right now."

"Don't come back here. Leave a message on a napkin on the last table by the back door—tuck it under the napkin holder. If you can't talk to him, talk to the nurse. Find out how he is, when he expects to be home, and tell him Morgan's okay—without saying it in so many words. Say whatever Agatha Christie would have Miss Marple say to get the message to him."

Sarah pulled out the paper with the hospital phone number, and returned to the restaurant. I watched her make the call from the safety of the hall, where I could also see the up escalator and anyone approaching from that angle.

As she hung up the phone, two men in suits rushed through the front door, and, one on each side of her, took her by the arms.

CHAPTER 15

I watched, horrified. Why had I involved her? *Please, don't let them hurt her,* I prayed. I started through the doors, determined to give myself up before I'd let them hurt a poor, defenseless eighty-six-year-old lady.

As I reached for the handle of the glass door, Sarah shouted. "Call 911! These ruffians are accosting me!" She continued to yell for help while she kicked one in the shin and whammed the other with her purse. A couple of patrons standing in line rushed to help.

The entire Mayflowers Gardens group—those who could move fast enough to get there—swarmed over the two hapless men, kicking, swatting, and yelling, until the men beat a hasty retreat out the front door. The look on their faces at the attack by tottery, silver-haired senior citizens was priceless. They'd likely have a hard time reporting *that* to Raven.

Bless her feisty old heart! I stepped back and waited, watching her thank everyone, then shoo them back to what they were doing. She looked out front to check on the men, then stopped at the cashier. The girl handed her something, and Sarah walked toward the glass doors, flashing a gold token in her hand where I could see it.

I hurried to the rest rooms and waited. When she rounded the corner, I threw my arms around her and hugged her tight. "Sarah, I'm so sorry I got you involved."

"Sorry? I'm having the time of my life," she exclaimed breathlessly. "How often does someone my age get to have this much fun?"

"Fun? You scared me out of my wits!"

She leaned against the wall and put her hand over her heart.

"Although the old ticker hasn't had quite that much exertion for a while."

"Are you okay?" I took her by the shoulders and looked at her carefully, at her bright eyes, the high color in her wrinkled cheeks.

She patted my hand and smiled. "No one in his right mind is going to touch an old lady in the middle of a restaurant. Confront her on the street where no one else is looking, maybe, but not in the middle of a crowded room. Our group will just stick close together, and they won't dare try that again. By the way, are you interested in hearing what I found out?"

"Of course. I was so concerned about you, I'd forgotten what provoked this whole episode."

Sarah's pale blue eyes darkened just a bit, and the wrinkles in her sweet face deepened even more as she pursed her lips and frowned. "It's not good news, I'm afraid. He won't be released until tomorrow, and only then if his headache is gone."

"Did you talk to him or the nurse?"

"I got right through to him."

"What did you tell him?"

"I said I was his Aunt Sarah and asked if he remembered me or if his head injury had caused a memory loss. That boy is quick. He caught on real fast. Said he remembered and asked how I'd heard he was in the hospital. I said his mother, my dear sister, had called to wish her granddaughter a happy sixth birthday, and when she found out, she called me. Wanted to know if I could keep my eye on her family since she was out of town and couldn't get back."

"Did he ask about Morgan?"

Sarah shook her head. "He asked what else his mom had told me. I knew he was dying to ask, but the smart lad waited for me to give him what I had."

So far, so good. "What did you tell him?"

"That his mother said her granddaughter was having the adventure of her life and she'd had a wonderful birthday party, except she missed her dad. She was entranced by a new pet, and all the other family members were healthy and happy as well."

"Good girl. Just enough to relieve his mind, but not enough to gi ⌐ Raven any information. Next time, if there is one, don't stay on the line more than twenty seconds. They can't trace the call in less time than that. That's why the muscle got to you so fast. They were right here where you were."

"Now what are you going to do?" Sarah asked, taking my hands in her blue-veined ones.

"Get Morgan out of here. We'll find someplace to hide until tomorrow, when I can get her back to her father."

"You could leave her with me, you know. I'd be glad to take care of her."

"I don't dare, Sarah. I've caused you enough trouble already—and it can only get more dangerous. They could hurt you or Morgan, trying to get you to tell what you know about me." I squeezed Sarah's hands. "Besides, this is my problem, not yours. Arnold entrusted his daughter to me. Whether I wanted the job or not, it's mine now and I can't abandon it, no matter how much I'd like to."

She smiled. "You do get yourself into some amazing predicaments. I'll go make sure the coast is clear, then send Morgan out to you."

I kissed her cheek. "Thanks. You've been a real lifesaver—again."

As Sarah ambled back into the restaurant, I stayed where Morgan could easily spot me through the glass doors when Sarah sent her out. But suddenly Sarah stopped at the drink dispenser and straightened. One hand slipped behind her back, waving—shooing.

No! I needed to get Morgan and disappear. I moved to the edge of the glass wall and ducked down, peering over the last table so I wasn't in anyone's line of vision if they looked out into the hallway of the office building.

Why was she waving me away? Who was there? Had someone actually called 911? Had the police come to investigate?

Sarah didn't return to her friends in the corner. She stood looking up at the menu as if she was going to order something else. Suddenly Raven appeared at her side! My heart stopped beating for an instant. I held my breath, not daring to stir for fear the movement would catch Raven's eye and he'd spot me.

Sarah turned to look up at him when he spoke to her. What was the man up to? Was he apologizing for his goons' behavior? Asking the time? Whatever was going on, she certainly had her wits about her. She offered her hand and managed to position him with his back to me. She'd really missed her calling, whatever she'd been in her younger life. She was good at this.

What should I do? Intervene? Get their attention on me instead of Sarah and Morgan? Give myself up to Raven? Then Sarah changed position and made a small shooing movement with one hand behind her. It took about one second to realize I needed to split. I wasn't one hundred percent sure, but I didn't think roughing up old ladies and little children in public was Raven's style. The Mayflower Gardens group wouldn't abandon Sarah, and she'd cry for help again if she needed it.

What was he talking to Sarah about? Querying her on her relationship with Arnold? The reason for the phone call? He'd know for sure now that Morgan was Arnold's daughter. Would that connect her to me? They knew I'd been there—I thought—but what else did they know? Maybe that was what Raven was trying to find out right now—the connection between my appearance at the house, Arnold, and Morgan.

I raced down the escalator, stopping at the street level to check up and down the street before leaving my cover. Very quiet this Saturday morning. Few people about, and they all seemed bent on doing something other than watching and waiting for me.

Slipping through the door, I headed away from the library, stopping once before I turned the corner, pretending to look in a window. No one followed. I glanced at my watch: a few minutes before ten o'clock. I needed to find some way to enter the library, get Morgan, and vanish—all without being seen.

How could I possibly do that with Raven there?

As I started to cross the street, the sun shining warm and bright on my bare arms and head, I remembered the satellite. How I wished I knew exactly what kind of surveillance it was capable of. I couldn't discount the very real possibility that it was at this moment observing me from crystal clear blue skies, beaming my location to whoever manned the monitors.

I hurried to the other side and slipped under a tree. It wasn't enough that Raven and Saucony were hot on my heels; now I had to hide from an eye in the sky. I took a minute to study the area, the little park I was in, its proximity to the library, and how much cover I'd have when I left the park.

Opting for a different route than I'd first planned, I dashed through the park, staying under the trees, until I came out on the other side of the narrow grassy area. I unrolled the hat from my bag, plopped it on my head, and crossed the street. The glass entrance on the corner seemed promising, so I hurried up the half dozen steps and through the revolving door.

A lovely little mall. Exclusive shops. Endless opportunities for disguise. Sarah and her group weren't leaving until two o'clock. I had until then to decide how to get into the library, and for Morgan and me to escape unseen.

Wandering the shops, I looked for items that might work as disguises. An umbrella—used mostly in southern California for protection from the sun—would become my protection from the satellite camera. I bought a couple of colorful scarves—good accessories, as they were lightweight so they didn't add to the bulk and weight of my already heavy bag.

Then I found it. Treasure of treasures. A wig shop.

These were no cheap acrylic forty-dollar wigs. These were fine European hair, several hundred dollars each, and at this point, well worth the expense. I tried on every style and color imaginable. A deep red, almost burgundy pageboy; long blonde tresses that could be worn down or in a ponytail; a silver-gray bob, short black curls, and everything in between.

I opted for the burgundy-red pageboy and the versatile blonde, paying for them with a phony credit card and fake San Diego driver's license from our files. I wore the red pageboy out of the store. It seemed more appropriate with my long, slim, short-sleeved black dress. I didn't think my pursuers had seen me in it yet. I'd have to keep track of who had seen me in what outfit so I wouldn't change back into the wrong one at the wrong time.

Time to try for the library. No doubt Raven had it staked out. Every approach would be covered, and probably every floor. Did he pull all his men from the train station and bring them to the library, or were some of them still scattered between here and there, watching for me?

I approached the gray four-story building from the south side, up through the park, toward the west Flower Street entrance. Sarah and her group would have used the north entrance, which was directly across the street from Carl's Jr. and The Green Burrito.

Aromas emanating from the grill reminded me I was starving. Why hadn't I grabbed something to eat when I was at Carl's Jr.? I was glad Sarah had fed Morgan. Poor child. I hadn't thought of food this morning.

A little French restaurant, definitely upscale from the fast food place across the street, sat almost at the doorway to the library on the west side. Little tables under lovely shady trees allowed diners to enjoy the sound of water cascading down the library park waterfall.

A great place for Raven to sit and wait for me.

On any other day, I'd be sitting at one of those tables, soaking up the warm California sun, enjoying the balmy May weather, listening to the waterfall, watching butterflies and bees dip and flit in and out of the colorful bank of flowers. Not today.

Before I reached the foot of the waterfall, I paused and studied the area. Which of these loungers, these people reading newspapers, taking notes, eating, or just enjoying the sunshine, was in Raven's employ?

The headline on a newspaper one man propped up caught my eye. In two-inch bold black letters it declared: *World Health Organization Fearful. Of course they're fearful,* I thought fleetingly. Hadn't I read about an Ebola virus outbreak somewhere? At least I wasn't contending with something as deadly as that. I only had mortals trying to kill me, not microbes.

The smell was too much. Not seeing anyone who looked particularly dangerous, I strolled around the little restaurant to a walk-up window and ordered a New York bagel and a lemonade. Retreating with them to a far corner of the park, I watched people come and go from the library as I ate. Not once did I see anyone in suits, anyone in Sauconys, or Raven.

Where were they? Inside? They wouldn't just leave. Would they?

If they'd withdrawn for whatever reason, now was the time to gather up Morgan and split. I dropped my refuse in the nearest receptacle and headed into the library.

I walked up the stairs, stepped into the cool, shadowy interior of the hall, and stopped just inside to allow my eyes to adjust to the darkness. Goose bumps shivered down my arms, a grim reminder that I could be entering the den of the lion.

CHAPTER 16

The security guard didn't give me a second glance. I proceeded cautiously, hoping to spot trouble before it spotted me. It didn't take long to find it. The man in the Harley shirt and navy Saucony shoes leaned on the information desk, chatting with the cute, dark-haired girl behind the counter. He glanced around, eyed newcomers, then turned back to his conversation.

The cross-shaped entry hall seemed the hub of activity, with people coming and going in every direction. I entered at the top of the cross. Saucony stood near one of the arms, where he could see anyone coming in either door. The two men who'd accosted Sarah loitered in the other end of the cross's arm, beyond the gift shop.

It was the lions' den, all right, and the lions were restless.

Saucony straightened when I walked into his line of vision. A quick glance to the right revealed a more alert stance with Sarah's boys. So they were checking out all females in my age and size category, not just the ones who resembled my description.

Time to attack the lion before he attacked me.

I headed straight for the information desk and Saucony, my eyes cast down so he couldn't see them. The tall man stepped aside to watch me.

"Pardon," I said, affecting a thick French accent. "Where might I find ze international boxing records and ze family histories?"

The dark-haired, dark-eyed girl consulted a directory and recited the floors and areas, pointing to her left down the long hall that made the foot of the cross.

"Zank you zo much," I said hesitantly, pretending to be assimilating the information.

"Wait." She scribbled on a piece of paper, circled something, and handed the paper to me, pointing to the floor plan of the library. "Go down that hall, get on the down escalator, and get off here. There'll be someone to help you."

"Zank you," I said again, turning away from Saucony's intensive stare.

I held the map up as though my life depended on following it, and made a left turn down the hall, heading toward the new wing with its skylights and huge, creatively decorated modernistic chandeliers.

As I reached the escalators, I paused, pretending to examine the immense fruit, ten-foot tall tulip, and bigger-than-life-size figures dangling from the chandeliers, then pivoted slowly to stare around me, as if in awe of this building and its unique architecture.

No sign of Saucony. No suits watching me. I'd passed inspection. But where was Raven? Had he left to look elsewhere?

In your dreams.

He'd be hanging around Sarah and Morgan. If he knew about Morgan—and I had to assume he did—he'd assume I'd come back for her. *If* he knew I'd promised to watch her. How much did he know, and how much was he assuming?

Fourth level underground—down gleaming steel escalators. At each level, each red tile and gray marble floor, I watched for someone watching for me. As I descended into the bowels of the earth on the shiny silver moving stairs, I thought of earthquake-prone Los Angeles, built on more faults than had names, and experienced a momentary flash of claustrophobia. But like most Californians who considered earthquakes as natural as sunshine and rain, I dismissed the thought and quelled the uneasy sensations that caused prickles up my arms.

Lower Level One—Support Services and Business Economics. No sign of Raven. No conspicuous suits or sports jackets standing guard.

Lower Level Two—Science/Technology/Patents. No suspicious characters.

Lower Level Three—Social Sciences/Philosophy/Religion. Clean.

Finally—Lower Level Four—the bottom of the building. Family History and Genealogy. No way out but up.

Visually searching as much of the history/genealogy department as I could see through the wall of glass while descending on the escalator, I was relieved to see no Raven in sight.

The senior citizens of Mayflower Gardens were scattered through the huge room, reading microfilm on magnified readers, poring over old, dusty volumes of printed family histories, pawing through card catalogs, and squinting into computers.

Following the red, yellow, and blue carpet that looked like three sets of miniature railroad tracks, slowly, carefully, I covered the entire department, making sure I didn't stumble upon Raven unaware. Where was the man?

Sarah and Morgan sat at a huge table, Sarah copying information from periodicals while Morgan thumbed through children's picture books. I went to the nearest computer station where I could watch them and much of the area, and called up "boxing" on the computer to appear busy while I watched for Raven or any of his cohorts. I had to be sure no one had Morgan and Sarah staked out before I approached them.

From time to time, Sarah glanced up, looked around the room, and then resumed her research. Finally she looked in my direction, and I pointed at myself while mouthing, "It's me."

She looked once, then again. Finally believing what she saw, she pushed her chair back, stood, and looked around the room. Apparently the coast was clear. She touched Morgan's arm and pointed to me. Morgan broke into a smile and scooted out of her chair, ready to run to me.

Suddenly Sarah bit her lip and grabbed Morgan's arm to keep her from moving. She bent down, whispered something to the child, and they moved away from the table—in the opposite direction, toward the rest rooms.

I buried my head in the computer, wishing again I'd remembered my colored contact lenses. I could disguise everything about me but my distinctive green eyes. All Raven had to do was look into my eyes, and his quarry was cornered.

I sensed rather than saw someone pause at my computer station; felt eyes on the top of my burgundy hair; smelled the fresh, clean scent of soap. I rattled the keys, typing new directions, a new search, anything to look busy and prevent me from looking up.

The presence didn't move. My danger antennae quivered. Chills swept along my arms, across my shoulders, and down my back.

Don't look up. Do not raise your eyes.

I stopped typing, waited for the computer to respond to my instructions, and chewed on a fingernail while I concentrated harder on the screen than I'd ever concentrated on anything in my life. Perspiration popped out on my upper lip, then my forehead. I could feel it puddling in my bra.

Keep cool. He's waiting for you to acknowledge his presence, to look up. He's waiting to see the one bit of evidence that will positively identify you.

I filled out the information slip on two books listed on the screen, nudged my bag farther under the computer table where it couldn't be seen, and suddenly stood. Rushing around the side of the polished wood cubicle with my head down, I forced the gray slacks and black jacket to quickly step aside or be run over.

Throwing an apology over my shoulder in the heavy French accent, I hurried to the reference desk with my requests. The librarian was on the telephone. With my back to Raven, I gazed at the wall of glass opposite me, waiting for his reflection to appear. It never came.

I turned to the librarian when she hung up the phone and handed her the requests, noting the cabinet top where she indicated the books would be waiting for me when they were retrieved from the stacks.

Now I had to go back to my cubicle. If Raven got curious enough to find my bag and search it, my cover would be blown. In these close quarters with nowhere to go, I'd be one dead doll.

I glanced down the aisle. He was leaning against the reference desk opposite my cubicle, talking to a librarian—watching—biding his time—waiting for my return. Did he suspect me, or was he just being that careful of anyone and everyone who fit Allison Allan's general description?

Hugh approached with a bunch of notes in his hands, smiled, and walked right on by. He hadn't recognized me. He'd been at the card catalog near the entrance—my next search, of course. I could watch Raven, he could watch me, and I'd have time to make a move if he came my way.

To look authentic in the genealogy and family history section, I'd started doing actual research. Not knowing how much Raven knew about my family, I didn't dare research my own maiden name,

Alexander, nor Karilledes, which was my mother's maiden name, so I opted for Dad's grandmother: Catherine Williams from Wales. It was her husband who was supposed to be Champion Boxer of the British Isles, thus my "boxer" search.

I pulled up a little bench, withdrew the drawer containing the Williams information, and my heart sank. Williams in Wales was as common as Smith or Jones in America. And Catherine was as common as Jane or Mary.

With occasional furtive glances down the aisle, I kept track of Raven keeping track of me. What about Sarah and Morgan? They'd been in the rest room an awfully long time—or had I missed their return to their table?

Then I heard Sarah's voice, a little too loud for a library voice, but loud enough so that she could be sure I heard.

"Come on, sweetheart. Let's go get you some new books from the children's department, and we'll return these you've already read. No sense in your being bored today."

I twisted on my bench as though to stretch, and looked up quickly. Sarah and Morgan were in the aisle directly between us, and Raven couldn't see me. Nor could I see if he would stay to watch me or follow them.

I shoved the drawer back, swivelled again so I faced the aisle, and pulled out another. As they sauntered out the door, I glanced up to see Raven suddenly materialize where they'd been seconds before—right on their heels. I dipped my head to examine the cards, watching the floor to see which way he'd go.

There was no sound, no footstep, no creaking shoe to let me know if he'd gone or was still watching me—waiting. Waiting for the chance to look into my eyes.

I muttered a lengthy list of frustrated French invectives, just loud enough to be heard by anyone standing within ten feet. If he believed my mother tongue was French, would that reduce the scrutiny? He'd know Allison Alexander Allan spoke fluent French, Spanish, Italian, Greek, Arabic, and Japanese, plus several other languages—that information appeared in any standard resume and was sure to be in any profile he'd been given. But Allison Allan wouldn't be thinking aloud in anything but English.

Or so should be the hypothesis.

I raised my head slightly, rolled it on my neck, and rotated my shoulders as if to soothe aching muscles. It was just enough to see the expensive Italian shoes and gray silk slacks. Just enough to know he was still watching me.

Why didn't he go away? Besides the obvious lure of one million dollars.

I swallowed hard, bit my lip, and quelled the tremor that began in my hands. He must not see my hands shaking. Must not know I was aware of him, that I'd recognized him, or that I feared him.

I scribbled a few book references on some scratch paper, shoved the drawer back in its place, and stood abruptly. Facing the card-filled drawers, I pretended to scan the labels all the way to the end of the stacks, in the opposite direction from Raven, and rounded the corner holding the paper up as if following where it led.

It led away from Raven. Away from the tall, blue-black-haired man with the distinctive white streak above one temple and dark, piercing, calculating eyes.

I needed to put distance between myself and this man whose sole mission at the moment was to find and kill me—distance, and as many people as possible so he couldn't get close enough to identify me.

My brain, too consumed with escape, wasn't processing this library system. I stopped at the far reference desk to ask where I'd find the books on my list. Out of the corner of my eye, I saw Raven strolling slowly up the aisle toward me. He stopped, picked something off the shelf, browsed the pages, then re-shelved it.

I hurried to the section containing the books I wanted, quickly located them, and left the isolated area almost on a run. As I flew around the corner into the main aisle, I collided with a solid mass of muscle dressed in gray silk slacks, black cashmere jacket, and white turtleneck.

Squeezing my eyes shut, I threw the books in the air and rattled a mild expletive, a tirade on people who didn't watch where they were going, and an abject apology in French, just in case the man did understand the language. Then I knelt to pick up the books that had scattered everywhere.

He reached for the books, grabbed one practically out of my hand, and straightened, waiting for me to stand. Waiting to give the book to me. Waiting to look into my eyes.

Slowly, deliberately, I gathered the books and started to get to my feet. A soft masculine voice apologized for not watching where he had been going.

I slung another insult at him in French for being a clumsy American who thought he owned the world and the right-of-way, and suddenly struggled, trying to get up.

"Oh, Monsieur. Ze knee. It locks up. I can't stand." Would he touch me? Would he try to help me to my feet? Or would he retreat and wait for another opportunity without having to touch me?

"Here, let me help." He took me by both elbows and lifted me to my feet—foot. Only one touched the floor. The other appeared locked into place, bent at an angle that nearly crippled any movement in my long, slim dress.

He leaned me toward the bookcase and backed away, wiping his hands on his pant leg. I gripped the corner, moaning in pain.

"Zank you. I can maneege now." Leaning down to work the knee, I muttered under my breath in fractured English, "Clumsy oaf."

Then I let loose a long litany of woes in French as I rubbed and massaged the knee, getting into my act so vigorously I nearly fell over. I watched his feet, stolidly planted in the same spot, having not budged so much as an inch. The only movement of his body was the subtle Lady Macbethian rubbing together of his hands in a futile attempt to cleanse them from having touched me.

"Monsieur, help, please, to ze chair." I pitched toward him and grabbed his sleeves with both hands to keep from falling to the floor. He had no choice but to catch me. I grasped him around the waist, pressed tightly against him, and felt a shudder of revulsion quiver through him.

Now you know how I feel about you, buster.

He backed me the four or five steps to the chair, dropped me into it, and hurried to the rest room. If I hadn't been so scared, I'd have laughed out loud. For the benefit of the librarian and a few other patrons who'd been watching, I continued to rub and flex my knee until, to the observer, it finally appeared to slip into place.

Then I fled to the rest room, where I could quiver and quake without an audience—and leave my recently swallowed bagel and lemonade in the commode. Why did I have to react to extreme terror by tossing my cookies? Next time Raven got close enough, maybe I ought to let loose on him. He wouldn't leave the shower for days, maybe even weeks.

Next time Raven got close enough . . . I shuddered at the thought.

CHAPTER 17

Would Raven leave me alone now? Or would he be more intrigued because not once in our interaction did he get a good look into my face? Time to disappear. You can only tempt fate so long. Maybe he'd forget about the French girl with burgundy hair and spend more time looking for Allison of the long, black, curly hair and emerald eyes.

What I really needed was to get out of the library with Morgan. Immediately.

Raven was nowhere in sight—apparently still washing his hands. Grabbing my bag from under the computer, I raced up the escalator two steps at a time, not waiting for it to bear me sedately the six floors to Children's Literature, second floor, main building. If Sarah could get Morgan outside without Raven's escort, and I could slip out, then maybe . . .

Morgan sat cross-legged in the front row of a group of children clustered around a storyteller. Sarah browsed the juvenile shelves, pulling books seemingly at random into her arms. I maneuvered through each of the nearby aisles, watching for Raven's men before I approached Sarah. Could I be so lucky? They appeared to be absent.

Wrong.

Hidden just out of sight, but where he could observe both Morgan and Sarah, lurked the man Sarah had kicked in the shins this morning. Awaiting another chance to get to her? Or simply dallying until I appeared?

I couldn't go near Sarah while she was being watched. Time to re-group. My whole intent in coming to the library—besides sanctuary, which had turned into prison—was researching jade to see if there was something special about a lion carved out of this semi-precious stone. No time like the present.

I pulled a couple of gemstone books off the juvenile shelf, scanned the information, and reshelved them. Informative but elementary. Back to the newer East Wing and down to Lower Level Two to Science.

What was the mystery of the jade lion? Why had Bart sent it to me? Why the instructions not to carry it with me or to leave it in the house? Maybe some knowledge of the stone would be enlightening.

The computer turned up a slew of books on gemstones. I found the section, watching carefully for anyone watching me, chose three promising titles, and settled in a corner where I could see the door and the escalator through the glass wall.

Kunz's *Curious Lore of Precious Stones* intrigued me, so I flipped to the entries on jade. Certain Chinese deposited jade amulets with their dead, as these amulets were supposed to afford protection to the departed. I shuddered. I needed protection from being put into that state.

The second book, Schumann's *Gemstones of the World,* featured facts, not fancy. The author said, "The name came from the time of the Spanish conquest of Central and South America. The natives called it a hip stone, as it was seen as a protection against and cure for kidney diseases."

Thank you very much, I'll stick with modern-day medicine.

Schumann's narrative continued: "In pre-Columbian Central American, jade was more highly valued than gold. With the Spanish conquest, the high art of jade carving in the Americas came to a sudden end. In China, this art was never interrupted."

"In 1863 in France, the gemstone which had been known for seven thousand years was proved to consist of two separate, distinct minerals, namely jadeite and nephrite. But since differentiation between the two is very difficult, the word jade is used to describe both. In prehistoric times, jade was used in all parts of the world for arms and tools because of its exceptional toughness."

That surprised me. I'd assumed that since the stone was so often carved into intricate designs, it must be fairly soft.

The third book, *Love Is in the Earth: A Kaleidoscope of Crystals,* by someone called simply "Melody," with musical notes adorning her name, was a heavy tome with one entry about jade, and an incredible amount of information on innumerable stones I'd never heard of.

I photocopied the entries in the books regarding jade, returned the books to the shelves, and studied a few more, copying a page or two here and there. Then I tucked myself back into the far corner to scan the information.

Melody stated that jade is known as a dream stone and a stone of fidelity, bringing realization to one's potential and devotion to one's purpose. That alone would have been reason for Bart to send the jade lion—I definitely needed to realize my potential as an agent during this fiasco, and devotion to my purpose would help save my life.

She also claimed it could bring accord to the environment, transmute negativity, and instill resourcefulness. Resourcefulness I needed. I considered Raven a negative, and would be happy to have him transmuted into the form of his namesake so he could fly far away and leave me alone.

The Smithsonian Treasury of Minerals and Gems, by John Sampson White, contained a puzzling statement: "Neither jadeite nor nephrite is particularly hard, but both are about as tough as steel." Quickly scanning the next few paragraphs to understand that statement, I came across one that leaped from the page.

"The most prized jadeite is a translucent, deep emerald-green stone that takes a brilliant polish, which gives it a bright finish. This is imperial jade, and the best qualities have uniform color. Imperial jade is rare and correspondingly valuable."

That description fit my jade lion perfectly. But Bart wouldn't have sent it for its value alone. Even if it were priceless, a one-of-a-kind piece, some ancient irreplaceable icon, he wouldn't send it to me. This bit of knowledge only increased my curiosity over the lovely lion.

Someone was coming. I stuffed my papers in my bag and abandoned the corner, realizing that privacy wasn't something I needed right now. A crowded room was much more to my liking.

I checked on Morgan and Sarah. Morgan sat entranced by the story lady, her beach cap still covering her blonde braids. Sarah, in the company of an assortment of other mothers and grandmothers keeping tabs on their charges during story hour, bent over her research spread on a nearby table.

Raven's henchman lolled against a window, now in plain view of Sarah. Threatening her by his presence? Or just reminding her she was being watched?

This kind of tension couldn't be easy on an eighty-six-year-old. I wrote a note to slip to Sarah the first chance I had. "Watch for opportunity to release birds to fly away. Confinement very unhealthy." I glanced at my watch. Nearly noon. I added, "Lunch time?"

Then I waited, watching Raven's man through the book stacks behind Sarah, waiting for him to turn, to shift his attention elsewhere just long enough for me to slip the note to Sarah and escape unseen.

He was attentive to his business, I'd give him that. I got chills just watching the intensity with which he observed his targets. Targets—that's what we were. How had I ever managed to entangle Morgan and Sarah in my problems? I'd vowed I wouldn't involve anyone in this mess, and now here I was, responsible for endangering a sweet old lady and a defenseless child.

I didn't even want to add to my burden of guilt that Arnold's hit-and-run might very well be my fault. I wouldn't go there now.

The man shifted, his eyes following a voluptuous young mother in a skin-tight tube top and cut-off shorts carrying a chunky child on her swiveling hip. I slipped from behind the shelf, dropped the note in Sarah's lap, and left before his attention returned to his assignment.

I found a chair across the hall where I could see the children's department and pulled the photocopies from my bag. When they left, I'd go, too. In the meantime, I had work to do, learning as much as possible about the mysterious jade lion.

Jade is found throughout the world, but the best quality jade has always come from Myanmar, formerly Burma. Nephrite is more common than jadeite. The most valuable is green, but the color ranges from white through the green shades to a rare lavender jadeite found in Myanmar.

Finally—an African connection. Deposits had been discovered in Zimbabwe, only a few hundred miles from where Bart was now, in Kinshasha. Whatever that meant to this whole puzzle.

Story time over, Sarah and Morgan, in a loose formation of grownups and kids, left the children's reading area for the escalators.

Sarah saw me, and with a slight nod of her head indicated that she was going across the street. If I could just get Morgan, and slip through Raven's fingers . . .

The man tailing Sarah left the window and followed her down the escalator. I followed him. Raven was nowhere in sight thus far, nor was Saucony at the information desk. The man in gray by the gift shop watched the stream of children flowing through the hall and out the 5th Street entrance.

I hurried past them and left the way I'd come in, by the Flower Street entrance. As I stopped briefly at the door for my eyes to adjust to the bright light, I caught my breath, ducked my head, and doubled over in a coughing fit.

Raven sat at one of the small tables, holding a newspaper, sipping a cup of coffee, and examining every person leaving the library. I headed for the fountain and drank long and deep. Raven's eyes bored holes in my back. I coughed some more, drank some more, and sat down on the marble fountain as if to catch my breath. Facing straight ahead, I could see him from the corner of my eye.

Allison Allan would know Raven, a well-known adversary of Anastasia. Allison would have seen the "Wanted" photos, studied them, memorized them. She would not sit quietly twenty feet from a man who could have been sent to kill her. Or so his thought process should go, causing him to dismiss this burgundy-haired French woman and pay her no attention.

In theory.

In actuality, he moved his chair back and stood. My signal to vamoose. I picked up my bag, and moved rapidly down the stairs into the garden, heading for the street. I heard his voice giving quiet orders into his radio.

Move it, lady. The natives are restless.

A taxi cruised down the street, heading for the corner nearest me. I broke into a run and waved my hand, yelling in French for it to stop. Then in English. Footsteps pounded behind me in close pursuit.

The taxi slowed, pulled to the curb, and stopped, windows all rolled down. I threw open the door and dove into the cab.

"Somebody's comin', lady. Wanna wait for 'im?"

"No! Get me out of here."

The driver pulled away from the curb before I had the door shut. A hand shot out and yanked the door open.

"Go!" I shouted, pulling with all my might on the door handle. If he got in the car . . . if he had a gun . . . if the light turned red . . . if someone was in the crosswalk . . .

The cab shot forward. Two hands grabbed the door post and hung on, clinging precariously as the taxi careened around the corner and shot down the street. Saucony! He loosed a string of expletives that burned my ears, yelling for the cabbie to stop or he'd kill him.

The taxi driver looked over his shoulder and slowed the car. I slipped my shoe off and pulled out a hundred-dollar bill.

"That man weel kill us both eef you stop. Here." Reaching over the seat, I shoved the money in his shirt pocket. "Thees ees to keep going while I get him off the car."

I grabbed my purse from the bag, grasped the fingernail file in both hands, and stabbed the back of Saucony's hand as hard as I could.

With an agonized scream he let go, tumbling into a stack of boxes and garbage awaiting pickup on the curb.

"Anozer piece of garbage to cart away," I said, wiping the nail file on a tissue.

The cabbie looked in the rearview mirror. "You okay?"

"Temporarilee. Where are we?" I looked out the window, not recognizing any of the buildings.

"Where do you want to be?"

"Paree would be nice right now. But how about ze Biltmore instead?"

"Gotcha. What is it about French women that drives men so crazy?"

"I do not know, but I weesh eet did not happen."

I hopped out of the cab and hurried into the elegant, historic Biltmore Hotel. The cool marble interior and fountain splashing in the center of the entrance calmed my pounding heart down to merely beating triple time.

A nattily dressed manager frowned as I clutched the ornate black wrought-iron banister, pulling myself up the stairs on quaking legs. I ignored him, steadied myself on the magnificently carved archway leading to the registration area, found the ladies' room, and tried not to lose my cookies again. It didn't work. This had to stop, or I'd ruin my digestive system.

Of course, it was a better alternative than facing Raven or Saucony. I shuddered thinking what horrible things Saucony would be dreaming up for me right now.

When I'd recovered my equilibrium, I examined my choices for a new disguise. Back to my original outfit: the denim skirt and white short-sleeved cotton sweater I'd had on when I got the message to leave the estate and run for my life. I brushed my hair till my scalp tingled, then pulled on the blonde wig and tied it at the nape of my neck with the red scarf I'd purchased this morning, pulling a few strands of the fine, silky hair loose around my face.

I turned the bag inside out again, put the burgundy wig on the bottom and my clothes on top of that, then slipped the papers back in the pocket. I tried to do something a little different with my makeup, but what I needed more than anything else was colored contacts. I looked in the mirror, decided I'd done all I could, and dropped my purse with the jade lion in the bag on top of everything else.

As I passed the gift shop, a bag, slightly larger than the one all my belongings were crammed into, caught my eye. I waltzed in, dropped my old bag in that new black one with the Biltmore logo, slapped the tag and fifty dollars on the counter, and left the hotel using the other entrance.

I headed back toward the library. How I wished I could make a run for the airport, get a ticket for the first plane out of the country in any direction, and put Raven far behind me.

But Arnold had entrusted his daughter to me. And I'd better get back to that little girl fast, before Raven and Saucony decided that she or Sarah might be persuaded to tell them something about me they wanted to know. Of course, neither Morgan nor Sarah had anything they could tell. That wouldn't make Raven happy.

And Saucony would be about as unhappy as a man could be right now. Back to the lions' den. This time one of the lions was injured. And more dangerous than ever.

CHAPTER 18

Entering Carl's Jr. and the Green Burrito from the business building entrance instead of the street entrance, I paused long enough to see who was where. Sarah and Morgan were at a table near the front door, where Sarah could see both entrances. But from my position, most of the dining room was around the corner, out of my line of sight.

Sarah glanced up, then looked away as I slowly made my way toward the line of people ordering their lunch. She raised her drink toward her lips, stopped, stared into it for a second, put the straw to her mouth, and looked at me while she sipped. This time she really looked.

I scanned the crowd. No familiar faces. I looked back at Sarah. She was staring at me. A quick perusal of the lunch bunch in sight revealed no one paying any attention to me but Sarah. I nodded to affirm her suspicions.

She slowly shook her head, made a subtle movement with her hand indicating someone was behind her, kissed Morgan on the forehead, and said something in her ear. As they gathered their wrappers and drinks and dumped them in the receptacle, I took a few steps backward toward the door so I'd be hidden from anyone in the interior of the dining room.

As I did, the door behind me opened.

My stomach turned a somersault. I didn't turn. I didn't dare. Moving slowly, I made my way toward the diminishing line of people ordering lunch. Whoever came in behind me was in no hurry. They didn't pass. I moved to the side of the narrow aisle, pretending to take my time searching the menu above the counter. The footsteps stopped.

Sarah and Morgan walked hand in hand toward the front door.

"Next, please."

That would be me. I ordered the Nachos Grande and a large drink, and while pretending to dig for my purse, I glanced toward the front door. Raven paused in the doorway, smiled, and held it open for Sarah and Morgan. He was sticking closer than mud to those two. How could I ever get Morgan out of here?

A male voice behind me ordered a double Western Bacon Cheeseburger, large fries, and a drink. I took my number and placed it on the table where Sarah and Morgan had been sitting, which offered good views of the front and back doors. Also a good view of the man who came in behind me, the man who'd been tailing Sarah and Morgan in the library.

They were closing in on me. I needed to get out of here, away from the library, away from Los Angeles, away from people who sought the bounty on my head. I pondered the same old question as I scooped melted cheese, hamburger, tomatoes, and onions onto a tortilla chip: who had offered the bounty? And why such a large one for me?

While I worked on the huge plate of nachos smothered with guacamole and sour cream, I decided the best way to handle our escape was to simply be bold. Not wait for an opportunity to sneak Morgan away, but just an in-your-face-I'm-out-of-here move right under Raven's nose. I'd spent too many scary hours this morning evading the assassin and his men. My luck couldn't hold out much longer.

Not knowing beforehand what I would do, I said a quick prayer for divine guidance, knowing without it I'd be doomed from the get-go. I bought a couple of salads, desserts, and bottles of water and put them in my bag. It couldn't hold much more, and I already felt like a bag lady carting all my worldly goods around with me. At least I was an upscale bag lady, with my new Biltmore Hotel bag.

I crossed the street, expecting the man behind me to follow, but he didn't. Did that mean he watched from the window and radioed Raven? Or that in my new outfit and blonde wig, I wasn't a suspect?

As I approached the library, the headline on the newspaper in the *LA Times* box caught my eye: ***Thousands Die As Infection Spreads.*** I experienced a momentary flash of sorrow for the unfortunate people suffering from whatever pestilence or plague had been unleashed on them. I sincerely hoped I wouldn't become a statistic—one more death in Los Angeles on this date. Or any other date soon.

It was close to two o'clock. The Mayflower Gardens group would be leaving within the hour. Not much time to make my move and disappear. I walked past Raven, who was talking to the man still stationed near the library gift shop. Both looked at me, but neither followed or seemed overtly interested.

So far, so good.

Sarah and Morgan were just settling down in the History and Genealogy section, with Morgan's children's books stacked high on the table in front of her. They seemed to have lost their tail entirely. Something was up. Why had Raven pulled their watchdog now?

Grabbing a piece of ever-present scratch paper, I scribbled a note to Sarah. "Leave Morgan here. Go upstairs and stay for fifteen minutes. If we get away, thanks so much for all your help, and I'll call you when I can. If Morgan is back here in fifteen minutes, my plan failed and I'll have to try something else."

Sarah read the note, hugged Morgan, and left the department. As soon as she was at the top of the escalator, I slid into the seat next to Morgan.

"How are you doing?"

She smiled up at me. "This is fun. Just like Buffy on TV."

"Buffy?"

"Buffy, the Vampire Slayer. She's always fighting the bad guys."

"Isn't that a scary program?" I asked, surprised that a six-year-old would be watching a show for teens. "Does your dad let you watch that show?"

Morgan giggled. "It's our favorite. We watch it every week, with popcorn and licorice. Then we talk about it—about all the bad guys and the bad things they do and why they do them."

"Right. Well, we're going to leave here and hopefully walk right by those bad guys. I'll go first. I want you to count to twenty, then follow me upstairs. Go straight ahead instead of turning to go out the front door. Wait for me at the fountain. I'll be right behind you, unless someone stops me. If I don't come, you come back down here and wait for Sarah, okay? Can you do that?"

"Okay. Then can we go see my daddy?"

"That's the plan. Are you ready?"

"Yes. One. Two. Three . . ." She started counting out loud, and marking the count off with her fingers, as well.

I hurried out of the department and up the escalator. None of Raven's men were in sight. Tiny fingers of fear tingled down my spine. Why? Did Raven have a new plan? Or was he giving up? Had he decided I wasn't here after all? *Yeah, right.*

Sarah met me as I hurried toward the reception area.

"They're searching floor by floor. I heard one of the men report by radio that the top three stories were clear. They're all on this floor right now." She glanced over her shoulder.

Sure enough. Raven and the two gray-suited watchdogs by the bookstore were conferring in the middle of the hall with two others who had joined them from rooms on either side. Saucony, his hand wrapped in a handkerchief, emerged from a door marked "Employees Only" and joined the others. As Raven pointed out their assignments, I followed Sarah down the escalator. We intercepted Morgan at the second level down, and she reversed direction.

Now what? Raven had kept Morgan and Sarah in sight all morning, but he hadn't bothered them, just had his men observe. That meant they were looking for me, waiting for me to join those two. What would happen to my friends if I didn't?

What to do? What to do? If only I'd been minutes earlier doing this, we might have been out of here by now.

I looked around the room. Rows and rows of bookshelves, filing cabinets, and tables offered no cover, but the wood-paneled cubicles containing the computers might be just the ticket. I peeked around the corner of one—this might do. Open on one side, enclosed by wooden paneling on three, with a shelf containing a computer and a desk-like shelf to hold books. Ample leg room under the computer, and an empty spot back in the corner under the desk/shelf.

"Sarah, if Morgan and I can hide until they're through searching, maybe Raven will give up and leave. I think we can snuggle back under these computers, but I'll need you and someone else to sit at the computer until Raven's completed the sweep, just to make sure we aren't spotted."

"I'll get Mabel to help."

"Thanks, love." I gave Sarah a quick hug. "I really owe you for this."

Sarah moved as quickly as she could to get Mabel, and, watching carefully to make sure no patrons saw us, I helped Morgan under one of the computer terminals in the center of the department. When she was comfortable, I told her she must not make any noise until I came for her.

"I'll just take a little nap back here," she assured me. "Duchess can sleep with me."

"Good girl. We may have to stay where we are for a long time, so remember how important it is that you be absolutely silent," I cautioned.

"Buffy could do it. So can I."

Waiting until a couple of patrons went down the aisle and I was sure no one watched me, I ducked under the computer terminal next to Morgan's. I wasn't nearly as comfortable as the little girl who easily fit, but figured it wouldn't be hours and hours that I'd have to hug my legs up under my chin and pretend to be a pretzel.

Sarah's shoes appeared in my line of sight, and she moved to the computer above Morgan. Mabel sat down at the computer above me and put her purse and file on the floor near my feet.

"You do get yourself into the most amazing predicaments, my dear," Mabel said softly.

"If I get out of this, it will be thanks to you and Sarah. Don't talk to me anymore. Pretend I'm not here."

Now all I had to do was sit and think. Sit and worry. What had prompted Raven to do a floor-by-floor search? Did they think I might have gotten away in the taxi? Was it just to make sure I wasn't here? Then would they go somewhere else? Where? To the hospital?

As long as I stayed in Los Angeles, Arnold and Morgan were in danger, as well as the senior citizens from Mayflower Gardens. Next question: How did Raven find me in the first place? That puzzle hung over me like a guillotine. Until I knew the answer to that, I couldn't be sure I'd ever get away.

How long would it take the six men to search the remaining three floors above us? Were they all searching, or had Raven stationed someone at the entrance to make sure their target didn't slip in or out unnoticed? When they'd finished searching, would they leave? So many questions my head ached.

Suddenly Mabel tapped her foot against her purse. "I see the dark-haired man with the white streak in his hair," she whispered.

"Gotcha," I said.

Sarah whispered something to Morgan. Everything quieted, except the rattling of computer keys in the two cubicles. I became acutely aware of every sound around me.

Footsteps shuffled by. Not Raven or his men. A pair of leather shoes squeaked down the aisle. I'd heard them several times before. In a few minutes, the soft crunch of wheels on carpet caught my attention.

"Mabel, I'm taking Carol and some of the others upstairs so we can get a head start. You and Sarah hadn't better be too far behind. Don't want to miss that bus."

"We'll be there, Hugh. Don't you worry," Mabel said.

Then I heard soft footfalls on the other side of the thin wood partition. They stopped. No more sound. No movement. Then more footsteps approached and stopped. Were they watching Sarah? Could they see me under the partition? There was about two inches of clearance between floor and partition. Was I far enough in to be completely hidden?

Another set of footsteps stopped. If I'd counted right, three men stood in the aisle just outside the compartment where I huddled. Coincidence? Or were they waiting for all six to get there, then they'd drag me out?

"Sarah, I hate to say this, but I think we'd better go. We'll miss the bus and our train back if we don't leave now." Reluctance quivered in Mabel's voice.

She was right. They couldn't stay. Not only would it be terribly inconvenient for them, it was also dangerous. A trip like this could be exhausting for a youthful, energetic person, especially given the early hour at which they'd embarked, much less someone in their eighties who probably napped each afternoon.

Mabel made a big show of filing her papers in her bag, chatting with Sarah as she gathered up everything she'd spread out. I could hear Sarah doing the same and answering Mabel in an unnaturally subdued voice which told me she didn't want to go. But she had to.

Would the men follow them out of the library? Part of me hoped they would, but another part hoped the sweet old dears would be able to go back to Mayflower Gardens without anyone hassling them for my sake.

Mabel shoved the chair up to the desk so I'd be hidden from view, and her footsteps shuffled down the aisle, followed by Sarah's. I suddenly felt alone. Abandoned. If *I* felt that way, how was Morgan faring in the next compartment?

Raven's quiet voice shattered my already shaky equilibrium. "She has to be here. It showed her coming in. Twice. She's here."

"What'll we do?" a disembodied voice above me asked.

"Smoke her out."

"How you gonna do that?"

"Burn down the building if we have to. But I'll have her, one way or the other, by tonight," Raven vowed. "I've spent too much time here already. The job wasn't supposed to take this long. Eliminate an unseasoned agent, grab the microdot, and leave town in a couple of hours."

"How do you suppose she got on to you?"

"No idea," Raven growled, "but she won't leave here alive."

"Think she knows what she's got?"

"Of course. Why would she carry it with her if she didn't? The fact that she has it proves her inexperience. She's had a couple of lucky breaks, but her luck's just run out." Raven paused as footsteps approached, then continued his instructions.

"I'll tell security we're ready so they can notify the fire department we're beginning the test. I want one of you on each floor. When the alarm sounds, examine every person—man, woman, or child—who leaves. You've seen everyone in the building. Look for someone you haven't seen. Flash your federal fire inspector's ID and detain them. Security's checking bags for people stealing books. You're checking faces. Keep that picture in front of you. Watch for the emerald green eyes—the facial structure. Pay no attention to hair. She can disguise that too easily. Don't let her slip through your fingers again, or it's the last thing you'll ever do."

Suddenly tiny muffled mewlings emanated from the vicinity of Morgan's hiding place. Duchess! I held my breath.

"What was that?" a voice above me asked.

"What?" Raven growled.

"Listen."

No one spoke. No one moved.

I prayed.

"I don't hear anything," Raven said. "What did it sound like?"

"Mmm, hard to describe. Little squeaks maybe? Little animal noises."

"This subterranean setting full of old newspapers and books is probably a haven for rats and mice," Raven said, moving away. "Let's get on with the search."

I could almost hear the shudder in his voice. His revulsion at being in the same room with rodents was evident.

"There it goes again." The man stopped. "Did you hear it?" He had good ears. Duchess's mewling was much quieter that time.

"No, and I don't care to," Raven said, moving down the aisle. I lost the rest of his comment as he moved out of earshot. As Raven's footsteps and those of his men receded, Duchess's little meows became more insistent.

Where was Morgan? Did I dare move from my hiding place to take care of the crying kitten? If she wasn't attended to, she'd lead the assassin straight to Morgan and me.

CHAPTER 19

The department became quiet. Was everyone listening to Duchess? Then a door creaked to my left. Someone dropped a book on a table and the copy machine whirred to life. The phone rang at the reception desk. The quiet hum of voices carried to my hideaway. Duchess's tiny little meows stopped. Thank heaven.

This activity would come to a grinding halt any minute when the fire alarm sounded. What would Morgan do when she heard the alarm? What was she doing now? Had she finally heard Duchess and was at this moment opening the litter box for the kitten?

How could I communicate with her without leaving the relative security of my cramped cubicle? Raven said one man would watch every floor. From inside the department or at the escalator?

My tendency to get claustrophobic in small, tight spaces kicked in. I squeezed my eyes shut and visualized the beach—my beach. My favorite rock. Waves crashing higher and higher as the tide came in. Envisioned the golden sun shimmering on the water, imagined it warm on my upturned face. Seagulls diving, screeching, and white sails billowing in the breeze that ruffled my hair and carried the salty spray to where I sat atop the rock.

Suddenly the fire alarm blared, echoing throughout the building. Frantic patrons scrambled for the escalator. A few ignored librarians' urging to leave immediately, taking time to gather precious files and papers. I could imagine the chaos from the sounds around me.

I watched Morgan's cubicle. No sound. No movement. Had she gone to sleep? We'd been up late last night and then up early this morning. Maybe she was tired enough to sleep through the fire alarm—and the search. I was torn between wanting her to sleep through the whole thing and wanting her awake to keep Duchess quiet.

As I waited for this fourth level down to be cleared of patrons and librarians and searched by Raven's men, I pondered his words. *"It* showed her coming in—twice." What? The eye in the sky? Had to be. An operative satellite with the ability to track individuals simply from a set of coordinates and a description programmed into a computer.

And he'd said I knew what I had or I wouldn't have carried it with me: a microdot. I'd examined the jade lion for a microdot. I didn't find one. But Raven's assignment had been two-fold. Eliminate the inexperienced agent—me—and steal the microdot.

My assignment was just the opposite: prevent him from getting his hands on the microdot—wherever it was and whatever it contained—and stay alive. But first, I needed to get Morgan back to her father and get out of town. Until then, it was a toss-up as to who would succeed in accomplishing their assignment: Raven or me.

Keep him from getting his hands on the microdot . . . it had to be on the jade lion, though I couldn't imagine where. It was the only thing I'd brought with me.

The History and Genealogy section grew quiet. Everyone should be gone. I waited for the search to begin. How methodical would they be? How thorough? Would they search every square inch or just do a quick pass-through, assuming that everyone had truly left as instructed?

I heard the voices first, too many to count, then the shuffle of feet. I listened for Raven or Saucony, the only two voices familiar to me. Within minutes I'd picked them out of the group of people doing a complete sweep of the floor—a thorough search, one said.

My heart sank. If they were truly thorough, there was no way they could miss us. I said a quick, fervent prayer for heavenly help as footsteps approached our row of computer terminals. Right now was not the time for my guardian angels to take a Twinkie break.

Security guards tossed sarcastic comments back and forth, questioning the motivation for the search. "Why would *federal* fire marshals conduct such an exercise?" I heard one ask.

"What's the point?" another queried.

A pair of spit-and-polished black shoes neared my cubicle, stopped, then moved closer. I held my breath. They stopped again. My heart beat triple time. A pair of black-clad legs bent at the knees. A face appeared. I'd been discovered.

I blinked. The face was familiar. The handsome brother of the mother on the train! My pretend uncle! He stared back at me, open-mouthed.

I put my fingers to my lips, pulled my wig askew to reveal the hairdo he'd recognize, and mouthed, "They're trying to kill me. Help me."

He sat back on his heels, looked around to see if anyone watched him, and glanced back at me. I pointed to Morgan's cubicle and mouthed, "I have a six-year-old with me. Don't let them find us."

He nodded and stood, holding my bag.

"What're you doing down there, Ramirez?" a voice nearby asked.

"I found another bag someone left. Checking in it for library materials. But it's clean," he said, placing my bag against my feet and moving away.

I tried to still my pounding heart. *Thank you, Father, for guardian angels, in whatever form they come.*

The search continued to the end of the room, then around the corner to the book stacks on the left and the magazine and periodical stacks on the right. I hadn't heard Raven or Saucony for several minutes. Had they gone? Or were they directing the search from another part of the floor?

Suddenly vigorous scratching resonated through the computer section. Duchess wanted out of her little basket—and she wanted out now. *Morgan. Please, take care of her—please.* The scratching stopped. The soft mewling began again, then quieted.

Voices reported from various parts of the area that their search was finished, all patrons and librarians cleared out. Footsteps approached, and the shiny black shoes appeared again, stopping in front of the computer on the shelf above my head.

Two olive-skinned hands quickly untied shoelaces, and as he knelt to tie them, he called to the man in front of him, "Got to tie my shoe, Valdez. I'll be right behind you."

"Stay where you are," Uncle whispered. "I'm on duty tonight. I'll lock this floor so the 'federal inspectors' can't get back in. When they're gone, I'll help you get out. But it will be a while."

"Thanks," I whispered.

Voices and footsteps receded, and the last sound I heard was Uncle's raised voice calling to someone, "I'm securing this floor. Doors locked." The lights went out. Then it was quiet.

I hardly dared move. Were they really gone? Were we safe? I let out the breath I'd been holding. Slowly, silently, I shifted my bag to one side, stretching my cramped legs.

A faint glow from skylights four or five stories above the escalators dimly illuminated the room. If the surveillance cameras I'd spotted in the corners of the rooms were working, there might be just enough light for anyone monitoring the remote TVs to see movement. I'd have to count on someone doing just that. Raven would make sure all eventualities were covered. But if I stayed low, below the camera eye, I might move around undetected.

Unfolding from my confinement, I stretched out on the floor, unkinking my pretzled legs, then snaked to Morgan's cubicle on elbows and stomach. She was sound asleep. Poor darling must have been exhausted to have slept through all that noise.

Duchess renewed her efforts to be free, so I released the basket from Morgan's arms and opened the top. A fluffy white ball of fur leaped into my face from the basket. I pulled open the little bottom drawer, and the kitten immediately scratched in the litter and became a contented cat once more.

I shifted Morgan into a more comfortable position, relieving the kink I thought she'd have in her neck when she woke, and surveyed the area. From my mouse's-eye view, I couldn't see any of the security cameras in the corners. That meant they couldn't see me, either. Now all we had to do was lay low, literally, until Raven and his men cleared out and Uncle could come back and smuggle us out of here.

Then what? There were still fifteen hours or so before I could call Bishop O'Hare to find out what was going on and get whatever instructions he had for me. Did I dare stick around Los Angeles until I could reach him? Or should I get out of town as quickly as possible, returning if and when he told me to?

I fed Duchess and played with her, letting her get some exercise while it was safe to do so. As she whirled and tumbled, chasing her tail and my fingers, I made a dozen plans, discarding most of them. Until we were safely away from the library, out of the reach of Raven, and Morgan was with her father, I didn't have the freedom to move as I needed to. When that happened, if that happened, then one of the plans might be viable.

I hated waiting. It gave me too much time to think. Too much time to wonder where Bart was at that moment, what he was doing, and if he was safe. How had my parents disappeared? Were they together? And where had Jim and Alma gone?

The quiet of the library, lack of sleep, and the adrenaline high of the chase hit me all at once. My head sagged to my arms and I snuggled down—just for a minute—closed my eyes—just for a second—and relaxed.

CHAPTER 20

The man with raven hair and dark, malevolent eyes moved closer. His evil smile of triumph sent chills down my spine, left my heart pounding harder in my chest with each step he took. I couldn't move, couldn't run, couldn't get away from the man who came toward me with one intent: to kill me. Someone held my hair, pulling, stabbing, keeping me captive as Raven came nearer and nearer. I fought, I struggled, but I couldn't escape from the sharp fingers tangled hopelessly in my hair.

"Allison, wake up. Everyone's gone." Morgan shook my shoulder as she tried to disentangle Duchess from the long, blonde wig hanging from her sharp little claws.

I sat up with a start and looked around, rescuing the wig from the playful kitten.

"You're sure we're alone?" I whispered, replacing the wig and becoming a blonde once more. "No one else is here? You haven't seen the man with the white stripe in his hair?"

Morgan started to stand, and I pulled her back down. "No. Stay low. We've got to keep out of sight of those cameras in the corners."

Her eyes got big and round. "Where did everybody go? Are we locked in the library?"

"As matter of fact, I think we are. What an escapade to tell your dad! How many little girls do you think have ever been locked in the library?"

Morgan looked at me, indecision clearly evident in her eyes.

"Don't you think this is a fun adventure? We'll stay hidden until a friend of mine comes to help us get away. Then we'll go straight to the hospital and see how your dad is. Maybe we'll even be able to take him home by then. I know you'd like that."

The little girl nodded solemnly, not quite convinced this was as much fun as I tried to make it sound.

"Are you hungry?" Maybe an impromptu picnic would take her mind off our precarious position.

"Yes." She brightened considerably at the question. "Can we go eat?"

"Better than that. We'll have a picnic right here in the library." I crawled back to my bag and pulled out the salads, desserts, and drinks. "Not exactly a banquet, but if, or when, they come back in here, they won't be able to smell what we're eating like they would if it was French fries and a hamburger."

"Allison . . . ," Morgan started, then she paused.

"What, love?" I asked, stopping what I'd been doing to give her my full attention.

"I miss my daddy." The cute little chin quivered, and her big blue eyes filled with tears.

I pulled her into my arms under the computer desk. "I know. You're ready for this to be all over so you can go home and have everything the way it's always been, aren't you?"

She nodded her head as she quietly sobbed into my shoulder.

"I want it to be over, too. And it will be. Very soon. But think of the things you'll have to tell your dad when you see him. You have a new kitten—who'll eat your dessert if we're not careful. And you've ridden on a carousel, played in the waterfall, fed the ducks and geese, ridden the train, and gone to story hour at the library. That's a lot of things for a six-year-old to do, don't you think?"

Morgan's sobs dwindled into sniffles. She looked up with moist eyes and nodded.

"And we're not through yet. You still have a bunch of story books we can read, and Duchess needs to be loved and played with before she takes another nap. So how about if we have our picnic, then we can read stories? Maybe by the time we're through with that, we can leave."

"Can I have my dessert first, before my salad?"

I tilted my head and looked at her forlorn little face.

"Daddy lets me sometimes," she said, a tiny smile beginning at the corners of her mouth.

"Honest?"

"Honest. He does."

"Why not? We'll both have dessert first. I've always wanted to do that." I opened the little plastic containers and stuck a fork in each piece of Oreo cheesecake.

"You've never had dessert first?" Morgan asked, her blue eyes wide with disbelief.

"No. Never."

"Wouldn't your dad let you?" she asked, leaning against the partition that surrounded the computer terminal as she dug into the cheesecake with enthusiasm.

"Actually, my dad was gone when I was growing up, but my mom worried about spoiling me, so she was pretty strict about things like that."

As I sat cross-legged on the floor under the computers, savoring the first bite of cheesecake, I glanced around for the suddenly absent ball of white fur. Duchess was nowhere to be seen.

"Where's Duchess?" I blurted the frantic question with my mouth full.

Morgan looked around. "I don't see her."

"We've got to find her quick. Those men could come back any time, and she can't be running loose."

I flattened to the floor to peer under the computers, tables, and chairs in our area. No Duchess.

"Stay low and look around this area. I'll cross the aisle and see if she's there," I whispered, snaking across the expanse of colorful carpet after determining I couldn't be seen by the surveillance cameras.

No Duchess.

Suddenly footsteps clattered down the escalator as shouts echoed through the building. I rolled back under my computer, motioning the frightened, wide-eyed child to do the same. I barely had time to toss our salad containers and water in my bag and gather our unfinished desserts before they were at the entrance to our floor.

"I'm hurrying, I'm hurrying," a familiar voice bellowed. "Give me a minute!" My pretend uncle noisily opened the door he'd previously made a big deal of locking, admitting some very impatient person to this fourth level down.

"Stay very still and be absolutely quiet, no matter what happens, Morgan," I whispered, pulling my bag up against my feet. "No one must find us."

"I swear I saw movement down here," someone yelled, the excitement in his voice carrying across the long room.

"Where?" Raven demanded, his voice coming closer. They weren't alone. The shuffle of feet and murmur of voices followed the two speakers.

"Number five camera," the voice answered. "That would be back toward the stacks."

"Did you reverse the video to check what was there?" Raven asked.

"No. I thought that would take too much time, and we might miss filming something when I turned the camera off to rewind."

The voices were now even with our computer terminals. Raven made no attempt to be quiet, no attempt to sneak up on whoever might be moving around. He'd boldly confront and capture whoever moved.

"Which way from here?" Raven stopped a few feet from my cubicle.

"There!" the other man shouted. "Look! It's the biggest rat I've ever seen in my life!"

"Where?" Raven said, his voice no longer belligerent.

"It ran right across the aisle, toward the periodicals." The man ran from where he stood, his diminishing footsteps pounding on the carpet.

"Search the room again," Raven ordered, "but I don't think you'll find anything. Rats don't sit around waiting to be caught. I'll be upstairs." Apparently he didn't like rodents any better than someone touching him. All must be germ carriers to him.

I recognized Saucony's voice giving orders, dividing the men into groups to search the room again. A pair of shiny black shoes stopped by my computer. Uncle? Or someone else? I held my breath. If they searched, really scoured the room, they'd find not only a little white kitten instead of a big rat, but two frightened females.

"You. What're you doing, just standing there?" Saucony demanded. "Get busy. Find that rat."

"Yes, sir. I'll take this section," the voice above me said. "Valdez, you search that next group of computer terminals."

Muffled footsteps moved along the carpeted aisle. The shiny black shoes moved a step closer, stopped, then stepped directly in front of my terminal. Directly in front of my hiding place. As the black trousers bent at the knee, I held my breath.

My pretend uncle's face appeared at eye level. "Are you okay?" he asked quietly.

I nodded. "Not a rat," I mouthed. "My white kitten."

The concerned look on his handsome face transformed into a big grin. "About two more hours," he whispered. "As soon as custodians arrive, we'll get you out."

"Thanks," I whispered.

"Find the rat, Valdez?" Uncle asked as he stood back up.

"No, and we won't, either. You know as well as I do there aren't any rats in this library, Ramirez," the other man said in a low voice. "I don't know what they've been smoking, but it must be powerful stuff. My wife cleans down here, and she'd have told me right away if she'd found any sign of rodents. No amount of money could get her back in here if there was the tiniest mouse, much less the biggest rat anyone ever saw."

"Then don't tell her about this wild goose chase, or she'll quit and you'll never get that new car paid for." Uncle laughed and the two headed back toward the door, followed by several other men murmuring among themselves at the incongruity of finding the world's largest rat in the Los Angeles Central Library.

"I saw it. I saw it on the monitor, and I saw it run across the floor when we came in," the first voice I'd heard insisted. "I'll stay down here and catch it if you don't believe me."

"I ought to lock you in down here and let it eat you, but you're needed at the monitors," Saucony growled. "Get back up there as fast as you can, and no more false alarms, or you'll be rat food."

The man protested all the way to the door. Uncle called out, "Locking the rat in," and I heard laughter as the door closed. I waited to be sure no one had stayed behind before crawling over to Morgan.

Her little face was ashen. "Is there really a rat here?" she whispered.

"Don't you know what he saw?" I whispered back, trying to keep from laughing out loud.

She shook her head and crawled into my arms.

"They saw Duchess prowling around and thought it was a big white rat. Wouldn't they be surprised to find out it's a little tiny kitten instead?"

"Are you sure that's what they saw?" Her big blue eyes filled with hope.

"I'm sure," I assured her, whispering the words against her ear. "There are some very valuable books here—some that could never be replaced. I promise there are no rats or mice in this library. Now we've got to get Duchess back in her basket before the camera catches her again and that man sees her on the monitor. Sit right here and be as quiet as you can while I try to coax her back to her basket."

It would be too dangerous to go looking for her. There would be more than one set of eyes scanning the monitors now—especially this fourth lower level. Not knowing what kind of audio the cameras had, if any, we couldn't take a chance on calling attention to our presence by moving around or making noise.

I pulled out the little drawer containing Duchess's dry food and gently shook it, hoping she alone could hear the quiet rattling. I waited. No Duchess. Again I shook the little tray. Still no kitty.

As I stretched out my arm a third time to rattle the cat food, the hair on the back of my neck stood on end, and tiny prickles of prescience froze my hand in mid-air.

CHAPTER 21

With my finger to my lips signaling silence, I motioned for Morgan to move quietly to me, then inched soundlessly back under the computer with her in my arms. There had been barely enough room for me. Two of us were packed in tight.

The tray of dry cat food sat under the computer terminal next to my bag in plain sight of anyone thoroughly searching the area, but I didn't dare reach for it. I cocked my head, listening for whatever had caused my danger antennae to react. There was no sound. The floor was quiet as a tomb. I shuddered. Bad analogy.

Morgan clung to me, her little body rigid. My fears were being transmitted to the child. Not good. When would this nightmare end so I could get her out of this terrifying situation and back to her father? No six-year-old should ever have to endure what Morgan had already, and who knew what was yet to come?

Suddenly I heard again the sound that had sent us scurrying under the desk like frightened mice. The soft squeaking of leather shoes. They came slowly nearer, then stopped. One of Raven's men had stayed behind! Goose bumps trickled down my arms. I held my breath. Morgan heard the sound, too. Her little fingers clutched my side where she'd been gripping my sweater. I hugged her tighter, pressing her head against my chest with one hand over her ear.

The squeaks resumed, coming up the aisle toward us. Again they stopped after a few steps. Was he listening? Waiting for something—or someone—to move, to make a noise?

Leather squeaked again. Step, squeak, step, squeak. He was near the librarian's desk, about ten feet from our computer station. He stopped.

There was no sound on the entire floor—except the wild pounding of my heart. It was so loud, if he came any closer, he'd hear it.

Without warning Duchess appeared, bouncing silently on little cat feet toward the tray of dry food. One tiny bite into that crunchy feast and we'd have Squeaky Shoe on us in a flash. I clicked my fingernails together once to get her attention, then wildly wiggled my fingers, hoping her playful nature could overcome her hunger for the moment.

She ignored my fingers and headed for the food.

Squeaky Shoe moved again. Step, squeak. Step, squeak. Duchess's ears twitched, and her little pink nose turned from the bite she was about to devour. Step, squeak. Her curiosity overcame her hunger, and she padded softly toward the mysterious sound located immediately behind me now.

As she neared the partition that separated us from Squeaky Shoe and discovery, she crouched in stalking fashion. When she crept within reach, I snatched her fluffy little white body and shoved her under my sweater, releasing Morgan slightly with one arm so there was room between us for the kitten.

Before Duchess could protest, I tickled her tummy and under her chin, knowing the only sound she'd make would be a contented purring. I hoped it wouldn't be so loud the man could hear.

He moved three more steps, then stopped. I held my breath. Duchess's purring filled the cubicle where we hid. Squeaky Shoe couldn't help but hear it. It sounded like a motor running.

The carpet crunched. The squeak came back in our direction, then stopped. The world stopped, waiting for someone to make the next move. Duchess stopped purring and started burrowing her way out from under my sweater. Enough of the fun and games. She was ready to eat. She no longer wanted to be enclosed in her little prison, tummy tickles notwithstanding. If I didn't let her go, she'd protest. But even her quiet mewling would be far too loud, considering our close proximity to the hunter standing above us.

Morgan rescued the struggling kitten and brought its little pink nose up to rub against her own upturned, freckle-covered one. She buried her face in the kitten's soft fur, and Duchess put her tiny paws on Morgan's cheeks. Both innocent little creatures stayed in that silent, loving position long enough for Squeaky Shoe to move down the aisle a few steps before pausing once more.

With Morgan sitting on my lap, small and light as she was, the circulation to my legs had been cut off for too long. My toes were beyond numb. Now they had sharp-pointed stars shooting all through them. I had to move. That would necessitate moving Morgan. But clothes rustle loud enough to reveal location, not to mention the noise a hungry kitten could make in the vicinity of crunchy cat food.

The minutes seemed endless as Squeaky Shoe moved slowly a few steps at a time, then stopped, listening, before moving again. When I heard the rest room door open and close, I quietly slipped Morgan off my legs. I sent her back to hide in her little cubicle with the whispered admonition, "Think about Buffy, the Vampire Slayer. What would she do if she had to play hide-and-seek from the bad guys?"

I put Duchess in her basket with a small amount of food and tucked the basket in my bag, covering it with clothes to muffle the sounds of the kitten eating. We'd barely settled back in our hiding places when the door opened and Squeaky Shoe returned to his patrol. This time he went down the aisle on the other side of the librarian's desk, far enough away that he couldn't hear our breathing or Duchess's occasional crunch of cat food.

I was hungry. I knew Morgan was, too. My mouth watered at the thought of the Oreo cheesecake, of which I'd only had one luscious taste. Even the pre-packaged salad sounded wonderful right now. But eating would be impossible with that man anywhere in the room.

Listening for his location, for the telltale squeak of his leather shoe, it dawned on me that I hadn't heard it for a while. Had he removed the noisy shoe, realizing it gave him away? Was he now patrolling in his stocking feet, able to wander as silently as Duchess on her little padded paws? I wouldn't dare try to warn Morgan, because the man could be standing directly on the other side of the partition and I'd not know it.

My stomach growled. I wrapped my arms around myself, trying to smother the rumbles that started. How much longer before Uncle came for us? How much longer would we have to stay crammed into these little cubicles, afraid to breathe, afraid to move?

Morgan was getting restless in her hiding spot. I could hear little wiggles, tiny sighs, and then her hungry stomach announced it was past dinnertime, too. What to do? What to do? If he came back up our aisle, any of these sounds would give us away.

An unfamiliar sound—one I hadn't heard the entire time we'd been here—echoed through the lower level. Suddenly the doors opened to a babble of voices, clatter-bang of wheels on metal thresholds, jangling keys, shuffling footsteps, and electronic whirs. A melange of sound and people poured into the too-silent History and Genealogy section.

A voice rattled rapidly in Spanish, giving instructions, assignments, and distribution of cleaning areas as the lights flicked on, flooding the area with illumination. Step, squeak, step, squeak. Raven's man strolled down the aisle on the other side of my partition, causing a major fright to a cleaning lady who'd had her back to him. She screamed, and I recognized the voice of Uncle calming her. I couldn't hear what he told her, but I'd liked to have heard how he explained the man's presence in a supposedly locked and empty room.

Suddenly Uncle's handsome features appeared as he knelt in front of my hiding place. "Did you catch the huge rat that terrorized this floor?" His dark eyes sparkled with amusement.

"Duchess is locked in her basket," I whispered.

"My wife, Luz, and her sister, Rosalie, traded floors with Vicki Valdez and her crew. When Vicki heard about the rat, she decided she couldn't come down here anymore." He laughed so heartily that I suspected he may have been the one who informed Vicki about the "rat."

"How are you going to get us out of here without Raven's men seeing us?" I asked, crawling around to get Morgan from her hiding place.

"Load you in this cart and take you up the elevator. Wheel you right out under his nose." The laughter faded from his eyes and his voice. "I don't know what you did, chiquita, but you certainly got the wrong people upset with you."

"I'd tell you, but the less you know, the better." I took his hand. "Thank you. This is twice you've saved me. Until you're better paid, bless you."

"I've slit the canvas. Crawl in, then hold the slits together. I'll load your bag on top so the camera will see what I've been doing down here."

In a wonderful baritone, Uncle began to sing a mariachi song at the top of his voice, and two other voices joined in from another part of the room. Morgan and I quickly crawled into the huge canvas cart and covered ourselves with the towels and linen already there. A heavy object was lowered onto my legs, probably my bag, and the cart moved forward. I held Morgan's hand, whispering that we'd soon be out of here and on our way to the hospital, but we couldn't talk again until we were out of the library.

"Scoot some of the things away from your face and make some breathing room, then don't move till they get us away from here," I instructed.

Each time the cart made a stop, something else was loaded on top of us. Items library patrons had left behind when the fire alarm sounded? Or books? With each addition, my claustrophobia index increased. How much longer could I quietly lie here, being smothered under all these linens and whatever else Uncle dropped into the cart?

I tried to go back to the beach—tried to conjure up that image of seagulls soaring freely above me and the crashing waves. It didn't work. I tried to imagine walking the golden hilltops above the estate, chasing after Bart when we were children. It didn't work. I put myself in Anastasia's Lear jet soaring high above the clouds, sharing an adventure with my handsome husband. That didn't work. Even Uncle's romantic renditions of my favorite Spanish songs didn't work. Beads of perspiration popped out on my forehead and upper lip. I fought to control the panic claustrophobia always caused. Struggled to get my mind on something else.

I mentally called up my to-do list and began checking off things I'd accomplished yesterday—or was it the day before?—before this horrible fiasco interrupted my life: Study scriptures. Check. Write in my journal. Check. Call my new companion to arrange visiting teaching this month. Check.

Deliver home-baked cookies to dear Sister Lassiter, who was abed with the flu. Check. I knew her kids wouldn't mind that they came out of the dairy case. They were warm when I delivered them fresh from my oven. Did I still get brownie points in heaven even if I hadn't mixed the batter myself?

What else? There was one other item besides my appointment with Dr. Simon. Something I needed to do for—when? For Sunday. Sunday! I needed to be in the nursery on Sunday! I'd planned to make copies of a handout for the children to color, buy snacks, and study the lesson.

I had to call someone to find a substitute who could prepare on short notice. Who could I call? The bishop's wife. Bless her heart, she'd know who could step in at the last minute and take over my class of ten delightful little souls, ages eighteen months to three years.

I loved being in the nursery. It was my first calling in the Church, and besides putting me within arm's reach of those perfect little people whom I could love as if they were my very own, it gave me an opportunity to teach simple, basic gospel concepts. It was the perfect place for me as a new convert—and as someone aching for children of my own with not much chance of ever having them.

The cart stopped. Uncle's beautiful baritone stopped. Morgan's grip tightened on my hand. What happened? I had so much stuff piled on and around me that I couldn't hear what was going on.

Suddenly the cart jerked forward and we moved fast, galloping over a metal bar, sliding across a marble floor, then bumping and bouncing over another metal object in the floor before coming to an abrupt stop. We were in an elevator. My stomach could tell. It tried to leave by way of my throat.

The elevator stopped just in time. I swallowed hard and willed myself not to be sick. Uncle started singing again as he pushed the cart over the metal grate and onto another marble floor.

Was it really going to be this easy? Could he just waltz right out of the library with us in this cart? Right past Raven and his men?

CHAPTER 22

We made so many twists and turns, stops and starts, and got on and off so many elevators that I was hopelessly lost, mentally unable to follow our path. Thus far, our journey had been unobstructed. My hopes rose with each minute that elapsed without detection.

Uncle's baritone stopped again, along with the cart. Voices above me argued about something, but the words were muffled by everything piled on top of us. A trickle of fear made its way through the miscellaneous items covering us, dripping insidiously on my nerves, eroding the newly acquired confidence built up in the long minutes since our safe departure from the fourth floor underground.

That voice. Saucony! I strained to understand the interchange between Uncle and Saucony. The cart jerked. I nearly lost hold of the slit through which we'd entered the canvas cart.

Saucony yelled at Uncle. His quiet reply was unintelligible. Saucony yelled again, and the cart jerked violently. Morgan grabbed my hand. I held on silently, willing her to feel comforted, willing her to be quiet, willing her not to move or cry out and betray us. Saucony wouldn't be in a mood to be merciful and gentle.

Whatever transpired above us, Uncle must have come out the winner. The cart moved again, and Saucony's frustrated voice receded in the background. We continued over a series of different kinds of flooring and seemingly endless miles of corridors, but Uncle's voice was strangely silent. Was he still pushing the cart?

I hoped my continual prayers for help weren't becoming bothersome in those celestial courts, since I needed help so very often to get me out of precarious situations such as this. Could I help it if I constantly found myself in way over my head? After all, I hadn't asked to be pursued by hired assassins.

Nor did I ask to be made responsible for this frightened little girl clinging to my hand. But I was, and it complicated things dreadfully. When we finally extricated ourselves from this phase of our current predicament, it was my plan to flee immediately to the hospital and deposit Morgan with her father. Hopefully I could take them both home, but if not, I'd simply call the Relief Society president of whatever ward they lived in, and let that benevolent society do their good deeds for a very needy nonmember family. Arnold *was* interested in my "special light"—which was nothing more than the light of the gospel—and he'd be able to see firsthand that gospel in action through those good sisters' ministrations to his little family.

I'd done what I'd felt was best at the time—taken care of Morgan, despite having someone breathing down my neck, trying to kill me, as I'd felt responsible for Arnold's accident. But it was time to get the child out of danger.

Now that I'd made all these wonderful plans, I hoped they met with heavenly approval. Too often, I'd discovered that what I thought was the very best way of doing something wasn't quite what the Lord had in mind. And it always meant I was in store for another heavenly learning experience—not heavenly in the sense that it was a divine and wonderful event. Instead, it usually meant another hard-learned lesson in being humble or obedient. My two major failings: I was far too headstrong and way too impulsive.

The cart slowed. A door opened, and night air crept through the upper part of the slit I gripped tenaciously. Who was pushing the cart? Until I knew who had control of our lives, I didn't dare move. My legs were numb, curled up tight in the bottom of the cart and stacked with who-knew-what. The hand that Morgan clutched had long since lost all feeling. My neck was kinked, my back had something sharp poking into it, and the hand that held the slit together would probably never open again. Still, I didn't move. Some terrible things are bearable because the alternative is even more unbearable.

The longer this unusual journey took, the more worried I became. If Uncle was pushing the cart, why hadn't he spoken to me? Why had he stopped singing? Or even humming? Were we being taken for the proverbial "ride"? Were we on our way to a rendezvous with someone Raven had assigned to get rid of us?

No. Raven would do the dirty work himself to make sure it got done. Since I couldn't see him pushing this cart as endlessly as this trip had become, I figured Raven wasn't the propulsion system. That didn't mean he didn't have something to do with whoever provided the horsepower, however.

All this conjecturing convinced me I could no longer lie passively in the bottom of the cart being pushed all over downtown Los Angeles. It was time to move. As the cart dropped off what had to be the sidewalk, I struggled to rid myself of the tons of linen and miscellaneous items piled on top of me.

"No, señora. Do not move. We're almost there," a voice whispered as the cart sped forward. Suddenly bright lights shone clearly through the canvas sides of the cart. We must be right in front of a line of traffic, crossing a street. Another jolt took us back onto the sidewalk on the other side.

A strange new voice. A very young voice. One of Uncle's men? Or Raven's? I didn't like not being in control. Granted, I had no other choice right now, but I didn't like it. It made me very nervous when I knew what was going on. When I didn't, it scared me spitless. And that was my condition at the moment.

Suddenly we came to a jarring stop. The lights were gone, and there were no traffic sounds. In fact, there were no sounds at all. Even the person pushing the cart was absolutely still. I waited. *Count to twenty. If nothing happens before that, I'm outta here.*

"It is clear, señora. We were not followed. You may come out." The young man had a Spanish accent.

Prying my stiff fingers from the slit Uncle had made in the side of the canvas, I crawled out onto a very dark sidewalk in a very dark alley.

"Can I come, too?" Morgan said, poking her head through the hole.

"Are you okay?" I asked, pulling the child to her feet. I felt her face and head. Somewhere in the bowels of the cart, she'd lost her beach hat. No big loss. I hoped we wouldn't need it, and I certainly wasn't going to paw through all that stuff again just to find it.

"That was a bumpy ride." She looked around. "I can't see anything. Where are we?"

I reached into the cart, felt the miscellaneous items until I found the overstuffed bag containing my purse and the jade lion, and rescued it before I examined our surroundings. "Good question. Where are we?" I asked our horsepower. "And who are you?"

The young man smiled. I know, because that was about all I could see of him in the dark. His white teeth.

"José Antonio Cesar Ramirez, at your service, señora. My father is the security guard who got you by the federal inspectors, then sent me to deliver you from them."

"And exactly where have you delivered us, José Antonio Cesar Ramirez?" Wherever it was, it must be the darkest spot in all of downtown Los Angeles. Where were all the lights in this famous "City of Lights"? Astronauts were supposed to be able to see its glow one hundred and seventy miles up in space. Seafarers thirty miles from shore were said to glimpse it beyond the curved horizon of the Pacific. I could hardly see my hand in front of my face, though I could now hear the beat of music nearby.

"Please, señora, call me Tony." His white teeth flashed again, wider this time. "We are just around the corner from Angel's Flight. I'm to put you on the cable car, and tell you to stay in the crowd at the Water Court until the music is over. Then you can go wherever you need to go as the people leave."

"What will you do?" I asked, loosening Morgan's death grip on my skirt and holding her little hand tightly in mine.

"I return this cart to the hotel where my sister is a chambermaid. She borrowed it to smuggle you from the library."

"Many thanks, Tony, for your help tonight. And please thank your father, and your mother, and your Aunt Rosalie, and your sister, and all the rest who helped us get away. We are much in your debt."

"I could tell they were very bad men, señora. They have bad vibes. You must hurry. And I must get Louisa's cart back to her. Go that way to the end of the alley. Angel's Flight will be right there."

José Antonio Cesar Ramirez loped off in the opposite direction, pushing the much lighter cart in front of him. Morgan and I headed for the light at the other end of the dark alley—in a hurry. This was no place for two females alone. We were running by the time we reached the sidewalk. And there it was, just as he'd promised.

Angel's Flight is supposedly the world's shortest railway—two cable cars that climb a thirty-three percent grade, three hundred and fifteen feet from Hill Street to the Water Court. As one car goes up, the other car comes down. The lower car was almost full. I dug in my pocket and found two quarters—the price of admission. No wonder Tony said to hurry. This was the last run of the night. Angel's Flight closed at 9 p.m.

We climbed aboard the pink cable car and took the last two polished wooden seats. The car was built on the same angle as the steep tracks so each set of seats was up one step higher than the previous one, all the way to the end of the car. The interiors of the cars couldn't have changed much since they were built in 1901, but the care they'd received was apparent as lights reflected in gleaming wood.

"Have you ever ridden these cable cars, Morgan?" I asked, settling my bag between my feet as the car inched its way up the steep incline.

"No. I can't wait to tell my dad." Her eyes were bright points of blue with little dark hollows under them in a pale, tired face. Her rumbling stomach reminded me we hadn't had dinner, and mine took up the chorus about the same time. I fully expected to hear Duchess join in, clamoring to be released from her basket.

The little station with twin cupolas at the top of the incline was the same dusty pink as the cable cars. It, too, retained its early 1900s flavor with gingerbread trim and painted accents. We paid our twenty-five cents and followed the sound of music behind the station/gift shop.

Morgan clapped in delight at the sight before us. Fountains danced and splashed around a marble half-moon stage. In the reflecting pools, huge floating hearts blossomed with bright red flowers, like lilies on lily pads. An eclectic menagerie of people clustered around white tables under square aqua umbrellas, or sat on concrete steps in the small amphitheater. The pavilion, lit with dozens of floodlights, was as bright as our alley had been dark.

The music, a lively combination of Latino, jazz, and reggae, echoed from the multi-storied buildings surrounding this lovely little oasis in the middle of downtown Los Angeles. A perfect spot to dine.

Morgan skipped through the aqua iron arbor that dripped with green vines and pink flowers, and we found a spot on the top step next to the curved railing—hidden from the entrances. I dug out our salads, cheesecake, and bottled water, and we feasted while the crowd clapped and cheered the young musicians, begging for more.

Much as I appreciated Uncle's help in getting away from Raven, I didn't feel secure in waiting one minute longer than necessary within the vicinity of my pursuer, so as soon as we'd finished eating, we deposited our refuse in the nearest receptacle and headed in the direction opposite Angel's Flight.

I flagged a cab, gave him a cross street a block from Arnold's hospital, and within twenty minutes, Morgan and I exited the car. She could hardly contain her excitement at getting to see her dad again. But instead of the relief I'd expected to feel right now, the hair on the back of my neck prickled, and butterflies performed wild acrobatics in my stomach. Something was not right.

CHAPTER 23

"Morgan, I think we'd better call your dad on the phone before we go into the hospital." I knew she wouldn't like the delay, but my danger antennae were sending warning signals I didn't dare ignore.

Before she could voice an objection, I spotted a hotel half a block away, in the opposite direction of the hospital, and pulled her quickly along with me. "What if he's already gone home? We don't want to waste time wandering around the hospital trying to find him if we can go straight home, do we?" I didn't give her time for an answer.

No derelicts hung about the entrance—a good sign—and though the once-posh hotel had apparently seen better days, it appeared to still be a respectable address. I discovered a bank of phones opposite the dark walnut registration desk and snuggled Morgan into one of the old-fashioned phone booths with me.

I expected to see "Reserved for Clark Kent" on the little brass sign above the seat, but on closer examination, it read "Five-Minute Limit on Phone Calls, Please." That reminded me I had another call to make. I dug out my coin purse, and, instructing Morgan to hold out her hands, dumped my nickels, dimes, and quarters into them.

"I need you to count to twenty as soon as I nod my head. Can you do that for me?" I asked. She nodded, and I dropped the first coin into the pay telephone. I dialed Bishop O'Hare's number—the only number in my ward I'd memorized. He and his wife had been our prime fellowshippers and contacts through our conversion and baptism.

"Hello."

I nodded at Morgan, and she began the countdown.

"Katie, I don't have time to talk," I blurted, purposely not identifying myself but knowing she'd recognize my voice. "Will you please call somebody to substitute for my nursery class on Sunday? Your husband sent me out of town, and I left so fast I forgot to tell anyone I'd be gone. They'll need a snack for ten little people, something to take home about the lesson, and they can do whichever one they want. Can you do that?"

"Of course. When will you be back?"

"Ask your husband. Thanks, love!" I hung up as Morgan said nineteen.

"Good girl. Now we're going to change phone booths, and I want you to do the same thing when I dial the hospital."

"Why are we using a different phone?" she asked as I shepherded her into the last booth in the line.

"So no one can connect the two phone calls I'm making. Hold out the money so I can put in the right change."

She held out her hands, and I dialed the number to Arnold's room. If he was still there, he should answer, since the little old man in the next bed didn't look in any condition to reach for the phone.

A male voice answered, but it wasn't Arnold. It was surprisingly strong and virile for someone in the hospital. I nodded at Morgan to begin counting.

"Mr. Trent, please." I tried to sound sophisticated and efficient.

"Who's calling?" the voice asked.

"Miss Sawyer. I'm his daughter's teacher. I need to speak with him about the open house at school. May I speak to him, please, if he's able to come to the phone?"

"He went home a couple of hours ago."

"Thank you." I hung up as Morgan said twenty.

Before she could ask the questions I could see coming, I opened the door, stepped out of the phone booth, held out my coin purse so she could dump the rest of the change back where it belonged, and pulled Duchess's basket out of my bag.

"Will you carry Duchess? I think she's tired of being buried in my bag. We need to hurry and find another taxi and go see if your dad is really home. The man who answered the phone said he was, but I'm not sure I believe him."

"Why not?" Morgan asked, clutching Duchess's basket tightly in her hands.

"He may have been visiting one of the other patients and didn't know your dad." That was a logical explanation. Unfortunately, I didn't believe it for a minute. Raven had Arnold's hospital phone tapped—I knew that from Sarah's phone call to the hospital from Carl's Jr. earlier today.

If Arnold really was home, he wouldn't be there alone. Even if he thought he was. Raven's men would have the place staked out, waiting for me. Now what? I had to get Morgan back with her father. I had to get out of Los Angeles. Tonight.

I stepped off the curb and hailed the cab that had intended to drive on past. The ancient cabbie stopped, leaned out his window and said, "I'm off duty, lady. On my way home."

"Which direction is home?"

"Naples." He sounded like he'd had a very long day.

"Want a fare to Long Beach? It's on your way." I flashed what I hoped was a beguiling smile. "And I give great tips."

He pointed at the cab waiting at the taxi stand on the corner. "Why don't you grab that one?"

"Frankly, I didn't like his looks. I'd feel safer with you."

"You saying I look harmless 'cause I'm so old?" The gray-haired man laughed. "Come on, then."

"No, you look like a kind sort of gentleman." We climbed into the cab and shut the door. "Two girls alone in Los Angeles after dark can't be too careful, you know." As soon as Morgan settled in, she took Duchess out of her basket to play with the kitten.

"I think I'm being fed a line, miss, but I'll take the bait, and count it as a double bonus if you're a good tipper." He smiled and winked into the rearview mirror. "Where to in Long Beach?"

"You know Woodrow Wilson High School? On Ximeno and 7th Streets? Then you can take 7th to Pacific Coast Highway and you're home."

I watched the cab at the curb as we passed, waiting to see if it followed us. It didn't. I checked out the back window frequently to see if we were being followed. Not that I could see. I relaxed back into the seat to find Morgan watching me, an inquisitive expression on her face. I was afraid she was thinking of all the stories she'd heard me tell.

How do you reconcile that kind of example with trying to teach a child honesty? Could she understand there were times when stretching the truth—or making up identities—was a means of covering your tracks so you couldn't be followed? Or that downright lying to the bad guys was the only way to stay alive? Could she understand we'd been living in the land of make-believe for the past two days?

But did that justify the lies she'd heard coming from my lips? Did that suspend the good habits of a lifetime? I'd always been uncomfortable with this aspect of an agent's life, but now I squirmed in my seat looking into those big blue eyes full of questions.

"I'll explain when we get home," I whispered. I opened Duchess's litter drawer, and the white ball of fur hopped in. "You'll have to clean it out when you get home. And you'll have to go to the store to get a big bag of kitty litter, some cat food, and a bigger litter box. Maybe even a bigger basket for her to sleep in."

"Oh, we won't need that. She can sleep with me," Morgan declared, opening the other drawer so Duchess could get at the diminishing supply of food. Fortunately, the kitten kept Morgan occupied the rest of the way to Long Beach, so I didn't have to answer any hard questions.

I paid the cabbie his forty-five dollar fare, plus tipped him an extra twenty. It was worth it to me to know he wasn't planted by Raven. He waved as he pulled away, leaving us standing under the streetlight across from the high school.

"Morgan, we're going to do some more play-acting. You get to be Buffy the Vampire Slayer again. We're going to go to your house, but we'll have to be very quiet so no one hears us come. I need to see if someone is watching your house."

"Why?"

As we headed down Ximeno to 6th Street, I tried to explain. "You've seen lots of bad men on TV—like Buffy has to fight. Some men like that are after me. I've had to make up a lot of stories—say a lot of things that weren't true so they couldn't find me. I don't want to lead them to you or your dad, so we're going to sneak down the alley and see if your dad is home, and if someone is there with him or is outside, waiting for me to bring you home."

"Will they hurt my daddy?"

"No. They won't hurt either of you." I prayed that was true—that they wouldn't harm Arnold or his daughter in any way. "They just want me. Do you have a special place, somewhere you like to go? A place where no one can find you?"

Morgan looked up at me. "You mean, like under the bush behind the shed?"

"Is that your secret hiding place?" I stopped under the streetlight at the corner of 6th Street.

Morgan nodded. "When I start missing Mommy, and I don't want Daddy to feel bad, I crawl under the bush and sit against the shed where no one can see me cry. I digged out a little hole, and Daddy's never found me there."

"Do you feel safe there? Even in the dark?" We crossed the street and headed away from the glare of the lights.

"It's a good hiding place," she said. "The bad men couldn't find me if I was there."

"Then that will be a perfect spot for me to leave you while I check around the neighborhood for bad guys. Two of us would make too much noise. Will you be afraid if I leave you alone for a few minutes?"

"I won't be alone. Duchess will be with me."

"Yes, she will. And you'll have to keep her in her basket, very quiet, so no one will hear her. How do you get to your secret place from here—without anyone seeing you?"

"We could go through Mrs. Foster's yard. She has a hole in her fence where I crawl through and play with her big ol' cat." Morgan pointed to the next house. "I take a shortcut down her driveway, behind the garage, and squeeze through the fence. Our yard's behind the fence, down a little hill."

"You can show me." I knelt down in front of the child, took her hand, and looked into her eyes. "But from here on we can't talk, and we have to walk quietly. Can you do that? Will you be afraid?"

She shook her head. "No. I'm not afraid here. I'm home."

"Then let's go," I whispered. Morgan took my hand and walked toward two strips of concrete leading to a garage at the back of the lot. Lights from Mrs. Foster's living room cast golden patches on the lush green grass, neatly trimmed, growing between and on either side of the concrete strip driveway.

Morgan led me without hesitation to the garage, then stepped around the side and headed into the darkness of the backyard. She stepped confidently from one flagstone to another and paused without speaking when I stubbed my sandal against one and stumbled briefly. When I regained my balance, she gripped my hand tighter and continued, slowing her pace slightly. The flagstones must be placed perfectly for her little legs, or she knew them so well she didn't have to feel her way as I was having to do.

My eyes, more accustomed to the dark now, recognized the fence with the lower half of a board missing. Faint lights from Tremont Street glowed softly beyond the hole. Morgan turned, silently handed me Duchess's basket, and crawled easily through the hole. She held out her hand, and I gave her the basket.

This would be a tight squeeze for me. I handed Morgan my bag, hiked my long denim skirt up, ducked my head, and stuck one leg through the hole. Half of me was on one side, the other half on the other. And the ground fell away on the side where Morgan stood. The little hill she talked about that ran down to her house wasn't so little.

Finally I stood on the other side, looking down into Arnold and Morgan's very dark backyard. Several trees hid most of the house from our view, but there were lights inside.

Morgan took my hand again and led me along a little cement ledge that couldn't have been more than twelve inches wide, probably the footing for the board fence. The hillside seemed covered with dense, long grass, possibly the ornamental kind that didn't have to be mowed.

Directly below, I could see the outline of the garage between Mrs. Pickins's house and Arnold's. Morgan led me quietly along the entire length of the fence to the end of their property and turned to follow the fence downhill. I envisioned myself slipping on that long grass and tumbling all the way to the bottom, but the concrete footing continued down the hill—not on a slant, but in about six-foot lengths, then a drop of two feet, like giant steps all the way to the bottom.

Just before we reached the bottom, Morgan stopped, turned, and stood still. I leaned down to see her face in the faint light cast from the bedroom windows. She pointed to a small building I hadn't seen in the darkness. I nodded, and the plucky child faded without a sound into the silent shadows.

I left my bag in the grass just off the cement steps where Morgan had disappeared, as much as a marker for where I could find her as a place where I could get my bearings when I came back this way in the dark.

I'd taken half a dozen steps in the direction of the house when a hand clamped over my mouth and a voice whispered close to my ear, "Don't move, girlie."

CHAPTER 24

My heart pounded violently. I froze, stunned into inaction. To have come so far . . . to be so close to returning Morgan without detection . . . only to be caught on this last leg of the journey. I knew they'd be here, but I thought I could sneak quietly past Raven's men.

"Don't be afraid, girlie. It's just ugly ol' Joe. You lookin' for that man up under the tree? I'm gonna let go. I don't think you wanna make a sound, do ya?"

Paralyzed by shock and fear, I stood motionless as he removed his hand. I finally recognized the voice of the old man Arnold fed at the back door after Morgan was asleep because he was so ugly he didn't want to frighten the child. If I'd been this close the first time we met, I'd have probably recognized the smell, too. Bad breath, probably no oral hygiene, and the odor of an unwashed body that must share its bed with a mangy old dog.

He spoke quietly against my ear. "When Arnold got out of the cab all banged up, that man followed, stayed in the shadows. Never went to the door. I figured he's up to no good. When you and Morgan sneaked through the back fence, I guessed he was waitin' for ya."

I leaned close to his ear. "Are you sure there's only one?"

He put his mouth to my ear again. "Sure. You needin' to get Morgan inside?"

"Yes," I whispered.

"Back door's unlocked. I'll get that guy's attention. You get her in."

Then Joe was gone, and I stood alone under a tree at the side of the house. Without waiting to see what Joe was up to, I headed for the shed, faintly outlined against the streetlights down the block.

"Morgan?" I whispered, not sure how close I was to her.

Suddenly she materialized out of the shadow and stood next to me with no sound other than the crunch of grass under her feet. I took her hand and headed for the back door. Out front, I could hear Joe singing an old sailor ditty, sounding more than a little tipsy.

The back door was not only unlocked, it was wide open. As I pulled on the screen door, it squeaked loudly. Morgan ran through the darkened kitchen and met Arnold as he rolled from his bedroom in his wheelchair. She dropped Duchess's basket and leaped into his lap, smothering him with hugs and kisses. I signaled silence and their tearful, joyous reunion occurred without a sound.

"I've got to go," I mouthed. "Will you be okay?" His broken arm was still in a cast, and with his shirt off, I could see just how banged up he really was. Various bandages, as well as unbandaged scrapes and scratches, covered his shoulders, and his midriff was swathed in tape to keep his broken ribs from moving.

He nodded and held out his hand. I took it, squeezed it, and bent to kiss Morgan's tear-stained cheek.

"You have a very intelligent, very brave daughter," I whispered. "I'm so sorry you had to be involved in my mess."

Arnold grinned. "You warned me." Then the smile vanished. "We'll handle it here," he said quietly. "I've got a friend who's a local cop. He's on his way over."

"Old Joe's a great ally, too. You know your line is tapped and your house is being watched?"

He nodded. "Don't worry. Just be safe. Let me know how you survive this."

I turned to Morgan. "Take good care of Duchess. Tell your dad all about our adventures, and take him to the church on Ximeno with the steeple that looks like a lighthouse. You were a real sport. Buffy would be proud of you."

Before I became maudlin, I hurried out the back door, stopping long enough for my eyes to adjust to the dark. I peered around the corner of the house and saw Joe, still singing to keep attention diverted to him, sitting on the sidewalk near the tree under which a man tried to blend in with the shadows.

Quickly crossing the lawn, I retrieved my abandoned bag,

retraced our steps up the concrete fence footing, back through the hole in Mrs. Foster's fence, and hurried out to the street. My immediate problem would be finding a taxi to the airport. Since cabs didn't cruise residential neighborhoods, my nearest access to one would probably be a phone in the little shopping center several blocks away.

Focusing my little remaining energy into the hike, I reformulated one of the plans I'd devised during those cramped hours under the computer in the library. Though I'd been praying for guidance as I made each of those plans, I hadn't felt particularly inspired by any of them. I still didn't. Did that mean it didn't matter which one I used? Or did it mean this was one of those instances when I was supposed to exercise my agency and act on my own, without continual guidance from above? I much preferred the guidance.

I did luck out. Or my guardian angels were still on duty at this late hour. A taxi dropped an old woman at a house a couple of blocks from Mrs. Foster's, and I snagged him before he drove away.

Twenty minutes later, I jumped out at Los Angeles International Airport. I still hadn't felt any heavenly guidance as to what I should do at this point. Apparently, I needed to handle this on my own. A really scary thought.

I chose Delta, knowing they have a lot of late flights to faraway destinations. Right now, I needed to be as far away from Los Angeles as I could get. On my way to the rest room, I glanced at the destination board. Three flights were possible if I could get on standby, or if they had empty seats: one to Memphis, one to Atlanta, and one to Chicago.

In the rest room I changed clothes again, opting for the reversible dress on the print side, removed the blonde wig that was driving me crazy, and brushed my hair till my scalp tingled. I stuck my head under the faucet, then under the blow-dryer, and dug into my bottomless bag for one of the vials of hair dye I'd purchased from the beauty shop when I'd had my hair restyled.

The green was the first I found, but I decided that would make my eyes stand out too much, so I opted for the blue. Brushing color onto the bleached ends of my hair, I wondered how Bart would feel to see the long black tresses he loved to run his fingers through replaced by a short cap of lightened curls with blue tips.

I tied the dress's fabric tie belt around my head gypsy-fashion, and put on the long, dangling earrings. Definitely a different look than I'd had before during this incredible nightmare. The final touch was makeup—not as wild as the Cleopatra look from Merle Norman, but definitely a change from my normal natural look. The only thing I couldn't change was the color of my eyes—the greatest tipoff to my identity—and I couldn't do anything about it. One of the things Bart loved most about my appearance could cause my demise, I thought ruefully.

Next stop: a ticket on the first flight out of Los Angeles. That would be Chicago, but it was booked solid and there were five standbys waiting already. I tried Memphis next. Same story. I crossed my fingers and said a prayer as I approached the desk where they had just posted the midnight flight to Atlanta. There was a seat available. One seat.

I booked it, not even blinking as she said eight hundred dollars plus tax and charges. Anastasia's expense account covered these fake credit cards and IDs I carried. And whatever it cost, it was worth it to get out of town. Out of the long grasp of Raven's tentacles.

One hour to flight time. One hour to midnight. I found a seat in a quiet, dimly lit corner of the boarding area where I couldn't easily be seen, and settled down to wait. I hated waiting. Almost as much as I hated running for my life.

A young woman hurried through the terminal, glanced around, and seeing my gloomy corner, made straight for it, looking over her shoulder a couple of times before crouching next to the window behind a couple of seats.

She glared at me as if to drive me away, then hunkered even lower behind a ragged backpack, trying, it seemed, to disappear into the shadows. She was younger than I'd first thought—much younger. Maybe thirteen, maybe not even that. Her makeup, her walk, her continual scowl lent years to what I'd perceived to be her actual age.

Her face would have been pretty, but her expression, an "I hate the world" look, spoiled it. Her spiked hair had dark roots, then an inch or two bleached nearly white-blonde, ending in bright green tips. Gold rings glinted in her nose and eyebrows, and rimmed her ears from top to bottom.

The denim miniskirt may have fit her once, but it seemed several sizes too big now, held up by two bony hips. As my Grandmother Karilledes would say, she didn't have an ounce of meat on her anywhere. The heather-striped knit tube-top was beginning to unravel at the bottom. Black nail polish on her toes peeked out from scuffed and worn sandals with huge thick soles, and matched the fingernails she nibbled between lipstick-blackened lips.

When she wasn't aware of anyone watching, her dark eyes lost their defiance, revealing the fear she hid with false bravado. Suddenly her eyes widened with panic. She glanced around, ready to jump and run, but there was no place to go. We were in a corner with one way out—straight ahead.

Looking to see what frightened her, I met the gaze of a man who sent shudders of revulsion through me. Greasy, stringy hair fell disheveled to his shoulders and covered one eye. His gray suit was expensive, though ill-fitting and none too clean. The once-white shirt looked wrinkled and gray, and was minus the tie you'd expect to see with such an ensemble. The thought flitted through my mind that he'd probably robbed some poor guy and stolen his clothes.

If that girl was running from this man, she doubtless had good reason. He took a step forward as if to search our quiet corner. In approximately four steps, he'd pass the aisle where two lines of chairs prevented him from seeing the girl. At that point, he'd only have to turn his head and she'd be in plain sight.

I stood, picked up my bag, and headed directly toward him.

Stop. What are you doing? You can't get involved. I ignored the little voice, knowing it was right, knowing I had no business stepping in here. But the fear—the sheer terror on that girl's face—propelled me forward. I held my elbow at an awkward angle, my bag dangling away from me, effectively blocking the man's entrance to the corner.

"Excuse me." I sidestepped—right into his path. He stepped the other way, and I again stepped into his path. "Oh, Ah'm sorry," I laughed, affecting a Southern accent and moving once again the same direction he did. "Shall we dance?"

The man glared at me, took me by the shoulders, and tried to physically move me out of his way.

"Y'all remove your hands immediately or Ah'll scream bloody

murder and have security on you before you can count to three," I said quietly. His dark eyes narrowed, assessing me, appraising my intent.

I started to count. "One. Two." I meant it. He knew it. Dropping his hands, he glanced once more into the shadows of our corner, and, turning on his heel, stalked off.

Legs shaking, I dropped into the nearest chair and took a deep breath, watching while he made a sweep of every boarding area, every waiting room in my line of sight, then continued on down the terminal. He never looked back.

From behind me, behind the seats, the soft sounds of sobbing broke my heart. I hurried to the window, sat on the floor beside her, and took the girl in my arms. Her quivering body resisted at first, then she melted against me and cried, great heaving, silent sobs that shook her frail body. Finally, the tears abated. I offered a tissue and she wiped her makeup-streaked cheeks, blew her nose, and looked up at me.

"Why was that man looking for you?" I asked gently.

She glanced around, eyes wide and wary as a deer ready to leap away.

"If you run, he'll probably be waiting for you. Why is he looking for you?" I repeated, offering another tissue for the tears that welled in her red-rimmed eyes.

"He wants to take me, ya' know, back to his pad. Wants me to hustle for him," she mumbled, sliding away from me. "That's not my bag, see?"

"What are you doing at the airport? Are you flying somewhere? Do you have a ticket?"

She raised her head, stuck out her chin, and looked me in the eye, defiance back with a capital "D." "Which dwarf are you? Query?"

I laughed, as much at the improbable question as the bravado that suddenly resurfaced in her eyes and voice.

"Nope. Just call me Dopey, for getting involved with you in the first place." I stood. "Have a nice life."

I walked out of the area, and out of her life. I didn't need extra baggage. I had three things to concentrate on, and helping smart-mouthed runaways wasn't one of them. The things I needed to be thinking about right now—the only things—were discovering the mystery of the jade lion, keeping it out of the hands of Raven, and staying alive. Nothing—and no one—must interfere with those goals, no matter how soft-hearted and soft-headed I happened to be.

Not knowing when I'd get to eat next, given the uncertainty of airline meals, I headed for the restaurants to fortify myself for the five-hour flight to Atlanta. Halfway down the concourse, I saw the malevolent-looking man in the ill-fitting gray suit coming toward me. That was enough to make my heart stop.

But right behind him appeared the face I feared most in the world—next to Raven. Saucony!

CHAPTER 25

Without hesitation, I veered into the women's rest room. One glance in the full-length mirror at the stranger with blue-tipped hair, pale face, and long, black and white print dress bolstered my confidence enough to peer out at the backs of the two men heading for the boarding area I'd just abandoned.

Neither had given me a second look. Not even the man on whom I'd threatened to call security. My heart did a flip. He headed toward the boarding area he hadn't had a chance to search thoroughly because of me. Back to find the frightened girl huddled behind the seats.

I raced after them.

Don't do this. She's not worth exposing yourself for. Stay out of it. You can't solve the world's problems. Leave it to social workers who get paid for that.

My little voice was right. I couldn't solve the world's problems, and I didn't need Saucony to find me, nor did I need the burden of this thankless waif. But I couldn't let her face that sinister-looking man alone.

A planeload of passengers disembarked right in front of us, slowing the progress of the two men, each searching for one particular face in the sea of faces flowing by. They were examining, inspecting each face as it passed. I had an immediate destination and sidled on by, hidden by the stream of tired humanity flowing from the plane.

The girl, still huddled behind the seats in the boarding area, looked up, her eyes filled with fear until she saw me. Then the sneer returned.

"He's coming back," I said, ignoring the look. "Crawl under the seats and curl up as small as you can get. I'll try to stand so he can't see you."

She flung her backpack toward the seats and rolled across the floor behind it, disappearing from view. I hurried to intercept Gray Suit. He was still checking out people, making his way more slowly toward this area. Pivoting, I searched for a glimpse of the girl. None.

I walked straight back, looking particularly at the place I knew her to be. She was well hidden. I wandered between the seats, as he might do, hoping that to anyone watching me, I'd appear to be simply strolling around with no apparent goal. Still no sign of her. Then I approached the seat where I'd been sitting when he came the first time. At that point, she was visible.

I increased my pacing as he advanced, watching for any other position from which she could be seen. Then I planted myself at the spot that would best keep her hidden, dropped my bag in front of the chair to conceal her further, and walked back and forth in a tiny circle, staking my claim to this section of carpet.

As the man approached, my heart beat faster. I hated confrontations. Would there be another?

With the sudden prickling of my skin, I remembered Saucony. How could I forget my own threat? I glanced down the concourse, looked for his head towering above the group of Orientals disembarking from another plane. I couldn't find him. A major mistake to not keep him in view at all times.

I panicked. With an enemy on two fronts, you must *always* know the location of each. Gray Suit arrived at the point where we'd met the first time. Suddenly Saucony loomed on the right, headed my way.

Double jeopardy!

That's what you get for meddling in other people's business.

I shut out the irritating little voice that was usually right. Bending to my bag, I pulled out my ticket and my sunglasses, pretending to need the glasses to read the ticket. Gray Suit advanced, glared at me, and continued to the back of the dimly lit area, searching in all the corners—all but the one I inhabited.

Saucony entered the area, intent on me, of course, since I was the only female in view. Stupid mistake. I should be out where I could run if I needed to, instead of being trapped with no other recourse. I glanced at the clock. Thirty minutes to midnight. At least ten to boarding time.

Think, lady. Use those leetle gray cells, as Hercule Poirot would say. It's your only way out.

Gray Suit returned, his search finished, and paused as he saw Saucony block his exit. He turned toward me as if to move aside and let the big fellow enter while he searched the one remaining location in which he hadn't yet been.

"Don't y'all come any closer!" I said, digging my umbrella out of my bag and brandishing it at him. "Don't y'all come one step close, or Ah'll scream."

Saucony stood absolutely still, watching the scene. I pointed at him. "That man won't let you abuse a poor country girl in this big, awful city, will you, mister?"

Gray Suit looked at Saucony, who had at least six inches and fifty pounds on him, and retreated a couple of steps.

"Not good enough, mister," I pouted. "Y'all got to leave me right alone. Go away, clear away, and leave me be." I waved to Saucony. "Tell him he can't terrorize poor defenseless women and get away with it."

Wordlessly, Saucony stepped aside and motioned for the smaller man to leave. Gray Suit did so immediately, tossing a hateful glance over his shoulder as he hurried by the big, grinning man.

"Thank you, sir. You're a real gentleman. Could Ah ask one more favor? Would y'all follow him for a bit and make sure he doesn't come back? My plane leaves in about an hour, and I don't dare leave here 'cause Ah'm on standby and they might call my name."

"Glad to help." Saucony followed the furious little man down the concourse. I headed for the rest room and lost my cookies again.

Trembling, I returned to the boarding area, saw no sign of either Saucony or Gray Suit, and bent to the girl still quivering under the seat.

"You must feel like a pretzel. I think it's okay to unwind now."

"Is he really gone?" she whispered without moving from her contorted position.

"Temporarily. But you'd better get out of here. Do you have someplace to go?"

She rolled from under the chair and snatched her backpack. "Who made you, like, my guardian angel?" I'm sure it was intended as a putdown—supposed to come out with scorn. Instead, her voice caught, and the fear inside her poured out in a squeaky little voice.

"Let's cut to the chase, chick." I stood. "I don't need to be helping you. I've got big problems of my own, and I nearly got trapped back here because I was watching out for you instead of me. Now, do you have a place to go?"

She blinked. Her mouth opened, then shut again.

"One more time, then I'm gone. Do you have a place to go? Were you on your way somewhere?" I didn't even try to sound patient or comforting or nice. I checked down the concourse for Saucony. I couldn't afford to be sidetracked again. Once was a mistake. Twice was unforgivable, because I'd probably be caught. Translation: dead.

"Like, I don't need your help, ya know." She hugged her backpack to her and tossed her head, sending shock waves through the green, gold, and black spikes on her head.

"Fine. The last thing I need is a problem with an attitude. I'm outta here." I grabbed my bag and headed for the line forming at the check-in desk for the midnight flight to Atlanta. Instead of turning my back on her and walking out of her life, as I should have done, I had to look one more time when I checked for Saucony.

Curled up in a ball, she rocked back and forth hugging her legs, tears running down her face, in plain view of all the passengers waiting to board the plane. In plain view of anyone approaching from the concourse to this boarding gate.

I turned my back, but my heart broke at the sight.

She doesn't want your help. You've got to get on that plane. You can't afford to miss it. Forget about her.

Oh, shut up, I told the irritating voice. It was right, of course. But I didn't have to like it. And I didn't have to listen. I stepped out of line, checked down the concourse one more time for Saucony or Gray Suit, and went back to the pathetic little girl with black streaks of mascara running to meet her black lipstick.

"What's your name?" I asked, sitting on the floor next to her and handing her a tissue.

"Rainbow." She wiped at her eyes, smearing the mascara even more.

I pulled out another tissue and worked at clearing the smudges from her face. "Where are you from, Rainbow?"

"Charleston." Gone was the defiance, the contempt, the bravado. A scared, vulnerable, lonely little girl remained, the barricades broken.

"South Carolina?"

She nodded.

"You're a long way from home."

She nodded again.

"Are you going home?" I glanced at the diminishing line at the ticket counter and the growing line at the gate. The tears started again.

"Rainbow, I don't have a lot of time. That's my flight everyone's lining up for. We'll leave sometime in the next fifteen minutes. If I can help, you've got to tell me how."

Rainbow looked at me for a long minute with tear-filled hazel eyes. "My friend was going to, like, turn a couple of quick tricks, ya know, and bring me enough money to get home. She said she'd be here by eleven. Like, if I don't get on this flight, I know he'll catch me. Hope must have told him where to find me, ya know. He must have beat it out of her—like, she'd never have told him otherwise."

"Do your parents know where you are? What you've been doing?" They called my flight, and the line of passengers began boarding the airplane.

She nodded. "They said to come home."

I stood, looked down the concourse, and saw Saucony emerge from Starbuck's with a cup of coffee in his hand, watching someone. I moved out into the boarding area where I could see the entire length of the concourse. Gray Suit was headed my way, checking boarding areas again as he came.

"Do you have ID, Rainbow? If there's a seat on this flight and I buy you a ticket, do you have a valid ID to show?"

She looked up, her eyes wide and her black mouth forming an O.

"Rainbow, your guy is right down the concourse. The man who's after me is there, too. I don't have time to waste. Talk to me."

The girl shook off her surprise and pulled an ID card from her backpack. The birth date said she was eighteen. I looked at her. She squirmed.

"Who made this for you? Never mind. Will they accept this?"

She nodded. Articulate child.

"Come on. Let's see if we can get you on standby." I ran to the ticket desk grasping her ID card and her hand, then shoved her in front of me, blocking Gray Suit's view of her if he looked this way.

"Are there any seats left on this flight?" I glanced at the name on the ID card. Rainbow Jones. Original, anyway. "Rainbow needs to get home as soon as possible."

The computer keys rattled. "Sorry. No more seats available."

"How about standby?" I insisted. "Can you put her on the standby list?"

"Full flight, and three standbys."

I leaned over the counter. "I know this isn't kosher, but can you see that man in the wrinkled gray suit and the long, stringy hair down there? He's forcing her into prostitution. If we can get on this flight, I'll take her to her parents in Charleston. Is there any way you can help me do that by getting her on this airplane?"

The airline rep looked down the concourse, saw the man coming this way, made a quick decision, and picked up her microphone. "Will passengers Child, Pierce, and Carrier please approach the desk at gate 52B? Last call for passengers Child, Pierce, and Carrier." Then she hit the computer again, made up a ticket, took my proffered credit card, and told us to board the plane. She'd send the rest of the paperwork, including my credit card, with the steward.

"Thank you!" I told the grinning rep. "You've garnered blessings in heaven for this." I shoved Rainbow behind a hefty lady, hiding her from sight, and told her to get on the plane, while I waited to make sure Gray Suit hadn't seen her—and Saucony hadn't seen me. Then I made a beeline for the jet bridge. Only two passengers straggled on behind me.

I caught sight of Rainbow climbing over a mother with a young child to take a window seat halfway back. My seat was near the front. As I stuffed my bag under the seat in front of me and fastened my seat belt, I thought it would have been nice to have adjoining seats—to be able to get to know her. I glanced at her ID card, still clutched in my hand, and wondered how she'd come from one coast to another. Alone? A runaway? Or had she come to stay with relatives?

As the flight attendant intoned the safety precautions, pointing out exits and showing how to use the oxygen masks if the cabin was de-pressurized, it suddenly dawned on me what I'd done. I'd taken responsibility for another life, when I was fleeing for my own.

Then a more frightening thought hit, sending ice coursing through my veins. Why had Saucony appeared at the airport right after I arrived? How had he known I was there?

CHAPTER 26

No one else boarded. No unexpected personnel or passengers. A good sign. The plane wasn't held up on the end of the runway as I'd been afraid it might be. It was a normal takeoff in every way. I held my breath until we were airborne. When I realized I'd actually left Los Angeles—and Raven and Saucony—far below, I breathed a sigh of relief.

But how had they found me? I'd expected the "eye in the sky" to keep track of me, but could it have tracked me at night? With all my costume changes? With our trek from the library hidden inside the laundry cart?

It couldn't have been coincidence that Saucony showed up at the airport—at the one terminal I'd chosen out of the dozens available—and so soon after I arrived. Even in my naivete, I couldn't stretch coincidence that far. It had to be something I carried that betrayed my whereabouts. That something could only be the jade lion.

When the captain turned off the seat belt sign, I pulled my purse from the oversized Biltmore Hotel bag, my only luggage on this flight for my life, and hurried to the rest room. I unpackaged the gleaming green lion, examining each layer of wrapping carefully, inspecting every square inch of the outer brown wrapper, then the two layers of Mylar. I opened the box on both ends and even checked the inside of the box. Empty. Clean.

I peeled off the brown plastic wrapping tape that had secured the ends of the box, thinking I might have missed something when I'd slit the tape with my fingernail file. Nothing suspicious there.

The bubble wrap surrounding the black velvet pouch seemed innocent enough. I even held it against the light to see if something had been inserted into one of the bubbles. Nothing. Dumping the lion out of the soft velvet pouch, I turned it inside out, inspecting the fabric between the seams. As far as I could tell, there was simply nothing suspicious at all.

That left Mr. Lion. But I'd already checked him.

I held him up to the light, turning him, twisting him, enjoying the feel of the polished stone in my hand, admiring the depth of color, the striking contrast of jade and almost translucent white on his mane and back.

"You're an attractive fellow," I told him. "Now if you'd just reveal the secret of your popularity. Why did Bart send you to me? Why does Raven want you so badly? What makes you so valuable?"

I ran my hands over him again, relishing the smooth, marble-like coolness of the stone, the ripples that made up his mane, the two dots that formed his eyes. As my fingernail traced the tiny carvings around his eyes, it snagged on something. Some tiny little thing that didn't seem to belong there—that didn't seem part of the carved eye. Something so small I couldn't see it in the dimly lit cubicle.

Suddenly someone knocked on the door.

"One minute," I called. Had I been in here that long? Or was someone desperately in need of the facilities and couldn't afford to wait patiently?

Tucking the jade lion back in his wrappings, I exited the Lilliputian lavatory and headed back to my seat, leaving the less-than-commodious quarters to the mother and child who were Rainbow's seatmates. Anxious to talk with the girl alone for a few minutes, I hurried down the aisle and found her fast asleep, snuggled under the too-thin navy blanket handed out by flight attendants, her spiked hair wildly colorful against the pure white of the tiny pillow. Our discussion would have to wait.

I sank wearily into my own seat. What had I gotten myself into this time? Why couldn't I have just left the girl to her own devices, to work out her own problems? Why did I continually stick my nose in other people's affairs? Constantly involve myself in things that were none of my business?

You're a softhearted sap. No one in their right mind, with their own life at stake, would take on the responsibility of an ungrateful wretch who'll complicate things more than you can imagine.

I reached for the newspaper tucked in the back of the seat next to me. The sleeping owner wouldn't mind, I was sure, and I needed to tune out the know-it-all voice belonging to my alter-ego.

I read the headline and shivered, unable to control my shaking hands as I read the article.

Ebola Twin Spreads Across Africa. Suddenly I remembered the headlines I'd seen—and ignored—the last two days! Thousands dying as the infection spread, the World Health Organization fearful. I quickly looked through the article.

They'd discovered a new strain of Ebola—"the untreatable, incurable virus so lethal that nine out of ten victims die, so agonizing as to defy description, and so terrifying that it has entered popular lore as a 'doomsday disease,'" the article reported. Like its twin, discovered in 1976 in Zaire, the new virus had surfaced with deadly results in that same country, now called the Democratic Republic of Congo. And it was rampaging through the capital city of Kinshasa.

Bart was in Kinshasa! Bart and Oz and Mai Li!

The temperature in the airplane dropped by at least twenty degrees. Cold chills ran down my arms. I couldn't stop shaking.

The leading scientist working on the epidemic had announced a breakthrough—a possible antidote to prevent the victim from bleeding to death within a few days of contracting the deadly disease. The day after the announcement, his laboratory had been bombed. The head of the scientific team died in the explosion, several of his assistants were severely wounded, and the lab had been completely destroyed.

I scanned the article for some reference to the formula being stolen. That was one of the headlines I'd read sometime in the last two days, wasn't it? Did it have to do with this article? Or had I been dreaming?

No. A separate article in a box in the middle of the page alongside the lead article covered that story. Dr. Olaf Svenson from the World Health Organization, a United Nations agency based in Geneva, Switzerland, had been working on the Ebola project since the virus was first discovered in the Ebola River region of northern Zaire and the southern region of Sudan in 1976.

The same evening the news of the promising formula broke on Kinshasa television, Dr. Svenson's home and his laboratory were broken into and his computers and files stolen. The next day, the laboratory and his home were bombed.

The group of terrorists suspected of bombing other capital city hospitals and clinics last month were suspected in this case. In an announcement earlier in the year, the terrorists had decried foreign intervention in any aspect of the former government of Zaire, and vowed to destroy the new government of the Democratic Republic of Congo, beginning with the desperately needed health care facilities that government officials were establishing.

According to quotes from a *Los Angeles Times* story, these terrorists included henchmen of former President Mobuto Sese Seko, who had terrorized and looted the impoverished country since taking power in 1965. Mobuto had billions of dollars in overseas bank accounts from diamond smuggling and graft, while a country with enough arable land and hydroelectric potential to feed and power the entire continent had been reduced to one of the world's poorest nations.

When Mobuto was deposed, health care in that African nation was virtually nonexistent. AIDS was epidemic, but even simple infectious and parasitic diseases caused half of all the deaths in Zaire, with four out of five of the dead being children under age five.

The new government of the Democratic Republic of Congo had been trying to change that. In fact, that was one of the reasons Bart, Oz, and Mai Li had been sent to Kinshasa. The group, Al Qaida, was one of twenty-eight new terrorist organizations that targeted United States citizens—the very terrorists Bart was to infiltrate.

Usama bin Laden, a tall, thin Saudi exile, led the Islamic extremist group, and was now on the FBI's Ten Most Wanted list, a five-million-dollar price tag on his head. Responsible for masterminding the 1998 bombings of American embassies in Nairobi, Kenya, and Dar es Salaam, Tanzania, in which two hundred people were killed and thousands injured, bin Laden with his full dark beard and mustache was now a familiar face to police agencies everywhere. But he had yet to be apprehended.

I tucked the paper back in the seat pocket, my mind racing through the facts I'd just read, retrieving information I'd studied with Bart when Anastasia received the assignment to help the new government of the DRC.

Suddenly I sat upright in my seat. Pieces of the puzzle fell into place so quickly it left me breathless. Some were still question marks, but—what if Bart had gotten in place inside the terrorist group before the bombing of the laboratory? What if he'd been able to spirit the formula out of the hands of whoever stole it? What if he'd encoded it on a minuscule microdot? What if he'd applied that microdot to the eye of the jade lion? What if he'd had that package hand-delivered to me?

That would explain an assassin of Raven's caliber being assigned to eliminate someone as inconsequential and unimportant as me. That would explain his preoccupation with "it," which he'd been assigned to get, and which I assumed must be the jade lion.

I leaned back in my seat. If they were after me, and were assuming I had the lion and the microdot, I had to assume that Bart's cover had been broken and they knew who he was—or they'd never have connected me with the lion.

If they knew who he was . . .

The thought was too horrible to finish. I forced it from my mind. Being paralyzed with fear or grief wouldn't get me out of my predicament. If I actually held the precious formula that would prevent millions of deaths, I darned well better make sure I got it into the right hands.

I went back over my list of what-ifs. Every single one seemed too probable. Every one fell into place too easily to dismiss.

I glanced at my watch. Four more nightmarish hours of this flight to endure. We'd land at eight o'clock in the morning Atlanta time. I could call Bishop O'Hare at six o'clock Pacific time, nine o'clock Eastern time. At 9:15 to be exact.

Five hours to go before I could make that phone call. Five mind-numbing hours of not knowing what had happened to my husband. Five hours before I'd get some answers to all these what-if questions. And the one I had to address immediately was the one that posed the most problems if I came up with the wrong answer.

Did Raven know I was on *this* plane?

I wiped my clammy hands on the blanket. If Raven could track me—and since Saucony had shown up at the airport so quickly, there was no doubt in my mind that he could—what kind of reception would Raven have waiting for me at Hartfield Airport when this plane touched down in Atlanta four hours from now?

CHAPTER 27

Tucking my own too-thin airline issue navy blanket around my shoulders, I leaned my seat back as far as it would go and closed my eyes.

Father, are You there? I desperately need a little heavenly help here. It's all well and good to leave me to my own devices when the issue isn't my life, but if You please, I could use a little less freedom of decision and a little more guidance right now. It may not seem important in the eternal scheme of things . . .

I opened my eyes. Of course it mattered in the eternal scheme of things. What if I made a totally wrong decision that allowed me to fall into Raven's hands? That would mean my demise. The end of my marriage. We still had four months to go before we could be sealed in the temple. Of course, Bart could do that work vicariously, but is that how we were supposed to end? Was my prescribed time on earth to be so very short?

Closing my eyes, I resumed my dialogue with Deity. *Father, just in case I am supposed to live longer than tonight or tomorrow, could I please have some direction? What am I supposed to do with Rainbow? How can I avoid Raven until I talk to Bishop O'Hare? What should I do with this hunk of jade that may contain the physical salvation of millions of Thy children?*

The proper procedure was to ponder the question, make a decision, then take it to the Lord for confirmation. My mind, muddled with so many questions, simply could not light on any one of them long enough to ponder anything. I couldn't concentrate. Images of Raven, of Saucony, of Rainbow's gray-suited pursuer formed together into one frightening phantom, relentlessly stalking the two of us. It mattered not where we ran, how far, or how fast, the specter appeared at every turn. There was no escape from his relentless pursuit.

Suddenly the flight attendant touched my shoulder, requesting that I put my seat in the proper upright position. I glanced at my watch, then out the window. We were descending into Hartfield Airport in Atlanta. I'd slept the entire flight. Zero hour had arrived, and I had no plan, no guidance, no idea what might be waiting as I got off the plane—or how to deal with it.

The flutter in my stomach had nothing to do with the turbulent air we encountered as we began the approach, and everything to do with the turbulence I expected to encounter as I disembarked from the safety of the plane.

Father, if I'm supposed to be making some of these important decisions on my own, please don't call off my guardian angels. I'll need them more than ever now.

I moved aside so my seatmates could retrieve their luggage from the overhead compartments, then stepped back to wait for Rainbow. Silent, bleary-eyed passengers streamed by—even the mother and child who were Rainbow's seatmates—but I saw no sign of the spiked hair coming up the aisle.

Had she slept through the landing? Slept through the jostling and shifting that came with gathering possessions and people? Though this was one of the more subdued groups I'd deplaned with, could anyone sleep through the pilot's and flight attendants' announcements? Through bumps and bangs of overhead compartments popping open and slamming shut?

When the last person straggled down the aisle, I headed back to find her. No Rainbow. Her seat was empty, her backpack gone. I'd watched every single passenger deplane, so I couldn't have missed her. How could you overlook black, blonde, and green spikes of hair?

A flight attendant approached, gathering passenger left-behinds. "Did you lose something?"

"Yes, a teenage girl with spiked hair. Did I miss her somewhere?"

"She was sleeping the last time I came through the cabin. I didn't see her get off. Have you checked the rest room?" she suggested.

Good idea. I slipped by the flight attendant and headed for the rest rooms in the very back of the aircraft. The first two were empty. The third was locked.

"Rainbow, are you in there?"

No answer.

I leaned against the door and raised my voice. "Rainbow, I'm not leaving without you, so you might as well come out."

Silence.

"They're getting the plane ready for the next set of passengers. In a minute, they'll unlock the door from this side and throw us both off the plane. Do you really want to get airport security involved? Or the police?"

I stopped. If we were escorted off the plane, Raven's welcoming committee couldn't lay hands on us until we were out of the hands of the police! It just might solve my dilemma. Then again, being escorted out of the airport would certainly call attention to us, when we might otherwise be able to slip by someone looking for a single dark-haired, green-eyed twenty-five-year-old instead of two young women with wildly colored hair.

The door opened slowly. Rainbow peeked out, biting one black-tipped fingernail. "Are the police here yet?"

"Not yet. Ready to go?"

"You don't have to baby-sit me, ya know." The defiance returned when she saw we were alone. "I can, like, get home from here by myself."

"I'm sure you can. But since I just invested over eight hundred dollars in you, I'm going to see that you do get home in one piece, and as soon as possible."

Rainbow opened her mouth to reply, and suddenly shut it. I turned to see what had changed her mind about mouthing off. The captain was heading down the aisle toward us, and he didn't appear to be in a jovial frame of mind.

"I'm, like, ready. I'll follow you," she said, avoiding both the captain's glare and my eyes. Authority figures seemed to intimidate the girl. Of course, the scowl on the captain's face didn't exactly thrill me, either.

I started toward the man, beaming a smile his way.

"Do we have a problem back here?" he called from halfway up the cabin.

"No problem. Rainbow was feeling a little queasy from the turbulence before we landed, and needed to get her stomach on straight before she got off." A logical statement. Might be true.

His face softened the tiniest bit. "Is she okay?" He had to ask me, since Rainbow was sticking very close behind me and I'm sure he couldn't see her at all.

I turned. "Are you okay?" I smiled at her and winked.

She poked her head around me. "I'm okay." She didn't look at the man, just muttered loud enough so he could hear her, then slunk back behind me again.

I turned to the captain. "She'll be fine. Still a little shaky. Any suggestions for post-turbulence trauma?"

He smiled. "I like that terminology. Yes. Something greasy. Fill her up with a hamburger and fries. Kids like that menu any time of day or night, I think. Need anything else?" By that time, we'd caught up to him. He stepped out of the aisle so we could pass, then followed us as we headed for the exit.

"Don't think so," I said over my shoulder. "Unless you're on your way out of the terminal. I wouldn't object to a good-looking escort off the plane and out of the building."

His laughter followed us up the aisle. "Okay. It's the least I can do for making the young lady sick. I'll even spring for the burger and fries."

His quick acceptance of my offer surprised me. Rainbow mumbled something behind my back, indicating this was the last thing she wanted. But it seemed a good precaution in case Raven had sent a welcoming committee. Someone might think twice if we were escorted by a big, tall, virile-looking man in uniform. They might be less likely to snatch my bag and eliminate me on the spot.

We paused at the entrance to the jet bridge long enough for the captain to grab his case and speak to the remaining crew. As we entered the terminal, I donned sunglasses and scrutinized the thinning crowd for someone watching this exit. At first, it didn't seem that anyone showed the slightest interest in the last stragglers off the flight from Los Angeles.

Then I saw him. Leaning against a pillar across the boarding area, a short, stocky man holding a newspaper in front of him glanced up occasionally, scanned the faces of those around him, then went back to his paper. This had to be the one.

I linked arms with the captain and Rainbow. Both looked at me with surprise. "Just keep walking, my friends, and don't look back. There's someone I don't want to talk to, and if we keep going, he may not see me."

"Trouble?" the captain asked quietly, matching his stride to my quickened pace.

"I hope not. Guess we'll see in a minute." When we reached the transporter, the moving sidewalk, I dropped the arms of my puzzled companions and looked back. I didn't see the man, but that didn't mean he couldn't see me.

"Thanks for being so kind, Captain. I'm sure this is above and beyond the duty of a pilot." Rainbow snorted on one side of me and the captain chuckled on the other.

"You're an interesting pair. A colorful pair. Thought perhaps I'd find a story here. My wife always asks if I've had any fascinating passengers she can write about in her newspaper column. So far in my last two flights, I haven't had any standouts or any stories. She'd appreciate you two."

Rainbow's head came up, and her hang-dog look of submission vanished. Defiance and anger sparked from her eyes. I stepped between the two so the captain couldn't see her face, and mouthed, "Don't say anything."

Her mouth snapped shut, and she turned her back to me with a dagger-filled glare. I glanced around and saw the short, stout man with the newspaper leave his pillar and amble down the concourse toward us. He didn't appear to be following. Since our gate was located at the end of the concourse, there was no other way he could have gone. He wasn't in a hurry. But he was there, nevertheless.

Turning to the captain, I said in what I hoped was a casual tone, "I assume all off-airport transportation is located by the baggage pickup, which is probably at the far end of the airport?"

"Did he see you?" the captain asked. He didn't miss much—or was I so transparent he could read me that easily?

"He's coming this way, but doesn't seem to be in a hurry." Of course, if there were more men stationed at other gates, or even at the exits, he wouldn't have to hurry. He'd just have to relay our location, and someone else could pick us up at the next position.

"Want to tell me about it? Maybe I can help." The captain turned slowly and looked over my head, checking the concourse behind us. "What does he look like?"

"Short, heavy, balding, checked shirt, tan jacket, khaki pants. And thanks, but if you can get us to the exit without being stopped, that's all I'll ask."

"I'd like to ask some questions."

I looked up into curious hazel eyes. "Fire away. I'll answer what I can."

Rainbow nudged me. When I glanced at her, she shook her head. Whatever her story, she didn't want it told. That was okay. I hadn't planned on telling mine, either. At least not the true story. He hadn't asked for a true story. Just a story he could tell his wife so she could pen an interesting column.

"First, are you sisters?" He glanced from me to Rainbow and back again.

"Besides the obvious sharing of hairdressers with an affinity for color, what is there about us that makes you ask that?" Question for a question. Bart hated it when I did that.

"Same slight build. You both have delicate features, though not really similar. Both have the same look in your eyes, the same—hmm—how do I describe it? A don't-come-too-close-or-I'll-run look."

I laughed. "Now you and your wife can speculate on what we were running from. Abusive parents, jealous, possessive men, the police? Any guesses?"

He checked behind me again. "Private detectives?"

I smiled up at him. "Maybe a hit man."

His eyes flicked down, met mine, and locked on, seeking an answer there, waiting for an explanation of my surprising statement.

"Maybe we're running from a rich Middle Eastern oil potentate who wanted to add us to his harem. When we discovered how stifling hot it was there, and how little freedom we had behind the black gowns and veils, we decided no amount of money could keep us there another minute."

The captain's gaze turned on Rainbow, who was smiling in spite of herself, then glanced over my head at the man still behind us, and back at me. "And the man?"

"Sent to kidnap us and take us back with him. The Sultan didn't like losing his newest acquisitions."

"The little guy doesn't look like he could handle both of you," he observed as we exited the moving sidewalk and walked briskly for the tram.

"He doesn't have to. He's got help, posted all along the way. He's just keeping an eye on us until we make for the door. Then he'll have his crew close in, shepherd us to the limousine, whisk us to the Sultan's private jet, and by tomorrow we'll be back in desert heat, black robes and veils, and servitude."

Rainbow quit laughing. This hit a little too close to home for her. The pilot didn't laugh, either. Not that he believed the story, but I could tell he felt there was some truth in the fabrication. He just wasn't sure what part to believe. I didn't help him out.

"We need to get lost when we leave here. Any suggestions? If we can get out the door without being followed, that is." I watched the short, stout man step it up a little, closing the gap between us. I hadn't seen him use a radio. Of course, I hadn't been watching him every minute. But if he needed to get closer, maybe he was the only one Raven had sent. That thought bolstered my spirits for a tiny moment.

Then I saw the small movement, the newspaper brought to his face, held near his mouth as though stifling a yawn.

"Do you fly in and out of Hartfield often?" I asked.

"It's my home base. Why?"

"You must know all the nooks and crannies and side doors passengers would never know about." I looked up into those increasingly curious eyes.

"What do you need?"

"A way out of here that he's not expecting. An escape route where he won't have men waiting for us."

The captain looked around, pointed at the little train just ahead, and guided us for it. When the doors opened, one on each side of the hallway, he quickly reversed our direction and we jumped on the train that would take us back to where we'd just come from. As the doors slammed shut, the short man dashed for the train. He was too late.

At the first stop, a minute or two down the line, the pilot pressed us toward the door. As soon as it opened, he pushed us through the crowd and headed back through the terminal. He commandeered the first airport cart that came along, directing the driver through several doors marked "Employees Only" and down long, deserted hallways where employees carried on their business out of sight of teeming passenger lanes.

Suddenly we burst out of doors and under an airliner being loaded with luggage and food carts, then beep-beeped our way past some flag men with flashlights and ear mufflers directing a plane into its slot.

We wheeled around one entire wing of the Hartfield Airport, and came out where a stand of taxis and airport shuttles and buses waited to accommodate the passengers streaming from the building.

The captain pointed to a shuttle just pulling into the number one position in a line of eight or ten shuttle dockets. The driver, grinning from ear to ear over his joyride, pulled up behind the Windy Hill Shuttle.

"Get on this. It takes you to straight through Atlanta to Marietta, to the Windy Hill Station at the Marriott Hotel. From there, you can either rent a car, or call, if you have someone to come for you, or get a room and hide out for a while. I assume you have money?"

"We do. And we thank you, Captain. I'll remember to fly Delta wherever I go. I've never had such personalized service." I shook his hand, grabbed Rainbow, and hustled her off the cart and toward the little shuttle bus that held only one or two dozen passengers.

The driver, just climbing out of the bus, asked for our tickets. When I told him we didn't have any, he pointed to a little ticket booth next to the shuttle. "Twenty-five dollars round-trip," he said.

I dug my purse from the Biltmore bag, found enough money for two tickets, and thrust it at Rainbow. "Take this, go to that window, and buy us two round-trip tickets to the Windy Hill Station. Hurry."

Rainbow, her eyes big and slightly dazed, dropped her backpack in the seat, took the money and bought the tickets, watching over her shoulder all the while. Had she been on the run long enough to spot someone who was looking for a particular person? Or was she just frightened, picking up on the fear that must be emanating in huge waves from me?

I watched the exits. Watched for the stout little man with the tan jacket and plaid shirt. For anyone who didn't look like a traveler either scurrying to catch a flight, or hurrying off one. Then I saw him. Them.

CHAPTER 28

Four men followed the short, fat, balding man in the plaid shirt and tan jacket out through the automatic doors. They spread out, checking taxi cabs, hotel shuttles, city buses. One especially sullen-looking man headed straight for the Windy Hill shuttle in the number one dock, while the three others made for each of the bus, taxi, and rental car areas. The man in the plaid shirt and tan jacket watched from the entrance, scanning faces in the crowded entry and egress zone.

Rainbow clutched my hand. "There are more. You weren't lying," she breathed in alarm. "Like, what do we do now?"

"Just sit tight and wait. If we get off, he'll see us for sure," I whispered as several people climbed aboard the shuttle.

"Like, what's with the 'we'? They're not after *me*. I'm gone, lady." She stood and made a move to get out of the window seat and into the aisle.

I grabbed her hand and pulled her back into the seat. "Sorry, Charlie. I'm taking you home to Charleston, and this is the first leg of the journey. They're looking for a different person than you see before you. They shouldn't recognize me, and they don't know about you, so you're safe in any case."

"Ha! If you're so sure about that, like, how come you're so scared?" Rainbow turned on me with a challenge in her voice and venom in her eyes.

"For the same reason that horrible man in the gray suit scared you. They want to do me bodily harm. And that, my young friend, is a frightening idea, considering the kind of animals they are." I turned from the belligerent teenager to watch the progress of the man heading our way. He'd crossed two busy lanes of airport traffic, and had one bus lane and one sidewalk to go.

The driver of the Windy Hill Shuttle slammed the back of the luggage compartment shut and walked to the front of the shuttle.

Come on. Come on, I demanded under my breath. *Let's get out of here.*

But the driver ambled around the shuttle, checking for what I couldn't tell, seemingly in no hurry to leave. I glanced at my watch. The posted schedule indicated that we were to depart at 8:30, arriving at Windy Hill Station at five minutes after nine. According to my watch, it was 8:32. I counted on making that timetable. That would give me just ten minutes to locate a phone and call Bishop O'Hare at 6:15 his time.

The sullen man, his morose expression unchanging, crossed the bus lane and stepped onto the sidewalk, leaving only twenty-five feet of pavement between him and the driver. The man wasn't ambling. He had a mission. Did the driver think this stone-faced man was coming to board the shuttle?

Get in, I urged the driver silently, teeth gritted, hands clutching my bag.

I glanced at Rainbow, who suddenly had nothing more to say. She sat wide-eyed, her tongue flicking over the faded black lipstick on her lower lip and back again, scrawny arms hugging her ragged backpack close to her thin body.

The driver checked his watch, finally turned his back on the approaching man, and climbed into the shuttle. As he reached for the handle to shut the door, the somber-faced man stopped in the open doorway.

"Taking the shuttle?" the driver asked.

I stopped breathing. *Please don't get on. Please don't search the shuttle. Please don't go with us.*

Peering inside as far as he could see, the man mumbled something and shook his head. At that signal, the driver slammed the door and started the engine. The man whose face seemed frozen in a dismal expression walked beside the shuttle as it backed out of the slot, staring through the tinted windows at the passengers. When the shuttle pulled forward onto the exit drive, the man examined the opposite side of the bus—the side we sat on.

I turned my head and looked out the other side of the shuttle, giving him no opportunity to glimpse my profile. As the bus accelerated down the drive, I looked back. He'd stepped to the next shuttle in line to peruse those passengers.

I breathed again, releasing the long-held breath, and felt Rainbow do the same next to me. Leaning my head back on the seat, I closed my eyes and uttered a silent, fervent prayer of thanks for our escape. For our temporary escape. I knew that's all it was.

The jade lion would lead them to me again and again until I got rid of it. But I couldn't even devise a plan until I talked with Bishop O'Hare. Hopefully, he'd tell me what to do. *Hopefully.* The Lord wouldn't really leave me to my own devices on this, would He?

I also had another plan to formulate: getting Rainbow home to Charleston, then leaving without being caught. There were too few roads in and out of Charleston to make escape easy.

Rainbow watched the Atlanta skyline flow by, her head leaning against the window, her lips drawn together in a thin line.

"Have you been here before?" I asked.

"Once." Neither her position nor expression changed.

"When you flew to California?" I guessed.

She looked at me. "I can get home by myself, you know." The attitude returned. "Like, who appointed you my guardian angel, anyway?"

I stared into dark, defiant eyes. "Do you believe in God?" I asked quietly.

The question caught her off guard. She blinked, then blinked again. I waited. Rainbow turned away, plucking at a frayed spot on the backpack with great concentration. I waited. When I didn't repeat the question, when I didn't move, she glanced back at me.

"Do you?" I barely breathed the question, not wanting to incite insolence, not wanting to send her scurrying back behind her mask of belligerence.

"I used to." Her voice, scarcely audible over the noise of traffic on the crowded beltway, cracked slightly. She continued to worry the frayed threads on the backpack.

The subject made her nervous, so I wouldn't pursue it. But I felt strongly about one thing she needed to know. "Think about this. I don't believe it was coincidence that brought us together in that terminal in Los Angeles. Someone loves you very much, and I believe I was guided by that Someone to find you, and help you get away from California." After planting that thought to grow and develop as it may, I turned back to the window.

I'd never been to Marietta, Georgia, but there hadn't been a break in civilization from the time we left the airport, so I supposed this was like any other metropolis. You couldn't tell where the city proper ended and the suburbs began. I loved the multitude of huge green trees lining the freeway, partially hiding the endless subdivisions on the other side of them.

My heart beat faster with each mile that flew by. I could feel it thumping inside me, ticking off the minutes, the seconds until I could connect with my only lifeline and find out what had happened to Bart, my parents, and the rest of Anastasia.

I'd banished all thoughts of Bart, forced myself to not think of what could be happening to him—or what might have already happened. I'd be paralyzed with fear and worry if I dwelt on it. But the closer we got to Marietta and the appointed hour to call Bishop O'Hare, the harder it became to ignore uninvited thoughts crowding in on my subconscious.

If Bart *had* grabbed the formula and sent it to me, they must have ID'd him for anyone to be after me. I couldn't come up with any other reason they were tracking me. Unless . . . was it possible the contract had been made on Anastasia *before* Bart got the formula— simply to eradicate all opposition to the terrorist group? And if Raven had been assigned to me, who on earth had been assigned to Bart? He was in *their* backyard—territory they knew intimately. What chance did he have of evading someone on their own turf? Someone who should be even more proficient than Raven? A shudder ran through me.

We zigzagged through the hotel parking lot to the Windy Hill Station, a small frame building nestled under huge Georgia pines where most of the passengers exited the shuttle.

"Everyone else for the Marriott?" he asked, looking in his over-sized rearview mirror. When the remaining half-dozen passengers affirmed this statement, he pulled away from the tan and green building and wound his way through azalea bushes and pines to the multi-storied Atlanta Marriott Northwest Hotel.

The minute the doors opened, I grabbed Rainbow's hand and pulled her off the shuttle. My first need was a phone, second a rental car, and then to flee Atlanta posthaste.

"While you're talking, I'll, like, visit the little girl's room," Rainbow said, checking out the posh lobby.

"I don't think so, Rainbow." I caught hold of her wrist as she spun away from me. "I need you to stay right here where I can see you."

"Like, I can't even go to the bathroom without you?" she wailed.

"Sorry." I pointed to an overstuffed chair near the phones. "Plant yourself there. I don't trust you."

"I know. I know." Her face tightened in an angry scowl. "Like, you've got a whole lot of money invested in me, and you want it back." She plopped in the chair and stared daggers at me. "I'll pay it back, like, every cent."

Ignoring her whining, I dialed the number of the bishop's office at the church. I knew he'd be anxiously awaiting my call. Not nearly as anxious as I was to make it.

"Hi, Bishop." I tried to sound strong and unafraid, neither of which I felt at the moment.

"Allison. Where are you?" The sound of his voice was like ice cream on a hot summer day—all comfort and goodness melted together—and just exactly what I needed right now.

"Atlanta." My weak, quivering knees gave way, and I slid to the floor.

"Atlanta? Georgia?"

"That's the one. But first, news from Bart? And my parents? Are they okay?"

"My questions first, Allison," Bishop O'Hare said quietly. "Did you get the package put in the safe before you left the estate?"

"Wish I'd known that was what I was supposed to do with it." I rubbed at the spot on my forehead where I could feel pressure building into a massive headache. "No. I have it with me."

The bishop groaned.

"Yeah, I know. That would have made things so much simpler. I think there's a microdot on it—I haven't tried to remove it, so I can't be sure—but I think it's enabling Raven to tail me wherever I go."

"Raven?!" The bishop was silent for a moment. "Well, you've come up in the world, Alli. How does it feel to have a million-dollar price tag on your head? Never mind. Apparently you're adept enough at this new game to stay one step ahead of him."

"Barely. What else is on the microdot, Bishop?"

He didn't answer. I ventured ahead. "Is it what I think it is?"

This time the response was immediate. "And that is?"

"Unless I'm carting around the most valuable chunk of jade in the ancient and modern world, I'm guessing it contains an item mentioned in world headlines this week, supposedly lost in a firebombing."

He whistled quietly. "Smart girl."

"So, what am I supposed to do with it?" I glanced up to see Rainbow making moves to the edge of her seat, probably preparing to bolt and run. Wearily I pulled myself to my feet, shaking my head, waving her back in her chair.

"Finish the delivery that was supposed to be made by Rip Schyler. Bart had it delivered to your home by special courier, with instructions for you to put it in the safe in the Control Center until Rip could safely slip in, retrieve it, and deliver it to Atlanta."

"Unfortunately, the only message I got was one Alma scribbled on the package. 'Somebody delivered this from Bart. I couldn't understand the messenger.' I tossed it in my bag as I ran from the house and didn't read Bart's instructions until I was on the train to Los Angeles. By that time, it was too late."

"Actually, you're in the perfect position right now. It needs to be delivered to the Center for Disease Control in Atlanta at six o'clock in the morning. Can you handle that?"

I hesitated. "Probably, but I do have one slight complication."

"Complication?"

"I, uh, have a companion . . ."

"Oh, Alli. Don't tell me you've been picking up strays again! Not now!" His voice was filled with disbelief, tinged with a little reluctant pride. The latter emotion originated from his calling as a bishop, the shepherd to his flock, always concerned with stray little lambs needing help. The disbelief stemmed from his experience as an FBI agent who knew that lack of focus on the issue at hand was not only dangerous, but often fatal, especially to newcomers to the perilous games agents played.

"Uh, yeah. But before we get into that, what about Bart?"

"Bart's safe. He called after he sent the package with the courier. Oz and Mai Li are trying to get out of Africa. Bart stayed with the terrorist group—he's 'helping' them find the terrorist who stole the formula, posing as one of Mobuto's trusted accomplices just released from jail. Apparently Usama bin Laden bought his story, with encouragement from a couple of other planted terrorists claiming they'd worked with him under the former dictator."

"When's he coming out?" I shivered at the thought of Bart anywhere near the infamous terrorist Usama bin Laden—that had to be worse than having Raven on my own tail. Much worse.

"He's working on two things—neither of which I can divulge." He added sympathetically, "You know he'll be home as soon as he can." Then his FBI persona returned. "Back to you. You need to be at the CDC tomorrow, six a.m. Remember Matt Runyon?"

"Of course. We worked with him on the amethysts and arson mystery." Memories of Matt's fatherly countenance triggered multiple emotions. Matt had attained "favorite uncle" status as he shared the terror of the chase, as well as our personal trauma when I'd lost our baby in February. The thought of seeing our friend from the Alcohol, Tobacco and Firearms division of the United States Treasury Department buoyed me up considerably.

"I'm faxing a picture to Matt. You'll need to connect with him so you'll recognize the man to whom you'll hand the microdot. Surrender it to no one else. Matt will give you whatever support you need. Here's his number."

I scrambled to scribble his number on the nearest available paper. As I turned my back on Rainbow, I saw her stand, her image reflected in the wide, gleaming brass trim around the phone units. I whirled and grabbed her by the waistband of her miniskirt, thwarting her escape.

"Got it?" Bishop O'Hare continued without waiting for an answer. "Call me at my downtown office tomorrow, as soon as you've delivered the formula. I'll wait for your call. Questions?"

"My folks?"

"No word. That, in itself, is good news. Good luck, Alli, and God bless."

I hung up the phone and pointed to the floor under the phones. Rainbow plopped herself down with a disgusted snort, which I ignored. I was getting antsy. I'd been here too long, and Raven and his men were too close on my tail to make it safe to stay in one spot for any length of time.

But I had one more phone call to make. One very important phone call.

CHAPTER 29

The phone rang—endlessly—but no one answered. *Misdial?* Hanging up, I carefully dialed again. *Please let him be there. Please let him answer. I can't stay here any longer.*

I counted the rings. On the fourteenth ring, I glanced at the clock in the lobby. No time left. Raven or his men could be here any minute. With trepidation and a very heavy heart, I knew I had to sever this link that had been so close to connecting me not only to a familiar and friendly voice, but to help, as well. As I reluctantly pulled the phone from my ear to put it back on the receiver, I heard a bellow through the earpiece. I jammed it back to my ear.

"Runyon here," the out-of-breath voice gasped.

"Matt." I was so glad to hear him I almost cried. "This is Allison Allan."

"Alli. Good to hear your voice," he panted before continuing. "Tell me to what good fortune I owe this call—while I catch my breath."

Another glance at the clock told me I didn't have time for friendly chitchat. "FBI Agent O'Hare is faxing you a picture of a man I'm supposed to meet tomorrow. Where can I connect with you to get it?"

"Where are you now? I'm picking up urgency vibes from your tone. Are you okay?"

"Marriott Hotel in Marietta, on my way to Charleston. Yeah, I'm okay, and should stay that way if I leave before my pursuers arrive." With my hand covering the mouthpiece, I told Rainbow to watch for the men we'd seen at the airport. She'd apparently caught the urgency in my voice, too. She stood immediately and peeked to check the front entrance.

"I can be in Charleston tonight," Matt said. "Hang on. Your fax is coming in now." Momentary silence on the other end, then an exclamation filled with disbelief. "Allison, how did you get involved in this?"

"You know my reputation for attracting trouble," I offered lamely.

"In spades. You've done it this time, babe. I've been keeping up with developments on this, but I didn't expect you to be involved." I didn't like the tone in his voice, and knew if he offered sympathy or anything resembling it, I'd probably dissolve into tears. I plunged ahead before he could.

"It doesn't have to be Charleston. I should be leaving there by early evening." I heard papers rustling, probably road maps.

"Okay. This should work. Just outside of Charleston, about a mile and a half off of Highway 17 on State Route 21, there's some old church ruins—Sheldon Church. What time do you want to meet me? Six? Seven?"

I did some quick mental arithmetic. "How about seven o'clock?"

"I'll be there with your picture. What else do you need?"

"Wish I could give you a list. There's no time. Just seeing you will be enough. By the way," I added as an afterthought, "what's the quickest way to Charleston from here?"

I scribbled frantically as he gave directions.

"Anything else?" Worry seeped into his voice.

"Thanks, Matt." I tried to sound cheerful and confident. *Don't be too nice. No sympathy. Keep it professional or I'll lose it.* "Gotta run. Literally. See you tonight." I slammed the phone down, wanting to cling to the false sense of security I felt listening to him, the comfort of knowing that someone who cared about me was within close proximity, that I wasn't entirely on my own.

"Let's get a car and get out of here." I grabbed Rainbow's slender hand and ran down the hall, following the gold arrow that pointed to "Rental Cars."

Miracle of miracles, we actually got the car and were on the freeway in just under fifteen minutes. Still too long there. Since I didn't know exactly how accurate that satellite was in pinpointing locations, especially if the target kept moving, I didn't want to delay leaving Atlanta. Setting the cruise control at eighty—five miles per hour above the speed limit—I took a deep breath and tried to relax.

One hundred thirty-nine miles to Augusta, then another hundred and seventy-five to Charleston; about five hours, give or take a little, from here to Rainbow's. I watched her, scrunched against the door, nibbling on one black fingernail.

"How ya doin', Rainbow?" I tried to lighten up, to flash a genuine smile instead of the cardboard one I felt pasted across my face.

She turned luminous dark eyes on me, now accentuated even more by the shadowed half-moons underneath. My heart nearly broke at the emptiness there.

"How long has it been since you've slept all night in a bed with clean, fresh sheets?" Direct hit. She turned her head away, but not before those dark pools of misery and loneliness filled and overflowed down her pale cheeks.

"Being on the run isn't any fun, is it?" I prayed for guidance as I tiptoed onto tender turf. "I hate looking over my shoulder, knowing that if I relax for even a minute—at the wrong minute—I could be dead." I glanced at Rainbow again, struck by how young she looked minus her mask of defiance.

"There's worse things than bein' dead." A statement without emotion, without inflection. A statement no young woman Rainbow's age should ever have to make from personal experience.

"How old are you, Rainbow? Twelve? Thirteen?" I glanced in the rearview mirror, making sure we weren't being followed, before I turned to watch her emotional response to my question.

Insolence flashed in those dark eyes as she whirled on me. "Like, if it's any of your business, I'll be thirteen in July. I'm old enough to be on my own, ya know. My mom was engaged at fourteen and, like, married at fifteen. Had me when she was sixteen and Abner Amos when she was seventeen."

"She loves you very much, doesn't she?" Just a guess here, but apparently a good one.

Rainbow's eyes widened. "How'd ya know that?"

"If she didn't love you a great deal, you wouldn't think of going home. If there was nothing there but an abusive father, you wouldn't chance going back." Guessing again, but it seemed logical.

"'Gator got my Pa when I was a baby. Grandpoppa's been my dad, dolin' out discipline—*with love.*" She accented the last two words as her slender fingers curled into tight little fists, then she turned away, hiding the emotion eating at her tender heart.

"Tell me about him."

She leaned her head back on the seat, apparently struggling with whether or not to open her life to a stranger. Then her face softened into a little-girl look as she surrendered her defiance to the memory of people who loved her, and whom she obviously loved very much.

"Grandpoppa, like, came to live with us when Pa died, ya know, to help Momma with me'n my brother. Momma was pregnant with Abner Amos when the 'gator snatched Pa right out of her arms." She turned to look at me. "Ab was a blessin' and a burden, my momma said."

Her eyes misted. "Ab's been a blessin' to me, too. He'd always tell me when Grandpoppa got on a tirade so's I could hide."

"Why did you have to hide?" I asked.

A van roared out of nowhere behind me, catching me off guard. I held my breath while it flew by, realizing I'd been so engrossed in Rainbow that I'd forgotten Raven's men. A lapse like that could get us both killed.

The black fingernail went to her pouty little mouth, now minus matching lipstick. She nibbled the nail for a minute before replying. "Poppa's a good man, ya know, but when he'd loose the devil from that bottle of Jack Daniels, he'd, like, beat Lucifer out of me, and try to beat the love of Jesus into me."

I stared at her, the pieces beginning to fall into place. "Is that what you meant when you said he disciplined you with love? And why you *used* to believe in God?"

Rainbow nodded solemnly. "Poppa, like, really does love me, ya know." Was this to convince me or her?

"Rainbow, Jesus Christ is a being of love and peace. That wasn't discipline, no matter how much your grandfather loved you. That was just plain abuse. Is that why you ran away?"

"I, like, didn't run away." She loosened the seat belt and tucked her legs under her. "My momma sent me out to stay with her sister in Pasadena. Momma didn't like my boyfriend hangin' around so much. Said at my age I needed, like, an education 'stead of a baby. But Aunt Flo was, ya know, so busy with her brood and her bridge club, I think she was, like, glad when I told her I had a friend who wanted me to move in with her."

"And did you?" My attention was now riveted on a black sedan in the rearview mirror that had slowly closed the gap between us.

"Did I what?"

"Did you move in with a friend?" I breathed easier when the sedan sped past. Rainbow hadn't answered. When I looked at her, she was watching me intently, fear clearly evident in those expressive dark eyes.

"Why're you, like, askin' all these questions? Why'd you buy my ticket? Who are you? Are you, like, really takin' me home?" Her hand crept to the door handle.

Poor Rainbow. I suspected she'd gone from the frying pan into the fire: from her grandfather's abuse, to her aunt's neglect, to a new and frightening kind of abuse and servitude, making her long on suspicion and short on trust.

"My name is Allison, and I don't like to see anything or anyone suffer. I'm interested in who you are, what happened to you and why, and I want to help however I can. I have money. You don't need to repay me for your ticket. I wanted to get you away from that scum chasing you. And, yes, I'm taking you home. I think you're probably wise enough to know how to avoid your grandfather's 'discipline' and smart enough to realize your mom was right. You do need an education, not babies, at your age." I glanced at her. The slender fingers still lingered on the armrest, inches from the door handle.

"Rainbow, I'm not going to hurt you or force you to do anything you don't want to do. You have the right to make your own decisions. I just want to help you get in a position to make the right ones, to help you start over on a better road. You're a bright girl, and brave, too, or you couldn't have survived that dark world in California. Tell me what I can do to help you. Name it. Anything."

"Anything?" She uncurled her legs and turned to me.

"Anything." I meant it. I hoped she understood that.

"Like, buy me lunch?"

I looked at the girl beside me. Some cultures would consider her a woman already—old enough to marry, have children, work in the fields beside her husband, and run a household, though she was barely more than a child herself. Right now she looked like a plain-tive, hungry pre-teen in need of a friend.

"Sorry. I was so intent on getting out of Atlanta, I forgot we hadn't eaten. What would you like? We'll stop at the first place you see."

"What about the men chasing you?" She frowned, and her black fingernail went back between her teeth.

"We'll take the chance that they won't catch us. Besides, the man in the airport saw me. I've got to change my looks. Do you want to look a little less California and a little more South Carolina when you get home?"

Rainbow's chin went up in defiance. "If they don't like what they see, ya know, I don't have to stay there," she snapped, her dark eyes flashing.

"Well, I'm not going to leave my hair looking like Sunset Strip. Why don't I give you a new look at the same time? You know the shock value of your appearance. How about meeting your folks halfway, and without a chip on your shoulder? There's something ahead. Want to stop there?"

"Yeah. Whatever it is."

I checked the mirror for cars behind us. Interstate traffic had thinned. We were currently the lone car on this stretch of road, every-thing else having passed us at ninety miles an hour. So far, so good.

We pulled into Arby's. Rainbow ordered the special: five roast beef sandwiches for $5.55, a large order of curly fries, large drink, and apple pie. I settled for the roast beef sub and medium drink, then watched in amazement as the girl tackled the meal. People at two or three other tables looked in amusement at the little girl with the big appetite.

"When was the last time you ate?" I asked as she mopped up the final drop of catsup with the last curl of fry.

She looked thoughtful. "Maybe yesterday. Maybe the day before. That pig told me he'd feed me when I got on my knees and begged for food. I told him I'd rather starve. He said that was all right with him."

Tears stung my eyes. I couldn't imagine, in my most horrific nightmares, what this girl had been through.

"Ready for a makeover?" I glanced at my watch. We'd taken longer than I'd planned to eat, but I needed to alter my appearance. Rainbow grabbed her backpack and headed for the ladies' room while I brought up the rear with my Biltmore Hotel bag and its precious contents.

Slipping off the reversible dress, I turned it from the black and white print side to the plain black georgette and offered it to Rainbow. She slipped it over her head. It hung loose on her slender frame, but covered the gold ring in her navel. I pulled on the white sweater and denim skirt in which I'd been dressed at the start of this misadventure.

I placed the vial of sable brown hair dye on the sink between us, and we brushed it through the brightly colored strands of our hair. I washed my face, grateful for the moisturizer, and did a quick smear of eye shadow and lipstick while Rainbow examined herself in the mirror. Without a word, she removed the earring from her eyebrow, and all but two sets from around her ears. Voilá. A skinny, normal-looking teenager. Cute, too.

She avoided my eyes. I didn't say a word, just grabbed my bag and headed for the door. She followed, with one last glance at her reflection. I think she liked what she saw.

I swung the heavy door open and held it for Rainbow, waiting for her to precede me back into the restaurant. The place was crowded now, noisy with people in line to order, and those carrying trays to tables.

A tall man, head and shoulders above most of the others, stood at the window, his back to us, scanning the parking lot. Panic pulsed through me.

CHAPTER 30

"Wait." I grabbed Rainbow's arm and pulled her back inside.

"They're here," she said, brandishing her backpack in front of her like a shield. It was a statement, not a question. She had a quick grasp of the situation.

I leaned against the door, thinking, then opened it a crack, checked on the tall man still looking out the window, and opened the door wider. He appeared to be alone. But he wouldn't be. Where Saucony was, could Raven be far behind? Maybe his cohorts were in the men's room next to us. They could be ordering food just around the corner, out of sight. Or they could be outside watching, waiting for us. Was Raven here, too?

"Stick close," I instructed, sidling through the door.

Rainbow nodded and followed on my heels, looking terrified. Exactly how I felt at the moment.

I'd parked by the side door. Saucony was watching out the front window. If we could make it to the car before he turned around . . .

As we passed the men's room, the door creaked open. I stepped double-time out of the hallway with Rainbow breathing down my neck. We made it to the door before the men emerged from the rest room. Their banter followed us as I jammed on my sunglasses and pushed open the heavy glass door. Rainbow slipped through as I hit the remote lock button on the car.

She fairly ran the last few steps, jerked open the door, and fell into the front seat. I tried to hurry, while not appearing to do so. Trying not to call attention to us, trying to be invisible, to escape without detection.

I tossed my bag in the backseat as I swung under the wheel, inserted the key in the ignition, and turned it as I shut the door and hit the locks. The transmission slid smoothly into reverse and I started backing out, watching the restaurant door and windows for familiar ugly faces. We might just slip quietly through their fingers.

Suddenly brakes screeched. A horn honked. Someone shouted obscenities. I'd nearly backed into a car entering the parking lot. The windows filled with faces. Paying too little attention to my driving and too much to my pursuers, I now had all their attention focused on me. *Way to go.*

I pulled forward into my parking slot and waited for the irate driver to proceed. He seemed determined to sit right there, belligerently blocking my way. Holding me up. Punishing me. I glanced at the restaurant, then back at the car. *All right. Enough already. You've made your point.*

"If anyone comes out of that building, tell me. This time I'll watch my driving. You watch the bad guys."

Rainbow nodded, her seat belt clinking and clanking as her quivering fingers tried to make the connection, securing her into the seat. I stared into the rearview mirror at the maniac gleefully laughing behind me. I threw up my hands in resignation, then leaned my head on the steering wheel. The brute got the message. I'd signaled defeat. He'd won.

"Someone's coming." Rainbow's voice came out high and raspy.

The obnoxious driver peeled into the parking lot and I put the car in reverse, checking carefully before I backed out. I glanced at the door as we pulled forward. Half a dozen laughing teenagers spilled out, inadvertently blocking the exit as they paused, watching the scene. A tall man right behind them pressed to get through. I didn't wait to see the outcome.

"Put your visor down and watch them in your mirror," I instructed. "Don't turn around. We don't want them to see us watching. Let me know if anyone follows while I get back on the Interstate."

I pulled onto the road and sped the short block to the on-ramp, cutting in front of an eighteen-wheeler making a left turn onto the same ramp. That torqued him, and he leaned on his horn. I seemed to be aggravating a lot of people lately. Not good. But neither was being caught by the likes of Raven and Saucony. Raven wanted the bounty on my head. Saucony just wanted my head for stabbing his hand with my fingernail file. I wanted out of this mess.

"Anyone coming?" I asked, maneuvering between a rusty old pickup idling down the road in the right lane and another eighteen-wheeler speeding toward us in the left lane.

"The truck's in the way. I can't see anything." Rainbow's eyes, wide with fear, were two dark circles in a thin, pale face as she clutched her tattered backpack.

"Keep watching," I said, checking the monster truck riding my bumper. "There should be several men in either a car or van. Saucony won't be tracking me alone."

Rain spattered the windshield, abated momentarily as if having second thoughts, then began anew in a blinding downpour, immediately flooding low spots on the road. I now had two eighteen-wheelers behind me, one in each lane, pressing, pushing me to drive faster and faster. I glanced at the speedometer. Eighty-five. I normally didn't drive that fast on clear, dry roads, much less on rain-slick pavement when I could barely see. My windshield wipers, flapping noisily from side to side, couldn't keep up with the deluge.

The trucks edged closer to my bumper. Raven and Saucony couldn't breach the barrier of trucks. I was temporarily safe from them—until I hydroplaned off the highway or slammed into the back of a car I didn't see in the blinding rain.

"Rainbow, holler the first exit sign you see. We've got to get off this road before we die." I'd need a long exit ramp. A long, straight one. At this speed on a rain-slick surface, I couldn't stop quickly enough on a short ramp or make the turn on a curved one. If I didn't get away from these faceless, insane madmen at the wheels of their lethally driven vehicles, it wouldn't matter how close Saucony and Raven got.

Something whipped by at the side of the road. "Was that an exit?" I asked, not daring to take my eyes from the rain-streaked windshield in front of me.

"I think so," she whispered, her face pressed against the side window.

"Not good enough. I've got to know, not guess, there's an exit ramp when I leave the highway."

Suddenly little orange beacons sprang to life outlining the right side of the road, almost directly in line with my right bumper. Visibility was so poor I didn't know I'd left the lane and inched onto the berm. Where were the stripes, the bumps, the noise to let you know you'd wandered off the highway?

"Yes. Yes!" Rainbow shouted. "You can get off here. It's an exit."

Immediately the bright beacons curved to the right and upward. I sent a prayer heavenward and gingerly turned the steering wheel to match the curve of the fluorescent orange road guides. The trucks shot past, their giant silver grills filling all three mirrors, dispatching an angry swirl of wind and water in our direction.

My pounding heart doubled the frantic rhythm of wiper blades slapping at the windshield; my clammy hands stuck to the steering wheel; and my mouth was so dry, my throat so tight that I could hardly swallow.

Easy. No quick moves. Ease off the gas. Don't touch the brake.

The exit ramp continued its gentle arc to the right while climbing up into the low-hanging clouds. I began a silent, pleading dialogue with Diety. *Please don't let there be cars at the end of wherever this leads. Please help me stop before I plow into something. Please help us stay on the road and not hydroplane through these deep puddles into oblivion.*

Huge trees on both sides of the road, whose reaching branches met in a canopy overhead, stayed the deluge enough for the wind-shield wipers to finally handle the water on them. I leaned forward, peering into the rain obscuring the narrow road.

Red taillights flashed ahead. I braked gently, glanced at the speedometer, then back at the road. Sixty—too fast. I touched the brakes ever so softly, then touched them again. Red lights flashed ahead. The car was stopping. I'd never be able to.

Gearing down, I tapped the brake, then navigated past the stopped car and stop sign. Unfortunately, the forty-five degree angle of the intersection didn't allow me to check traffic approaching from the left. I held my breath and veered into the left lane of the road.

Mixed blessings. No traffic coming at me from either direction, but a bridge loomed straight ahead. The car slid across the lane, across the tiny shoulder, then bounced off the steel girders of the ancient bridge and back into the traffic lane. Gripping the wheel with aching fingers, I pressed my foot gently on the accelerator, just enough to feel the tires grip the road again, and eased into the right lane.

The bridge narrowed as it arced over the river, allowing two very slender lanes for cars at the top, then as the bridge ended, the road widened slightly and curved back to the right, beside the river.

I pulled off at the first wide spot in the road, trembling from head to toe. When I could breathe again and my heart had slowed to a decent beat, I murmured a quick "thank you" to my guardian angels and glanced at Rainbow. She stared straight ahead, her fingers locked around the backpack.

"Are you okay?" I asked, touching her arm.

She turned, looked at me with wide eyes and a frightened face devoid of color, and took a deep breath. "I thought we were, like, going in the river."

"I'm glad I didn't know that river was there. That would really have freaked me out." I glanced in the mirror. No lights. No cars. No one following us. Was it possible Saucony had missed us as we exited? Could he be tooling down the Interstate right now, thinking we were still in front of those murderous trucks?

"Since there's no ramp onto the highway here, we'll just have to backtrack to the next one. That might put us behind the men who are after me, instead of in front of them." I retrieved the long blonde wig and pulled it over my now dry, newly dyed sable brown locks. "And since they've just spotted a brown-haired girl they think is me, I have to change my appearance again, and hope they didn't get the license number. On second thought . . ."

I dug the umbrella out of my Biltmore bag, jumped out of the car, and rubbed some mud on the license plates, hoping it wouldn't wash off too quickly in the rain. Then I washed my hands in a puddle and ducked back into the car.

"Why are they after you? You never told me." Rainbow's fragile face had regained a little color.

"I have something they want." Pulling back onto the narrow two-lane rural road, I headed for the next route leading to the freeway.

"Why don't you, like, just *give* it to them?" she said, her disbelief apparent at my stupidity in keeping something someone wanted enough to chase me across the entire United States.

"That wouldn't help. They also want my life." I glanced at the girl to see her reaction to this news.

She pivoted in her seat and leaned forward. "Honest? Like in the movies? The mob's after you? They've sent, like, a hit man?"

"Unfortunately, that's about it. Except it's terrorists, not the 'mob.'" Stopping at an intersection, I peered through the rain, trying to spot the Interstate. Unless my sense of direction was totally screwed up, this should lead us back to the highway.

We rode in silence as we crossed another narrow, ancient bridge over the Ogeechee River and Interstate 20 loomed out of the rain and mist. Easing onto the ramp, I accelerated to a safe speed in the driving rain and set the cruise control. Rainbow's silence piqued my curiosity.

"No comment?" I asked, examining traffic as it flowed by me. I didn't want Saucony slipping up behind me if I could help it.

"Why do they want to kill you?" Her voice, tremulous, timid, was barely audible over rain pounding on the roof of the car and tires splashing through puddles. I could almost see the wheels turning in her head; she was probably wondering if she was in more trouble now than she'd been in California.

"I belong to an anti-terrorist organization. *Our* business is putting terrorists *out* of business." I glanced at her again, wondering what effect, if any, this information would have on the young woman.

Rainbow sat quietly, chewing on the black fingernail whose polish was badly chipped by now. "Why?"

"Why what?"

"Why do something that makes people, like, want to kill you?"

How to answer that enigmatic question? "I'm not sure I can explain how I feel. These people don't value human life, property, or anything except their own power. Their lust for control is so all-consuming, they'll destroy whatever's in their path—including infecting thousands, possibly millions, of people in Africa today with an incurable disease. But if a cure isn't found, that disease could literally wipe out the population of the world."

Rainbow's eyes widened. "And you can really do something about it?"

I nodded. "But I have to be in a certain place with a certain item first thing in the morning. So I'm going to drop you at your home, then be on my way. The sooner I'm in and out of Charleston, the less danger there'll be to you and your family."

Her pale young face paled even more. "They'd kill me and my family?"

Brilliant, Allison. Scare her to death!

"No," I hastened to assure her. "They want me. They know nothing about you or your family."

"But you said . . ."

"If I take you home and leave Charleston immediately, I'll be gone before they even know where I've been. There'll be no way to connect us. However, if I hang around, they might trace me there. So I won't dally when we arrive." I hoped that alleviated her fear.

She sat quietly, her face turned away, looking out the rain-streaked window. I checked traffic again, making sure we weren't being followed. Then I sat straight up in my seat. They wouldn't follow me. As soon as they determined I was, in fact, Allison Allan, they'd force me off the road, grab the jade lion—and Rainbow and I would be history.

"How'd they know you, like, came to Atlanta?" Rainbow asked, swiveling in her seat to face me. "And which road we took?" She stopped. "You look funny. What's wrong?"

"Do you watch science fiction?" I asked, wondering how to explain. Then I realized Rainbow was a child of the new millennium, more familiar with modern technology than I'd been at her age. "You know about satellites that act like eyes in the sky? Connected to computers that compile and report what the satellite sees?"

She nodded, her dark eyes wide, lips parted.

"I think an item I'm carrying, the item the terrorists want, contains a microdot that's relaying my position to a satellite, and back to those men. That's the only way they could have tracked me everywhere I've gone. What I don't know is how accurate it is. Can it pinpoint this car exactly, especially in this storm, or just relay the general direction we're heading, and whether we're moving or we've stopped?"

Rainbow thought about this, her forehead wrinkled in concentration, the ever-present fingernail between her teeth.

"I want out." Stated quietly, with finality, it left no doubt of her total aversion to continuing with me for another minute.

"I can't let you out in the middle of this monsoon, in the middle of nowhere," I protested. "You'll be safe enough until I can get you home."

You can't make promises like that. You don't know whether you can get her safely one more mile, much less a hundred and seventy-five.

As we approached Augusta, the traffic increased dramatically, pouring onto the Interstate from every ramp. A lighted sign overhead directed me to the I-520 bypass to Highway 278 and Charleston, South Carolina.

"I want out. Now." The girl's cold, flat statement startled me out of my concentration on traffic, road, and rain.

"Rainbow, look around us. We're in the middle of four lanes jammed with traffic. I couldn't get to the side of the road to let you out if I wanted to. Besides, it's raining cats and dogs."

"Better drenched than, like, dead." Defiance and anger radiated from her voice and eyes. The old Rainbow was back—the Rainbow I'd first encountered in the Los Angeles airport. How did a twelve-year-old—correction: nearly thirteen-year-old—develop such a hard edge in so few years? Then again, if she'd thought she'd found safety with me, and suddenly discovered more danger than she'd experienced in California, she had reason to be upset.

I took a deep breath. "Rainbow, this is how it is. I'm delivering you directly to your doorstep in Charleston. Meanwhile, I have my hands full with traffic and hazardous highway conditions, driving an unfamiliar car on unfamiliar roads, and watching for my pursuers. I don't need problems from you. I'm sorry if you're uncomfortable, but I'm not in a position to do anything about it."

"I'm not staying in this car, like, another minute." Slender fingers reached for the door handle. "If you don't let me out, I'll jump."

"Now, that would be really smart," I said sarcastically. "If hitting the pavement at sixty-five miles an hour didn't kill you, the ten cars slamming into you before they could stop would certainly do the job."

Then I repented of my anger and continued with a little more compassion. "Look, I'm sorry you feel so threatened you'd risk your life jumping rather than staying. I can't guarantee nothing will happen before we reach Charleston, but I can guarantee you wouldn't survive the jump."

Rainbow slouched silently, sullenly against the door, her face turned away, that everlasting fingernail between her teeth.

I let her sulk, concentrating on making the tricky exit off I-520 onto Highway 278. A frisson of fear filtered through me as we left the high volume of traffic on the Interstate, from which I'd derived a false sense of security. Surely the satellite would be high-tech enough to pinpoint our route. As to whether it could keep close track of us in this storm, with the heavy cloud covering—another question. Maybe we were temporarily safe while the storm continued.

Rainbow, curled against the door, appeared to be asleep. Fine. I needed all my concentration on the road and route changes, and no distraction in this downpour by a distraught teen threatening to jump. As I turned the heat up so she wouldn't get chilled, my thoughts strayed to Bart.

Had he been able to keep Usama bin Laden's focus from him? My stomach knotted as I thought of the bearded leader of Islamic extremists, wanted in nearly every country in the free world for vicious, senseless acts of terrorism. Why did my husband have to be in the most dangerous place in the world—at least as far as I was concerned? Why couldn't he do what had to be done from a distance, instead of in such close proximity to the despicable leader of Al Qaida?

Then I thought of the Ebola plague—or its evil twin. It would be so like Bart to wade right into the middle without a thought for his personal safety. Any child he found needing comfort or attention would get exactly that, and Bart would never think to mask or protect himself from the danger of contamination. I guess that was one of the myriad reasons I loved the guy so much—his total unselfishness. His devotion to perceived duty. His devotion to me. And the list could go on and on.

But I'd been distracted by introspection—a dangerous preoccupation when my attention should be focused on my surroundings. I needed a plan, needed to know the route to Sheldon Church from Charleston. Definitely didn't need to be studying a map on some dark rural road in the middle of nowhere.

I checked the gas gauge. Better stop for gas while things were relatively quiet. The last thing I needed was to run out of gas, especially if the clouds lifted . . .

Stupid!! What was I thinking? Satellites couldn't photograph through cloud cover, but they had no problem tracking electronically under the heaviest clouds. It could pinpoint me no matter where I went, as long as I had the jade lion in my possession. Raven could know at all times whether I was in front of or behind him. And there wasn't a thing I could do about it.

So far as I could tell, the lion contained only one microdot. That meant it held both the formula and the tracking device. I had neither the equipment nor the expertise to separate them.

Suddenly, as if conjured up by thoughts of my pursuers, a black van, parked beside the intersection, pulled onto the road behind us. Coincidence? Or had Saucony—and Raven—found us?

CHAPTER 31

I sped up, exceeding the sixty-mile-per-hour speed limit on the two-lane road. Better to be stopped by a cop than rear-ended by Raven. The van accelerated, caught up, and stayed on my tail. Panic pounded through me with each heartbeat.

Keep cool, a little voice instructed. What do you do on a lonely stretch of unfamiliar, rain-slick road with parties unknown riding your bumper? *Get to civilization and find the police.*

Thus far, we'd passed a tiny town about every ten miles since we exited US 278 onto US 78, most only a wide spot in the road. I required one with a gas station, a policeman, and more than one little street to afford some maneuverability. The last one had consisted of a post office, a few empty buildings, and some houses. Of course, it was hard to tell in the blinding rain.

Did it always rain this hard and this long in the South?

The van stayed on my tail, too close for comfort but making no aggressive moves. Were they tailgating, waiting for an opportunity to pass? Or was it Raven's men, waiting to make a positive ID before moving in for the kill?

The road curved through dense green vines covering everything in sight: utility poles, trees, barns, fences—apparently anything that didn't move. I'd read about it on my last trip into South Carolina. The green stuff was Kudzu, a native plant of China and Japan. It had been imported—I couldn't remember why—and had quickly had taken over the South. It made the rural road resemble a jungle with the green darkness creeping, in places, to the very edge of the pavement. Farmers waged a constant battle to contain it.

A road sign, illegible through the rain, alerted me that we were on the outskirts of a town. I glanced at my gas gauge. *Please let there be a gas station—open and operating.* I braked to notify the driver behind me that I was slowing. He was so close I was afraid he'd drive right up my tailpipe if I simply took my foot off the gas.

"Bamberg," a lighted sign proclaimed through the downpour. "County Seat of Bamberg County." Surely this could accommodate my current needs.

Rainbow stirred, stretched, and looked out the window. "That's one thing I liked about California, ya know. The rain didn't last for days on end. Any chance of, like, a rest room in the next couple of minutes?"

"Keep your eyes open. We need gas, too."

She wiped the condensation from the window and peered out. "Where are we?"

"Bamberg. Do you know it?"

"We're an hour from Charleston! I have an uncle, ya know, who lives here. There's a service station and mini-mart somewhere."

"Is there a police station?" I watched the van in the rearview mirror, still riding my bumper, the rain too heavy to identify the driver.

Rainbow bolted upright and whirled to face me. "Did they find us?"

"I don't know. Van's tailgating us. I figured it wouldn't hurt to pull in to the nearest police station and see if they followed us. Do you know where it is?"

Rainbow stuck her fingernail between her teeth. "All these little places have, like, a town square. That's where the courthouse is."

"But you don't know about Bamberg?" I slowed to the prescribed thirty miles per hour, feeling like we were going so slow that anyone in the van could jump out and catch us.

"Never noticed. Like, I didn't need the police." She managed to sound both apologetic and proud. "There." She pointed through the windshield. "Mini-mart's up there."

I held my breath, signaled a right turn, and pulled off the highway, watching to see if the van followed. If it did, I'd whip back onto the road, head for the center of town, and hopefully find a square with a visible police car. If it didn't, I'd refuel the car, let

Rainbow have her rest stop, and check out road maps to become acquainted with the lay of this unfamiliar land.

To my relief, the van accelerated and disappeared down the road. I released the breath I'd been holding, drove under the canopy, and stopped. It took a minute for my legs to stop quivering enough to get out of the car. While the gas pumped and Rainbow ran inside, I located Bamberg on the map, and about sixty miles beyond that, Charleston. I found US Route 17, and, following Matt's directions, spotted Sheldon. Its isolated location didn't instill much warmth and comfort.

Rainbow hadn't emerged when I'd finished filling the gas tank. *Dummy. What if she's jumped ship? Why didn't you think of that?*

I ran inside, battling with the little voice on one hand saying, "Good riddance. You don't need that extra baggage," and the other one arguing, "Don't abandon her. She needs you."

I needn't have hurried, or worried, on Rainbow's account. Leaning on the counter, laughing and flirting with two good-looking boys, she straightened as I pushed open the heavy glass door. "Look who I found! My cousin, Billy Joe, works here now. This here's his best friend, John Paul."

"Hi, guys." I wondered how to approach our departure. Would Rainbow be willing to get back in the car, or would she want to remain with her relatives?

"I'm, like, ready to go when you are. Rest room's back there." She waved toward the back of the mini-mart. When I came out, Rainbow had already said her good-byes. In high spirits, she nearly beat me to the car.

"You're in a good mood," I noted, pulling back onto the highway.

"Billy Joe says Grandpoppa had a stroke a while back. It, like, took away the use of his right arm, and the doctor, like, took away his Jack Daniels, so I can go home now! Don't have to worry none about gettin' beat within an inch of my life." Joy transformed her.

"Did he really beat you like that? Didn't your mom stop him?" I couldn't imagine my own mother allowing anyone to lift a hand against me.

"Momma never dared stand up to him. She'd, like, disappear till it was over, then she'd stay up all night rubbing me with her grandma's ointment, sweet talkin', trying to soothe the hurt, telling me he really was a good man, that it hurt him as much as it did me. Hogwash," she declared. Then she tossed her head back and threw her arms in the air. "But that's all over, and I can go home without worryin' about it anymore."

"Where do you live in Charleston?"

"Didn't I tell you? Magnolia Plantation and Gardens. It's, like, the oldest public garden in America. Been in the Drayton family since 1676—three centuries and thirteen generations." Pride tinged her voice and lit her eyes.

I stared at Rainbow. "Your family owns it?"

She gasped. "Like, what do you think we are? Some kind of rich?" She flopped her head back on the seat. "I was raised there, ya know, like, it's my home. But, no. We don't own it. Just help manage it and work it."

"That's interesting. I grew up on an estate, too. My mom and I managed it." I laughed. "I just found out she owns the estate. All the time I was growing up, I believed it belonged to a missing movie star, and we were managing it till her return. Last year I discovered my mother was that missing movie star."

Rainbow's mouth dropped open. "Your momma's a movie star?"

"Well, she used to be. A long time ago. What do you do on the plantation?"

A casual glance in the rearview mirror revealed a car approaching from behind—fast. Rain diminishing to a drizzle allowed me to count six heads silhouetted by the car lights behind them. Another panic attack. Another shot of adrenaline.

Decision time. Speed up, not letting them get close enough to identify or force us off the road? Or let them pass, taking a chance it wasn't Raven's men?

"What's the matter?" Rainbow whispered, flipping down her visor to check in the mirror.

"Make sure your seat belt's buckled. I'm not lolly-gagging around to let that car catch up to us." I stomped on the accelerator. The burst of speed propelled us down the highway enough ahead of the pursuing car to quiet my pounding heart.

I checked the speedometer. Too fast again. Much too fast for rain-slick roads. I slowed, trying to maintain a safe distance between us and the car full of men. Suddenly the adrenaline coursing through me moments earlier dissipated. I slumped in my seat, spent, limbs like limp spaghetti.

How much longer could I do this—so little sleep, no real rest, running for my life, and afraid for all those around me? I wanted Bart. I wanted to go home, home to our cozy honeymoon cottage, lock the door, and never leave. I wanted out of this horrid business— this crazy, on-the-edge lifestyle where one tiny slip meant death.

Then I remembered the tests at the hospital. What irony. If Raven didn't get me, if I survived the contract he had on me, something even worse could slip insidiously into our comfy little cottage and snatch me away, and all of Anastasia combined couldn't do a thing about it.

"Allison?" Rainbow's hesitant voice brought me back from my uncertain future to my present depleted state. "Are you okay?"

I shook my head. "Nope. I'm exhausted. I'm sick of this ridiculous lifestyle and everything to do with it. I want my husband. I want to go home. I don't want to do this anymore."

Rainbow's dark eyes were wide, her mouth agape.

"Now, tell me about Magnolia Plantation while I keep an eye on that car behind us. Did you love being a part of something so beautiful? Was it neat caring for historical treasures?"

Rainbow snorted. "Love it? Like, I might as well have been one of those slaves they used to use."

Her words shocked me. I'd always felt it a privilege to help Bart's mom polish the crystal and silver, the walnut paneling, and etched glass French doors. I'd loved doing any little thing Alma let me do in the upkeep of the mansion, and begged Mom for more responsibility in running the estate.

Rainbow's answer puzzled me. "Why did you feel that way?"

"Like, what did I get out of it but work, work, and more work? Nothing belonged to me. Never would. Even the flowers weren't mine, though I planted, tended, weeded, and loved them so they just had to grow."

"Tell me about the gardens." Keeping the prescribed distance between my car and the one following us, it was apparent they weren't using cruise control. Their speed varied from sixty to eighty miles per hour. That bugged me. I didn't want to go eighty. Even with the sun peeking through the afternoon clouds, the roads were still wet—too dangerous to drive that speed.

"You want the whole spiel?"

"What do you mean?"

"I memorized the thing they give the tourists, you know—the history of the place. Like 'family tomb built before 1700, vandalized by soldiers in 1865.'"

"Fire away." I loved historical places. I loved beautiful gardens. And I was a captive audience for at least another thirty minutes, maybe more. Better to have my mind on something pleasant instead of the direction it was wont to go.

"You've got to see it to appreciate it, you know, but it's right on the Ashley River. There's the Sixteenth-Century Maze, Eighteenth-Century Herb Garden, Barbados Tropical Garden." She stopped. "That's where the first owner came from after he left his family's estate in England, you know." She continued, ticking them off on her fingers: "Audubon Swamp Garden, Topiary Garden, Biblical Garden. That has a statue of David in a Star of David, and Mary's in a cross of flowers. Those are my favorites. There's lots of plants from the Bible."

I glanced at the girl whose eyes were glowing to match the awe in her voice. Checking the mirror, I was alarmed to see the car closer than ever.

"Sorry to interrupt, Rainbow, but how close are we? Do I drive into Charleston?"

"Oh, no. We live ten miles this side of Charleston." She peered out the window. "Where are we?"

"Approaching Ridgeville. Should I stay on this road?"

"There's a couple of ways to Magnolia. You're wantin' to lose those guys, right?"

"Of course."

"Might throw 'em off if you turn at Ridgeville and take, like, that next road. Plantation's on it anyway."

"Watch for the turnoff. I'll see if I can lose them so they don't see us leave Highway 78. Sure you know the way?"

"Do birds fly? 'Course I know the way."

Slowing down only to turn at the intersection, I sped up on the connecting road. If the car followed, if they found us, I'd know it was Raven's men. On the other hand, they'd been following for miles and hadn't made any overt move to overtake and run us off the road. Maybe my jitters were groundless.

Rainbow chatted about Charlie, their resident alligator who'd killed her father. His offspring, born and raised in the blackwater cypress swamps of the plantation, all had names. She described the observation tower above the five-hundred-acre wildlife sanctuary, the petting zoo housing her furred and feathered friends, and the wild-flower garden.

She talked about statues nestled among trees and shrubs or planted in the middle of a square of grass with no apparent access, visible only across a hedge. But she knew the way into them all.

"Rainbow, what a marvelous place. You played in those gardens growing up?"

She look startled. "Yeah, sure."

"And you don't see anything unusual about that?"

"Like, what's to see? Momma had me plantin' and weedin' from the time I could tell the difference between weeds and flowers. When I wasn't hidin' from Poppa, that is. Oh, turn here."

Following her directions, I relaxed a bit at the certainty in her voice, and the absence of the car full of men. Maybe they'd had nothing to do with Raven. Maybe I was so paranoid that I couldn't tell the difference between pursuers and incidental travelers.

I listened to her prattle on about the plantation. "Rainbow, what are you going to do when you grow up?" I finally asked.

She stared at me, her luminous dark eyes strangely blank.

"When you get out of school? What do you want to do? To be?"

She remained silent, her expression unchanged.

"Haven't you thought about what you're going to study?" I pressed. "What you're going to do with your life?"

"Never thought I'd live this long, what with Poppa's beatin's and then that scum in California." Her voice, flat and unemotional, intrigued me.

"Well, think about it now. If you could be anything in the whole world—do anything—what would make you happiest?" I glanced at her face, half hidden by the shadows of the huge branches bridging the road above us. Mist drifted through the trees in the half-light of late afternoon, giving a ghostly ambiance to the scene.

"Right there," she pointed. "Turn in that gate. I'll get us through without payin'."

I drove through the gate, where we were waved onto the plantation by a surprised gatekeeper.

Rainbow laughed, delighted at his expression. "Won't they all just be so surprised to see me?"

"Have you thought about my question?" I pursued the avenue down which I'd been heading with regard to her life plans.

"Anything?" she said in a dreamlike voice.

"If you had all the money in the world and could do anything you wanted, what would you be? A teacher? Doctor? Astronaut? Dancer? What?"

Her pensive expression was suddenly replaced by a mask of indifference. "Don't matter much what I want. Won't get it anyway, so why pretend? Turn here."

The narrow lane wound beneath centuries-old oak trees with branches as big as tree trunks. The low-hanging sun peeked through a thinning cloud, tinting everything it touched a rosy hue.

I parked the car and turned off the ignition. This would have to be fast. I couldn't believe I'd lost Raven's men, if it had been them. That would be too good to be true. Actually, I couldn't believe Raven himself wasn't breathing down my neck. But the longer I stayed in one place, the higher the odds he'd show up.

"Home. Now what?" I asked, watching conflicting emotions play across Rainbow's face: delight at being home, apprehension at her mother's reaction, uncertainty about her future.

She turned to me. "Can you, like, stay for a few minutes and let me show you around? Just a little. It'd take too long to see the whole plantation, but, like, just a few of my favorite spots?"

I glanced at my watch. Three forty-five. I didn't have to meet Matt at Sheldon Church until seven. I'd be cutting it close, but . . . "Sure. Let's go. You don't want to see your mom first?"

Rainbow jumped out of the car and slammed the door. "I need a little dose of Magnolia first." Her laugh, nervous and uncertain, explained everything.

"Lead on. Show me your beautiful Magnolia Plantation." I hesitated. Should I leave the jade lion in the car, or take it with me? I'd only be a few minutes. Surely it would be safe that long. I locked the car.

Rainbow grabbed my hand, dragging me through an arbor and across a picturesque pole bridge. Tall, stately green trees and colorful flowering shrubs duplicated themselves, mirrored in the still water. A glimpse of Eden.

We hurried down a well-defined path winding through beautiful gardens, past "Miss Julian," an historic cotton barge displayed on the river bank, and turned a corner to be blinded by the sun gilding a wide, slow-moving river directly in front of us.

Suddenly a cry pierced the still air as the water under a huge, ancient oak came alive with wild splashing.

The cry came again—an anguished cry for help.

"Grandpoppa!" Rainbow ran for the tree.

Branches trailed into the water, and to one of these low-hanging branches a gray-haired man clung tenaciously while an alligator thrashed fiercely in the water at his feet.

"It's Charlie. Charlie's got Poppa!" Rainbow flung herself down the grassy embankment and grabbed her grandfather's arm. "I've got you, Poppa! I've got you!"

CHAPTER 32

I slid down the bank to the river's edge to help Rainbow in the deadly tug-of-war for her grandfather's life.

The huge alligator, its tail lashing the water into a froth, imbedded its long, snaggly teeth in Grandpoppa's leg, shaking its ugly head back and forth, trying to jar the old man loose from his precarious grasp. Leaves peeled away as the desperate man's grip stripped them from the branch.

"Allison, I'm slipping! I can't keep hold on Poppa!"

I grabbed a cane lying next to some orange day lilies on the riverbank, and with a whoop Tarzan would have loved, slid into the river, slapping the cane on the water and yelling at the top of my lungs. Charlie's bulbous black eye didn't even blink as I swung the cane with all my might and whopped him across his ugly long snout. Again I raised the metal cane and brought it crashing down, this time right across his eye.

He only renewed his effort to shake Poppa loose from the tree. Blood flowed from the old man's leg, staining the river a deep crimson. Rainbow, in the river up to her waist now, clung to her grandfather, crying hysterically, screaming for help.

Again and again I whaled at the beast with the metal rod until my arms ached from the effort. Charlie seemed impervious, never loosening his death grip on the bloodied leg. Rainbow sobbed Poppa's name over and over. The old man's grasp on the branch had stripped everything off to the very end. There seemed nothing left to grip.

Suddenly a voice shouted from the bank above us, and another joined in. Two men slid down the grass, grabbing Rainbow and her grandfather. Three more men appeared. One grasped me around the waist and tossed me out of the river onto the bank, while two plunged into the water with long, thick branches they'd broken from the tree.

They beat the water and the alligator. Someone wrested the cane from my tired hand and thrust it into the mouth of the gator, then twisted. I saw at least one tooth go flying before the beast loosed his grip on the old man's leg and slid down into the water, leaving a v-shaped ripple on the gilded river.

One of the men ran to call 911. Another pulled his shirt off and wrapped it around Poppa's leg to stem the bleeding. I couldn't move. I lay on the grassy bank, muddy, wet, and shocked by the sudden realization that I'd actually gotten into the water with an alligator and attacked it with an old man's cane.

Rainbow held her grandfather's head in her lap, wetting his gray-bearded face with her tears, sobbing inconsolably while he stroked her hair and tried to shush her.

"Oh, Poppa, Poppa. I love you. Don't die," she crooned over and over, wiping his face, then wetting it with more tears. "We beat Charlie. We cheated him. He didn't get you, like he did Daddy."

A tall, thin, dark-haired woman bearing a striking resemblance to Rainbow appeared at the top of the riverbank.

"Rainbow?"

That one word, spoken so quietly I might not have heard it if I hadn't watched the woman utter it, brought Rainbow out of her hysteria. She looked up at the woman, wiped away the tears still streaming down her cheeks, and sat still as a stick.

I glanced at the newcomer, then back at Rainbow. No one moved. Even the Spanish moss dripping from the tree above us stopped its swaying. The whole world seemed on hold while these two assessed each other.

"Momma?" Rainbow breathed the word into the stillness. It seemed a question, an invitation, an offering, a flag of peace, a testing of the waters, all in one quiet whisper.

The woman flew down the bank, fell to her knees, and enveloped her daughter in her arms, rocking back and forth, oblivious to the old man's head bobbing back and forth between them. The third man, kneeling next to Poppa, gently slid him from Rainbow's lap, supporting the injured man in his arms.

Rainbow's mother held her daughter away from her. "Let me see you. Why didn't you tell me you were coming? How'd you get here? When?" Then she hugged her child again in a joyful embrace.

Time for me to disappear. Poppa appeared none the worse for his injuries, though it would probably require several stitches to sew him back up; but the old man looked like a rather hearty specimen. He could probably handle the shock to his system, especially with loving care from Rainbow and her mother.

I hurried to the car, grabbed my Biltmore bag, and ducked into the tourist rest room to change into dry clothes. My wardrobe choices had diminished drastically. Rainbow wore my black reversible dress, which had given me two different looks. My white sweater and denim skirt were muddy, smelly, and soaking wet. That left only the snug-fitting jeans and T-shirt I'd grabbed in Marshall's. And soggy sandals.

Between dipping arms and legs in the sink and wet paper towels, I managed to leave the mud behind. Thank heaven I'd grabbed a spare set of underclothes before I left the house when this nightmare began. Fairly presentable, I hurried back to the car.

The ambulance had arrived, attendants had Poppa in the back, and Rainbow's mother clung to her hand as she boarded to go to the hospital with her father. "You'll stay here? You'll be here when I get back? Promise?" Worry, evident in her voice, as well as love and concern for her daughter, were mirrored in dark, expressive eyes much like Rainbow's.

"I promise. I'm not going anywhere anymore, Momma." Rainbow waved good-bye as the door shut and the ambulance pulled down the tree-shaded lane.

Tossing my bag into the backseat, I looked at Rainbow halfway across the parking lot, no longer resembling a lost child. "You'd better get into some dry clothes."

"I'm going to, like, right now. If you'll wait, you can take your dress." She hurried across the parking lot, peeling it over her head as she came. Her arms and legs, as well as her tube top and mini-skirt, were as mud-streaked as the dress. "Thanks, Allison," she added. "You didn't have to do this. I know I was, like, a lot of trouble."

"As long as you got something good out of it, it was worth it." I took the proffered dress and gave Rainbow a quick hug. "You'll be okay now?"

She nodded, her eyes tearing up. "I thought about what you said—your question. What did I want to be? What would I love doing? I want to stay right here on the plantation and learn how to be a gardener. You know, a . . . ." Her voice trailed off as she tried to find the word she needed.

"A horticulturist?"

"That's it. I've always wanted to do some really neat things here. If I learn how, Magnolia Plantation can have the most beautiful gardens, like, in the whole world." Her enthusiasm made her dark eyes sparkle as nothing yet had.

"Then do it. I'd love to have you show me the rest of the plantation's gardens, but I don't dare stay any longer. Can I come back someday and have you show me around?"

"Yeah, I'd really love that."

I hurried to my car and left without having seen the beauty a brochure I'd spotted in the rest room called "The South's Complete Plantation Experience!" This was my second time in Charleston—and once again I hadn't even set foot inside the city touted as one of America's most beautiful.

That notion, coupled with what the next several hours might bring, plunged me into dark depression. I hated being dirty. I hated being on the run. I hated being afraid for my life—and for my husband's safety. I hated having Bart on the other side of the world all the time. In short, I hated this lifestyle. Whatever possessed me to think I could be an Interpol agent?

Speeding down the road Rainbow said connected with Highway 17, I felt self-pity seeping through me like the mist creeping through the ancient oak trees edging the road. Why did I have to end up with this stupid jade lion? Why didn't Bart send someone who spoke English so Alma could have followed Bart's instructions? At least then I could have just gotten lost somewhere, and Raven couldn't have followed me twenty-five hundred miles across the United States.

Why me? Why? Why? Why?

Why not? a little voice asked.

"Go away. I don't want to hear anything you have to say."

You're tired. You're hungry. You're scared. You're all alone. It's natural to feel negative at times like this.

"I don't like 'times like this.' I don't like anything about this situation."

Come on. Where's that Pollyanna persona? It wouldn't hurt to smile and show a little gratitude.

"Gratitude! I'm beginning to smell like a fishpond. I itch all over. One of the world's top assassins is on my tail. And it's beginning to rain again. Stupid weather. Just what do I have to be grateful for?"

For one thing, you're alive. And Raven is nowhere in sight. You're going to meet Matt in an hour, and in another twelve hours you can get rid of the lion and the microdot.

"Go away."

Aren't you glad you listened to me at the airport? Things turned out nicely for Rainbow, don't you think?

I relented a little. Yes, things had turned out nicely for Rainbow, and it hadn't cost me anything besides a little time to help her out. I checked the rearview mirror. And Raven—or Saucony—were conspicuously absent.

The depression abruptly disappeared, replaced by fear surging through me, sending goose bumps up and down my arms. Why were they absent?

Nothing had changed. Raven still wanted me and the jade lion and what it contained. So where were they? Short of the satellite dropping out of the sky, there wouldn't be anything to prevent them from their relentless pursuit. An accident? That would be too much to hope for. And the odds were about the same as my winning the lottery.

So. What happened to my pursuers?

I mentally catalogued all the possibilities, even stretching my imagination to include such fairy tales as the possibility that the contract had been canceled. Or maybe Saucony and Raven had argued over who got to do away with me, and ended up killing each other.

Sorry. Even for your vivid imagination, that's too far out.

"Please go away. Aren't you supposed to be an unobtrusive little thing that pricks and prods quietly?"

Ordinarily. But you've been too overwhelmed to hear me. I had to become intrusive to be heard. If you'd kept wallowing in self-pity, your senses would have been totally dulled to the danger you're in.

A sobering thought. Right on the money, too. So why *had* my pursuers disappeared? And where were they? I had no doubt they knew what I had in my possession; Raven had said as much in the library. And the closer to Atlanta I got, the more worrisome it should be for them. They'd want to stop me well before I neared the city and the CDC.

Prickles of prescience tingled up my arms. They *knew* I'd have to get the microdot to the Center for Disease Control in Atlanta. There were only so many roads from Charleston to Atlanta. They didn't have to follow me every minute. They simply had to plot my course via satellite and computer, then lie in wait somewhere along the road.

Switching on the overhead light, I held up the map to check my route. Three hundred and twenty miles to Atlanta from Charleston. Somewhere between here and the big city, someone waited for me. With that in mind, I'd better decide very carefully which of the half-dozen routes would be the busiest, the fastest, the safest—thus the least likely to provide a place for successful ambush.

I begged for some quick inspiration—some guidance on which would be the best route to take. Nothing came. I felt my prayers weren't getting past the thick cloud covering. Ironic. When I so desperately needed help, my prayers couldn't penetrate the heavens as easily as that satellite that kept me in constant danger. What was wrong? Why did I feel so alone? So abandoned?

Wasn't I worthy of guidance? Had I told so many lies that heavenly help was temporarily discontinued? Knowing what God thinks of liars, that wouldn't surprise me. But it had been "in the line of duty." Didn't that make a difference? It had been to save my life. Didn't that count for anything—or did every lie count the same? And against me? Depression darkened my mind and soul again.

The rain eased slightly. My headlights illuminated a sign: Gardens Corner—one mile. My turnoff to meet Matt. The thought of Matt's familiar face, his friendly smile, and cheerful, affectionate nature warmed my heart. A friend, an ally. A safe harbor, if only for a little while.

I turned right at the corner, then watched carefully for the turnoff to the ruins of Sheldon Church. Suddenly I was upon it. A bright red Jeep Cherokee and a teal sedan stood next to the fence. No parking lot, just a wide spot in the road. I could see a family with several children reading inscriptions on tombstones. No sign of Matt.

The rain had slackened to a drizzle now, but I grabbed my bag from the backseat to retrieve my umbrella, and brought the bag along. Matt might want to see the jade lion. Maybe even deliver it to the CDC himself! That thought brightened the dreary day considerably.

I left the car, locked it, and tried to dodge huge puddles on the packed dirt "parking area." Why bother? My sandals were already soaked from their dunking in the Ashley River.

A sweet, peaceful feeling enveloped me as I stepped onto the green, well-cared-for lawn. There were no sidewalks, not even a path worn in the grass leading to the ruins. Gray mist hung low in the massive oaks surrounding the red brick shell that remained of Sheldon Church. Four tall brick columns, which once had probably supported a portico and formed a porch in the front of the church, stood partially hidden in the mist.

The children quietly read names and dates from the gray marble tombstones, going as a group from one monument to the next. There was no running through the trees, no climbing on the marble sarcophagi. No loud calling to one another. The reverence invoked by these old ruins amazed me.

I looked for Matt inside the roofless church. It was empty. Walking back out through the huge arch that once must have contained front doors, I discovered a marble plaque:

Church of Prince William's Parish,
known as
SHELDON
Burned by the British army 1779
Rebuilt 1826
Burned by the Federal Army 1865

Had this church belonged to wealthy plantation owners? Or to the common people who worked the plantations? What sacrifices had they made to rebuild, only to have it burned again barely forty years later? War exacted such a terrible price on people.

An engine turned over, and the teal car pulled away. The family, quietly talking among themselves, headed for the Cherokee. Suddenly I was alone in the ruins, with only the ghosts of Sheldon Church for company. At least, I hoped there was no one else here. Except Matt. Where was he?

If he didn't show soon, I'd have to leave. I couldn't afford to hang around a deserted churchyard. Perfect place for an ambush.

I circled the ruins, watching for movement in the trees, feeling the fog deepen, creep closer, obscuring trees, enveloping columns and tombstones and even the stone sarcophagus nearest me. I shuddered. If it got any worse, I wouldn't be able to find my way back to my car. Silence, heavy as the fog, muffled every sound. If someone came up behind me, I wasn't sure I'd hear him.

I didn't. I felt his presence before I ever heard a sound. Whirling around, I came face to face with Matt Runyon as he stepped through one of the arched window frames.

"Matt!" I threw myself at him, hugging him around the neck until he should have hollered uncle. Instead, he held my shaking body in his arms, patted my back, and whispered over and over, "It's okay. It's okay."

I pulled away, suddenly embarrassed by my unprofessional conduct. As I opened my mouth to apologize, he put a finger to his lips. I shut my mouth and listened. I couldn't hear anything.

Taking my hand, he led me away from the ruins, away from the road, toward what I thought should be the trees behind the old church. The fog was so dense by now that I couldn't tell one direction from another.

We stopped, probably a hundred feet from the ruins, under the wide branches of an ancient, gnarled oak with Spanish moss dripping nearly to the ground. A perfect umbrella of green spread above and around, enclosing us in a protective shelter.

"Were you followed?" Matt whispered.

"I don't know. They've been everywhere I've been—turned up every time I tried to shake them. They could be right behind me—or waiting somewhere down the road."

"Then we'd better make this fast so you can get on the road again." He pulled a folded sheet of paper from his pocket.

Acute disappointment stabbed at my heart. I'd hoped he'd go with me, or take this horrible piece of jade and what it contained off my hands. My hopes were dashed with his quick instructions.

"The microdot goes to this man, and this man only. Don't wait for him more than hour. If he doesn't show up by that time, get out. Report to O'Hare immediately, whether or not you're able to deliver it. He'll give you instructions if the doctor doesn't come."

"You mean there's a chance I won't get rid of this in the morning?" I couldn't believe it. I didn't want to hear this. I wanted to be rid of this albatross as quickly as possible and be done with it.

"Anything can happen. Planes delayed. Accidents on the freeway. Let's just say, barring anything unforeseen, you'll be rid of it at 6 a.m. tomorrow morning. And hope it happens as planned."

"Amend that. Hope it happens according to *our* plans, not Raven's."

Suddenly a bullet whistled between us. Matt shoved me behind the tree as a second bullet tore into his shoulder. He flung himself against me, and we toppled to the ground as bullets splintered the tree, showering us with fragments of bark and leaves.

An explosion shuddered through the ground. I peeked around the tree. A dull red light glowed through the mist in the direction of the gate. My car. They'd just blown up my car.

CHAPTER 33

Matt grabbed his bleeding shoulder with one hand and pointed into the mist with the other. "Run!"

Scrambling for footing, I grabbed his arm, dragging him to his feet. Spurred on by shouts and footsteps pounding toward us, we raced in the direction he'd indicated, trying to keep the protection of the tree between us and the bullets that ripped at the wood and thudded into the ground around us.

As we raced through the fog, Matt jerked free, fumbling for his gun. He was right-handed. He'd taken the shot in his right shoulder, rendering that arm useless. But he needed his left hand to compress his wound.

I grabbed the gun from his hand and pushed him toward the thick undergrowth just ahead. Having the good sense not to argue with me, he stumbled across a small creek separating the lawn from the thicket and disappeared into the dusky darkness and deepening mist.

Suddenly the shooting stopped. I couldn't see them. They couldn't see me. They must be listening for us. I jumped the creek and plunged into the thicket as quietly as possible, hoping the wet ground would absorb my footfalls, hoping the fog would obscure sound and trail.

Brambles tore at my bag, my clothes, my skin. Not sure I was even heading in the right direction, I tried to the follow the path of least resistance, the thinnest part of the tangle of branches and vines. I should have caught up with Matt by now. I stopped, listening. All I could hear was my heart pounding wildly in my ears and my own rasping breath.

Then I heard voices behind me. And cursing. They'd crossed the creek and were thrashing noisily through the thicket, straight for me.

"This way, Alli." Matt's whisper came from the right. I veered in that direction, blindly navigating through ankle-deep puddles, Kudzu vines, briars and stickers, and Spanish moss that dangled like spiders' webs in my face.

"Here." His voice, faint but straight ahead, came as a guiding beacon in the ever-deepening gloom. With my gun hand held above my face, shielding my eyes from attacking branches, I headed for the familiar comfort of Matt's voice.

Suddenly I stumbled over something large, pliant, and frightening. Matt, crumpled against a tree, his legs spread across the opening in the vines, lay ominously still.

I dropped to my knees. "Matt," I whispered. No answer. "Matt." I shook him. Still no response. I pulled his jacket away from his shoulder. Blood pulsed from the bullet wound. Grabbing several sopping wet leaves from the nearest vine, I stuffed them inside his shirt against the jagged wound. I needed something to tie them in place.

Rummaging in my bag, the only thing I could find was the soggy black dress Rainbow had worn into the river. I twisted it a couple of times lengthwise, then looped it under Matt's arm and tied the ends together on top of his shoulder, tucking the hem and the neckline under the knot to apply pressure. Not wonderful, but the best I could do at the moment.

I felt for a pulse. Weak, but discernible. Now what? I'd never be able to carry him—surely couldn't drag him through this tangle of vines and thicket. But could we stay here?

I glanced around. It was nearly dark, made even more so by the low clouds and heavy mist. Maybe, just maybe, it might work. I pulled Matt around behind the old tree, under some heavy Kudzu vines. Quietly opening my umbrella, I covered him with it, then camouflaged the umbrella and the area with as many vines as I could soundlessly manipulate.

Voices came and went in the fog as I worked, sometimes frighteningly close, then moving away. But Raven wouldn't give up until he was certain we'd left the area—or he found us.

Rain filtered through the leaves overhead, slowly at first, then increased until the downpour drowned all other sound. My work finished, I crawled under the umbrella with Matt. I sat with my back to the massive oak tree and pulled his head and shoulders onto my lap, cradling him in my arms under the protective covering of umbrella and Kudzu. The gun I tucked in the pocket of my jeans, with the handle hanging out where it would be immediately accessible.

I felt for Matt's pulse again, found it a little stronger than before, and tried to check his wound without disturbing it. Unable to see anything, I slid my fingers gently under his jacket. Thanks to the umbrella and leather jacket, his shirt was dry, except for the sticky area around the hole in his flesh. But there didn't seem to be any fresh bleeding.

"Not bad for a green agent," Matt whispered.

"You're conscious!"

"No way would I miss being held in the arms of a beautiful woman. Have they gone?"

I bent to Matt's ear. "I don't know. I haven't heard anything from them in a while, but it's raining so hard they could be standing next to us and I wouldn't know it."

"We need to get out."

"Where to?"

He pulled my head down closer to his mouth. "Beaufort Island. You need to get me to the Marine base, to the hospital there. Then we'll work on getting you to Atlanta. That's one appointment you can't afford to miss."

"You have a car stashed somewhere nearby, I hope."

He didn't answer for a minute. "You don't happen to have a motorcycle license, do you?"

I straightened up and leaned my head against the tree. *Oh, no. Please, not a motorcycle.* Bending to whisper in his ear, I begged, "Tell me you're kidding. Please tell me you're kidding."

"No motorcycle license, huh?" I could hear the smile in his voice.

I took a deep breath. "My last experience involving a motorcycle also involved a tree. We aren't compatible."

"We'll worry about that later." Silence. Then, "What time is it? How long was I out?"

"Want me to strike a match and look at my watch?"

"Funny girl." He shifted, shifted again, then slid his arm under my hand that rested on his chest. "Feel my watch?"

I did.

"There's a button on the outside about two o'clock. Make sure you have the top button—two o'clock position. Push it."

"What happens if I get the wrong one?" I whispered.

"It's one of Bond's castoffs. Q didn't finish briefing me. I haven't dared try the rest."

"Funny man." Since I didn't know if he was pulling my leg, I made sure it was the top button before pushing it. The watch face, a soft blue, illuminated enough to read—7:45.

"We'd better get a move on." Matt started to get up.

"Wait," I whispered, grabbing his good shoulder. "What about Raven?"

"He's handicapped by the rain. We'll take advantage of it. Help me out of this tangle you've woven around us."

He had a point. If Raven couldn't find us because of the storm, now was the time to move. Besides, sitting on the wet ground in the downpour, even the umbrella couldn't keep us dry. I couldn't get much wetter.

I crawled out from under the umbrella, folded it, helped Matt to his feet, and we stood quietly in the dark, listening. All I could hear was the relentless pounding of the rain.

"Let me fix your arm so you don't start bleeding again as you move." Removing the dress I'd tied under his arm and around his shoulder, I fashioned a sling and secured it around his neck. I'd hoped to simply wrap his arm to his torso with the long dress to keep it from moving, but the dress wasn't long enough. Matt was bigger than he looked.

"Where's my gun?" he whispered.

"In my hand."

"Give it to me."

"No way. You take care of your shoulder. I'll take care of the gun."

"Allison . . ."

"Just get us out of here, Matt. Don't argue."

He didn't answer. Then, "Man, I hate this. Push the top button on the left side of my watch, will you?" He thrust his arm against me.

I fumbled down his sleeve to his wrist and felt for the top left button. A compass appeared on the blue dial.

"This way." He stepped away—and silently disappeared.

I turned in the direction the compass had pointed and walked right into him.

"Sorry. I can't see a thing," I whispered.

"Good. Neither can Raven. Hang on to my jacket."

I hitched my bag on my left shoulder and grabbed the bottom of Matt's leather jacket with my left hand, leaving my right hand free of any encumbrance but the gun. Not that I could see a target in the dark, but if Raven did suddenly appear, at least I'd be ready.

We stumbled through vines and brush, holes with water up to my knees, and waded rocky creek beds, stopping every few minutes for me to check the compass on Matt's watch. This wet jungle seemed never-ending. I pictured the map in my mind. We'd probably traipsed halfway to Gardens Corner by now. Maybe farther. At least the rain had slowed to a drizzle instead of a downpour.

Where had Matt left his transportation? And exactly what kind of wheels did he have? I shuddered at the thought of a motorcycle. Surely he'd been joking, pulling my chain. If not . . . well, I didn't want to think about it. I concentrated on something more pleasant. Physical discomfort.

My jeans, soaked and plastered to my body, began to chafe against my thighs. My feet were a mess. Sandals were no substitute for hiking boots. Acceptable for fording rivers and streams, maybe, but even then, I couldn't stand the thought of what I might have picked up as we squished through the mud. This was the South, after all. Famous for all sorts of lovely little creatures that . . .

Matt stopped abruptly. Peering over his shoulder, I saw a faint light straight ahead, flickering like a candle sputtering in the wind. He didn't move. I stepped silently to his side. He stood watching, hardly breathing. I couldn't see his face, but tension radiated from his taut body like a hot California sun. I caught the vibes, and they weren't good.

He reached for me, found my arm, and ran his hand down it toward the gun. I pulled it away and put my mouth next to his ear. "I'm a crack shot, Matt. Trust me here."

I knew I asked a lot. No agent, man or woman, wants to depend on anyone else for his life, even another agent. But it was especially hard for a man to put his life in the hands of a woman he'd never worked with before—to depend on someone whose qualifications might look good on paper, but whose reactions and skill were personally unknown to him.

Matt put my hand to his cheek and nodded, indicating we'd communicate with signals, not chancing whispers. Still holding my hand in his left hand, he held two fingers against my palm and tapped it, then rested his hand in mine. His two fingers formed a "V." What did a "V" mean? He read my hesitation as not understanding. Smart guy.

He touched my outstretched palm twice. Two. Two what? I gazed toward the flickering light as I tried to puzzle out his meaning. The light had disappeared. We were again surrounded by total darkness.

Then another light flickered. Even in the rain I could smell the cigarette smoke. That was a lighter flickering. Two men. Two men smoking, waiting for us to come out of the woods.

I brought Matt's hand to my face and nodded. He grasped my hand, held it against me, then pointed my arm to the right. Then he pulled my hand to his chest and pointed left. I put his hand against my cheek so he could feel my nodded acknowledgment of his communication.

Leaning against me, he bent to the ground. As he straightened, I heard a soft metallic click. The sound of a switchblade opening. I was relieved he was armed, that he wasn't totally helpless with only one good arm, and weakened from loss of blood.

As he moved away from me, I felt a sudden sense of abandonment, of being alone again, left once more to my own devices. I didn't like the feeling. I'd pressured my father to let me become a fully trained Interpol agent so I could work with Bart. Not with another agent. Not alone. My career with Anastasia wasn't meant to be the solo job it had turned out to be.

Time to focus. To concentrate. Two men waiting for me. It won't be Raven—he'll be warm and dry somewhere—but it will be his men. Possibly Saucony. The man with a hole in the back of his hand. The man who'd like to wring my neck—or worse.

I reached out in the darkness and felt for Matt's leather jacket, found it, and kept pace with him as we crept toward the unsuspecting assassins silently smoking only a few feet from us. The glow of their cigarettes became our beacon, our homing device. They stood about three feet apart, one on either side of what I suddenly realized was a trail. I'd been so intent on my misery, I hadn't noticed we were no longer fighting bushes and vines.

When we were five feet from them, Matt stopped. I knew the routine. At the count of three we'd each go for our man. I felt for the nearest tree, found it, silently deposited my bag of precious cargo behind it, and returned to Matt's side. He held out his hand, waiting for me to take it. I found it, expecting his count, but instead he wrote something in my palm with his finger. He raised his finger, then repeated the action.

Two zero. Twenty. I repeated the number in his palm. He stretched out his hand again. I covered it with mine. I felt one finger raise, then the second, and the third.

This was it. I took a deep breath and felt Matt do the same as we moved away from each other and toward our target, counting silently to twenty. On fifteen I'd managed to get behind my man, sixteen, seventeen, in place, eighteen, I raised the gun high overhead, nineteen, twenty. I brought it down hard, just as the man flipped his cigarette and shifted.

I waited to hear him collapse on the ground. He didn't. I caught a couple of halting steps—he was staggering. I knew when he straightened and turned toward me. I blocked out the string of oaths he let loose. Saucony! I'd recognize that voice anywhere. Thank heaven it was pitch black. I couldn't see the murder I knew would be in his eye, and he couldn't see me.

I heard him stumbling toward me, heard his big hands tearing at vines, shredding off leaves, groping in the dark for me. He was hurt, not moving quickly, steadily, quietly as I'd expected. I stepped out of his path, waited for him to get abreast of me, then swung the gun again. This time he went down. All the way down. He didn't move.

I rushed to the path and bumped into Matt's leather jacket. "Matt?" I whispered.

"You okay?" he asked.

I threw my arms around him and hugged him tight.

"We've got to stop meeting like this," he said quietly in my ear as he patted my back. "What if your husband catches us?"

"I'm so glad you're okay," I whispered, still clinging to his neck. "And Bart would hug you just like I did, you old tease."

"Ouch. Don't call me old," he said softly. "And watch the shoulder. Come on. Let's get out of here. But be careful and be quiet. There could be more waiting ahead."

I grabbed the tail of Matt's jacket again and let him lead us down the path. I'd have to remember to ask him how he could find his way so well in the dark

The bag! I'd forgotten the Biltmore bag and its precious contents—the jade lion and the invaluable formula! All my money—ID—disguises. Everything in the world I needed right now I'd left somewhere back there on the trail. In the dark.

CHAPTER 34

I tugged sharply on Matt's jacket. "I left the bag!"

Not waiting for reaction or instruction, I wheeled around and headed back down the narrow trail. How would I find the right tree in the dark? There were hundreds lining the path. I didn't even know how far we'd come—a couple of hundred feet? Half a mile?

I hurried as fast as I dared in the dark, one hand still clutching Matt's gun, the other outstretched to protect me from walking into a tree. Unfortunately, that didn't prevent me from tripping over whatever lay across the narrow trail. As I went down hard on all fours, the gun skittered down the muddy path, out of reach.

I reached back to see what I'd tripped over and touched wet jeans covering a human leg. *Or subhuman as the case may be,* I thought as my mouth suddenly went dry, wondering if it was Saucony or the man Matt had taken care of.

My heart thumped wildly, loud enough to wake the dead—or the unconscious. I started to chastise myself for having to come back into the arms of the enemy, then stopped.

Focus. Find the gun. Find the bag. Flee.

Moving away from the body, I stretched out in the mud, feeling ahead of where I thought I'd landed to where the gun must have slid. It shouldn't have been hard to find on the two-foot-wide trail. But it wasn't there.

I covered the area again, this time reaching a foot or more into the grass on both sides of the trail. No gun. I backtracked, beginning at the legs of the man stretched across the path, working my way through the mud. If I had my bag, I had a penlight in my purse. But

I didn't dare leave Matt's gun to go search for the bag. If I left this area now, I'd never find it again, even with the legs as a guide.

Suddenly a low moan came from somewhere to my left. Saucony! Recovering from the knock on the head I'd given him. I had to get out of here!

I dropped to my stomach in the mud, spreading my arms wide across the trail, then fanned them up and down—like making snow angels. I inched forward, feeling my way up the trail, taking in the grass, weeds, vines, and brambles lining the path.

The moans increased in volume, in addition to rustling noises. Saucony was reviving. Where was the gun? Suddenly my fingers touched something hard, angular, cold. Success! I grabbed it, stood, and counted off about eight feet back up the trail.

Exploring behind every tree, I listened for Saucony to get to his feet. He'd probably have a flashlight, and he wouldn't be shy about shining it on his surroundings—which would include me if I didn't find that bag in a hurry and scram.

Where? Where had I left it? It had to be close. Moans turned to curses. From the noise, he must be trying to sit up. Hurry. Hurry. It had to be here. Right here. But where?

Thrashing and cursing blocked out every other sound. Any second I expected to find myself spotlighted in the middle of a flashlight beam. Hurt or not, Saucony was too much for me to handle, especially given the score I figured he'd want to settle with me.

You do have a gun, you know, a sarcastic little voice reminded me.

Right. As if I'd want to kill a man. I could have done that the first time. Go away.

Then I found it. The Biltmore bag! The jade lion. The whole reason for this fiasco. I grabbed it and whirled back down the trail, hoping to slip by Saucony before he became aware of me, before he was lucid enough to be a danger. Before he found a light.

No such luck. Just before I reached the man in the path, a sudden beam of light illuminated the trees above Saucony. I jumped out of the path behind a tree. The light played erratically around the area, revealing a glimpse of the man holding the light, still stretched out in the trees where he'd fallen when I clobbered him, then the man Matt had left sprawled on the trail.

Saucony held the beam on the man, only two feet from the tree behind which I hid. Another oath, then he struggled to his feet. The light shone on the ground, then flashed capriciously around the area while he pulled himself up with the help of a nearby tree. I hightailed it down the trail before he could concentrate the light again on the body of his buddy. Distance between us, as much as possible, as quickly as possible, became my main concern. This would be one dangerous foe from here on.

Now to find Matt. I should have counted steps when I left him. I gained a new appreciation for blind people as I fled down the muddy trail in total darkness. What must it be like to never be able to see where you were going? To never be able to see anything?

I slowed as I went, listening for any sound that might reveal Matt's presence. Then I had a terrible thought. What if he'd passed out again? What if he was lying somewhere off the trail, bleeding to death? I'd never find him in these miserable, wet, stygian conditions.

Forget being quiet. Forget Raven's henchmen. I had to find Matt.

"Matt?" I breathed in a stage whisper. "Matt, where are you?" I moved slowly down the trail, peering into the inky blackness. What I wouldn't give for a nice, bright, full moon right now. Then I remembered my penlight. Did I dare use it, with Saucony on the rampage a few hundred feet behind me? Did I dare *not* use it? I needed to find Matt so we could get out of here—so we could get him to the hospital.

I leaned against a tree, dropped the gun in my bag, and rummaged through it to find the penlight in the pocket of my leather purse.

"Alli?" The voice, weak, unmistakably Matt, came almost at my elbow.

"Matt! Where are you?"

Something touched me. I shuddered. Even *knowing* it was Matt, it frightened me to have a disembodied hand suddenly grip my arm.

"Did you find it?" His voice, strained and quiet, told me more than he'd ever verbalize about his condition.

"Yes. Where's our transportation?"

"Up the trail. I'll need your arm."

He slipped his left arm over my shoulder, and with my right arm around his waist, we stumbled down the muddy trail as quickly as his waning strength would move his legs.

Ahead, where the trees apparently ended, a few small lights glittered. Just before we reached the edge of the woods, Matt stopped.

"Lean me against this tree. The motorcycle's just behind it, covered with Kudzu."

"Matt, I hate motorcycles."

"Then you'd better start carrying me. If I don't get to a hospital pronto, you'll be burying me." The flat, forced voice told me he wasn't kidding.

Heart in my throat, I found the motorcycle. Thank heaven it wasn't a Harley. It was small enough for me to handle, but large enough to do the job. I pushed it onto the trail, stopped for Matt to get on the back, and as I glanced down the trail one last time before starting it, I saw a flash of light.

Saucony was on his feet. Probably raging mad, and moving this way.

"Saucony's coming. Should I start it now and vamoose, letting him know we're leaving on a motorcycle, or wheel it—"

"Start and go," Matt said, leaning all his weight against me.

"Do I need to tie you on?"

"Not if you hurry up and get out of here." He reached around me, turned the key and put my hand on the throttle. "Can you handle it?"

"Say your prayers." I did. This wasn't my thing. I hated motorcycles with a passion, mostly because I felt so out of control—and I hated not being in control of my life. Under normal circumstances, I'd do almost anything to steer clear of them. This, however, was definitely not normal circumstances. In fact, I wasn't sure what those were anymore, not having experienced "normal" for such a long time.

"Where are we going?" I said over my shoulder as I headed down the dirt road, through somebody's field, and toward the lights.

"Gardens Corner, up there. Then on 21 to Beaufort Island. Marine Base is just across the bridge."

"How far?"

"Fifteen, twenty miles."

We didn't talk again. I concentrated on dodging puddles on the muddy road, then navigating through the farmer's maze of barn and sheds. I found the highway, and hit the throttle. Matt's head lolled on my shoulder, and his grip loosened around my waist. Just what I'd need—to have him pass out, fall off, and be run over by a stupid car before I could get to him.

Please, Father, could I have a little heavenly help here? Even if You've left me on my own, don't desert Matt now. He's one of the good guys.

Maybe a Harley would have been better, I thought as we flew down the highway. *One with a windshield.* At least my hair was so short it didn't blow in my eyes. Then it started raining again, a soft, misty moisture that increased with each mile until I had to slow our speed considerably. That could give Raven and Saucony a chance to catch up. With each car approaching from behind, the tension heightened until my nerves were ready to snap.

To my great relief, the Marine Air Station materialized through the rain. That relief was complete when security even let us through the gate—which I wasn't at all sure would happen. One of the guards guided us to the hospital when I explained, not patiently, that it would be faster than sending an ambulance to fetch Matt.

The hole in his shoulder was repairable, the bullet had not done a tremendous amount of damage, and other than losing a lot of blood, Matt's prognosis appeared good. Finally I relaxed a little. My dear friend would live, be able to return to work fairly soon, and for the first time in days, I felt a modicum of safety. As long as I stayed on base, surrounded by marines, Raven couldn't get to me, could he?

I washed the first layer of mud off while they stitched Matt up. And picked off a dozen or more slimy, creepy leeches that had attached themselves to my feet and ankles as we waded through those swampy, muddy creeks. I shivered and shuddered each time I had to touch the repulsive little creatures. Where was Bart when I needed him? A thoughtful nurse suggested that I scrub those areas with antibacterial soap, available in the rest room, keep them clean, and watch them carefully for the next few days.

I'd just gotten one unpleasant task out of the way when another presented itself. Before Matt started coming out of the anesthetic, an intense vice commander of the base erupted on the scene, demanding to know who we were, what had happened, and why we'd chosen his particular base hospital to have the bullet removed. Since gunshot wounds are always investigated, he'd been informed and come personally for answers.

Unfortunately, Matt wasn't exactly coherent yet, so it fell to me to provide explanations. I gave him as much information as I felt comfortable revealing: Matt had been shot by men trying to stop me from delivering a vital formula to the CDC in Atlanta. The commander of the base was a friend of Matt's; they'd worked together on a couple of cases, and he would probably be able to finagle a military plane to get me to Atlanta. Which, of course, cocooned me in feelings of safety and comfort, emotions rarely experienced of late.

The vice commander—not too much taller than my five-feet-four inches, but with every muscle marine-toned—shot that balloon down immediately. "Captain Blevins is away, I'm in charge in his absence, and there will be no military aircraft used for civilian purposes." He wasn't even nice about it.

"Sir, I don't consider this a civilian purpose," I said quietly, fighting to stay composed in the face of this pompous little man brandishing his authority like a sword.

He snorted. "*You* don't consider? You have no say. This is a military installation. You are a civilian." He made it sound like a dirty word. He paused and glared, daring me to further oppose him. I bit my tongue to keep from blurting out what he could do with his attitude and authority, not to mention his base. Then he dropped a mini-bomb on my world.

"I'm placing you both under house arrest. You will remain at this hospital with Agent Runyon until we have a full rundown from headquarters on your activities with Interpol. You will not leave this facility until you have my approval. Is that clear?"

I was speechless. Could this arrogant, overbearing, self-important little man actually believe that he could keep me here? I had a formula to deliver that could save the lives of millions of people. Didn't he think that was more important than his autocratic hold on everything and everyone on base right now? Apparently not.

Then again, maybe being confined to base—and the safety it offered—might not be such a bad deal. I sighed. Except that I had to get that formula to Atlanta and to Dr. Svenson.

"Is that clear, Mrs. Allan, or whatever your name is?"

"I understand your command, sir." But just because I understood it didn't mean I had to obey it. This dictatorial marine wasn't my boss. I had my own orders to follow. As soon as he disappeared, so would I.

The two marines who accompanied the vice commander were ordered to stay with us until relieved of that duty. They were not to let us out of their sight without express permission from this czaristic little man who flaunted his authority like a matador flashing his cape in front of the bull. Then he stormed out of the room, leaving two smirking marines, one irate woman, and one ATF agent in a white fog of anesthetic.

Now what? I had to get to Atlanta. I didn't have time to wait for Captain Blevins to return and offer a military plane. That help might never materialize. I couldn't afford to wait and see.

"Matt. Matt! Can you hear me? Wake up, please. I need a little advice here." But Matt wasn't in any condition to offer advice. And if I waited for the anesthetic to wear off and he was coherent enough to help, would it then be too late?

Evaluating my situation, I glanced at the marines. I didn't think it would be too hard to slip away from them, but getting off base, renting a car, and actually arriving in Atlanta without Raven cutting me off along the way didn't seem as simple.

One of the marines, Crawford, shook his head. "I'm sure sorry, ma'am. Chance of anything good happening with the vice CO involved is zip. He's afraid it might affect his career." The second guard, Murphy, nodded his agreement at Crawford's assessment.

I walked to the rain-streaked window and stared out into the wet night, watching raindrops dance in puddles under the streetlight in the parking lot. "I know it didn't seem important to what's-his-name, but I've got to be in Atlanta at the Center for Disease Control tomorrow morning to meet the man who needs this formula." I turned back to the guards. "The Ebola virus is killing thousands of people a day in Africa, and unless Dr. Svenson can control it, there will be nothing to stop it from coming here."

Crawford and Murphy looked at each other, something unreadable passing between them. Murphy coughed. "Don't Interpol and the ATF carry a lot of weight? Exactly how much rank can you pull, ma'am?"

"Meaning?" I asked, puzzled.

Crawford stepped forward. "My girl's just getting off duty. We could smuggle you off base. I've got a speedboat. If you could guarantee I wouldn't be charged with going AWOL, I'll take you to Savannah. That might throw off the men on your tail."

"How long would that take? I have to be in Atlanta by five a.m." I pictured the map in my head. Charleston and Savannah were only about two hours apart in driving time. Beaufort Island was between them. But on a stormy night, I wasn't sure I wanted to trust any small boat on the ocean, even for a short trip.

"If we got things in motion right now, I could have you there by midnight. That would give you five hours to get to Atlanta—just about what it takes." The big blonde marine drew himself up to his full six-foot-plus height and flashed a wide smile. He certainly looked capable enough. He also appeared ready for an adventure and anxious for excitement.

I looked at Matt, still lost in an anesthetic fog. No help would be forthcoming from him. I was on my own again.

"Ma'am, get us both off and I'll ride shotgun," Murphy said.

I checked out the big African-American marine with the smile as wide as his partner's. Yes, I'd definitely feel safe with these two, but I wasn't keen about that boat trip in the dark.

"Say the word and we'll get started," Crawford urged.

"Where's your boat?" I asked.

"Lady's Island. I can call and have it ready to go when we arrive." Crawford's smile widened.

"How far is Lady's Island?" I still wasn't convinced the ocean route was the answer.

"On the other side of town. Fifteen minutes at most."

"You have a car to get us off base?" I asked.

He nodded.

I mentally ran through the scenario, trying to envision all the pitfalls, the least of which would be a very nasty encounter with the vice CO if we were caught before we got away. The worst I could come up with was an uncomfortable, dangerous couple of hours on the stormy sea. Nothing at all compared to facing Raven and Saucony.

"I'm sure we can get you off the hook with the base commander," I said slowly. "Maybe even get you nominated for a commendation for service above and beyond the call of duty. However, I'm not sure even Interpol and the entire Treasury Department can help you deal with a despotic boss who'll probably see this as mutiny against his orders, or dereliction of duty, or something equally as serious. And you'll be in jeopardy from the men chasing me."

"We'll handle it," the enthusiastic marines said simultaneously. The blonde one took in my appearance. "Including some clean clothes for you, ma'am. Give me twenty minutes."

"Okay, Crawford," I said, committing to the plan, even feeling a bit of enthusiasm myself. Was it the mention of clean clothes? "As soon as he's lucid, Matt Runyon can run interference with Captain Blevins. But from the impression I got of the vice CO, even an order from his commanding officer won't soothe his feelings at having his orders ignored or disobeyed, especially if you get patted on the back for it. Are you prepared to deal with that?"

They looked at each other, grinned, and nodded. "I'll be at the entrance in twenty minutes," Crawford said, and with a sharp salute slipped out of the room, leaving Murphy behind.

"Is this a good idea? A speedboat in the dark on the open ocean— in the rain?" I asked.

"If you can't trust the marines, who can you trust?" Murphy said with a wink.

"Good question. But it's not the marines I'm worried about it. It's that great big expanse of stormy sea that's got me concerned. Boats and water I'm used to. I grew up on the ocean. I also learned a healthy respect for it. That included knowing when *not* to be on it." But it seemed it was no longer optional. The plan had been put into operation.

"I need to make arrangements to have a rental car waiting in Savannah," I said, thinking out loud. "If you drop me at midnight, nothing will be open. In fact, nothing is probably open right now, except at the airport, and that's not a convenient transfer—from the waterfront to the airport."

"Mrs. Allan, I'm sure Crawford's bringing Janet's roommate to stay with Mr. Runyon while we're gone," Murphy said. "She could have Mr. Runyon make those connections for you while we're on our way to Savannah."

"And if he sleeps through our entire boat trip?" I looked at Matt, who was totally oblivious to his surroundings, and relived the uncertainty of the wisdom in making this trip.

"Then she'll have to get a few people out of bed and make sure you've got transportation by the time we arrive in Savannah." Murphy's confidence boosted mine.

"I guess if he can't make the arrangements, I'll just take a taxi to the airport and rent a car there." I didn't like that idea. That would give Raven too much time to track me. I needed to hit town and be gone before he could pinpoint my location. I didn't doubt that by now he waited outside the gate to the base. And Saucony would be with him. I wasn't sure which of the two I feared most at this point. Maybe a wild boat ride into the night wasn't such a bad idea after all.

Crawford showed up minutes later with a cute young female marine to stay with Matt. He'd be pleased to see her pretty face when he woke up, and that might distract him from worrying too much about me. We left instructions to pass along to Matt when he came out of the anesthesia, including our estimated time of arrival in Savannah and location where a car was to meet us. Then we hurried out into the misty night, where a car with the official Marine Corps seal on the side and lights on top awaited us. At the wheel of the security police vehicle was a dark-haired girl in a marine uniform.

Murphy opened the back door for me, then climbed in the other side. Crawford joined the woman in the front seat and introduced us. "Mrs. Allan, this is Janet, my fiancée. She'll be our partner in crime tonight." He grinned over the backseat as Janet nodded in the rearview mirror.

"They'll have the boat ready at the dock when we get there," Crawford continued. "I also ordered a couple of Ollie's specials. Figured you might be kind of hungry."

Another military police car suddenly joined us. Janet did a thumbs-up and pulled away from the hospital, with the second car falling in behind. "Just in case," Janet said, smiling. "Mrs. Allan, when we get to the gate, please duck. Maybe we can fake out the guys waiting for you."

Before we reached the gate I doubled over, out of sight of anyone watching cars leave the base. In the well-lit area, it would be easy to not only count heads in the car, but actually see faces if someone watched with binoculars.

Several blocks from the base, I straightened up. The other military police car, still behind us, pulled over to the side of the road and stopped.

Janet, watching in the rearview mirror, sped up. "Get down again, please, Mrs. Allan," she instructed. "We've got company." Car lights filled the interior of our car. Someone was right on the bumper.

CHAPTER 35

"I think your friends found you," Crawford noted. Through the space between the seats, I saw the big Marine unholster his gun. "Exactly how dedicated are they to doing away with you?" he asked over his shoulder.

"Extremely. The only consolation—the only safety I have—is that they need, intact, this very precious item I'm carrying, so they can't just run me off into the river or blow up my car with me in it. Otherwise, I'm sure they'd have collected their money long before now."

The car's headlights were hidden, so close was their car to ours. Then it smacked our bumper, nudging us toward the edge of the road. Janet picked up her radio with one hand while she tried to keep the car on the pavement with the other. As she accelerated, distancing us slightly from our attackers, she spoke calmly into the radio. "Okay, Henry, move back in. Do your thing. And detain them for at least thirty minutes so we can get these people safely on their way out of town."

Before she'd put down the radio, a siren wailed behind us. Henry, apparently in the other military police vehicle that had lagged behind to lay the trap, moved in fast. With a screech of tires, our pursuers swerved off the road onto a side street. I raised up in time to see Henry's lights flashing right behind them.

Just adding more fuel to the fire. There was no way I'd survive another encounter with Saucony and Raven. I'd caused them far too much trouble. They must both be so tired of this ridiculous chase that was supposed to take only a few hours, and so angry at this little troublemaker named Allison Allan, that it could only be resolved one way—them or me.

I shuddered at the thought. I hated confrontations. I hated knowing what this would all boil down to in the end. And hated knowing there wasn't a thing I could do but face the music when the final dance was played sometime in the next few hours.

Crawford was right. It didn't take long at all to drive through Beaufort. We crossed a long bridge to Lady's Island, and pulled up at a restaurant named Ollie's On The Bay, set back under huge old oak trees dripping with Spanish moss.

Murphy ran inside to retrieve our food while Crawford hustled us around behind the restaurant to a small dock anchoring a dozen or more boats. Most were old fishing boats, so the bright red racing boat stood out conspicuously.

Janet handed me a shopping bag. "These may not be a perfect fit, but they'll be an improvement over your muddy things, and much more comfortable. Jump in the boat and change. I'll keep Crawford busy for a minute."

She and Crawford pored over a map on the gleaming prow of the candy-apple red boat, whose metallic finish gleamed in the lights from restaurant and dock. It must have had two dozen coats of lacquer to shine like that.

Janet was a size or so larger than me, so the jeans and sweatshirt were comfortably roomy—much better than the ones I'd grabbed off the rack at Marshall's in Long Beach. The tennis shoes, with the aid of the thick socks she brought, almost fit. What a relief to be in clean clothes and warm, dry shoes instead of soggy sandals.

"Thanks, Janet. Give me your address, and I'll get these back to you as soon as my life becomes normal again."

She waved her hand. "Don't worry about it. They're just some old things I've had in the back of my closet. I'm actually glad to put them to use."

I could smell Murphy's bundle before I saw him coming. It smelled heavenly. When had I eaten last? With Rainbow on our way to Charleston? Murphy stowed three large white Styrofoam containers under the seat. The engine roared, drowning out all attempts at farewells.

While Crawford backed the boat out of the slip, Murphy handed me my dinner, directing me toward a cozy corner just under the dash, where they'd piled several blankets. "I suggest as soon as you finish your meal, you curl up and get whatever sleep you can between here and Savannah. You're lookin' at a four- to five-hour drive to Atlanta once we get you to a car."

I turned and waved at Janet as we nosed out into the Coosaw River, feeling a momentary jab of loneliness. *How can you be lonely in a little boat with two big, strapping marines?* I thought, shaking off the melancholy. *Only nine more hours, more or less, and this will all be over, one way or the other. You can stand on your head for nine hours, Allison Allan. Get a grip.*

I tucked my Biltmore Hotel bag up under the dash. Then, snuggling on the floor out of the wind, I opened the Styrofoam container and studied the food that smelled so wonderful. I did like to know what I was eating before I put it in my mouth. Murphy must have read my mind. He leaned over, pointing to the box. "Seafood platter. Little of everything. Calabas shrimp, buttermilk flounder, crab, scallops, and the most delicious crab cake you'll ever eat."

"Thanks, Murphy. Right now I could eat an alligator, I'm so hungry."

"Think you might have a little bit of that, too, if Crawford ordered the usual. Deep-fried strips. Pretty tasty."

I'd certainly rather be eating an alligator than the other way around. I wondered how Rainbow's grandfather fared, and whether or not Charlie would pay for this latest attack. Personally, I'd have destroyed him after he'd killed Rainbow's father. I wouldn't have waited for his second attempt to have the family for dinner.

Murphy was right. The crab cake was the best I'd ever eaten, the flounder was delicious, the Calabas shrimp were what I called popcorn shrimp, and I did find some little deep-fried strips that must have been alligator. I enjoyed every bite. Murphy passed me a can of soda to wash it down with, then collected my empty containers.

We were winding between islands, not on the open sea yet. Not full throttle. I curled up on the blankets, pulled a couple over me, and decided it was time I left things in the able hands of the marines and my guardian angels. If they couldn't handle it, who could?

Exhaustion immediately gave way to sleep. I think I must have been aware of the increased roar of the engine as Crawford opened up the throttle, aware of the boat bouncing over the tops of the waves, thawumping down hard before becoming airborne again, but I didn't even open my eyes to check our location. I'd seen Hilton Head Island on the map, and knew we had to pass that before we reached Savannah. One more famous place I'd miss seeing, and I didn't even care.

I awoke to liquid dripping on my head from the dash above me. Icy cold water ran down my neck and jolted me upright. It was raining—a soft, misty dampness that seeped in and around and through everything. I looked over the edge of the boat and was surprised to see lights on both sides of us—we were on a river. No wonder I was getting soaked. No speed, no wind to blow the rain over the top of the windshield.

"Welcome to Savannah, Mrs. Allan," Murphy grinned.

"Already?"

"We'll just make your midnight rendezvous. Myra called from the hospital. Runyon finally woke up—said to deliver you to the Waterfront Park, and his men would meet you by the Old Cotton Exchange. That should be it right up there."

Peering through the mist, I could just make out the lights along the Park. As Crawford throttled down, I saw the Waving Girl Statue, then the old brick and stone of the buildings along River Street and Factor's Walk.

Crawford eased the boat against Waterfront Park, and Murphy jumped out to hold it while Crawford searched the nearly deserted plaza, then returned to the boat. Two men materialized out of the shadows and hurried toward us. Crawford's gun suddenly appeared in his hand. I felt no shame in hiding behind the big marine. I was tired of being chased and shot at, and leery of all strangers.

Satisfied with their identification and assured that they were, indeed, Matt Runyon's ATF men, Crawford handed me, then my bag, up to Murphy on the plaza. I gave Crawford a mock salute and shook the big, black marine's hand. "Thanks, guys. I hope the next leg of this operation is as easy as you made the last one. Kind of wish you were going along with me."

"Ma'am, we need to get you out of Savannah as soon as possible," one of the men said, motioning toward a car.

Murphy jumped back into the gleaming red racing boat, and both marines turned and waved as they headed toward the mouth of the Savannah River. I allowed myself to be led to the dark sedan waiting in the shadows and put in the passenger seat. Agent Ledford settled behind the wheel. "I'll drive you out to I-16, and then you can take it from there, Mrs. Allan."

"Actually, I can drive myself from here. I really don't need . . ."

"Runyon specified that we needed to get you out of town before we turned you loose." Stopping at a red light, Ledford turned toward me with a puzzled look. "Don't know what you did, or who you did it to, but it musta' been a real doozy. We don't get calls like this very often."

"Like what?" I asked, not sure exactly what he was talking about.

"We were to drop everything else we were working on, meet you with a car, hustle you out of town, and then forget we ever saw you." He pulled away from the light, checking in the rearview mirror to make sure his buddy in the other car was still with us. "Care to enlighten me a little?"

"Guess if you'd had a need to know, Matt would have told you." I leaned my head back on the seat and sighed. Mystery. Intrigue. I'd always loved it—had thrived on the excitement of ferreting out the secrets, discovering the clues, puzzling out the solutions. But at this point, I'd had my fill.

If I ever got caught up in something like this again, I needed my head examined. Better yet, I needed to be locked away so I wouldn't be a danger to myself or anyone else. I'd had enough of mystery, intrigue, terrorists, jade lions, microdots, assassins, and everything that had anything to do with any of them. Enough to last two or three lifetimes. I'd resign from Anastasia as soon as I saw my father again.

"Here we are," Agent Ledford declared, stopping the car in the parking lot of a root beer and ice cream parlor. The other car pulled directly behind us and stopped. "There's the on-ramp for I-16. Weather report says you'll have rain on and off all the way to Atlanta, with patches of fog, so drive carefully. Need anything? Drink? Snack? Munchies to keep you awake?"

"Why are you supposed to forget you've ever seen me?" His comment had puzzled me when he made it, but now it worried me. "Did Matt actually say that? In those words?"

Ledford's hand hovered above the door handle. He glanced at me, his expression guarded, eyes shadowed by his hat brim. "Don't recall if he used those exact words, but that was the gist of the message. Do everything we could to get you safely on your way, then go about our business as if you'd never been here."

"You don't get an order like that every day, do you? Really makes you curious when you hear something like that, doesn't it?" I watched a slow smile creep across his face.

"Especially from someone like Runyon. Now there's a down-to-earth, by-the-book guy, and when he runs something like this by you, calling in all his favors, you just gotta wonder what the real story is. And who the lady really is. Then she turns out to be a real looker who shows up out of the night in a red racing boat with salt-and-pepper bookends that look like defensive tackles. Yeah, Runyon will have some heavy explaining to do the next time I see him."

"Let's just hope you don't hear anything about it—until Matt can explain it. It's not the kind of thing we want popping up in tomorrow's *Atlanta Journal Constitution*, is it?" With that, I opened my door and walked around to slide into the now empty driver's seat. "Thank you, Mr. Ledford. What you've done tonight made a great contribution to the survival of the world. Now if I can do my part successfully, we'll all sleep better tomorrow night."

I buckled my seat belt, knowing Ledford watched every move I made, knowing I'd done what no agent in his right mind would ever do, should ever do. I'd piqued his curiosity beyond all forgetting. This would bug him until he had to know what it was all about. Ledford wouldn't give Matt an hour's rest until he had the whole story.

Not that I didn't trust Matt. I did. With all my heart. But that bit about "forget you ever saw her" didn't sit well with me. I didn't want to be forgotten. If something happened to me between here and Atlanta, I wanted everyone in the world to know about it. I didn't want to end up in a swamp somewhere, with no one having any idea where to start looking for me.

Life was too uncertain for those who ran in my circle. Something unexpected could happen to Matt before he got home tonight. My two marines, my "salt-and-pepper bookends," might never hear any more of this, and basically only Matt knew where they'd taken me. I wanted these two agents to remember me, to remember everything they could about me: the time they dropped me off, where they left me, what kind of car I drove, what I wore, what I carried. I wanted to leave a starting place for a search, if it came to that.

I rolled down my window. "Ledford." He bent down. "If I don't show up at the Center for Disease Control in Atlanta by 6 a.m., you may have been the last good guy to see me alive. Put that in your pipe and smoke it. Sleep well. And thanks for everything."

I rolled up my window and pulled away, leaving Ledford standing in the middle of the parking lot, staring after me. A dirty trick to play on the poor guy—but a sure way to leave an indelible impression.

Traffic was light on rain-slick I-16 leaving Savannah. A big green mileage sign flashed by: 252 miles to Atlanta. The digital clock glowed one minute after midnight. Five hours to reach Atlanta, find the CDC, reconnoiter the area, and devise a plan to deliver the microdot to the good doctor who was supposedly blown to bits earlier this week. And elude Raven and Saucony in the process.

Piece of cake.

CHAPTER 36

I set the cruise control on sixty, slower than I'd prefer driving on the Interstate, but as fast as present road conditions allowed. Then I concentrated on Raven. With the help of the ATF and the marines, I'd managed to elude Raven and Saucony one more time. Now I was on my own.

I'd have a head start on Raven, but just how much of one, and how long I could maintain it, was anybody's guess. Unless someone shut down the satellite that continued to feed my location to Raven, he'd be aware of my arrival in Savannah, and now my exit. He'd know I was on my way to Atlanta, and being acutely aware of my cargo, he'd also know my destination.

Did that mean I wouldn't have to worry about them until I arrived at the Center for Disease Control? Would they simply go directly to the CDC and wait for me to show up? Or would they try to intercept me and retrieve the jade lion with its invaluable microdot?

What would I do if I were Raven?

Make sure Allison Allan never arrived in Atlanta. An ambush somewhere between here and there would be the perfect solution. It would be too risky to wait. They didn't know what kind of reception might be waiting for me in Atlanta.

For that matter, neither did I. None at all, I suspected. But Raven might not know that. It was to his advantage to get the jade lion and the microdot as soon as possible, and exterminate me before any of us got anywhere near the big city.

So how would he catch up to me? Or was he already ahead of me? In the time it had taken us to get to Savannah by water, he could have chartered a private plane, flown to Savannah, and rented a car. He could be anywhere down the road in front of me—or behind me.

Or he could have sent Saucony ahead to set up an ambush and he'd stayed behind me, or vice versa. Yes. That was the most likely. I wasn't confident the marines had been able to hold them in Beaufort, not sure they'd even caught them. I couldn't count on that. Or that the marines had been able to delay them significantly.

I peered through the darkness, through the rain-streaked windshield at the long stretch of wet pavement ahead. They were out there somewhere. Waiting for me. Waiting with some kind of trap. Just waiting for me to drive right into their hands.

So what are you going to do about it, lady? You have no gun, no protection, no idea where they are or what they'll try. Just what are you going to do?

Forewarned is forearmed. I needed to know exactly what lay between here and Atlanta. Not much, if I remembered right. First I needed a map. My other one went up in flames with my car at Sheldon Church.

I saw a light ahead—a truck stop. Perfect. I pulled off the Interstate, grabbed the Biltmore Bag, and ran through the mist to the brightly lit café, rest room, gas station, and shower combination. First I hit the rest room; then, wandering the aisles, I checked the shelves for anything I could use for protection, anything that could be turned into a weapon.

When I checked out, my arsenal included half a dozen portable fire extinguishers designed especially for automobiles and trucks, a half-dozen plastic bottles of motor oil, a map of Georgia, and a detailed map of Atlanta.

I stocked up on goodies—ice-cold soda and crunchy munchies to keep me awake and alert. Then I consulted the map in the bright interior of the store, noting only one city of any size between here and Atlanta—Macon—and it looked like I would actually bypass that. Lots of lonely, open highway. Lots of opportunity for Raven and crew.

Waiting for a couple of truckers to pay their bill, I tagged along behind them with my bundles so I didn't make an easy target leaving the lighted area. My skin prickled at the thought of guns pointed at me, eyes watching that I couldn't see. I hit the remote button on the car keys and unlocked the doors halfway across the parking lot, ran the rest of the way, and tossed my parcels in the passenger seat.

I locked the doors and wasted no time getting out of there and back on the highway. The rain had let up a little, becoming nothing more than a fine mist, so I set the cruise control at seventy-five and put the "leetle gray cells" to work imagining every trap Raven could possibly devise—and how I could thwart each of them.

Traffic had been light, only an occasional car or truck, and most were moving as fast as weather conditions allowed. Some idiots never paid attention to either traffic or safety rules, thus I wasn't surprised to see a mini-van tailgating a sedan just ahead of me.

But there appeared to be no reason for the van to be so close to the car. There was no other traffic around. This was a four-lane divided highway. Plenty of room to pass. Plenty of opportunity. Must be somebody playing dangerous games.

I couldn't see the driver of the van as I passed, nor could I tell how many passengers there might be with him, but the van's head-lights illuminated the interior of the sedan, and I could clearly see the frightened expression of the woman driving it. She was alone in the car, and from the look on her face, she must have been terrified out of her wits.

Suddenly the van whipped around the car and sped up, catching me in an instant. Now it hung on *my* bumper, driving so close it would have run into me if I'd touched my brakes. I accelerated. The van accelerated. I eased off the gas pedal. The van slowed, exactly matching my speed.

Again I slammed my foot on the gas pedal. I watched with trepidation as the speedometer clocked seventy, seventy-five, eighty, eighty-five miles per hour. The van stayed with me, never getting a full car length behind me, and usually so near I couldn't see its headlights.

Was this Saucony? Raven wouldn't play like this. He'd determine identity, close in for the kill, get his microdot, and vanish. Saucony would want revenge. He'd taunt and torment me before he exacted that vengeance.

There was no other traffic on our side of the freeway. The other car, the sedan that looked like mine, had disappeared somewhere in the darkness behind us. It was just me and the madman at the wheel of the van. I let up off the gas again and caught a frightened breath as I felt the van bump me slightly before it backed off.

I grabbed a couple of the bottles of motor oil, propped them upright between my legs, and removed the tops. Rolling down my window, I jammed the gas pedal to the floor. The car leapt ahead, leaving a momentary gap between me and the van. I stuck the bottles of oil out the window and turned them upside down, weaving back and forth across both lanes of the freeway, dumping the oil on the wet pavement as I went.

Suddenly the van hit the oil on the highway and careened off the road. Lights flashed on the trees at the edge of the road, then back across the pavement. I didn't wait around to see what happened. If it was Saucony, I didn't want to be anywhere near if he recovered and got his vehicle back on the road. If it wasn't, I didn't need to be in the vicinity of a madman.

When I could no longer see lights of any kind in my rearview mirror, I slowed to a manageable speed while my heart slowed to a reasonable beat. As the adrenaline rush dissipated, I melted into my seat, totally spent, bones like limp linguini. Thank heaven for cruise control, or I'd have had to pull over and wait until I had some life back in my quivering legs.

A snack. A sugar fix. Some quick energy. I needed something. I drank a long gulp of soda, felt for the snacks I'd bought, and found a candy bar. A Baby Ruth. Peanuts and chocolate and caramel and heaven-sent goodness. Who said comfort didn't come in a wrapper?

I savored every bite, and by the time I'd finished, the world didn't seem like such a horrid place after all. I'd survived sharks, hurricanes, volcanoes, assassins' bullets, planes being blown almost out from under me. You name it, it had nearly got me. But I'd survived. And I would this time.

With a little help from my guardian angels.

I wished I knew where Raven was, what he was plotting. I wished I knew the layout of the CDC. I wished I could make plans ahead of time and have everything fall into place. Actually, I just wished I felt a little more in control. Even another Baby Ruth wouldn't give me that.

Where was the trap, the ambush, any sign of Raven or Saucony? My eyes ached from the strain of scanning the roadside, waiting, watching for the attack. My head ached from trying to put myself in Raven's mind, from trying to envision what kind of entrapment he'd devise. My body ached from sitting in one position for so long. It was a miserable night.

What was Bart doing now? My conditions, bad as they seemed to me, would probably be sublime compared to his circumstances. I shouldn't complain. I was warm, dry, not hungry, and, for the moment, apparently out of the crosshairs of my would-be assassin's gunsight.

Bart's situation would be precarious. Each breath could be his last while he was anywhere near Usama bin Laden. Why did he thrive on danger? It invigorated my husband. It exhausted me. What had I gotten myself in for when I'd married that adorable—and adoring—blonde, blue-eyed hunk of suntanned muscle? Since our marriage, I'd not only experienced the happiest, most blissful, joy-filled days of my life, but also the most frightening, worry-filled, physically threatening, and dangerous hours I could ever have imagined. Not in my wildest dreams could I have concocted the stories that I'd actually lived through in the last eleven months.

Did I want to put myself through a lifetime of this kind of torture? Moot point. Not a consideration tonight. If I survived tomorrow, and the next few weeks . . .

I thought of life without Bart, tried to picture me in any other situation, and decided it didn't matter. For better or for worse, for richer or poorer, in sickness and in health, until death do us part—at least for another four months until we could get to the temple, and then for time and eternity—I wanted to be at his side. Nothing else mattered. Even innumerable broken bones and situations like this.

Miles and hours passed uneventfully, and before I knew it I was on the outskirts of Atlanta. This worried me. Did they know something I didn't? Why weren't they trying to stop me? Or had Saucony tried and failed? But where was Raven? It didn't seem feasible that he would let me drive right up to the CDC and deposit my prize without a great deal of effort on his part to stop me.

I found another well-lit gas station and pulled off the Interstate to refuel my car and locate my destination. According to the map, the CDC was nestled in an area above Emory University called Druid Hills—a straight shot up I-75/85 from here.

Trickles of trepidation tingled down through my hands to my fingers as I pulled back onto the freeway. It was now four-thirty a.m.—just an hour and a half before I was to meet Dr. Svenson. I needed to scout the area, make certain I could get in and get out without Raven trapping me. Was Raven waiting? Surely he could pinpoint me via satellite. He'd know which route I'd take coming in. I could stay on the Interstate only so long, then I had to get off. An ambush at any given intersection this time of morning would be too easy.

When I pulled up at the CDC Visitors' Center, I didn't like the layout of the place. Perfect arrangement for a trap—for me. As the guard stepped out of his gatehouse and waved me forward to check my identification, the hair prickled on the back of my neck. I knew that face. I couldn't remember where or when, but I'd seen the man before. Recently. I drove quickly away.

New plan. If I left the jade lion and its precious microdot somewhere, Raven could trace it and retrieve it. If I kept it with me, he could trace everywhere I went. I needed some time and space. I needed to *set* the trap instead of walking into Raven's.

I headed for the Interstate again—my only safety zone. What to do? What to do? Just before the on-ramp, I spotted a cab parked at a gas station. An idea hit me. I whipped around and pulled up next to the taxi.

"Are you on duty?" I asked the man pumping gas into his tank.

"Just going on."

"I'm sure you get some really strange requests, but I'll bet this will be one of the strangest you've ever had."

"Lay it on me, lady, and I'll let you know." The man, probably in his late sixties, grinned across the trunk of his car.

"First, are you bonded?" Was that what I needed to know? What I wanted to ask was if he was trustworthy. How do you phrase that in politically correct terminology?

"Bonded? How do you mean?" The grin disappeared, replaced by a scowl.

"Let me start again. I'm about to ask you to drive around for one hour with a package of mine, then come back here and return it to me. I'm not saying this very well because what I really want to know is, can I trust you to do just that? To not open the package? To not ask any questions? And to be back here exactly an hour from now? I'll not only pay the cab fare, I'll toss in a great bonus."

The scowl dissipated slightly, and suspicion crept into the man's eyes. "What do you consider a great bonus?"

"One hundred dollars?" It was question, not a statement. He knew it.

"Why?" His eyes narrowed into wary slits.

"Why what?"

"Why do you want me to drive around for an hour with your package?" He hung the gas hose back on the pump and replaced his gas cap.

Anything less than total honesty right now would probably get me no for an answer. I took a deep breath and blurted it all out. "Because there's a transmitter in that package enabling someone to follow me. I need one hour before I meet them—one hour to get some things done without being followed. I'd like you to get on the Interstate and drive my package around so the people following me will think I'm lost or something. Then I'll meet you back here in one hour and give you your fare plus one hundred dollars."

"Am I going to get shot at?" The man walked over to my car and leaned down.

"No. At least I don't think so. Do you usually get shot at driving in Atlanta?" I tried a cheerful smile. It probably wasn't very convincing.

"Not usually. But you're right, this is definitely one of the craziest requests I've had. Okay. Give me the package. But first, let's see the hundred dollars."

I dug my purse out of the Biltmore Bag and waved a hundred-dollar bill. Then I pulled the box containing the jade lion out and started to hand it through the window. I hesitated.

"Second thoughts?" he asked, apparently sensing my indecision.

"I just need a little assurance here. I can see the name of your company, and the phone number on your cab, but can I have your name? And your home phone number? What if you have an accident? I need a way to find you. This is really important, and I'm not sure I'm actually doing the right thing. In fact, maybe we'd better forget the whole thing."

"Cold feet?"

"What I have is very important. Not monetarily. Just important. What if you lost it? What if someone hijacked your cab and stole it? No. Forget it. I'm responsible for it. I guess I'll just have to figure out another way to handle this. Thanks anyway." I put the package back in my purse and reached for the gearshift.

"Wait a minute, lady. Let's talk about this. You need some help. I can help you. What's the problem? You don't trust me? You wanna call my boss and talk to him? My wife? My five kids? I'm trustworthy. Okay?"

I looked up into sincere gray eyes. Yes, I needed help. And I'd been sitting here too long. Raven could have located me by now.

"Okay. Take it. Don't park anywhere. Just drive on the Interstate until it's time to meet me back here. And don't talk to strangers. Whatever you do, don't let anyone take the package from you, okay? Hurry. Go now, before I change my mind."

I thrust the priceless package into his hands and watched with a sick feeling in the pit of my stomach as he jumped in the cab and whipped out onto the Interstate. I couldn't dawdle either. As I pulled away from the service station, all I could think was: *What have I done? What on earth was I thinking to put something that valuable into the hands of a perfect stranger? Had I endangered him as well as the world in letting the microdot out of my hands?*

CHAPTER 37

Okay, "leetle gray cells," do something besides tell me what a stupid thing I just did. Figure out how we're going to get that microdot into the doctor's hands without getting caught.

I drove toward the CDC Visitors' Center, duly noting a pre-dawn graying of the sky in the east. Suddenly I passed a marvelous, massive old oak tree sheltering a bus stop. Wooden benches formed a large circle beneath it. Like so many ancient oaks in the South, the girths of its low-hanging branches were bigger than some trees. "Branch" was actually a misnomer. You could probably sleep on the limbs without worrying about falling off, they were so thick.

A streetlight offered just enough illumination, but not too much. Hmm. Near the CDC, but not too near. Business park area, so there wouldn't be much traffic for the next couple of hours. I drove around the corner and came back. A plan formed. Would it work? Nothing to do but try it. At this point I had no ATF. No marines. No Anastasia. Not even a weapon. All I had was me. If I didn't set a trap for Raven, he'd set one for me.

Somewhere down the road, I'd seen a Wal-Mart superstore. They were usually open twenty-four hours a day in the South. I retraced my route and found it just on the other side of the Interstate. In the paint department, I picked up TEC's Premium Resilient Tile Adhesive Clear Thin Spread, supposed to set up super-sticky within fifteen to thirty minutes. Perfect. I selected several gallon cans of thick latex paint, along with a couple of brushes and an opener. Cotton gloves from the garden department, a couple of long-sleeved shirts and pants from the women's section, size unimportant, some clothesline and fishing line, two pairs of boots, a pair of reading glasses, a small gift box, and two Styrofoam wig stands filled my basket.

At the checkout stand I tossed in a package of sweet rolls, and on the way out I grabbed a handful of newspapers, not caring that they were yesterday's. I'd have to work fast. The sun would be up soon, and my little tableau needed to be in place before daylight.

I parked the car near the tree, leaving the door open with the motor running, then unloaded everything on the bench behind the tree. Dumping out the Biltmore bag and Wal-Mart purchases, I "dressed" two dummies stuffed with wadded newspaper. Each received a wig from my bag on its own wig form tucked into the shirt collar. I painted faces on the styrofoam with my makeup. I shuddered to think what I was about to do to these beautiful, expensive wigs.

Each woman received a pair of gloves, pants tucked into boots, one got the floppy hat, and one a scarf. The head coverings wouldn't protect the wigs from my diabolical plan. Oh, well. Write it off as an Anastasia expense for saving the world.

One of my ladies would go in the backseat of the car with a sweet roll stuck in her gloved hand, and the other on the streetlight side of the bench, holding a newspaper.

I tied fishing line to each hand of the lady holding the newspaper and climbed the tree to thread them through a branch overhead. My puppet strings. If Raven suspected dummies, suspected a trap, I hoped movement would dispel that notion.

I painted each dummy with tile adhesive, carefully smearing it along the areas where an assailant would most likely grab when they went for the ladies.

The cans of paint, fire extinguishers, and leftover motor oil needed to be in the tree. Not that I had a plan for the last two items, but one never knew when one thing might not work and another might. Thank heaven for the low-hanging branches and high-backed benches. I tied the rope to the paint can handles, climbed up on the back of the bench, and crawled onto the lowest branch. Then I hauled the paint cans up, hand over hand, and positioned them on the wide arms of the tree, three above each lady. Couldn't worry about what would happen to the rental car when I dumped all that paint right by the door. The extinguishers and oil I lined up on the lower branch to position later.

Only one car had passed this quiet street so far. I glanced at my watch. Five twenty-five. Time to retrieve the jade lion and the microdot. I'd have to finish my preparations when I returned.

I arrived at the service station just as the taxi exited the freeway. To say I was relieved to see it would be a gross understatement. I grabbed the package, opened the box, unwrapped the jade lion from its multiple wrappings, and ran my fingernail over the eye. Yes. It was still there: the formula to curtail the spread of the deadly Ebola virus—and the tracking device that would deliver Raven into the waiting arms of my ladies.

I looked up into gray eyes watching my obsessive behavior with unveiled humor. "Everything just as it should be?" he asked.

"Yes. Thank you. What's my tab?"

"Seventy-five dollars," he said without flinching.

I slapped two hundred-dollar bills in his hand. "Here's your seventy-five—and I'll even increase your tip. Thanks. Now we'd both better disappear." I wanted to tell him how important the item he'd had for the last hour was to the world. But I didn't. I just drove back down the road and parked under the tree again, door open, motor running. Part of the trap, but an escape vehicle if I needed it.

I placed one dummy in the backseat, her legs out the door and facing the lady on the bench, being careful not to come in contact with the sticky stuff I'd smeared all over her. I stepped back to observe the total effect. My ladies actually looked rather real in the half-light of dawn and the streetlight's dim glow.

I climbed the tree, wedging the package containing the jade lion between a couple of smaller branches above my head. It took several precious minutes to string the fishing line from the lady's hands holding the newspaper, as well as the clothesline attached to the paint buckets, back to my perch. I removed the lids from the paint cans and rigged them above the lady sitting innocently below. No chance for a trial run; I just hoped I'd positioned the paint in the right places and had figured the pull strings right.

I needed something more. I checked my little arsenal and opened the remaining bottles of motor oil, drizzling them over the grass from my perch high above, walking out on the huge arms of the tree to cover a larger area. Might do some good, might not. But it was worth a shot.

A police car cruised by, slowed, and the officer rolled down his window. I maneuvered my literary lady's hands to open and close the newspaper. It looked like she had just turned the page of the paper. My sweet-roll-eating lady, half in and half out of the car, didn't move.

The police car moved away. I took a deep breath. So far, so good. But where was Raven? He should have been here by now. He'd been breathing down my neck for days, relentlessly pursuing me from one coast to the other. Now that I was ready for him, where was the man? Had all these preparations been for naught?

I'd designed the plan trying to put myself in Raven's mind, trying to think as he'd think, conforming to patterns he'd seen me establish. I'd always stayed close to people, being careful never to be caught alone. Thus I hoped he'd think I'd parked under this tree, by an occupied bus stop, to wait for my contact and deliver the formula, close enough to talk to the lady while I waited.

The streetlight clicked off, startling me. Good—although by the time anyone showed up, the sun might be shining directly on my creations, revealing what they really were.

I glanced at my watch again. Five forty-five. Fifteen minutes until I had to meet my "dead" doctor, the one whose demise had been announced in newspapers all over the world, to give him back his precious formula.

What if Raven didn't show? What if he was down the road at the Visitors' Center, waiting for me to come there? Or had set a trap for me between here and there? If he wasn't here by six o'clock, what would I do? Leave my elaborate little trap to go find the doctor? That would expose me to whatever Raven had planned.

Why wasn't this working as I'd anticipated? Raven was supposed to track the lion via satellite. It would lead him here, where he'd expect me to deliver it to the CDC. He'd come to the tree—directed by the satellite—and I'd catch him. But this was supposed to already have happened. I needed to be finished with this part in—I checked my watch again—ten more minutes.

A car approached, drove slowly by the tree, and continued down the road toward the CDC. My doctor? My point of contact? What would happen if I missed him? Could I get inside the building if I missed him out here? The guard at the Visitors' Center hadn't looked any too friendly. Where had I seen that man? At the airport?

The car returned. A dark red sedan. It slowed as it approached the tree, then stopped. I glanced at my watch. Eight minutes to six. Was this Raven, or just someone looking to catch the bus that stopped here?

Both front doors opened. The driver stood, stretched, and leaned an elbow on the top of the car as he looked up and down the street. Saucony. I couldn't see the man on the passenger side clearly; branches and leaves blocked my view, and I couldn't tell whether he remained in the car or had exited. I watched, horrified, as two more men emerged from the backseat.

Oh, no. No, no, no! I'd only figured on Raven and Saucony. But against four men? Four guns? And what did I have? A half-dozen cans of paint. *Brilliant, Allison. Well, lady, whatever you get, you deserve for thinking you could play with the big boys and not get hurt.*

I really was tired of this game. Tired of living on adrenaline. Tired of constantly being in jeopardy. Tired of matching wits with some of the most diabolical minds in the world. Then I had another thought.

A million-dollar bounty on me—Allison Allan. How about them apples?

As I watched the men amble toward the tree, I froze. I just sat there, watching those men advance, watching my plan look more and more foolish with each step they took. How clever I'd thought I'd been. The glue would set up nice and sticky by the time Raven arrived. What made me think he'd stoop to touch anyone, much less a lifeless dummy?

The strings threaded through my cold, clammy fingers stuck to them. Which ones went to which buckets? *Think, lady. Get cracking, or you'll be as lifeless as your ladies down there.*

I squeezed my eyes shut. *Okay. I can do this.* I took a deep breath and mentally ran through my plan, wondering as I did so why I'd thought it would work, why I'd thought it was so brilliant. As I opened my eyes, three advancing men silently stepped into the dark shadows under the towering tree. Two approached the lady on the bench below. Saucony turned to the lady in the car.

"Good morning. We seem to be lost. Can you give us directions?" How could that creep sound so humble, so sincere, so polite?

No time to wait for Raven to get into place. One, two, three. Now!

I pulled the strings when the men reached for the dummies. Paint buckets tipped, spilled, and tumbled off the arms of the tree. Direct hit. Three great big bad guys, covered with red, blue, green, and purple paint, were stuck fast to my super-glued ladies, and slipping and sliding all over the oil-slick grass and each other.

I closed my ears to the language and grabbed two of the fire extinguishers, taking careful aim. Raven would look up into the tree, might even shoot up here before he saw me, knowing whoever set the trap would be here. I'd need to beat him to the trigger.

He'd stopped short of the tree, watching, listening. I couldn't move, couldn't breathe for fear I'd give away my position. But surely he knew I was here.

"Shut up," a familiar voice ordered. The three men grappling on the ground stilled instantly.

Slowly, carefully, Raven approached the tree, prepared to collect his million-dollar bounty. The one on my head.

A thousand thoughts raced through my mind in the split second before Raven raised his gun and pointed it into the tree—at me.

Wonder what the doctor's prognosis would be when he saw the results of the tests? Would it matter?

I'd loved well—and been loved in return. Bart would never forget me, but maybe he could find another love.

But I didn't *want* Bart to find another love. I wanted to be his *only* love—forever.

I squeezed the triggers with every ounce of strength I had in me—and some that came from somewhere else—splattering Raven before he could get off a shot, covering him with a thick coating of white foam. I just kept spraying, covering every inch of all four men: face, eyes, nose, mouth, clothes, guns.

I hurled the empty canisters at the assassins, then grabbed two more, burying the four men sprawled in the oil and paint in another layer of foam. When those canisters were empty I seized the last two, covering them all over again. Raven slipped and slid to his feet, screaming in pain and frustration.

The sun rising above the treetops at that moment reminded me of the time—and what I still had to do. I grabbed the little package containing the jade lion and climbed down the tree, jumping from the high bench back across the horrible mess I'd created on the ground to a clear spot. A shot rang out, missing me by inches.

Racing around the tree to my idling car, I stumbled and fell, dropping the package. It rolled out of my reach. As I sprawled face first in mud and oil and paint, a bullet tore into the ground beside me. I scrambled to my feet and grabbed at the package. Another shot rang out. I dived and rolled toward the car, clutching the box to my chest.

How could anyone see to shoot at me? They should be blinded by the foam. Then I realized Raven was shooting toward any sound he could hear. I rolled one more time, as quietly as possible, grasped the nearest boot of the dummy sitting in the back seat of my car, and tossed it beyond the trunk. Raven, on one knee, ear cocked for the next sound, shot at the boot as it hit the ground.

I didn't have time to lie here and be shot at. I needed to keep that appointment with Dr. Svenson—if the good doctor hadn't already entered the CDC and become inaccessible.

Anything else I'd touch on the dummy would probably rattle her newspaper stuffing. I needed one more diversion. Cramming the box under my sweatshirt, I tucked my shirt into my jeans, then slipped off my tennis shoes, tossing one as far as I could throw it while I got to my feet. Raven turned as it hit the ground and fired, missing it by inches—an incredibly accurate blind shot. I tossed the other shoe so he had to turn further, putting his back to me as I slid into the driver's seat. I didn't wait to see how close he came to that one.

I rammed the car in gear and tromped on the accelerator, shutting the door as the car leapt forward. Bullets slammed into the car, shattering the rear window. The car screeched onto the street, around the corner, and out of range of Raven's wrath.

I took a deep breath, delighted to breathe. Delighted to be alive. Six-fifteen. I'd missed my appointment. I raced toward the Visitors' Center at the CDC. Maybe he was late. Maybe the doctor hadn't arrived yet. Planes were late. Traffic caused delays, and Atlanta traffic on the beltway was notorious.

But as I turned the corner, a long, white limousine pulled through the gate, which closed immediately behind it. The doctor! He must be in that car. I'd missed my contact. I felt . . . useless. Ineffective. Drained.

I wanted my husband. I wanted to go home. I wanted to spend the rest of my life doing something else—anything but playing Interpol's games.

CHAPTER 38

There was one thing I *could* do. I drove to the CDC gate to ask the security guard to call the police. I held my breath, hoping the familiar-looking guard wasn't on Raven's payroll. I lucked out. The guards had just changed shifts, and I'd never seen this one before. I asked him to tell the police to pick up some men shooting up the neighborhood down the road, and to check them out with Interpol. At least one would be a valuable catch.

I turned my car back to the street and was trying to decide what to do next when another car approached the gate. I glanced at the car as the driver rolled down the window to show his identification to the guard.

Bart?

It couldn't be!

"Bart? Is that you?" I yelled as I threw open my door and ran across the pavement.

"Princess? Is that really you? What are you doing here?" He met me halfway, ignoring the mud and oil, ignoring the guards, ignoring everyone but me. He threw his arms around me and whirled me off my feet. I clung to his neck, laughing and crying, trying to kiss him, trying to wipe the oil from his face that I smeared there, making it worse instead of better.

"Whoa. You've not only changed your hair, you've added some sharp points to your anatomy. Something's poking me." Bart released me and I retrieved the box, the package—the jade lion that had caused this whole mess.

"Here. You deliver it. It's the jade lion with the formula. I don't want anything more to do with it." I shoved the package into Bart's hand.

"You're the courier? I thought Rip Schyler had the assignment." Bart gathered me in his arms again and hugged me tight. I hadn't felt this sensation of being deliciously safe, wonderfully warm, and totally loved for so long that I'd forgotten it existed. I took a minute to absorb it, to revel in it, to let it seep through my whole being before I began my explanation.

"Your mom couldn't understand the man who delivered the package. She thought you'd sent it to me, and she brought it down to the cottage. I got home from the doctor just in time to get Bishop O'Hare's call to get out fast. As I ran out the door, I tossed the package in my bag. So not only did I have your little 'treasure' to protect, but I had Raven on my tail all the way across the country."

Bart froze, a scowl darkening his face. "Raven? Don't you move from that spot. Let me get this in the hands of the man who knows what to do with it, and then I need to hear about Raven. I'll be right back."

My husband peeled the outer wrapping off the box—the stamped, addressed brown wrapper—and tossed the box to me. He jogged across the pavement, bent in at the window of the car, handed the man in the passenger seat the paper, spoke to him for a minute, and turned back to me. The man—the one in the picture—emerged from the car. Dr. Svenson. The man I was supposed to meet.

"But what about the microdot on the lion? Doesn't he need that?" I said, running to meet my husband.

"Not that I know of." Bart looked puzzled. "We put the formula on a microdot under the stamp. Is there another on the lion?"

"There's something I thought was a microdot on the lion's eye. I thought that was how Raven tracked me." I opened the box and peeled the layers of wrapping off, handing the jade lion to Bart to examine.

I couldn't believe it. I'd been chased, stalked, and hounded, all the way across the United States by an assassin intent on killing me, and all I'd had to do was get rid of the lion to get rid of the assassin.

Bart held the lion up to the sun and inspected the eye that I pointed out. "Tell me about Raven. How did you manage to elude him?"

"I barely did. Right now he's just down the road, covered with foam."

Bart nearly dropped the lion. "He's *where?*"

"I set a trap, rather than be trapped. I guess we really should see if they're still there—see if the police got to them before they got away."

Bart hopped in the passenger side of my car, I slid back into the mud and oil-covered driver's seat, and we raced down the street to where I'd left four incredibly messy men. I glanced at the clock. Six twenty-five. Approximately twenty-five minutes since I'd covered the men with paint and foam. They'd probably all hightailed it by now.

As we turned the corner, a police car barricaded the street in front of us. Bart jumped out and headed for the center of the melee. With all the police in the area, I couldn't count bodies. I glanced up the street. I couldn't see Raven's car.

I didn't need a body count now. I knew at least one was missing: Raven. *Way to go, Alli. Let the one get away who wants to collect the bounty on your head. Now the nightmare will continue ad infinitum.*

Slowly I climbed out of the car, totally depleted, my excitement at seeing Bart tempered by Raven's escape. I was cold, wet, and miserably dirty. What else could go wrong?

I got stopped by a policeman who said I couldn't go in there.

"Would it make any difference if I told you I'm with Interpol, that man you just let through here is my husband, also with Interpol, and I'm the one who caused all this mess?"

"Not unless you have some ID to prove it." He wasn't smiling. Of course, it didn't help that I looked like something left over from a war zone. And probably smelled worse.

"See that bag over there that says 'Biltmore Hotel'? That's where my purse is with my ID. Of course, I dumped paint all over it, so everything is purple and red . . . Oh, forget it. I didn't want to get involved anymore, anyway."

Talk about anti-climactic.

I went back to the car. No clean clothes left. I'd dressed the newspaper ladies in everything I had.

Add "totally unappreciated" to my list of grievances. And hungry. I rummaged through the bags on the floor and found another Baby Ruth. Fate hadn't abandoned me completely. I started the car, put the heater on full blast, and settled back with a mouth full of chocolate and caramel goodness to watch the police in action. They'd cuffed the filthy dirty men and seated them in a circle away from the paint and oil mess under the tree.

I was really irritated that I'd let Raven escape. Not only would it complicate my life, since he wouldn't give up that million-dollar bounty easily, but it was totally unprofessional to incapacitate the bad guy and then walk away and let him disappear. Of course, no one ever accused me of being professional, and they certainly wouldn't this time.

I popped the last bite of Baby Ruth into my mouth and peeled some of the drying mud from my jeans. I wasn't looking forward to reporting to Bart or the rest of Anastasia—especially Dad. Mom would be more understanding, but Dad was professional from his gray hair down to his size-ten shoes.

It didn't matter that I was so concerned with getting the microdot to the doctor that I didn't think of anything else. Or that I was being shot at and running for my life. I should have taken care of Raven. The others were probably small potatoes who didn't matter much. But I should have at least tied their leader up, or shot him in the leg with his gun so he couldn't leave. Or something.

What could I have done? My "leetle gray cells" were very tired. They'd done about all the thinking they were capable of at the moment, so I gave them a rest, assured that any minute someone would tell me what I should have done. I wouldn't have to wonder much longer.

Bart chose that moment to return to the car. "The police would like you to come and ID these guys."

"I only know two—Raven and Saucony. Actually, I only know one. And I'm afraid I let him get away."

"Raven didn't get away. He's here with the others."

I couldn't believe Bart. "Raven—coal black hair with a white streak in it?"

Bart opened my door and held out his hand for me. "Raven. The man on Interpol posters. Assassin extraordinaire. Wanted all over the world. White streak in black hair. One and the same."

"He's there? He didn't get away? But the car is gone. Somebody got away."

"Come on. See for yourself. Boy, you sure created a mess up here. I don't think these guys will ever be the same again." Bart pulled me to my feet, holding both of my dirty hands in his, and grinned at me. "Have I told you lately that you are one incredible lady? I thought I knew how terrific you were, but to take on four armed men with only paint cans and fire extinguishers?"

"And motor oil," I added.

He kissed the very tip of my nose—probably the only clean spot on me—and pulled me past the policeman who'd refused me access to the scene. I suppressed an impulse to stick out my tongue at the uniformed man, ignoring him instead.

"I hope they won't ever be the same again. I hope they have to take off at least two layers of skin to clean that off, and I hope . . . Bart!" I stopped short. "What can the police charge them with? They have to have committed a crime to be arrested. I stopped them before they could get their hands on the formula."

"I'm sure they'll all have a rap sheet a mile long. And Raven is a high-profile killer. Several countries will want him extradited to face charges in their jurisdiction. Can you identify him?"

It was easy enough. Raven was the man rubbing his hands together as if washing them, then rubbing them over his wet face. Saucony hadn't fared much better. Tears streamed from their red-rimmed eyes, and the newspaper they rubbed on themselves to get rid of the foam had left printer's ink streaked everywhere. Saucony gave me a quick, curt glance, mumbled some obscenities under his breath, and went back to rubbing off the burning chemicals.

"Hi, Raven," I said. "Nice to meet you under these particular circumstances." I couldn't believe it. Here he sat, handcuffed—nabbed, snagged, snared. Caught. I expected to feel jubilant. I expected to want to sing and dance and shout, "Nanny, nanny, nanny!" in his face. But I didn't.

I actually felt sorry for the man who'd tried to kill me. Not being clean hurt him worse than it did me. And his eyes and skin must burn like crazy. His fetish for cleanliness might actually drive him insane.

I looked up at my husband, who watched me intently. "Yes, that's Raven," I clarified. "And this is his right-hand man. I don't know his name—I called him Saucony because of his shoes—but he's been with Raven all across the United States. I'll press charges of attempted murder if you want." I looked around, puzzled. "But if they're all here, who took the car?"

"If they left the keys in it, somebody probably hopped in, drove it off, and is in the process of stripping it right now," Bart said.

I nodded. "Can we go now?"

He slipped his arm around my shoulder. "Yes, we can go, Princess. You can't identify these two?"

I glanced at the paint-streaked men and shook my head. I retrieved my purse, abandoning the paint-spattered Biltmore Hotel bag under the tree. Bart took my hand and led me back to the car.

"You look exhausted," he said, wrapping his arms around me and pulling me against him.

"I am. I thought I'd want to flaunt my victory in their faces, but I didn't. I just want to be clean, and to have you hold me in your arms. And never let me go again." I leaned my cheek against his chest and sighed. "But I still have a phone call to make. I'm supposed to call Bishop O'Hare to let him know I made the connection with Dr. Svenson and delivered the formula. And you have to tell me how you ended up with the doctor."

Bart handed me his cell phone. "Use this."

The phone rang in California only once before the bishop came on the line. "O'Hare."

"Mission accomplished."

"Allison! Thank heaven. I was beginning to worry. You delivered the formula to Dr. Svenson?"

"And found my husband at the same time."

"How are you feeling?"

Strange question. "Why?"

"Because I ran into Dr. Simon at the hospital yesterday, and he told me he'd been trying to get hold of you. Asked if I knew where you were. When I told him you were out of town, he was particularly upset. Said he had some news you needed to hear and was concerned about getting it to you as soon as possible. Why didn't you tell me you . . . ?"

I interrupted. "Did he have the test results?" I held my breath and looked at Bart, hoping the fear that flooded my system didn't show on my face. It must have. Bart reached for my hand and held it tight.

CHAPTER 39

"I don't know about the test results," Bishop O'Hare said, "but he did have some news. Call him the first chance you get. When are you coming home?"

"Definitely not today. Maybe not tomorrow." I glanced up at my husband. "In fact, not until we have to."

That was a stupid question I'd asked. What with doctor/patient confidentiality, of course Dr. Simon wouldn't have revealed anything to Bishop O'Hare, even though Dr. Simon knew he was my clergy—and even though I knew they were good friends and associates. Still, it didn't stop my heart from leaping into my throat at the possibility of news resolving this emotional issue.

"Better follow doctor's orders, Alli," Bishop O'Hare said quietly. "Dr. Simon said you were supposed to take it easy. I doubt you've done that. Now would be a good time to start."

"I think I will. A nice hot shower for several hours—it'll take that long to get clean again—then bed for several days. See you in a week or so, Bishop. Here's Bart." I handed the phone back to my husband and sagged against the car, my knees suddenly weak. I replayed the bishop's words, his tone of voice. What could I read into that? Good news? Bad news?

Bart finished his update to the bishop. "They're slowly tightening the circle around Usama bin Laden, the terrorist who put out the contracts on Anastasia's agents. The various hit men who were involved have been apprehended. Raven was the last of them, and Alli corralled him and three of his associates all by herself this morning. Wish you were here to see her innovative little trap. My wife is brilliant." Bart beamed down at me.

I needed to hear that bit of praise, needed to have a little self-confidence restored after my scathing self-criticism a few minutes earlier.

"Nothing more on this end. You can read the report when we've filed it. Right now, I've got a lot of catching up to do." Bart disconnected and slid his arm around my waist. "I think you deserve a little pampering. What say we find a nice hotel and check out of the world for a couple of days? I don't think the head of Anastasia would disapprove. What do you think?"

"If you're not ashamed to be seen in the company of a muddy, oily wife in clothes that don't fit, I can't think of anything I'd like better."

Bart laughed as he gently settled me into the passenger seat of the car. "It's not the first time, nor even the second time you've come out of the mud like this, and I'm sure it won't be the last, what with your propensity for finding trouble—or should I say, falling smack into the middle of it?" He shut the door and went around to the driver's side, ignored the oil on the seat, and sat down—on the jade lion.

"Here." He tossed it at me. "A little souvenir from Africa."

"Let me get this straight. If I'd simply thrown away the lion and all the wrappings, and kept just the brown paper with the stamp, Raven couldn't have found me?"

"Dr. Svenson could answer that better than me, but, yes, I think that's right. He'd planned to mail the formula to the health authorities in Europe, but he discovered one of his technicians smuggling things out of his lab. So Dr. Svenson had taken the formula and gone to meet a doctor friend to give it to him, when his lab and home were fire-bombed. His friend got him out of the city, then called another friend who notified Interpol. That's how I connected with Dr. Svenson. We decided it would be wise to get him out of that part of the world and here to the CDC, where he could work without interruption or danger."

"That doesn't explain how the tracking device got on the lion."

"My guess is that either he placed it there when he prepared it for mailing, thinking it would be a way of tracking it if it became lost in the mails, or his assistant did, thinking it was a way he could get control of the formula once it left Dr. Svenson's hands. When I told

Dr. Svenson I could get the formula into Anastasia's Control Center for safekeeping, and have it delivered to him at the CDC, he agreed that would be wiser than taking a chance on someone recognizing him as we traveled out of Africa."

"So when you put the little card with the note to me in the velvet pouch, you had no idea there was a tracking device on the lion?"

"None. I intended it to remain in the Control Center until Rip came for it. Dr. Svenson's assistant must have known the device was attached to the lion. We discovered he worked for bin Laden, who also hired Raven. That had to be how Raven knew about it." Bart reached for my hand. "I'm sorry you had to go through all this alone—the tests, the uncertainty, and then being chased from coast to coast by an assassin." He ran one finger down my cheek and brushed off a little dried-on mud. "Your ingenuity amazes me."

Bart started the car.

I leaned back in the seat and sighed. "When you have no weapon, you have to put the 'leetle gray cells' to work." I closed my eyes. "It doesn't have to be a four-star hotel, you know. Just a hot shower, fluffy towels, a soft bed, room service, and you. That's all I need."

"That's it?" Bart said as he pulled away from the police scene. "That's easy."

"Well, that's it for the next two days. After that, I'll need some clothes. Mine are all back there under the tree, covered with paint."

"Or covered with mud and oil," Bart pointed out.

"These aren't mine. They belong to a marine from Beaufort Island."

"Marine? I hope you're not tired, because you don't get to sleep until I've heard every detail of your escapades."

"Sleep?" I opened my eyes wide and sent an innocent look toward Bart. "Who said anything about sleep?"

Bart laughed. "You're a quick study, Princess. That was my line." Bart reached for my hand and squeezed it. "I think I like your new hairdo. Of course, it's kind of hard to tell, covered in mud as it is, but it makes you look sort of pixie-like. Sort of contradicts the dedicated super-agent that you've become."

I took a deep breath. "About that super-agent. We need to talk."

Bart pulled onto the Interstate, scanning the road ahead. "Help me watch for a hotel. The sooner we get you cleaned up . . ."

"Love of my life, you're not listening."

"Of course I am. You said we need to talk. Before we can talk, you need a shower and one of my special shower scrubs. Then breakfast." He flashed that boyish grin at me. "Room service, of course. We'll follow doctor's orders. Not let you out of bed for at least the next two days."

"Dr. Simon said to take it easy," I objected. "He didn't prescribe bed rest."

"Did you hear me say bed *rest?* I thought I said I wouldn't let you out of bed . . ."

I laughed. "Sorry. I'm a little slow this morning. I don't remember the last time I had a good night's sleep. My brain's muddled."

"That's on the agenda, but not until I've had an instant replay of every minute since you got my message and left the estate." Bart tenderly rubbed at a smudge on my face. "You are incredible, Princess. Taking down four armed men single-handedly. You're going to be as great an agent as Else."

"Bart, I'll never be an agent like Else. I don't have her instincts. I don't have her reflexes. I can't shoot first and consider it later. I don't even like to *think* about shooting someone, even when they're trying to kill me. I'm terrified the whole time, especially when I'm afraid I'm not worthy of heavenly help."

Bart pointed at a high-rise hotel just beyond the next exit. "That look okay?"

"Sure. Anything with a hot shower will do."

"Princess, we're all scared. If we weren't, we wouldn't stay on our toes, wouldn't be sharp enough, alert enough, to stay alive." Bart exited the Interstate, executing the tricky entrance into the hotel parking lot. "Besides, sometimes we have to suffer to learn what we're capable of doing—draw on our inner resources, reach and stretch and find out what we really can do. We know He won't do for us what we're able to do for ourselves, and He knows our capacity better than we ever will." He pulled next to the entrance.

"You stay right here while I get a room." He bounded out of the car and disappeared through the double glass doors, emerging minutes later holding a card key between his fingers and flashing that smile that always melted my heart. He slid into the driver's seat.

"We're in luck. They just happened to have the penthouse suite available. Breakfast will be delivered in one hour. That should give us just enough time to scrub off your beauty pack." He wrinkled his nose. The mud, and whatever else I'd wallowed in, was becoming more aromatic by the minute.

"Can you imagine people actually smearing this stuff on themselves on purpose?" I peeled a mud cake from my elbow. "Of course, it may be a higher class of mud than this."

Bart laughed as he started the car. "Aren't you glad you're so beautiful that it's not necessary to torture yourself with all that gunk? Let's see. He said there's a back door and elevator. I thought you'd prefer that to parading through the lobby in your current state."

"That was thoughtful of you. Or were you just ashamed to be seen with a dirty wretch like me?" I teased.

Bart maneuvered into a parking space near the back entrance, shut off the car's engine, pulled the key from the ignition, then turned to me. His blue eyes were serious as he leaned across the console and kissed me. "Princess, I'm never ashamed to be seen with you, no matter what you look like."

I touched a dirt-streaked hand to his face, prickly with at least two days' growth of beard. "Thank you. I love you, too. But I can't stand me much longer, so I don't expect you to. Let's find that shower."

I didn't even stop to explore our sumptuous room, nor look out the wide expanse of window that must have had a marvelous view. I headed straight for the shower, leaving a trail of mud-caked, oil-stained clothes along the way. Bart followed, picking them up as I dropped them.

"Think I'll just dispose of these before they contaminate the fresh air in our lofty nest. Be right with you." He disappeared out the door.

I jumped in the shower, turned on the hot water, and luxuriated in the process of coming clean again. When Bart joined me, I'd already shampooed twice. He emptied the tiny shampoo bottle and worked the remaining shampoo into my hair, his magic fingers making my scalp tingle.

"You don't have much hair left," he observed. "Was there a good reason you got rid of all that wild, wonderful gypsy hair I love so much?"

"Raven was the reason. I figured a drastic change of hairstyle might throw him off a bit. You should have seen me when it was streaked with blue tips."

Bart backed me under the spray and rinsed the suds away tenderly. "I wish I'd been there. The thought of you, alone, with Raven in pursuit . . ." He shuddered and shook his head. "I needed to be with you."

"And I needed you with me," I said, "but I got by. With help from some guardian angels. I couldn't have done it without all the help I had from that department."

"What form did they take this time? Human or otherwise? I want to hear about every one of them. But first, you deserve the specialty of the house."

Hmmm. Bart's massage just about made everything I'd experienced the last few days worth it. I started listing people who had turned up in the right place at the right time to help get me through a sticky situation: the Mayflower Gardens group, the Hispanic mother and her little family who provided cover on the Metrolink, and her good-looking brother, my Hispanic "uncle" and all his family at the library. Even old Joe at Arnold's house.

"Your guardian angels were certainly busy rounding up all that help," Bart said when I was about halfway through my list. "I guess you didn't need me after all."

"I always need you," I assured him. "But when you're not there, somebody has to protect me from the bad guys who populate your world. So my guardian angels just have to provide whoever's handy to do the job. I much prefer the real thing."

Bart leaned forward and kissed my nose, then I turned him around and rubbed and scrubbed the scars that crisscrossed his back and shoulders. When we were first married, I'd cried at the thought of the terrible beating he'd taken in that Tibetan prison from a vicious Red Chinese guard. The scars looked so tender that I'd almost been afraid to touch them. Now I worked my fingertips over them lovingly.

We wrapped in the luxurious full-length white terry cloth robes provided by the hotel just as room service knocked with breakfast. Pecan waffles smothered with butter pecan syrup, fluffy scrambled eggs, strawberries and whipped cream, and hot raspberry white chocolate to drink.

"Mmm. You'll spoil me if you're not careful. I might think I've died and gone to heaven if this keeps up." My waffle melted in my mouth. Exquisite.

"I'll do everything in my power to spoil you. You deserve it." Bart's warm smile faded. He played with his scrambled eggs for a minute before he looked up, his blue eyes filled with concern. "You haven't told me about the tests. What did you find out?"

I swallowed hard. "Nothing. The results won't be back for a few days. But we're not going to think about it until we talk to Dr. Simon. Whatever news he has, we'll hear it together. At least I won't have to handle that alone." I reached across the breakfast cart and clasped Bart's outstretched hand. I clung to it, unable to speak for a minute. "Thanks for being safe, for not getting yourself killed in Africa. And thanks for coming home now. I needed you here. I'm not as brave and independent as I thought."

"Sure you are. There was just too much all at once this time. Eat your waffle while it's hot, then I want the full story from start to finish."

But we had so much to talk about, we dawdled long after our food was cold, eating a bite here, a bite there between relating our stories, until we finally gave up and put the cart outside the door. I kept the strawberries and whipped cream for later.

"Ready to hear Dr. Simon's news?" I asked, almost afraid to face what he had to say.

Wrapped in his white terry cloth robe, Bart stretched out on the sofa and held open his arms to me. "Come here. We'll snuggle down and face it together."

I sat on the edge of the sofa facing him. "What if the cyst is malignant? What if they have to do a mastectomy? A radical one? What if I'm scarred and ugly?"

Bart pulled me into his arms. I clung to him, afraid not only for my life, but afraid for us. For what might happen if all my worst fears came to pass. Would Bart still love me? Still find me attractive? Or would I be so disfigured he wouldn't be able to look at me? I didn't consider the possibility that I might not survive the coming ordeal.

My husband cradled me in his arms while I soaked his robe with my silent tears. Then he tenderly wiped my face and tilted my chin up so I had to look into his eyes. "Princess, you know I love this beautiful body of yours. But that's not the most important part of our marriage. You wouldn't worry I'd stop loving you if you lost an arm or a leg, because you know I wouldn't. Why are you so worried about how I'd react to a mastectomy? Do you think you'd be less of a woman? Is that the secret fear behind this?"

I wiped my wet cheeks. "You'd think I'd have analyzed my fears and feelings—that I'd know how I feel and why. But I don't. I guess I'm more afraid that you'd find me repulsive than I am of the actual cancer. How's that for logical?" I tried to laugh, but the sound caught in my throat.

Bart reached for his cell phone. "What's Dr. Simon's number? Let's get this over right now so you won't have to worry and wonder another minute."

I recited the number, one I'd had to call far too many times in the last few weeks. Bart got through to the receptionist, waited, and finally Dr. Simon came on the line. Bart positioned the phone between us so we could both hear.

"Dr. Simon, this is Allison Allan. Bishop O'Hare said you needed to speak with me. That you had some news?"

"Allison. I'm so glad you called. I have great news for you—on two fronts. First, they rushed the test through for me, and your cyst is benign."

A fresh new batch of tears poured down my cheeks, but this time they were tears of relief. Tears of joy. I thought my heart would burst with elation.

Dr. Simon continued. "And the next bit of good news is something I just read in a medical journal on fertility. Have my receptionist make an appointment at your convenience, and we'll discuss it. I think we may be able to do something about that little problem, too. No promises, but certainly some fresh new ideas contained in the article and some innovative procedures that may help your particular circumstance. How are you feeling?"

"Better right this minute than I've felt in weeks. Thanks for the news. When we get back to California, I'll come right in. Thanks, Dr. Simon."

Bart dropped the phone on the carpet and kissed my neck. "Feel better now?"

"I don't think I can explain how much better."

His lips worked their way up the side of my cheek. "Like you've just conquered the world?"

"Even better than that."

He kissed my eyelids, first one and then the other. "Flown to the moon and back?"

"Much better."

His lips found mine. I melted against him. This must be heaven. Earth could never be this rapturous, this totally bliss-filled, this absolutely divine.

Bart leaned back and looked at me. "I love you."

"More now than an hour ago?"

He frowned. "What was an hour ago?"

"Before my shower?"

He laughed. "Probably. But that's just a temporary physical thing. And speaking of physical things, I think you were going to tell me something."

It was my turn to be puzzled. "About what?"

"You said we had to talk. I think it may have had something to do with being an agent. Or with not being one?"

I stared at him. "How did you know what it was about?"

"Because I've heard those rumblings before, at the end of every job we've done. You vow you'll never do that again."

"Well, this time I mean it." I rolled off the sofa and paced the length of the sitting room. "I'm through pulling horrible, slimy, bloodsucking leeches off my body. I'm through having a price tag on my head and being chased all over the world by some crazed gunman. I'm through being pushed down a rain-slick road by giant trucks and going without sleep all night, and living in jeopardy every minute, worrying about every knock at the door and every footstep behind me." I stopped in front of the window, looking out, but not seeing the view beyond. Bart waited quietly for me to finish.

"But most of all, I'm afraid of being deserted by the Lord because of all the lies I have to tell all the time." I leaned my forehead against the cool glass. "I felt like the heavens were closed to me, that He wasn't listening to me anymore. That I wasn't worthy to have my prayers answered. I just can't live that like."

"Okay." Bart came up behind me and wrapped his arms around me.

"What did you say?" I turned and looked up at him.

"I said okay."

"What does that mean?"

"You can do whatever you want. If you want to quit, you can. How many times have I told you I want nothing more than to have you stay home, where you're safe and sound, and raise our children? That would make me perfectly happy." He pulled me close and nibbled my neck.

"Wait a minute." I pushed him back so I could see his face. "That was too easy. You agreed to that too fast."

"What did you expect me to say? You know how I feel. How I've always felt. I worry about you every minute we're on a job. I can't concentrate thinking about what could happen, what I'd do if someone got in a lucky shot. How I'd live without you." He shook his head. "No, Princess, I won't be unhappy at all to have you turn in your resignation and become a full-time wife and mother. Nothing would make me happier in this whole world. There isn't anything more important you could do, either."

I opened my mouth to respond, but he kissed me and pulled me closer, then continued before I could get a word in. "And as for not being worthy to have your prayers answered, did you ever consider that maybe you just didn't have the confidence in yourself that He had in you? Did you forget that whatever you need to do, He's there for you when you ask as long as it's a worthy cause? You asked for His help, and He sent what you call your guardian angels to assist."

I thought about that for a minute. Probably true. Then I had another, not-so-pleasant thought. I pulled away and looked up at him. "And while I'm changing diapers—if we're so lucky—you'll be in some exotic spot, with some beautiful agent, or spy, living life on the edge, loving every minute of it."

Bart cocked his head and raised one eyebrow. "Could be. It's been known to happen."

I couldn't think of a thing to say to that. This conversation hadn't taken the course I'd expected, and I didn't quite know what to do about it. "I'd miss out on those slow boat trips through tropical islands," I said ruefully. I didn't like the thought of that.

"I guess you would." Bart nodded thoughtfully.

"I'd be worried sick about you."

"Probably." It was Bart's turn to look out the window.

I sighed and leaned my head against his chest. "So what's the answer?"

Bart put his hands on my shoulders and looked down at me. "How about if we just leave it in the hands of the Omniscient One? We'll do whatever He decides is best."

I studied those azure blue eyes, so filled with trust. "Sounds good to me. Everyone keeps telling me I don't make very good decisions anyway."

"Then let me make one for you right now. The best one you'll make all day." Bart scooped me off my feet, strode across the room, and dropped me on the bed.

"Are you sure this is a wise decision?" I laughed. "I haven't had a good night's sleep forever. If I'm horizontal, I may not be able to stay awake to tell you the rest of my escapades."

"I'll take my chances," Bart said, stretching out beside me. "Now, where were we in your narrative?"

I slipped my arms around his neck and pulled him close. "How about right here?"

"Perfect."

ABOUT THE AUTHOR

Lynn Gardner is an avid storyteller who does careful research to back up the high-adventure romantic thrillers that have made her a popular writer in the LDS market. For her first novel, *Emeralds and Espionage,* she relied on her husband's expertise as a career officer in the Air Force, interviewed a friend in the FBI, and gathered extensive information on the countries in which her adventure took place. Additional extensive research in Hawaii, San Francisco, and New Mexico allowed her to create exciting stories with realistic settings for her other novels.

When Lynn's scheduled trip to Thailand and Sri Lanka was canceled because of raging fires in Southeast Asia, her son and daughter, who both work in the garment industry, were able to visit these countries, and with specific instructions from Lynn on sites she'd researched, gathered the information and took the pictures she needed to make *Sapphires and Smugglers* as vivid as all of her others have been.

For *Amethysts and Arson,* Lynn traveled solo 6000 miles, from coast to coast, through sixteen states to discover historical or important targets in the major cities of the South for her villain arsonist to destroy.

Jade and Jeopardy takes place on her home ground, and back to the East coast to a few favorite locations she fell in love with on previous research trips.

Lynn and her husband, Glenn, make their home in Quartz Hill, California, where Lynn is director of the stake family history center. They are the parents of four children.

Among her many interests, Lynn enjoys reading, golfing with her husband, traveling, beachcombing, writing, family history, and spoiling her five granddaughters and three grandsons.

AN EXCERPT FROM THE SOON-TO-BE RELEASED NOVEL
BY NANCY CAMPBELL ALLEN

A TIME for the HEART

The young woman carried the small basket of fruit into her queen and set it before her, curtseying as she did so.

"Thank you, Queliza," the queen murmured, smiling at the young servant. She was seated upon her ornate throne in her personal quarters in the spacious palace, which was positioned to the right of the ceremonial temple.

Queliza liked the new queen. The king's first wife had been thoughtless and demanding. After her death, the king had chosen for his bride a young woman from a neighboring city. The new queen was young and kind, and treated her servants well.

"That is all I will need for now," the queen said. "I will have you summoned should I require something further."

Queliza curtseyed again and quietly left the room, her heart giving a little leap of excitement. She had some time to herself! Perhaps, if she wandered around the plaza a bit, she might spy the object of her recent affections . . .

* * * * * *

C laire O'Brian viewed the empty spot on the shelf with something akin to dismay. She was either losing her mind, not altogether a far-fetched possibility, she wryly admitted, or someone had moved the artifact without her knowledge or authorization. Surveying the room, she looked carefully over each possible hiding place before turning again to the shelf where she'd last placed the ancient pottery bowl that had been unearthed and documented the day before.

A pesky, pulsating ache that began behind her eyes gave Claire the promise of more intense pain to follow. She pinched the bridge of her nose with her thumb and forefinger, closing her eyes and muttering, "I am a competent adult. I am an extremely competent adult."

She turned at the sound of the door behind her being opened and closed. Claire narrowed her eyes as a young woman entered with an unnecessarily dramatic flourish.

"So you're missing some stuff?" the girl asked without preamble.

Claire mentally sighed and attempted to fix a smile on her face, hoping the expression didn't look as much like a grimace as it felt. "Hello, Devon. Nice to see you, too." Devon Stark had a habit of bursting upon the scene, any scene, with an air of faux importance. Her presence at the Guatemalan archaeological dig called "Corazon de la Ceiba," or "Heart of the Jungle," was a nuisance, but a necessary one, as it was her uncle's money that funded the project. Devon herself had been the first stipulation. "I'll supply money for the project if you can find a position for my niece," had been the less-than-subtle demand. Needless to say, Claire had given Devon a job.

Too much personal garbage attached to this place, Claire mused as she rubbed her forehead. Devon's wealthy uncle was the other half of Claire's former relationship. It had ended on a good note, though a slightly unsettled one—at least on his part. Claire had wanted out, he'd wanted her to stay, and she had to suspect that he'd agreed to fund this dig more as a means of keeping track of her than out of respect for her abilities.

"Yes, Devon," she finally replied. "I'm missing some stuff. I don't suppose you've seen it? The most recent thing missing is a piece of pottery, a bowl, cracked in many places but largely intact. The main piece is gone, and so are the smaller pieces that need to be reattached."

Devon shook her brown hair off her shoulders. "I haven't seen anything," she stated, then turned and left, slamming the door.

Claire stared at the vacated spot, pursed her lips, and nodded slowly. Everything in life was attached to a price. In order to continue unearthing the ancient city of Corazon de la Ceiba, or "Corazon," as the staff had come to refer to the place, they had to put up with Devon. A seventeen-year-old girl wonder who had never bothered to crack a science textbook, who insisted on wearing full makeup and leaving her hair down in humid, ninety-degree weather, and who was "enjoying the experience of a lifetime her friends would just be so jealous of," in her own words.

Claire raised her eyebrows and blinked, turning her attention to her former dilemma. The artifacts were carefully catalogued and marked, placed in the temporary lab Claire supervised, then readied for transportation to a more formal lab in Guatemala City. The current incident of missing artifacts marked the third time the site had seen theft under Claire's direction. The five or six pieces that had previously gone missing had yet to be found, and Claire literally lost sleep over the fact. She closed her eyes in resignation. She was destined for a restless summer, it seemed.

She left the lab, locking the door behind her, and made her way to the office of her employer and the head of the dig, Justin Hodges. She didn't bother to lift her eyes to the splendor that surrounded her—the lush green colors of the jungle, the thick trees surrounding all sides of the ruins. The large Mayan temple positioned approximately a football field away from her current position, flanked on either side by two smaller but equally impressive buildings, was partially buried in mountains of dirt and rock that receded into the dense jungle overgrowth.

The floor of the site was a grassy expanse, punctuated periodically by large, carved pillars that rose from the earth, each with its own story to tell. Several buildings, nearly a dozen, were positioned around the ancient plaza of Corazon de la Ceiba. The archaeologists could only speculate as to the purpose of some; many were still partially buried in the earth and needed to be excavated.

Part of Claire's frustration with the limited number of her staff was that this process would take a long, long time. The buildings still holding their many secrets would have to wait until the crew and their helpful workers could get to them.

At the center of the dig was a ball court—a long strip of stone resembling a concrete athletic court that looked from the air to be the shape of an "I," flanked on either side by two small, rectangular buildings situated atop tiered staircases.

The lab where Claire did much of her work was one of several buildings Darren Stark had taken upon himself to have built on the site, with the intention of turning Corazon into a "research" site of sorts in the years to come. These buildings were temporary but sturdy. They were wooden, whitewashed, and red roofed, and were positioned at the end of the ruins opposite the ancient temple, where they would be out of the way and unobtrusive.

There were two larger buildings to be used for dorms; there was a small but functional kitchen in another building, where dinners were cooked by a woman named Rosa who lived in a nearby village; and there were several small, separate units to be used for offices. The electricity necessary for running machinery and equipment was supplied by generators, and the site boasted two very nice latrines, as latrines go, and a private, but not *entirely* primitive outdoor shower, which functioned by filling a large tank on the "roof" with rainwater.

For the time being, Darren wanted the staff kept small, and so the buildings were empty, for the most part. Justin Hodges used one for his office, Claire claimed another small building for a bedroom, and the remainder of the buildings were divvied up amongst the remaining staff, which consisted of three masters students, Darren's annoying niece, and a world-famous French epigrapher.

One benefit to having so few people on hand was that everyone was entitled to his or her own bedroom. One serious drawback, however, was that there was so much to be done, and not enough people to help.

She usually found amusement in the contrast between the splendor of the ruins and the crisp charm of the more modern buildings; however, at present, her brow furrowed in a deep frown as she reached the small building that housed the office, and gave a perfunctory knock at the door before cracking it open and peering inside. The object of her quest was seated behind his desk, staring into space. He blinked at Claire's greeting and motioned her to enter.

Justin smiled wearily as Claire took a seat opposite his desk. "Any lu k?" he asked, his expression hopeful.

"No, but then I haven't exactly torn the place apart, yet." Claire wiped at her forehead, shoving her damp bangs out of her face. "I've decided I wouldn't be nearly so stressed about this if it were cool outside."

Justin chuckled and glanced at her in sympathy. "Only a few more hours 'til the temperatures start dropping." He paused at Claire's grim expression. "It's not hopeless, you know. It's probably just the local amateurs at their best. And if that's the case, we'll put a stop to it, and the artifacts will stay where you put them."

Claire shook her head. "I don't know," she admitted. "I can't see pothunters getting into the lab so easily. I always lock it if I'm leaving and the students aren't there either." She paused, frustrated. "It's making me angry. More than just a little."

Hodges nodded. "We'll figure it out, Claire. Just keep doing your job, and we'll get things figured out."

Claire nodded, trying to hide her stress. Her job. Lately, her job description seemed to be growing by leaps and bounds.

* * * * * *

Bump St. James smiled at the man who was perusing Bump's wet bar, which was full of nothing but diet drinks.

"Where's all the good stuff?"

"I got rid of the good stuff. You'll have to make do with what's there, I'm afraid." He laughed at the expression on the face of his young companion, who had formerly gone by the street name of "Doc." Bump currently used the man's given name on a regular basis in an effort to help the younger man make a new life for himself.

"It's not so bad, Jon."

"Not so bad! Man, I've only been gone for six weeks! What have you done?" Jon's face was the very picture of panic.

Bump's mouth quirked into a gentle smirk. "You've been in rehab. You're not supposed to go looking for alcohol the minute you walk in the door."

Jon scowled. "I was just going to smell it."

"Smell it?" The hoot of laughter was loud and contagious. Jon's answering smile was quick in coming, and it warmed Bump's heart.

"Buddy, you go around smelling the stuff and you're done for. Stay away from it, trust me."

Bump's mirth died away and he motioned for Jon to sit in the overstuffed chair, opposite his own position on the couch. "It wasn't just for your sake, actually."

"What wasn't?" Jon made himself comfortable in the chair, propping his feet on the matching ottoman with a sigh and settling back.

"Getting rid of the alcohol. I've made some, um, lifestyle changes since you've been gone."

Jon's eyebrows shot upward of their own accord. He cleared his throat. "What kind of changes, exactly?"

Bump absently rubbed the arm of the couch. "I've joined the Mormons."

The pause was lengthy and defining, in and of itself. When Jon finally found his voice, the incredulity within it was blatant.

"Why?"

Bump laughed. Why indeed? "I'll explain it sometime soon. Let's just say that neither of us is going to be doing any drinking anymore."

Later that evening, Bump asked himself the same question Jon had given voice to earlier. Why? He knew the answer, had felt the rush of emotion when he'd been given the missionary discussions under the tutelage of his friend, Liz O'Brian, and her new husband, Connor. But *why* was probably a question he'd be asking himself for some time to come.

As he wandered around his Seattle high-rise apartment, switching the lights off and readying for bed, he reflected back on his baptism of a month ago. The feeling had been extraordinary. He believed the principles he'd been taught, was still studying his new scriptures with the single-minded goal of learning as much as he possibly could, and he felt the truthfulness of it all when he prayed.

It was the Mormon culture he was having a hard time with. The Church members had been extremely nice in welcoming him into their fold. They'd been kind and friendly and more than a little curious. He was just so different, and felt it himself. They all seemed very content to . . . *conform*. His life had been anything but ordinary; his acquaintances worldwide were varied and often odd.

He wondered how he'd ever fit in enough to feel like he belonged.

Chapter 2

Queliza stepped out of the palace and into the bright sunlight, looking over the whitewashed plaza in hopes of spying the young man who had sought her attention time after time in the recent past. Of course, he was the son of the king, and therefore hopelessly out of reach, but her heart thumped when he spoke to her. He was so very handsome . . .

* * * * * *

Claire entered the office with a single-minded purpose the following morning. She sat at Justin's request and regarded his tired face. His eyes were lined and careworn, making him appear older than his mere forty years. She was determined that the recent mishaps in her laboratory not affect him.

"I'd like to bring someone in on this, Justin."

His thoughts were obviously elsewhere; the effort it took to bring the present into focus was evident. He blinked. "What? Bring someone in on what?"

She leaned forward, catching his glance and holding it. "I know you're stressed. I understand your responsibilities to this dig, and I know the funding is precarious, at best. We don't need pothunters making things worse." She paused for breath, searching his face for signs of agreement. "My brother and his wife are good friends with a high-tech security expert. They've suggested he may agree to a trip down south for awhile."

Justin braced his arms on his desk with a sigh. "I don't know, Claire. If Stark gets wind of any problems, he may back out altogether. What's he going to think if we can't handle things on our own? If we have to count on an outsider to help us take care of a few pesky problems?"

"They're not pesky, Justin. The police have basically told us we're on our own with this. We're missing valuable artifacts that are of no use to us gone. I know my work." She ran a hand through her hair and sat back. "I don't make mistakes with important things. I rarely make mistakes with unimportant things." She punctuated her remarks subtly by tapping her palm on the arm of her chair. "I don't like what's happening; I feel like something's just not right."

She shook her head at his silence. In the short time they'd worked together, he'd shown himself to be an archaeologist of immense talent. She valued his friendship. He was one of the few people she could relax around. With other people, she felt the necessity to maintain a cheery exterior at all costs, and the demands she placed on her own performance were high. Justin was one of the few people who knew she was a perfectionist to a fault. Everyone else found her carefree and highly entertaining; it was a burden that was beginning to wear.

Claire knew she wasn't the only one who was having problems. In addition to the issues they faced with their volatile benefactor, she knew Justin was going through a messy divorce that was tearing at his heart. He rarely saw his child, a daughter, and when he did, it was under the close scrutiny of his estranged wife, who seemed determined to drain his very lifeblood before their relationship formally reached an end.

"Please, Justin." Claire's brow creased in concern. "This is one more thing you just don't need. Let me take care of it. I'll have Connor contact the guy and see if he's even interested."

"And what would a high-tech security expert be able to do for us here?"

"Well, it's not just that; he's also an excellent PI. I've heard nothing but rave reviews about him from Connor and Liz ever since their debacle with drug dealers in Peru." Claire shrugged. "I don't know. I keep thinking he might be able to see things around here clearly because he'd be fresh and new to the place, you know?"

"And how do we pay the man? You'll never get this past Stark."

Claire smiled grimly. "How 'bout you let me handle Stark. If I can get him to agree, will you support me on this?"

Hodges shook his head in resignation. "You are persistent, Claire. Yes, I'll support you. Just don't get your hopes up; Stark will never go for this in a million years."

* * * * * *

"So what you're telling me is that there are problems beyond your control, Claire? Is that what I'm hearing from you?"

Darren Stark. It was so very like him to be sanctimonious. Claire gritted her teeth, clutching the phone until her knuckles whitened. All thoughts of showing a happy face to the world came to an abrupt halt each time she spoke with her ex-boyfriend. She hoped the air escaping her flared nostrils wasn't evident to the man on the other end of the line. She didn't want him to know that her reaction to him mirrored that of a stampeding bull. She was certain he'd find a way to turn it around on her, to suggest that she was just unable to handle life without his controlling presence.

"You know, Darren, there was a time I thought you understood just what it is I do for a living. I help run an archaeological site. I'm an on-site Conservator. I'm busy with the preservation of extremely old and valuable artifacts. I don't have time to scout around, playing detective." Claire sat in the chair behind Justin's desk, grateful he'd given her some space to make the call. Had he been witness to her end of the conversation, she feared he'd have mouthed the words, "I told you so." Justin had been right; Stark would never agree to spending money on an outside PI.

"I'll tell you what, Claire. You come to Paris and we'll discuss it."

Claire rolled her eyes, then closed them in frustration. It was his favorite request, and one he repeated every time they spoke, which was as little as she could manage without jeopardizing her job security. "I don't need to go to Paris to discuss this with you. I can do it from here." She paused. "You know I can't leave, Darren. I need you to stop asking the impossible of me. I have work to do here, and I'm doing a job you're paying for."

"I miss you, Claire." The voice was soft and vulnerable. She knew it too well; he'd perfected it and used it on her before. Fortunately, she was wiser for it.

"You don't miss me, Darren. You miss having someone to lord over." *I never did fit well into that role. It's a wonder we lasted as long as we did.* "Now give me the go-ahead to call this guy and we'll see if we can't save you some money. You do realize that each artifact that goes missing costs you, if only in name recognition? Everyone who's anyone in archaeology knows the great Darren Stark is funding this dig and will be generously donating the finds to museums. Every little piece of pottery that's stolen is one less artifact with your name on it."

The responding chuckle was subtle. The ensuing pause was lengthy and wasn't subtle in the least. It was designed to make her hold her breath, hoping, and she hated the fact that she was. "You call your PI, Claire, and see what he can do," he finally responded. "But I'll only give him a month or so. I'm not going to pay the man to sit around forever if he doesn't start turning up something."

"Thank you, Darren." To be forced into thanking him for anything was galling, but necessary. "I'll let you know what I find out."

"You do that. Incidentally, how is my niece?"

"Oh, she's great. Devon's great. Quite the little helper."

"Well, good. I'm glad to hear that. You take good care of her for me, will you? She's an awfully long way from home."

Yes, at whose insistence? "That she is." *You probably sent her here as a way to wreak your revenge on me . . .*

"You take care of yourself, Claire. I'll see you soon."

A TIME FOR THE HEART
COMING THIS SUMMER TO LDS BOOKSTORES